Mitsubishi Melody

Lt. John O'Donnell, USN ret.

John O'Donnell

Self-Published in the United States
Printed by McNaughton and Gunn, Inc.
P.O. Box 10
Saline, Michigan 48176

ISBN   0-9656874-0-6

Mitsubishi Melody--Fiction

Book Cover by Ruey Fang Syrop and Duflon Design

Acknowledgments

First and foremost, my thanks to Genie Lester, publisher of *Infinity Limited* magazine for her meticulous and skillful editing. And to her husband, Kenneth for sharing his computer expertise.

None of this could have happened without the tireless help of California's librarians, most especially those men and women on duty in Castro Valley, Hayward, San Leandro, and San Lorenzo libraries. The articles the reference section dug up for me from news media reports, circa 1930's and 1940's, together with various history books written by foreign authors, provided the basis for this book.

To my wife, Evelyn, who passed away while I was writing this novel, my never-ending appreciation for her timely suggestions and continuous encouragement.

Mitsubishi Melody is dedicated to the "Fleet Reserve Association," most especially to those American sailors, marines and coast guardsmen who had to pay the ultimate price in death, hardship, and terrifying memories.

About the Author

Born in Washington, D.C. and raised in Conshohocken, Pennsylvania, Lieutenant John O'Donnell enlisted in naval aviation as a seaman at the age of seventeen on October 14, 1944, for what turned out to be a twenty-three year career. During the more than two decades in the service, John, now a retired naval aviator and graduate of the University of California at Davis, spent seven years in Asia, flew in dive bombers, torpedo planes, patrol bombers, military transports and fighters, piling up over 6,000 flight hours plus 752 carrier landings. His last tour of duty was in Fighter Squadron 154 on board the U.S.S. Coral Sea where he flew seventy six missions over North Vietnam in the F4 Phantom.

John has been a resident of Castro Valley, California for over twenty years, ten of them with Safeway Stores' Brookside Division and twelve with East Bay Regional Parks District Board of Directors..

Mitsubishi Melody is a fact-based novel, told from the Asian point of view by the author writing as if he were a footloose, Japanese, ex-minor-league baseball player, turned utility navy pilot, named Kiyo Debuchi.

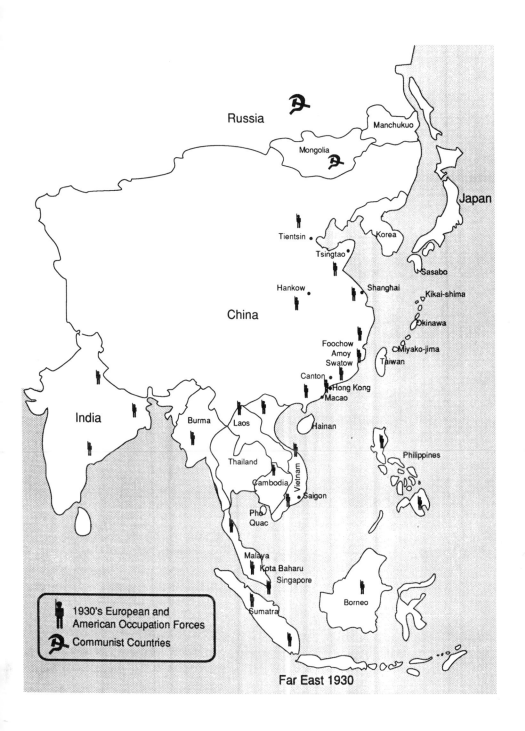

Far East 1930

Chapter 1

The First Punch

Using Volcanic Mount Aso as a reference point, I flew over the island of Hirado Shima before crossing Kyushu's coastline on the way to my latest assignment. Taking the shortest route to the Sasebo Naval Air Station in the latter part of November, 1941 forced me to pass over a fleet of warships heading for the open sea. Had I known how much impact this strange set of circumstances was going to have on my life, I'd have bailed out without bothering to put on my parachute.

The biggest occurance during my lifetime up until now had taken place in 1923, the year the gigantic Kanto earthquake killed 140,000 people. But I was only seven years old at the time, and anyway, I had been nowhere near the fault line.

I'm Kiyo Debuchi, a utility pilot; I have to fly all types of aircraft-- army, navy--anywhere, at anytime. Fortunately, variety fits my personality. There's no celebrity status attached to this job, just lots of flight time.

Before I joined the navy, I was a utility infielder for the Kabuki Kites, a minor league baseball team. As I said, I like variety.

According to Jane Howell, an American acquaintance of mine, I have auburn hair, chocolate-colored eyes, a peanut shell complexion, and a quirky smile. I didn't need her to tell me I'm shorter than the average male from her country.

As I brought the tan and orange Ki-27 Fire Dragon fighter plane in on final approach, I thought about the first time I encountered Jane.

I ran into the red-haired, green-eyed, vivacious woman while on a vacation trip to Hawaii. Even from a distance, the hairdo she called a poodle-cut caught my eye. And I especially remembered her light-blue, silk suit with its square, padded shoulders, topped off with a dark-blue Basque beret.

I wondered if she'd have bothered with me if I'd been honest enough to inform her that my own mother regarded me as nothing but a footloose, girl-chasing sailor.

My soul-searching was suddenly cut short by the tower operator screaming at me to add power.

It was my first landing in the Fire Dragon, and unluckily, in a hurried effort to get slowed down, I put on the brakes too fast, enabling the Aichi dive bomber behind me to overtake my aircraft. Its spinning propeller sliced a jagged hole in the rear section of my canopy, narrowly missing me, as I scrunched down in the corner of the cockpit to make myself into the smallest possible target.

After an angry and noisy confrontation with the base honcho about my overly cautious concern for the length of the runway, I left quickly for the harbor area to escort, time permitting, a lady physician to the air base. My schedule was tight because of a training flight I had to squeeze in before becoming her source of transportation.

I waited impatiently on the beach alongside Dr. Kimiko Hattori as she bit into her shapely lower lip. Behind her, the front page of the *Sasebo Sentinel* blew across the sand, its headlines screaming: **Corporal Hiko Daizen has throat slit with bayonet aboard the *Ikeda Maru*.**

Earlier in the day I'd read the rest of the article, which said: "The murder weapon with 'Trademark Killer' carved in its handle was found stuck in an artillery shell next to the body. A reliable tip reported it looked like a hideous cross or an evil prankster's idea of a gravestone.

"Military authorities wondered if there was any connection between it and last month's murder at the giant Yokohama Naval Base, where the killer had also left a bayonet at the scene."

Kimiko said she was torn between utilizing all of the five hours she had remaining to buy gifts for the big New Years celebration or putting part of the time to use touring the *Ikeda Maru* before it left the dock. "After all," she murmured, "it is my boyfriend Michi Sakamoto's first trip on a military transport."

But then again, I thought, there was a ten mile train ride ahead of us to consider if she was going to be on time to fly with me.

Snuggling deeper into her turtleneck sweater to ward off the early morning November air, Kimiko said she wished she'd put on something warmer than the tan-colored, black-belted, just-below-the-knee culottes.

Suddenly, the cool sand shifted under my feet and seemed to put Dr. Hattori's senses on red-alert. Her eyes grew wide. Was this the start of another one of Japan's many earthquakes? Or, was it, hopefully, and more likely, a fiddler crab.

While procrastinating over the choice between loyalty to her boy friend or purchasing New Years presents for her traditon-bound mother and elderly father, Kimiko's dark eyes remained alert to nature's unstableness.

The second time her indecisiveness caused her to shift her eyes back to the *Ikeda Maru*, Kimiko shook her short, jet-black hair and claimed her boy friend's determination to volunteer for hazardous duty on a ship that had a murderer on board had her rattled.

"It's ridiculous," she called to the sea gulls in her low-key contralto voice, "for a twenty-nine-year-old woman, a physician at Karatsu General Hospital to be so hesitant. What would my patients think of me?"

Relying on her disciplined background, designed to anticipate the worst, she dug her toes into the sand, her youthful figure primed to challenge mother nature. Regardless of Dr. Hattori's inner turmoil, she kept her eyes fastened on the military transport.

I could see she had finally made up her mind, so I took her arm and moved her toward the ship.

An officer standing at the top of the gangway waved us aboard. I accepted the invitation in order to find out what my cousin, Lance Corporal Jun Kaine, had to put up with.

Out of curiousity, I followed Kimiko to her boyfriend's new living quarters. The former first-class passenger's stateroom had pine-paneled bulkheads and a teakwood deck in lieu of the cedar walls and tatami mats I had grown up with in Kobe. The resonant bong of the ship's bell sounded harsher to my ears than the strident clang of the more familiar crosstown streetcar.

Of more immediate concern, according to the menacing-looking Inspector Geki Ibuse who shared the cabin with Sakamoto, was the probability of having a murderer on board.

While we were looking at a map of Malaya that Sakamoto had placed on the wall, Ibuse claimed that Corporal Daizen was found with his throat slit, tossed like an old sack behind boiler number 6. The chart, I noted, depicted in graphic terms the tremendous amount of Malayan territory Britain had handed over to the Dunlop Tire Company.

When we stepped outside to begin our examination of the ship, my cousin joined us. I told him his description of the Inspector had been accurate. Most people would mistake the man at Michi's elbow for the villain. The army's foremost investigator's smile resembled the business end of a great white shark. His eyebrows were best described as a tarantula caught in a light socket. His eyes were the color of left over coffee-grounds.

I turned and asked Geki Ibuse if he had any leads.

"There have been unsubstantiated rumors circulating about a beautiful Mongolian lady named Hisako Bayar. And somehow or other, the port city of Shanghai may be involved," he snapped.

A short time later, having strayed from the crowd for a moment, I caught a glimpse of a shadowy charactor scuttling along the corridor leading away from the personnel office. All this talk about murder has put my nerves on edge. I thought, shivering.

The tour was over by the time I caught up with the group entering the anchor chain compartment, a place that gave me a creepy feeling. I guessed the strange sensation was due to either the presence of Inspector Ibuse or that odd hint of mothball again.

When the time came to say goodbye to Kimiko, Michi Sakamoto apparently realized how much he cared for her--and the slim, dark-haired man had held her in a grip that would have made a boa constrictor smile. He seemed to be locking the scene in his memory bank when he stared at the little wind-blown, red and gold-colored maple leaf perched in her hair, a sign that winter was bearing down.

After taking a deep breath, he tore himself away so she could leave the ship. He followed her halfway down the gangway before he slowed enough to regain his composure. With concern showing in his every movement, he reluctantly stopped and waved goodbye, all the while watching Kimiko's lips form that intimate farewell, *sayonara*, before he turned and disappeared into the folds of the over-crowded transport.

With rampant rumors of Western submarines being sighted throughout the Far East, I fully realized the danger of being on a troop ship. However, since the Professor was naive about naval matters, I was afraid he'd develop a false sense of security when they joined the cruisers and destroyers waiting offshore to escort them.

For a man who worshipped on the altar of freedom as he did, it was only natural for him to enthusiastically support "Operation Asian Independence."

The notion of taking on the British lion was no longer just an idealistic possibility, I reasoned as the harbor lights faded in the early morning light. It was, instead, a definite objective.

What if, I wondered, after gulping in some salt air to clear my mind, the first step to free Asia ends in blood and gore instead of concrete results. Michi had good reason to believe the American B-I7 strategic

4

bombers stationed in the Philippines were preparing for a strike against Japan sometime in early December.

After the tug boats had nudged my cousin's ship away from the collision mats at pier 5, Kimiko made a final gesture. She pushed a loose strand of hair out of her eyes, scooped up a handful of water, and flung it towards the departing vessel in disgust. Then she put on her calfskin sandals and grabbed her suitcase, determined to do some serious shopping at Echigoy's, the world's first and oldest department store.

"I might even have time for one of those American silent films featuring that nutty Harold Lloyd, if I hurry," she said.

I looked at my watch. "I'd better get going," I said, taking off for the train station. "I have to be airborne within the hour. I'll meet you at the airfield after I get back.

I would have missed the train if the lady conductor hadn't spotted me and signaled the engineer to hold up.

It wasn't long before I was adding throttle to an underpowered Nakajima Kotobuki engine mounted on my squadron's blue and yellow-colored utility aircraft.

Using the top of a ship's smokestack as an altitude marker, I weaved my way through the mass of transports.

Pretending I had a real torpedo aboard, and aware that it would need time to stabilize before hitting the water, I climbed high enough to clear the lead destroyer's mast for the final portion of the run.

Doing my best to feel combative, I focused on dropping the inert weapon in the empty space between *Enchanted Shadow* and *Midnight Star*, the two destroyers chosen as the target boundaries.

My radio-gunner trainee, frowning in the rear cockpit, quickly lost the desire to practice aiming his unloaded 7.7 mm machine gun at the tormenting army Ki-43 Peregrine Falcon fighter plane, when the taller foremast of the hospital ship, *Whispering Wind,* burst into view. I must confess to having muffed that play like a rookie infielder when I mistakenly used the shorter topmasts of the destroyers to judge my height.

Yelling I had planned to use the highest boom as a pylon all along, I frantically banked around it.

With the army fighter on my tail, I pulled away from the fleet with a bad taste in my mouth, even though the dummy torpedo split the distance between the targeted ships as briefed.

5

"I thought the hospital ship would be stationed further back," I said over the intercom, extending my hand to pat the side of the aircraft.

Reaching up with my fingertips, I closed the non-slam canopy and waited for the Peregrine Falcon to complete its barrel roll around my plane before I headed back to the airfield to pick up three passengers and a different aircraft.

"Utility aircraft from Riptide. That pass the fighter made under your plane looked pretty scary from down here."

"He just wanted to keep the navy from getting bored," I answered lazily, caught relaxing against the air-foam cushion seat as two more Ki-43s came screaming in to put together a formation of three for their flight home.

A rainbow still visible to the east and dark clouds moving in from the south fit into my present mood--which went from upbeat to something approaching despair.

The gloom caused by the fiasco with the hospital ship wasn't to be my only embarrassment of the day.

While landing, I had just floated past the halfway mark on the runway when the tower operater called in a demanding voice,

"Set it down, Dreamer!"

How did he find out my nickname, I wondered, as I planted the plane on the airstrip. The affectionate, (at least I think it was affectionate) title had been given to me by my ball club. They thought I was being impractical and unrealistic about my ability to play all positions. The more aggressive members of the team said I participated too cautiously, some even said, timidly.

I shook off the rest of the negative images, and condensed all my anxieties into one harrowing thought: Would I have the guts to throw the first punch if they threw me into the fray to pinch hit for a combat pilot?

Chapter 2

Pep Talk

Standing by the ship's railing, thirty year old Professor Michi Sakamoto, recently commissioned a lieutenant in the Japanese Army, felt a splash of water on his somber-looking face. The spray had much more moisture in it than the droplets normally carried by the wind.

Why the difference? he wondered, wiping the liquid off with the back of his hand. The fragrance left on his skin by the mini-shower caught him by surprise. "If I didn't know better, I'd swear it smelled more like Kimiko's perfume than seawater," he chuckled.

The spray didn't bother the farm boys aboard the *Ikeda Maru*. They were involved in dealing with the first swells from the unrestrained ocean waves as the ship left the more sheltered waters of the harbor entrance for the open sea.

Michi moved out of the way to let a couple of soldiers, who gawked in astonishment at his height, pass by. He was still chuckling when his thoughts were interrupted by a yell from the squeaky-voiced Lance Corporal Jun Kaine. "Watch the port side!" Kaine cried, frantically hunting for a corner to hide in. "There's a blue and yellow aircraft headed this way at low altitude."

"It's carrying a torpedo! This may be the start of the Pacific War," Sakamoto commented, seemingly unconcerned about the damage an aerial torpedo could inflict on a thin-skinned transport like the *Ikeda Maru.*

"Don't say that," the normally cheerful Kaine whimpered, hunching down in case there were explosives.

Inspector Geki Ibuse grinned maliciously as the Lance Corporal breathed a sigh of relief and a shout of joy when he spotted the red suns on the underside of the blue and yellow Kyushu aircraft. With the initial scare over, Jun Kaine stood there looking foolish, realizing Japan was still within viewing distance. And any hostile aircraft were probably thousands of miles away.

He felt nervous being in the vicinity of Inspector Ibuse. But having heard from his fellow platoon members that the large scholar-soldier standing next to the investigator was the friendly type, the sociable draftee decided to take a chance. "Professor, do you know anything about the history of this ship?"

7

"*Hai,*" Sakamoto answered in his well-modulated, baritone voice, puffing out his chest as if he were the former ocean liner's owner. "The *Ikeda Maru* , was named for a town near Osaka--it was the pride of the N.Y.K. cruise ships. It carried passengers all over the Pacific until the Western oil embargo forced them to stop."

"It sure doesn't look like a sea-going castle anymore."

Kaine reached around the professor to take a swipe at the ship's only airborne stowaway, a housefly. "Was N.Y.K. a big company?" he asked.

"It was the largest shipping company in the world, with offices in San Franciso, Chicago, Los Angeles, and New York. They even had full-page ads on the back covers of the more popular American magazines," Sakamoto said, almost getting trampled by the sergeant in charge of the personnel office hurriedly exiting hatch 34.

"I'll be right back after I check in with the Sarge," Kaine said, knowing he was required to verify his family record, which was part of his service jacket.

"I'll be here on deck," Michi answered, bowing in return as the Lance Corporal departed.

As he caught up with the noncom, the Sgt. said. "You left your snowshoes tied up to your bunk," not bothering to mention how absurd snowshoes were for the upcoming climate. "Why did you bring them?"

"You'll see."

Oh, well," the Sergeant grumbled. "Nobody's going to steal them. The private in the bunk across from you carries a paper umbrella. And there's another soldier who has a fishbowl, complete with fish. I wonder if the rest of the platoons have this many weirdos?"

As he paced up and down the weather deck waiting for the teen-aged soldier to return, Lt. Sakamoto caught himself rubbing the two stars mounted on the yellow and red striped collar patches. Kimiko had pinned them on the same day the army command asked him to give a series of inspirational messages that would explain why the upcoming hostilities were unavoidable.

Although Michi Sakamoto had no particular relish for the military. He realized, as he ran his fingers through his wind-scattered, thick, black hair, that his family, by virtue of being students of Western history for the last fifty years, had provided him a unique background for looking at the hidden meaning to Western actions.

Startled by a sudden noise behind him, Michi spun around, ready to fend off an attacker. Instead, it was the Lance Corporal returning. He appeared to be about nineteen years of age, and was coming forward with

8

a series of hesitant steps.

"Come on over," Sakamoto beckoned, shifting his eyes down to take in the unlined face, innocent eyes, and skin coloring that would have made him invisible in a wheat field.

"Sensei," the teen-aged soldier started to say, using the more formal title for a professor or doctor. "I mean, Lieutenant," he mumbled, not sure of how to address him.

"Either one will be fine," Sakamoto said in warm, well-educated tones. "Walk with me to the bow of the ship. I need the exercise. In my position," he assured him, "you don't have to worry much about military standards."

"I'm interested in Japanese history," the soldier said, hurrying to keep up.

Michi smiled good-naturedly.

"I wasn't given a travel brochure on Malaya. In fact, no one even asked me if I wanted to go. Can you tell me why we're headed there and anything about the physical features of the region? I can't find anyone with Malayan blood aboard this ship that has ever seen his ancestor's place of birth."

"Well, Lance Corporal Kaine," Michi said, with his feet spread apart and hands clasped behind his back. "The geography is easy. It's a seven hundred mile long peninsula in the South China Sea. Much of it consists of tropical rain forest. The why is something else again. It's a long story, and it'll take most of the two week trip to satisfactorily answer your question.

"Look through that break in the clouds to the south, Kaine-san," he said, stumbling over a coil of line . "You can still make out the outline of the full moon."

Jun Kaine nodded with satisfaction at the fast fading display of earth's little companion. "Will the West fight savagely to keep us from freeing Asia?"

"Absolutely!" the Professor revealed, "There are only three independent, non-communist countries left in the Far East. Soldiers like yourself are going to have to fight bravely to make up for that deficit"

Kaine slipped past Sakamoto to stand in the front part of the ship. To get the feel of being an old-time sailor, he placed the palm of his right hand over his eyebrows and pretended to peer through a heavy mist for the first sign of danger.

"Unfortunately," Lt. Sakamoto said, leaning on the rail to observe the turbulant sea. "China won't be much help. That sleeping giant has been carved up by the Europeans and our own country into spheres of influence to a point where it resembles a poor man's colony more than a free nation." Not content unless there was lots of space between himself and what he perceived to be water of unimaginable depth, he moved back a couple of feet.

"It sounds confusing," Jun Kaine admitted, turning his dark eyes everywhere but towards the Inspector, who seemed to have materialized out of thin air.

"Why doesn't China declare war on us?" Inspector Ibuse asked from his position on the opposite side of the bow.

"The Chinese Communist did!" Michi replied, wondering why Ibuse was eavesdropping. "And have fought a guerrilla campaign against Chiang Kai-shek's Nationalist Chinese and our army for a number of years," he hiccupped.

"How did we get into our present predicament with the Western powers?" Jun asked, following Sakamoto down the starboard side of the ship.

"Mainly through the reluctance on the part of the West to recognize the past economic achievements of our culture--and *that's* where we'll begin our motivation story," Michi said, pleased that he found a technique to use in persuading the men to fight extraordinarily hard for Asia's freedom. He pushed aside the unwanted thought that his assignment might cause them to take unnecessary chances.

These neophyte soldiers had been reared to put a premium on concensus and politeness, he thought, hoping to find the right words to fire up the new draftees. Changing the priorities of men who had been previously taught to cherish symmetry, strike the correct balance, and preserve a love of nature presented him with a real problem. Flexibility was the key--there was no firm, diplomatic goal for them to rally around, just a desire to free Asia from foreign rule.

"Six hundred years ago we were already pre-eminent in shipping and commerce throughout the East China Sea," Sakamoto explained, stopping to spread his arms out wide enough to include the ocean. "These waters we're sailing over," he said exuberantly to drive home his point, "were dominated by Chinese and Japanese traders and pirates long before the first European merchants and soldiers ever came around the Malayan peninsula."

"You're really tall!" Jun Kaine suddenly exclaimed, as he looked up to ask another question.

"Tall enough to kiss the Sun Goddess," Michi said immodestly, staring up at the sky.

"Why didn't Japan go to Africa and Europe?" Jun quickly inquired, not knowing whether to laugh or be scandalized by the flippant remark about the Shinto religion's most important diety.

"There were enough opportunities for trade right here in the Far East," his instructor replied, after pulling on his lower lip to find the answer.

And I'll bet Kimiko's knee-deep in packages at one of those department stores right now, Michi Sakamoto added to himself.

* * *

After she'd finished shopping, Kimiko had completed a twenty minute train ride before getting off at the station in front of the Sasebo Naval Air Base.

"You're right on time, Dr. Kimiko Hattori," I said, stepping forward to welcome her, trying to appear cheerful after my hectic flight in the blue and yellow utility plane.

"*Ho,* Naval Air Pilot First Class Kiyo Debuchi," she said, releasing the suitcase when I reached for it.

"I'll escort you to the plane."

"Are nurses Mariko and Atsu here yet?"

"They're waiting at the aircraft,"

"Are you the pilot for this flight?"

"*Hai,*" I said, not bothering to tell her I was nearly yanked from the hop after narrowly missing the hospital ship's mast.

"You look a little stressed out?"

"My commanding officer has stomach trouble and is in a foul mood."

"Is that the plane?" Kimiko asked, pointing at the aircraft we were approaching.

"You bet," I said. "It's a three passenger Gasuden KR-2."

"What's a Gasuden?"

"That's just a nickname for the Tokyo Gas & Electrical Company."

"Can't we get a Nakajima or Mitsubishi product instead?" Kimiko asked, looking apprehensively at the little biwinged arcraft.

"Not to worry. Gasuden has won awards for building top-notch electrical parts and heat-retaining glassware. I'm sure they've put that same degree of craftsmanship into this aircraft."

"It's got 'Mitsubishi Melody' written in chalk on the nose," she said. "Does that mean anything?"

"I believe I can make this engine sing as sweetly as the more

11

expensive models," I said, my hand automatically going to my jacket pocket where a piece of chalk was stashed. I had hopes some day of flying with the Four Ghosts aerobatic team. They fly Zeros, a Mitsubishi product.

The faces on the two nurses had the same fearful look as Kimiko's when she greeted them.

The three attractive medical women looked like stairsteps, I thought, the taller, heavier, high-cheekboned Atsu, the smaller Kimiko, and the petite Mariko who had to stand or her tiptoes to make five feet.

The line mechanic had memorized their names and was making mental notes to tell his buddies later on about the volatile wiggle on Mariko Ito, the trim little package whom they addressed as Dr. Kimiko Hattori, and the self-assured pace on the long-legged, busty Atsu Ogata.

I'll bet that big one could fire up a blow torch just by staring at it, I thought.

"There's not much room for luggage, Doctor," Atsu said, her dark hair ruffled by the wind.

"Atsu better sit up front, *Sensei*. If you don't mind," Mariko suggested to Dr. Hattori. "She's the biggest."

"Quite right," Kimiko said, looking at the small size of the plane's rear seat. She turned in time to thank the mechanic with her dark vibrant eyes for finding room in the small luggage compartment for their gear.

"Climb in, ladies," I said, offering them a hand. "If it will make you feel any better, Tokyo Gas and Electric also built marine engines.

"Marine engines are used on water," Mariko stated, "and that's not what I want to think about when I'm flying over the ocean."

Sitting side by side in the back seat, Kimiko whispered to Mariko, "I wonder how many flight hours this pilot has?"

"He doesn't come off as a very stable charactor to me," Mariko judged. "I don't know what kind of aviator he is. But he's nice-looking, and *what* a beautiful voice."

"He's not even as tall as Atsu," Kimiko observed, with what she hoped was a disinterested whisper.

"I'll fly you out to the aircraft carrier *Sky Dragon*," I told them as I started the engine. "From there, I believe one of the destroyers will take you to the hospital ship *Whispering Wind.*"

"Mariko's going to Miyako-Jima," Kimiko said.

"How come you and Atsu didn't go out with the ship when it left port?" I asked, catching Mariko's dark, bedroom eyes looking back at me in the rear view mirror,

"This is a special project and it didn't get approved until it was too late to go aboard. The hospital ship left ahead of the convoy."

"Fortunately, it gives me the opportunity to make a carrier landing," I said, embarrassed by the clatter from the 150 hp Jimpo engine's poor imitation of a lovesick tomcat.

"Don't lean too hard against the side," Kimiko warned her seat companion. "It seems to be made of wood."

Out on the runway, at full throttle, the plane vibrated and sounded out of sync.

"Here we go," I informed them in my most theatrical manner. "Hang on."

"What's he mean, hang on?" Kimiko whispered. "The plane's barely moving."

Atsu, in the forward seat, tried to distract her mind by picking out familiar objects in Sasebo harbor. "What's that noise?" she asked when we were airborne.

"Not to worry," I said soothingly. "That's just the wind blowing past the struts."

"You mean the wings have ribs on them like an umbrella to keep them from blowing off? How fast are we going?" Kimiko asked, as the harbor slowy receded.

"We're maintaining a cruise speed of 97 knots," I assured them.

"It's a good thing the convoy hasn't been at sea very long," Atsu murmured.

I cringed after discovering the prop didn't have variable speed control. That meant I had to manually change the prop pitch every time I moved the throttle.

"Have you told Michi you're going to be in the convoy, albeit far to the rear?" Mariko asked Kimiko.

"I'll tell him whenever I think he has a need to know," she replied with a wink. "I had them classify the project in case having more women aboard disrupts the mission. Did you write your husband when you volunteered for the project, Mrs. Ito?" she asked.

"No, I'm going to use your approach," Mariko said, laughing. "As far as he knows, I'll be stationed in Miyako-Jima for the duration of hostilities."

My thoughts strayed to the only one of the three of them without a steady male in her life, the good-natured Atsu, whose eyes matched her overall physical appearance: large and dark. She wore that starched and glistening white nurses' uniform like it was tailored for her. That made me suspect that there's been a nip somewhere to accentuate the bosom, and possibly a tuck to slim the waistline.

And the cap. On anybody else it would look uninteresting, but on her, the shape of her forehead and the length of her hair make it seem rakish. Or, maybe she really did tilt it a little.

"I've got the carrier in sight," I said, after twenty minutes of flying time.

"I've seen postage stamps that were bigger," Mariko informed us as she looked down at the ship.

"No problem, this plane has a very low landing speed." I didn't bother to mention that I had very few carrier landings in it.

"What's it feel like to land a Zero fighter plane on an aircraft carrier?" Atsu asked, her inquisitive dark eyes lighting up at the thought.

"I'm not allowed to talk about combat aircraft," I replied, not wanting to go into past foul-ups.

"*Sky Dragon*, from Air Taxi with three ladies aboard."

"Air Taxi, from *Sky Dragon*. Orbit one mile to the southwest. We are launching Aichi dive bombers."

"Air Taxi, *Tadachi ni,*" I said, using the catch-all term for I understand and will comply.

Since none of the women had ever flown before, I decided to treat them to a trip inside a big, puffy cloud.

"Going into that cloud was equivalent to straying needlessly from a well-marked trail in the wilderness," Mariko complained.

"I see the convoy up ahead," Atsu said from her excellent vantage point. "I can't spot him of course. But, from what you've told me, Kimiko. I imagine Professor Sakamoto is down there giving a speech on foreign policy."

"Did you get good marks in history at school?" Mariko asked me.

"No. I hated remembering dates. I hope Michi makes it interesting."

"You mean like trying to make the year 1530 into a spellbinder?" the doctor asked.

"What's 1530?" Mariko asked.

"That's when the European pirates, I mean Portuguese, reached Japan in trading vessels," Kimiko said. "They had expanded to Asia on a mandate from heaven via the Pope."

This orbiting is a bore, I thought. Maybe I can stir up a little excitment.

"Somewhere out there in the Dutch military-controlled East Indies, three thousand miles southwest of the convoy," I told the ladies, "I visualize, a hard-eyed, jack-booted major, representing the Netherlands

Army Airforce, listening intently as the Dutch Admiral gives his first report on Japanese ship movements from one of the Royal Netherlands submarines.

"I picture him squeezing the arm of the chair to contain his excitment, as he leans his wide-shouldered body forward to catch every word. The Admiral says, 'A Japanese convoy has departed Sasebo, heading in a direction that could eventually put it in a position to challenge the British Empire in Southeast Asia.' And like the army major of my imagination, he fingered his white-enameled Maltese Cross."

"Will they attack the fleet along its route?" Atsu asked.

"Not unless Queen Wilhelmina changes her mind. It's more likely that the present plan calls for holding off on hostilities until the Japanese attack the British forces."

"Will the Dutch fight even if Japan fails to invade them?"

"Absolutely, If Britain loses its ability to keep its occupation forces in Asia it will make the Dutch army's job of keeping the freedom-fighters in line much harder."

"You're a good story-teller," Kimoko remarked.

Chapter 3

Hachijo Island

"I'm glad that low-flying aircraft turned out to be one of ours," Kaine said from his spot on *Ikeda Maru's* weatherdeck, "We'll be seeing enemy planes soon enough.

"Kaine-san, I have a meeting with the Admiral's aide. But I'll be back in a few minutes if you'd like to talk some more," Sakamoto said, anxious to instruct such an inquisitive mind.

"You bet, Professor, " the small town inductee promptly agreed as the historian departed, "I don't have a drill period today."

After an initial inquiry, a bosun's mate took Michi Sakamoto to the foot of the ladder leading to the staff's living spaces.

"Lieutenant Sakamoto reporting as ordered sir," the tall professor said, knocking on the cabin door.

"Come in. Good morning, Sakamoto-san," the aide said, acknowledging his presence. "The Admiral wants to broadcast your messages."

"I've been on NHK radio a few times."

"I want you to know, even though I'm disappointed at having my own choice for historian turned down, I wish you the best of luck. You have a good name in the academic world. As a political appointee, I expect you to make the men aware of their heritage and the importance of this initial drive to free our fellow Asians from the martial law policies of the West.

"With the approval of higher authorities, we've set up a low-powered transmitter and a special frequency for you, The Admiral wants the men in this fleet to understand why we're taking the lead in this endeavor and why it's important to go into battle with a can-win attitude."

"I understand."

"Map out a strategy that will have them spoiling for a fight before we reach our destination. Encourage the troops to ask questions. There's bound to be some men aboard who aren't afraid of the microphone."

"Yes sir."

"That's all, Lieutenant. Pick up your equipment and detailed instructions at the radio shack. I'll be monitoring your transmissions."

The weather had taken a turn for the worse. The wind was stronger, and the sea had gone from ripples to an occasional whitecap. Dark clouds were in the vicinity of the two warships on the southern horizon.

Walking toward Jun Kaine with a microphone and extension cord in his hand, the Professor pondered over the issue of European entry into Japan. It was a very complicated subject, and he wished to explain the sequence of events in a meaningful manner.

"Ho, Professor," Kaine's youthful-sounding voice called out, picking up where they had left off. "What caused the trading to stop?"

"I'll give you the information chronologically. In 1590, the Dutch and English established a trading post at Hirado. Kaine-san, do you know where Hirado-Shima is?"

"Hai. It's an island a couple of miles off the northwest coast of Kyushu," the squeaky voice of Jun Kaine answered. "What did the Dutch think of us?"

"They were surprised to learn that far from being a backward country, economically, Japan was on a par with England. Japanese trading villages were already changing into the larger commercial towns that followed.

"The chief radioman gave me a long microphone cord and a list of the places where I can plug it in. Keep asking questions. We're going to check on the ability of the fleet to pick up this short range transmission."

"Were there any corporation names during those times that I might recognize?"

"Hai. Mitsui, for one," Sakamoto said, his voice bouncing in cadance with his movements. "It's the world's oldest big-time place of commerce. It was started before the Pilgrims ever landed in America. By the seventeenth century, it had become the first business establishment to create chain stores. More to the point of economical stability, Mitsui opened a bank ten years or so before the Bank of England was established."

"Outstanding!" the eager as a puppy Kaine said, standing outside the paint locker.

"Mitsui had very conscientious bookkeepers; their records are still available in a secure fireproof library. And, something few people realize, Mitsui wasn't hostile to having women in management."

"You mean I may have to work for a woman in civilian life?" Lance

17

Corporal Kaine complained. "Where does it stop? They already have too much power."

"It's quite possible you will. Those who do not wish to give birth are in line for promotions in the larger companies."

"There's a lot steel surrounding us."

"That shouldn't bother the transmission. The antenna's up on the tallest mast. But to get back to the subject. A more liberal civil code is being contemplated by the legislators."

"Being bossed around by females is nothing new to me," Jun sighed, "my parents kept trying to have a son. After seven girls--bullseye, identical twin boys. But with seven older sisters and a mother, all telling me to sit up straight, pick up my clothes, and comb my hair--dodging females became an art."

"What was the worst part?"

"Trying to get in front of a mirror. I have plenty of horror stories," he confessed. "And if that's not bad enough, I was born and raised in Hachijo where they have a matriarchal society."

"Although Hachijo is an extreme case, the philosophy is not new in Japan," Lt. Sakamoto advised. "The man of the house is boss, as long as he doesn't act like a boss. Have you ever heard the name Yone Suzuki?"

"That has a vague ring to it."

"Twenty years ago, she commanded sixty-five companies and was one of the richest women in the world--if not the richest."

"I'll bet she had plenty of boyfriends," Kaine chuckled.

The Professor disdained to comment on that. He continued, "By 1638, because of improper American and European intrusion, Japan stopped some of its overseas trading with foreigners."

"You did say, *some*, Professor."

"Among other considerations, the Westerners always demanded special privileges--not competition."

"What was our strategy, *Sensei?*" the soldier from Hachijo Island asked.

"We pulled away from what we perceived as underhanded trading techniques in order to save Japan's economic status," Sakamoto replied. "But since we needed to import and export to live, the DeShima trading port was left open. Trade continued on a regular basis with China, Korea, Okinawa, the Dutch, and even secretly with those parts of Asia that were controlled by the European military." The Professor paused.

"Are you nervous at the thought of walking down the dark passageways at night with a killer on board?" Kaine asked, his mind

18

jumping to another concern.

"Sure. When you don't know the reason for a murder, and the killer's still at large, your brain invents all kinds of weird scenarios."

The sky cleared momentarily and a squadron of Ki-27 fighter planes appeared in the background, which gave the approaching ship's navigator an excuse to comment.

"According to NHK radio, those army fighter planes have been highly successful against the Italian and Dutch volunteers in China," the Commander announced. "But as a navy man, I'd rather read about Ghost Leader. Please go ahead with your discussion on trade, Professor."

"The Netherlands and Asian countries still had a virtual monopoly on trading with Japan. In fact, it was so profitable, the Dutch sent over six hundred ships of their own and even hired American vessels flying the Dutch flag to take their merchandise to Japan."

"One of those Fire Dragons is headed this way faster than a tremor on an earthquake fault," Kaine warned.

Chapter 4

Dolly

When I recognized Tomi's voice, I placed myself in a position to intercept his Ki-27 on its inbound heading. I was betting that he was going to put on a one-man airshow for the amphibious fleet.

"Tell us what that little tan-colored plane with the orange nose is doing," Mariko requested.

"Tomi thinks it's his chance to be in the spotlight," I assured them. "He'll check to make sure *Dolly's* oil temperature and manifold pressure are in tolerance before doing any aerobatics."

"Dolly?" said three voices at once.

"The last time I saw the man that's flying that plane was at Central Coast Air Base in Thailand. Tomi, my old college classmate, now an Army First Lieutenant, had been busy selecting a suitable theme for the nose art on his Nakajimi Fire Dragon. 'Should the design be comical?' the five foot, six inch, graceful pilot had mumbled. 'No, that's not appropriate. Death is too serious a subject. Erotic? No! This plane is anything but romantic. Profane? I could put something irreverent about the Emperor, but then, somebody would be sure to squawk. I've got it!' he had yelped. 'Something significant, suggestive, purposeful.'"

"'Debuchi-san,' Tomi hissed like an alley cat. 'You have a degree in linguistics. Is this the way you spell *Dolly* ?'

"When I verified the spelling, he turned to the sergeant, 'Paint that name on the nose, and surround it with cherry blossoms. That American president's wife had no more love for the British army than I do.'

"'Yes sir!' the accomodating flight line sergeant had said, believing it best to humor him. He obviously thought the First Lieutenant had lost his marbles."

"You're a linguist?" Dr. Hattori asked when I finished my story.

"Hai. I specialized in Dutch and English at Rikkyo University"

Taken by surprise, Tomi finally spotted my rickety-looking Navy KR-2, and catching a glimpse of the women passengers, he quickly pressed his mike button. "Riptide, this is Black Magic Two One Five. Requesting permission to cross over the convoy?"

"Black Magic Two One Five," from Riptide. "Permission granted."

He pulled away and waved goodbye when I smiled. The peppy Nakajima engine emitted a deep-throated roar.

"What's he doing?" Kimiko asked.

"If I'm not mistaken--he's tightened up his five-point safety harness, has pushed the stick forward, and opened up the fuel valve."

"It's a sporty-looking plane," Mariko said.

"It's a Ki-27b, the army's pick as the style-leader of 1941. If I know Tomi, he intends trying something more exotic than the standard loop."

Nearing the convoy's mid-point, he went into a vertical climb.

"Tell us what's happening," Atsu suggested, trying to keep the plane in sight.

"Even while he's concentrating on holding the wings level and the nose straight up, he's aware of the dangers involved in toying with the rapidly falling airspeed."

As the plane's momentum decreased, I felt my left eyebrow cock and my face muscles tighten in harmony with Tomi's efforts to maintain vertical flight.

"It should look good from the deck of the *Ikeda*," Kimiko said.

"At extremely low speeds, the plane becomes unstable," I said. "His right wing is down. His hands are fighting to maintain control.

"He has no airspeed--this is no time to get flighty, *Dolly*--if you'll pardon the expression, ladies."

Out of habit, I gave my safety harness one final tug. For a few seconds the Nakajima fighter plane hung in the air--then began to cartwheel.

My passenger's thrill at watching the plane go straight up was replaced by a feeling of alarm when the Fire Dragon hesitated, and then by absolute terror.

"It's spinning end over end!" Mariko yelled.

"Bail out! Bail out!" Atsu screamed.

Instead of leaving the aircraft, Tomi's body would be squashed against the side of the plane under the force of centrifugal action, as he fought to bring the Ki-27 back to a stabilized horizontal position.

"He's not going to make it," the anxiety-ridden, black-eyed Mariko announced.

"Yes he is," Atsu insisted, as if her cheerful attitude made her more knowledgeable. "It's stopped rotating," she observed.

"If that was a cat," Mariko squealed, "it's just used up one of its nine lives."

After three complete turns, Tomi had eased his foot off the rudder pedal to stop the cartwheeling, and had closed the throttle to prevent a rapid buildup in speed. Applying back pressure to the control stick, he managed to coax the plane into level flight before heading outbound.

Although the sky is a huge lake, where moons, planets and faraway suns go sailing by in drill formation, I thought, when my racing heart had slowed down, I realized it was nothing but a playpen for men like Tomi.

"That hammerhead stall looks scary," I explained to my female passengers. "But he was never in any real danger. You should see the Navy's Four Ghosts aerobatic team in action. I hope to fly with them one of these days."

"That sounds exciting," Mariko said

"Only the top naval aviators get the opportunity."

"Oh, by the way," Tomi said, as he departed the area, "If you want to hear Sakamoto's spiel, dial in the Iris frequency on the auxiliary receiver."

"Auxiliary sounds like an inferior product," Kimiko said.

"Luckily," I said, "the navy purchased an auxiliary receiver that's more than capable of amplifying weak signals into audible ones. It happens to be manufactured by a top notch company." I tuned to *Ikeda's* special frequency to test the reception, turned it up to full volume and placed my earphones over the back of the my seat.

"What's an Iris frequency?" Atsu asked.

"It's a code word. All fleet frequencies are named for flowers. For instance: Rose might mean l00 megacycles. Let's listen in."

"What was Britain's reaction to the trade restrictions?" "That's my Hachijo Island cousin," I said, his voice booming in so loud and clear I had to turn down the volume.

"What? Oh yes. At times, British ships sent their crews ashore to take private property by force,"

"That's Sakamoto," Kimiko said, leaning forward attentively.

"Then Britain began planning for a large naval base in Singapore, to expand its trade markets in the Far East with the help of its armed forces. A permanent military presence would ensure that trade was under the control of the Global Empire.

"In case I haven't mentioned it before. The Global Empire is a term to used to describe Great Britain and all the land she has taken by military conquest. Their empire is so large it doesn't fit under the normal category."

A message on the main receiver automatically overrode the lecture series on the auxiliary.

"Riptide from Black Magic Two One Five. You'll need a relay aircraft if you want to reach low-flying planes with your Iris transmissions. I'm at two hundred feet altitude and the signal faded just as I lost sight of the fleet."

Rather than fly around in a circle, I decided to give the women a good view of both the Malayan-bound convoy and the hospital ship.

Chapter 5

Unequal Trade Treaty

According to the information we heard on the auxiliary unit, the discussion group was relaxing with bean-jam buns, rice and vegetables in the former second-class passenger's dining saloon. Professor Sakamoto was still talking.

"A fleet of warships led by Commodore Perry sailed across the Pacific to coerce our people into giving preferential treatment to America's manufacturers, and California newspapers mentioned the possibilty of the navy shelling Japanese cities."

His speech was punctuated by the sound of feet striding across the metal decking.

"Judging by the the background noise," Atsu said. "A lot of off-duty personnel must have shown up to hear the Professor's comments."

"Anytime a large number of men are involved," I conjectured, "the odds go up that one of them could be Corporal Daizen's killer."

After taking the squeal out of the backup receiver by retuning it, I could again hear the Professor talking.

"Commodore Perry's warships are usually given credit, by America, for opening up Japan to the West, or some other such nonsense. But if one wants to be honest, it was nothing but robbery. Japan was never isolated, and never did stop trading. It received scientific literature and news of Western accomplishments through the Dutch, and continued trading throughout the Orient."

A soldier identifying himself as Corporal Mishima asked. "Didn't America want to buy and sell?"

"An analogy to America's idea of free trade would be an underworld figure entering a business establishment asking for preferential treatment. When he doesn't get it, he threatens to break the owner's kneecaps and smash-up the place."

Kimiko tapped me on the shoulder. "After hearing the Professor's answer, Kiyo, I'll bet you're eager to get into battle."

"I'm ready to do my part," I answered, half-heartedly.

Sakamoto's voice interrupted our comments.

"The United States wanted to set Japan's import-export tax rates to benefit themselves,"

"Maybe I'll transfer to the infantry," Atsu said jokingly.

I listened closely to the radio.

"Do you have anymore thoughts on Perry's trip to the Far East?" my cousin Jun asked.

"Hai."

"Did Perry himself make threats?" someone growled, in a voice reminiscent of his role on the battlefield.

"He promised to blow up the cities surrounding Tokyo Bay unless the Japanese gave the U.S. special concessions on trade," Sakamoto answered.

"We should have mailed them a Habu snake," Mariko suggested, her ears going red with outrage.

I knew the tongue-in-cheek Mariko was familiar with Okinawa, the home of that deadly reptile. "As your great grandmother probably informed you," I said, glancing in her direction. "Using the Marines, Perry invaded Okinawa and forcibly sold the peaceful island's administrators protection insurance."

The Professor needs to wave the flag more, I thought, if he wants an all out effort from the draftees.

"Did the Americans get their own way in Japan?" Lance Corporal Kaine asked, barely audible as we approached the outer limits of the Iris frequency range.

"Hai. **Our nation was cowed into signing the first of the unequal trade treaties with America in 1864--Japan had been mugged, and could do nothing about it. Instead of pistols, cannons were used. Instead of in a dark alley, the robbery was done in broad daylight for all to see."**

"Dates again," I grumbled.

A sudden shout temporarily overloaded the amplifier.

"Platoon 4 and First Assault Landing Team members G through S--shower time!"

"That's Sergeant Ogata from platoon 3," Atsu said, "Sgt. Ogata is my Uncle Benjiro," she reminded us. He's a joker, he'll probably put bath salts on the floor.

There was a sound of stampeding men.

"I'm going to stop by my bunk to get my soap and towel," I thought I heard Kaine say, breathlessly, transmitting inadvertently.

I listened for the clack, clack of his wooden clogs on the hard deck, but the mike wasn't sensitive enough. I sorely missed that familiar racket on the flagstone sidewalks back home.

In my imagination, the quieter slap, slap, slap of a pair of rubber zore would be the killer.

With all those men shouting, it sounds more like they're going to a gymnasium than a public shower," Atsu pointed out, still irritated with the unequal trade treaties.

I didn't bother to tell her that the first American consul was a believer in gunboat diplomacy. It wouldn't help her disposition any.

"It doesn't sound very smart to me," she said. "Why does America support Britain, a country that holds one-quarter of the world hostage? Have they forgotten that the Englishmen set fire to the White House during the previous century?"

"Hai," I said. "And also the the treasury, state, and war department buildings. First lady, Dolly Madison, the heroine of the day, did manage to avoid complete catastrophe by saving a few historic items, but the British destroyed all the rest, including her clothes and jewelry. However, this didn't bother the upper-crust in America; they loved European royalty enough to make excuses for them. Even today, if Britain's King-Emperor asks them to kiss his arse, they'll say which cheek, and how often."

"That's a colorful way to put it," Dr. Hattori said.

"Please cut off the auxiliary receiver, so we can talk without being interrupted," Mariko said, impatiently.

The last words I heard as I reached for the switch were,

"Professor, I'm Yeoman Nitta. Have you heard about the gorgeous lady I met in Shanghai before I joined the assault landing team? She was from the People's Republic of Mongolia."

"Michi will be embarrassed that he let that comment slip through," Kimiko said.

"I recognized the voice of that quarrelsome Quartermaster Kato from Beppu's Hell Springs," Atsu said. "I once patched him up after a fight."

"I had the yeoman for a patient," Mariko said. "Do you remember when Nitta and Kato got into a quarrel at St. Lukes Hospital? It started innocently enough.

"Kato said, 'It'll be a pleasure throwing the British army out of Malaya. For every Malayan that has been murdered, raped, or burned out from their homes by the British,' he had promised, 'two Englishmen will die.'

"'I'll give you something to holler about!' Nitta yelled angrily.

"'A paper-pusher like you ought to join the Handerchief Theater. That way you'd be able to cry your eyes out and get paid for it.'

"'I'll use a handerchief all right,' Nitta said, 'but it'll be around your neck, wise guy. And stop squenching up your eyes. They look like sun-dried prunes.'

"'You think you're tough,' Kato said, 'just because your mother was one of the construction workers that helped build Sasebo Naval Base. Well, I've got news for you. It's not hereditary.'

"'Don't you say anything about my mother,' the Yeoman warned.

"'What did you do for a living before the army drafted you, sleezeball?' Kato shouted.

"'I sold lottery tickets, jerkhead,' Nitta flung back, 'which is more work than you could ever handle.'

"'That's a nothing job,' the senior quartermaster informed him. 'I was in training to be a racetrack manager before I joined up.'"

"Do you know how the Western trade treaties worked?" Kimiko asked me, when the nurse had finished her tale.

"If I remember right, the West set Japan's tariff rates, so that imports from America were low-priced and exports to the West were expensive. Under that scenario, Japan was flooded with cheap American products."

Kimiko's coal-black eyes lit up with a sudden recollection. "We still have some of that junk in a trunk at home. But the one piece of information that Sakamoto gave out that stuck in my mind," she said, "is the fact that America was the first country to use land mines."

"Our warships, transports, and aircraft are on a mission that would have been unthinkable a couple of years ago," I said, hoping to divert the conversation back to the present time. "Taking on the responsibility for ending British military occupation in Asia is a big step."

Maybe too big, I thought to myself.

"Flying in a circle is about as exciting as chewing sand," I grumbled,

"Did you know," Kimiko asked, "that Britain's royalty once said that military force brought their empire into existence and military force would keep it under British rule."

"With the auxiliary receiver in the off position," I said, "we won't hear the usual afternoon announcement about the pride the Emperor feels

27

in his armed forces."

"No one seems to be excited about that pronouncement anyway," Mariko noted. "What does he do besides be emperor?" she asked.

"He presents a silver wine cup to everyone who reaches one hundred years of age," Atsu Ogata replied. "He's a very gentle-looking man. He visited my village once, and everybody was impressed with his mild manners. He's actually a marine biologist and has won several scientific awards for his achievements. The army tries to elevate his position to use as a motivating tool, and the West translates the word *Kami* into 'God,' instead of a meaning closer to 'revered one.'"

"I wonder if they know that three emperors had been exiled," Mariko said, bending her head to get a good view in the hand-held mirror. "Another emperor sold pens and autographs, and there was one whose body lay unburied for over a month due to lack of funds."

"That doesn't sound like he was much of a god to me," I said. "What gave the West such a false impression of our emperors?"

"The millions of Westerners who saw the operetta *Mikado* by Gilbert and Sullivan, came away with a distorted view of the power of the emperor--and now it's very difficult to change that perception."

"How do you know all this stuff?" I queried.

"My older brother took up the study of religion as a hobby, and I was exposed to more information on the subject than I wanted."

Chapter 6

Too Many Planes

Catering to the whims of an unruly stomach, Mariko leaned her head against the canopy.

"I wonder what it would be like," she asked, looking at the ocean, "to stalk an enemy convoy from under the sea, report its position, then wait for permission to send a warhead into the hull of one of its ships."

"Mariko-san," I asked, approaching the question with the same caution I used with poisonous snakes. "Are you ill?"

"No, Debuchi-san, I'll be all right in a minute. Can this plane receive commercial news broadcasts?"

"*Hai,*" I informed her, tuning in a commercial radio station located in the upper floor of Canton's *Red Bamboo* restaurant that broadcasts in several languages. "This one generates one of the strongest signals in the Far East."

The distant voice came through weak but clear:

"**The United States will back the Dutch and British military controlled governments in Asia if Japan tries to free them from the European army. "It's already supplying the occupation forces with armaments."**

"**This is truly a catastrophe for Japan,**" he continued with a shiver in his voice, "**because the last thing it wants is a war with the American giant.**"

"What's the alternative?" Atsu requested.

"There is none," I replied, failing to think of a credible answer. I crabbed the aircraft into the wind, which had gotten strong enough to blow the sea into ten foot waves with heavy spray and numerous whitecaps. "If we don't knock out their fleet and air power, they'll use it to stab us in the back while we're fighting the Global Empire."

"Look how dark it is to the south of us," Atsu noted.

Mariko's long lashes looked gigantic attached to such a tiny face. "The storm clouds are moving towards the convoy," she said.

"How did you become interested in medicine?" Dr. Hattori asked.

"My father worked for the Sankyo Pharmaceutical Company," Mariko explained.

"Didn't that company provide the financial backing for Honda's racing cars? Specifically, the one that Honda-san crashed in the All-Japan Automobile Speed Championship?"

"Hai," she said, fluttering her long lashes.

I switched the dial back to the Iris frequency. Professor Sakamoto was speaking from sickbay.

"I'm down here with Captain Ohira to see how Corporal Mishima is doing. As most of you have heard by now, he was stabbed as he left the shower room."

"Inspector Ibuse is going to be a mighty busy man," Kimiko said.

"He only has Yeoman Nitta to help him," I said, agreeing with her assessment of the situation.

"Do you think there might be more killings?"

"Hai," I said. "Unless Inspector Ibuse can figure out the killer's motive."

"It's a small world," Kimiko said, "Inspector Ibuse's wife used to work for the bookstore at Doshisha Women's College of Liberal Arts where I took my first classes."

I had taken a wide detour to show my passengers the size of the assault fleet.

We watched a destroyer race ahead of the fleet to plant a target buoy. The Aichi bombers overhead now faced an additional distraction. The ships would be passing down both sides of the target as the planes maneuvered toward their objective, I surmised from the ship's radio transmissions.

High above the convoy, the squadron looked for the outlines of the large, red buoy.

Behind it, the approaching task force formed an impressive sight, as the ships split and steamed by the floating bullseye.

The lead Aichi dive bomber climbed higher into the cool, bleak sky, rolled over lazily, then plunged seaward.

I couldn't risk tearing the wings off the KR-2, so I eased the nose over and pretended the target was London's Whitehall Palace, where the lives and deaths of millions of Asians were determined daily.

"What are you doing?" Kimiko yelled just as I got the propeller hub lined up with the buoy.

"There are at least a dozen planes diving toward us," Mariko barked at me in an unladylike manner.

Clenching my teeth to show my determination, I dove at a slightly steeper angle.

"A plane just hurtled past our wing tip," Atsu screamed.

I shoved the throttle forward and yanked back on the stick in an effort to get out of the way of the next bomber. Too late. I passed right over the target site as it released its non-explosive, practice bomb.

"There's an ugly-looking object headed our way," Mariko cried, tilting her head upward to keep it in sight.

My vision was partially blocked by the proximity of the fast-moving object. Panic time.

Evasive action was paramount, so I bent the fragile Gasuden aircraft into a turn it wasn't built to withstand.

The women hollered as the g-forces squeezed them against the back of their seats.

The wings creaked under the strain, the engine labored and threatened to quit--but I managed to dodge the projectile.

"You should be locked up," Kimiko said unkindly.

Being familiar with the boos of disgruntled fans, I ignored her.

"There are planes scattered all over the sky," Mariko said, as she cowered in her seat before turning angry.

The last Aichi bomber started, and held, what appeared to be a good dive--then suddenly went steeper, steeper than squadron doctrine allowed.

"There's a plane coming straight at us," Atsu yelled.

"No problem. We're low enough to stay out of trouble," I said, looking up at the fast-moving aircraft.

"That plane veered off to keep from colliding with us!" Kimiko roared.

"Pull up! Pull up!" I hollered. Too late! The Aichi pilot, his aircraft, and the buoy became one in a crunch of metal and torn flesh. The radio-gunner bailed out at the last moment, and hit the water trailing a half-opened chute.

I slammed my open hand against the windshield. Two aviators lost their lives. Were they victims of target fixation? Or did that last maneuver of mine break the pilot's concentration?

"Won't you be in trouble for getting so near those diving aircraft?" Kimiko asked.

"I can handle it," I assured her. "Trouble's nothing new to me," I bragged. "I once tried to do a favor for a woman I met while I was in flight school. She's now associated with NHK radio.

"My best buddy worked for Mitsui while I was a taking flying lessons, and when the company came up with a new chemical fertilizer, she sweet-talked me into giving the farms adjacent to the airbase a helping hand."

"Crop dusting?" Atsui asked.

"She convinced me that I should be a good neighbor before becoming Japan's most fearless aviator," I continued, not bothering to mention that I was unable to resist the flattery of a beautiful woman. "I eased into Mitsui's agricultural plant with my friend's pass and grabbed a bag labelled, 'Smart Crop fertilizer.'"

"Did you get caught?" Atsu asked.

"No. I slipped past the guard at the base that night and put the fertilizer into my assigned aircraft, not realizing until the following morning that I'd put the bag in the wrong cockpit."

* * *

"You're not going to believe what this navy's coming to, Cadet Debuchi," the instructor pilot growled at me during the preflight inspection. "I've got a sack of fertilizer leaning against the control stick."

"Let me get rid of it for you, sir," I volunteered, pretending to throw it on the ground before tossing it into the forward cockpit.

"Get rolling Debuchi," he commanded, saying that he was thankful his new orders would take him away from flight cadets like me. "Find an area to practice your aerobatics," he said.

I headed the training plane in a direction that would take us over the greatest number of farms. Unfortunately, I inadvertently pushed the bag with my foot as I started my first roll to the right.

"That's enough," the instructor commanded after my tenth snap roll. "Do something different."

I told him I was trying. The fertilizer bag was hopelessly jammed between the control stick and the left side of the aircraft. Desperate, I smashed the heel of my shoe into the wedged sack and managed to tear a hole in it.

Fertilizer and noxious fumes showered the two of us, the plane and the farms underneath during the next two snap rolls, but it also reduced the sack's contents to a point where I could move the stick to the left.

* * *

"Close call," Mariko said. "But a happy ending."

"Not exactly," I admitted. "It had been too dark in Mitsui's plant for me to read the smaller print on the bag. It turned out to be batch five of an experimental test."

"It didn't work?" Kimiko asked.

"The farms won't have to use fertilizer for the next one hundred years."

"Congratulations." Atsu said.

"Just one small difficulty," I said, turning pink. They won't be able to grow crops for the first half of that."

"What was the outcome of that incident?"

"The training commander was threatened with severe punishment, until he convinced the court martial that I searched out tragedy like fat people do sugar."

I'm beginning to believe it," Mariko mumbled. "What was the woman's name?"

"Ruriko."

"She's my younger sister," Kimiko said.

I was glad I hadn't made any derogatory remarks about her.

"Your story sounds about as likely as the existence of a Japanese Sandman," Atsu kidded.

How did she know I stretched the truth on occasions?

"Air Taxi from *Sky Dragon.* We have a clear deck. If you're in a position to come aboard, we can fit you in before the dive bombers arrive."

"*Hai hai,* from Air Taxi," I said, passing over the *Ikeda Maru* at an altitude of two thousand feet.

Having heard there were women coming aboard, sailors jammed every section of the superstructure, the gun platforms, and the unused portion of the flight deck to get a view of their temporary guests.

"What are those red stripes on the back part of the ship?" Mariko asked as I descended towards the flight deck.

"It means danger, keep clear of the ramp."

"We're headed right for it," she cried.

Except for a pirouette when I hit the right brake harder than the left, I considered it an uneventful landing. My passengers, their fingers cramped from clutching the arm rests, thought otherwise.

Captain Naifu was quick to greet and lead Kimiko away.

"That landing scared me a little," she said.

"If he had so much as caused a single bruise on any one of you three women, I would personally have had him keelhauled," I heard the Captain promise.

"What is keelhauling, Captain?"

"The next time the carrier is drydocked, we'll tie a line around Debuchi and push him down the starboard side of the ship. Then we'll slowly drag him across the bottom of the vessel at the spot where the barnacles are the most plentiful. To complete the ordeal, we'll pull him up the port side. With any sort of luck, he'll be good for nothing but fish food," the Captain said in a happy state of mind. "Unfortunately," he added sadly, "that particular punishment has been outlawed."

"I'm glad," Kimiko said.

"Your orders have been changed, Doctor," the Captain said, getting serious. "The head of Karatsu Medical Center needs you back there as soon as possible. Nurse Atsu Ogata will transfer over to the hospital ship, and Mariko Ito will go to Miyako-Jima temporarily."

A gunner's mate almost fired his 20 mm weapon at the sight of Mariko's legs exiting from the plane. Smiling sheepishly, he quickly joined in the applause for the queen-sized Atsu.

A flight deck mechanic with a smudge on his cheek rushed forward to escort the tiny but shapely Mariko to the hanger deck. Atsu was greeted by Inspector Ibuse, on board to check on a recently transferred sailor who had known Corporal Daizen at another duty station. "I see he managed to get you here safely," Ibuse said with a crooked smile he considered flirtatious, unmindful of Atsu's frown.

"Does Debuchi fly one of those?" she asked, pointing to one of Silent Storm's white Zeros.

"More or less," the Captain replied, overhearing her.

"But on a more important note," Ibuse queried, not at all intimidated by Atsu's size. "If I get sick, will you nurse me back to health?"

"I don't know of any germ that would dare attack you, Inspector," she answered.

I pushed the mechanic aside, and, with a touch of gallantry, handed blankets to the two women so they could cover their legs while getting into the swaying seat.

"Thank you," Atsu said, turning her large, dark, expressive eyes in my direction, adding a smile when I blushed.

"Did he *have* to give them something to cover their legs?" the gunner's mate asked no one in particular.

34

Watching Atsu Ogata swinging in mid-air as she sat rigidly in the little chair carrying her to the destroyer did nothing for Mariko's frame of mind. In contrast to the gentle rising and falling of *Sky Dragon, Midnight Star* bucked and heaved.

" If Ken, your pilot-husband, knew you were here," the unmarried Atsu said, looking back at the tiny figure on the carrier deck. "He'd drop a bomb on you."

The sailors disbursed when it became apparent that the ladies knew how to tuck the blankets in to maintain their modesty--but not before an argument started on the *Midnight Star* between those who thought Mariko deliberately showed a lot of leg getting off and those who thought it was accidental.

I got into a conversation with the smudge-cheeked mechanic I knew from a few years back.

"Didn't you have a red-hot sports car in flight school?" Nogi asked, circling around to get in front of me.

"I had a 1937 Datsun roadster."

"Wasn't it tan with red trim on the headlights, fenders, and dashboard?" he asked, using his hands to point out the relative position of the colors. "A black interior, large hub caps, running board, and a rumble seat?"

"That's the one."

"No wonder people remember it! Was it a big seller?"

"I think they sold something like fifteen thousand of them."

We paused to watch them stow the transfer lines used for the delivery of perishable food supplies to *Midnight Star*.

"Have you been listening to Professor Sakamoto?" I asked.

"Hai."

"Has he said anything to make you eager for battle?"

"Hai. He said that Japan watched the Westerners carve up China to obtain exclusive railroad rights, mineral rights, telegraphic services, and whatever else they could extract by violence."

"Anymore?"

"The American Armed Forces swept across the Pacific, taking control of Hawaii, Johnston Atoll, Midway, Wake, half of Samoa, Kingman Reef, Guam, and finally the Philippines," Nogi replied, ducking when he heard a pop out of the tiny explosive shell from a transfer line propellant. "The United States now had men and ships stationed some seven thousand miles from its own borders."

The destroyer pulled away and headed for the hospital ship.

"Do you ever see Shiroko anymore?" the mechanic asked.

"Only in my dreams." Turning away while shouting goodbye, I was unable to prevent my mind from drifting back to the time when the delectable legal assistant Shiroko Daizen took me to visit Nagasaki Municipal Hospital.

* * *

"It's within walking distance," she had said, thanking me for my expression of sympathy concerning her mother's death. Little did I know at the time that her brother Hiko would be murdered later on.

The six-block stroll was pleasant. The fragrant cedar trees, the lotus ponds, and the minature gardens had hypnotized people passing by into taking time to stop and enjoy one of earth's simple treasures. Its natural beauty lulled them into forgetting the possibility of typhoons and earthquakes.

Walking up the wide, marble steps to the brand new Nagasaki Municipal Hospital entrance, I understood why the community felt such pride in a building dedicated to the health of children.

Going through the door first, I followed the tradition of *bushido* and checked for evil-doers. Then turning around, held out my hand to her in a manner befitting a scholarly samurai, indicating it was safe to enter.

"Arigato, Koibito. I beg you to treat me as kindly in the future," Shiroko said, playing out the little charade with downcast eyes.

I hoped the, "thanks, sweetheart," expressed by Shiroko, was a clue to our future relationship.

The on-duty nurses looked me over, some boldly, but most with their hands on their mouths pretending shyness--none had forgotten to bow and smile at Shiroko in a fashion that showed their affection for her.

Spotting an office employee, Shiroko pulled me towards the female bookkeeper. "Kiyo, I'd like you to meet my new friend, Miiko Arishima. She was a traffic director before the gas embargo and now works in accounting keeping tabs on pediatrics."

"Please stop by and have a look at the baby ward," the attractive Miiko said with a gentle smile. "We'd like you to see our pocket-sized patients before you leave."

"Oh, I intended to," I said, never having given it a thought, but nonetheless charmed by Miiko's soft, lisping, Kyoto accent.

"Since he's so eager to see the babies," Shiroko said. "I'm going to take him there right away. See you later, Miiko."

36

"Isn't she nice?" Shiroko asked, dragging me down the passageway. "Her boy friend's a soldier on the *Ikeda.* His name is Jun Kaine. He's either a lance corporal or will be one, I don't know which."

"I'll remember his name," I said, smiling to myself when I thought about how my cousin had spent his off-duty hours.

"The tiniest ones are on the left," she said pointing to the glass partition. "The babies on your extreme right will be leaving the hospital in a day or two."

"They're outstanding," was all I could come up with. "There's so many of them."

"Were you in Nagasaki around February or March?" Shiroko asked.

"I might have been. Why?"

"I swear that baby with the auburn hair looks just like you."

Talk like that makes me nervous. I hoped she was teasing me.

A tremor ran through her as she turned her face up to me. "The Westerners won't bomb baby hospitals, will they?"

"No," I lied, "The children will be safe."

"Here's my address if you ever get to Hainan," she said as I turned to depart. "I don't live in Yulin, but have an apartment in Ya Xian, a little tourist town a few miles north of the air station."

* * *

Once the cargo nets were hauled in, I dropped my thoughts of Shiroko and directed my attention toward a group of idle sailors in time to hear one of them remark, "Finding an Asian or Pacific Islander that isn't ruled by the white man's armed forces is a rarity, but those past invasions do bring up a technical point though. Did America declare war before shooting any of the residents?"

"Not according to Sakamoto. Nor did they when they shelled our coastal cities," the aviation ordnanceman proclaimed, shaking his head in disappointment when he found out there would be no mail.

This convoy, I thought, looking from horizon to horizon, will enable the Asians to roll back the armies of Britain's King-Emperor's mighty empire like a cheap rug.

The Captain's steward filled us in on the latest gossip an hour later.

* * *

"Would you describe our Malayan thrust as a sneak attack?" Dr.

37

Hattori had asked, according to the steward's story.

"Look around you," Captain Naifu insisted. "You couldn't possibly hide a fleet of this size."

"Do the Westerners expect war?" she queried. "If you don't mind me asking these questions, Captain."

"After all that's happened in the last month, any commander in the Pacific who isn't ready to fight without an engraved invitation being sent from London or Washington should be tranferred to guard duty in a retirement home."

"Maybe the Americans have a scheme of their own," Dr. Hattori said, unhappy with Naifu's report that she couldn't be flown back to Sasebo until morning. In the meantime, she was to have the executive officer's cabin. The XO had already moved in with the operations officer.

"From all indications, the Americans, with the whole-hearted approval of Britain, were ready to launch a B-l7 surprise attack on our homeland, either from China or the Philippines. Everything is in place but the ammo," the Captain said.

"Do you think we can beat them to it?" the doctor asked, appearing uncomfortable when Naifu told her she was the prettiest medical person he'd ever known. She reached towards the night stand for the radio's on/off button at that point to break up the tension.

"If we're lucky," he said.

The steward slipped out to spread the news that the Captain was making moves on the doctor.

* * *

The *Sky Dragon*, operating just to the rear of the convoy, had its combat air patrol on reduced alert status, but instead of being asked to sit in the cockpit of a Mitsubishi A6M fighter, I was ordered to take the KR-2 to Kikai Air Base in the northernmost section of the Ryukyuan Island chain.

I reported a submarine after I got airborne.

"Open your eyes," *Sky Dragon* ordered. "That's a cargo net full of tomatoes accidently dropped over the side by *Ikeda Maru.*"

Pouting, I continued on my way.

The tiny, oblong, Kikai-Shima Island looked lonely. It had barely enough flat land for an airstrip. It had no villages nor even a coral reef like that on neighboring Okina-Jima.

The first thing I saw when I taxied into the bantam-sized air base, to what was jokingly referred to as the parking area, was not the familiar blue and yellow utility plane, but an army Ki-43 Peregrine Falcon that had not yet been assigned to a squadron.

Chapter 7

Kikai-Shima

As the convoy steadily moved toward its stated goal of freeing the Far East from Caucasian domination, I thought of myself as being up at the plate in the ninth inning with two strikes, two outs, and my team six runs behind. Our fate rested in the hands of the perennial world champions from Amsterdam and London.

Our manager's signs had been stolen. If I swung my bat at a sinker ball, the Western league was prepared to throw its latest multimillion dollar acquisition from Washington into the pennant race.

Like me, the men in the fifteen knot convoy had plenty of opportunity to dwell on the consequences of losing.

Although the fleet and the *Ikeda Maru* managed to settle into a comfortable routine, I was not so lucky. I had a frightening experience on my fifth hop of the day when I was ordered to bring a load of Aichi aircraft parts to *Sky Dragon.*

The flight was short, and I had to dump fuel in preparation for landing with a heavy load.

Unfortunately, pleasant thoughts of Shiroko during a hot summer day on the slopes of Mt. Fuji were shattered when I forgot to turn off the dump switch and stayed in a steep bank too long. The wispy memories of her standing in a paper-thin, white komono, with the sun spotlighting her taffy-colored skin and curvy outlines vanished as I flew through the escaping fuel. Sparks from the exhaust torched-off the stream of gasoline pouring from the trailing edge of the wing. Although it didn't explode, the ignition was nevertheless scary--and the torrent of firey liquid continued until I got the dump valve shut off. I would need a quieter period to recall Shiroko's lustrous black hair falling in soft waves about her shoulders, her eyes mocking my feeble attempts at being romantic.

I landed the KR-2 and its supplies without further mishap.

The crewman on the carrier referred to the KR-2 as the Sandpiper, a shorebird with a slender bill and a piping call.

"I thought the war had started when I saw the firey streaks in the sky," the mechanic responsible for tying down the aircraft told me later.

The color in his face had receded along with the flame in the darkened sky.

"And I thought the plane blew up," I countered, making room for the other sailors gathering around the aircraft, one of whom pictured himself as the resident intellectual. Politics quickly became the topic of the day.

"Do you agree with Sakamoto?" the brainy bluejacket asked. "I certainly do, especially when he paraphrased Churchill as saying that England's claim to Asian possessions, mainly acquired by violence, largely maintained by force, seems less reasonable to other nations than to Great Britain."

The question was too highbrow for me. I turned to the Captain's steward standing on the edge of the circle. "Anything new?"

"Dr. Hattori was eating alone in her stateroom when she saw the flash in the sky out of the porthole.

"No gossip?"

"Captain Naifu was bothering her again," he said in a hushed voice.

Trying to include all the troops that came out to greet me, I asked. "Anything more from Sakamoto?"

"During what the West referred to as 'China's Boxer Rebellion,' a foreign force including five thousand Americans fought their way from the coast to Peking. They burned, looted, and killed in that city," an ordnanceman divulged.

If the West ever condemns another nation for brutality, I thought. Peking should be mentioned to put it in perspective.

"Captain Naifu, pretending to be interested in the radio, moved his chair next to Dr. Hattori's," the Steward said, eager to stay in the conversation.

If I was correctly reading between the lines of what he was saying, Kimiko had better keep her scapel handy.

"I might mention that 1901 was the fifth year of the Osaka bicycle boom," the mechanic said, wanting to be in the center of things. "Those bikes were exported in large numbers, scaring American and Britain manufactures."

Hoping to top them all, the aviation ordnanceman shouted to be heard. "Japan had big investments in Hawaii, the Philippines, Sumatra, and Taiwan, to name just a few. As a long range speculative venture, we even bought three thousand acres in New Jersey."

"New Jersey!" I exclaimed. "What's that?"

"It's a state on the east coast of North America," someone who claimed to have been a straight 'A' student in geography volunteered.

"Because of Japan's victory over Russia, nationalist parties sprang up throughout Asia," my friend from the radio shack claimed. "Their chant echoed throughout the orient: the White man is not invincible.'" His tone reminded me of Yeoman Nitta's voice on the radio. He sounded like he belonged on the loading docks instead of an office.

I changed the subject by telling the group a sea story about an exciting night's liberty in Cam Ranh Bay a couple of years ago. "She was French," I told them. "Glossy dark-brown hair, come-hither eyes, a see-through blouse, high heels--and legs," I said with a professional sailor's gleam in my eye. "I *mean* we are talking legs."

The crowd disbursed, deflating me.

"Keep an eye on the doctor, my friend," I said to the steward before he left, "and tell me about it when I return."

"Where are you going, Debuchi-san?"

"I'm taking the KR-2 back to Kikai-Shima to bring out a target for the fleet. I don't know what kind of plane I'll be flying. The blue and yellow aircraft is down for repairs."

I took off when the moon broke through a heavy cloud bank to the west.

The weak luna light reminded me of the first time Yukiko and I had viewed a full moon together. It was while walking home from her monthly poetry contest, a popular event in Kagoshima.

The small detachment at Kikai was so bored they were shooting off fireworks.

Did Japan's treaty with Russia, Great Britain, and the U.S. protecting the fur-bearing seals have any affect on this place, I wondered, almost tripping over an artifical fern. "Ah, so! I smell chestnuts roasting," I told the mechanic begging me to bring in some charcoal on my next trip.

"Any excitment?" I asked the wind-burned sailor dishing out baked sweet potatoes.

"I can't claim its as quiet as a cemetery around here. The place is too small for a burial site. However, we did have a girl from NHK that claimed she was a sports writer. Her name was Ruriko Hattori."

"Baseball?"

"No. Fishing. She wanted to talk about surf casting.

I ate a helping of steamed fish loaf, turnips, and pickled quail eggs, and washed it down with powdered green tea and Nippon beer while sitting under the wing of the army's Ki-43.

"What's the latest rumor?" I asked.

"A Dutch submarine was spotted off shore last night."

Chapter 8

Peregrine Falcon

My turnaround time in Kikai was minimal, what we would call a hit and run in baseball. As the tiny island quickly faded into the background, I tuned the Peregrine Falcon's radio to *Ikeda's* command center.

"Before you know it, we'll be off the coast of Hainan in preparation for an amphibious landing exercise and a practice forced march through the forested areas," the Captain announced over the radio. "As part of our overall training, we're proceeding with a scheduled gun drill for the cruisers and destroyers. One of the army's Ki-43s is presently inbound with the targets.

"The utility pilot flying the plane is well-known to this command. He has volunteered to put on a one-man air show to demonstrate why the army thinks this plane is superior to the navy's A6M, better known as the Zero. A receiver has been jumpered into the loudspeaker for your enjoyment."

I watched the thinly scattered clouds below me flash on and off like a Western Christmas tree, as my aircraft lights illuminated them.

Five miles from the fleet, I looked at the fuel gauge with satisfaction. The external fuel tanks were empty, but my fuselage cells were nearly full.

Noticing a grease spot in the lower, left-hand corner of the windscreen and a popped circuit breaker on the non-essential panel, I reached over and wiped off the thick lubricant with my left elbow, then pushed in the circuit breaker with the index finger on my right hand.

Except for a sore rear-end from too many flights in one day, I figured I was about as ready as I was going to get. Even if I hadn't finished chewing my chocolate-covered carmel.

"Riptide, this is Black Magic Two One Five," I said, retaining Tomi's call sign. "Where do you want the target?"

"Black Magic Two One Five, from Riptide. Take a heading of one four five. I'll tell you when to drop."

"Two One Five, *Tadachi ni.*"

I banked to the prescribed heading, eased off on the throttle, and waited.

"Black Magic Two One Five, this is Riptide. Drop target!"

A mile from the fleet, I hit the release button on the control stick and felt one of the two florescent-painted, external tanks leave the aircraft.

Seeing the empty tank hit the surface intact, I climbed and headed for the opposite side of the convoy. "Riptide, I'll circle to the north away from action until you're finished shooting."

"Riptide, *Hai.*"

Unfortunately, my shortcut took me over a destroyer on the outer fringe where the second tank decided to come loose.

"Look out below!" I hollered.

The destroyers *Enchanted Shadow* and *Midnight Star* opened up on the easternmost target after firing flares to illuminate the area. They bracketed the designated drop tank with the first salvo and sank it with the second.

The bigger warships, including the eight inch guns of the heavy cruiser, *Painted Veil,* fired in unison, blowing the second object to smithereens on the opening volley. "Good shooting," I muttered, thinking they've had a lot of practice somewhere along the line. And with no flash from the smokeless powder pinpointing their position to enemy ships, they'll have a distinct advantage at night.

"Black Magic, we're done firing. Thanks for supplying the targets. Our ships would appreciate seeing what the Peregrin Falcon can do."

"Congratulations on your first-rate shooting. For those of you who have never seen the Nakajima Ki-43, " I said, turning on all the extra lights mounted on the leading edge of the tail and wings, this is the army's secret weapon in case the navy declares war on its sister-service.

"I'm utility pilot Kiyo Debuchi," I said, moving the rudder back and forth like a dog waging its tail. "and I've had the pleasure of ferrying this plane since it began replacing the Ki-27. In contrast to the navy's Zero, which you hear so much about--thanks to our hard-working public relations department--the newer models of the Falcon will have head and back armorplating and self-sealing fuel tanks in the wings."

"Won't that extra weight slow down the Peregrine Falcon?" the Captain. a navy booster wanted to know.

"Not by very much. It's being flown by Manchukuo and Thailand as well as the Japanese Army Airforce," I allowed, climbing at low speed to demonstrate its excellent stall charactoristics. "I've reached the top of a loop. Most Western fighter planes will spin out if they enter a vertical maneuver at the speeds I used.

"I still have control," I said, rolling the aircraft right-side up at the apex of the arc to illustrate an Immelmann maneuver.

"Look out *Ikeda*," I warned with a snarl, dropping the aircraft's nose.

Flying directly over the fleet to demonstrate the aircraft's superior acceleration, I rammed the throttle to the firewall. *Dolly Madison's* cream-colored airspeed needle sprinted across the black dial like a ten-year old child running through a graveyard at night.

"Check that out, Admiral" the General hollered as the aircraft's lighted silhouette leaped forward. "I'll bet it can outrun a Zero while sitting in the chocks."

"I've seen a Datsun dig out from a stop sign faster," the Captain taunted.

"How much credibility does a sailor have?" the General countered.

"It's easy to win a race against thin air," the Admiral suggested in a loud voice. "Against a Zero it would be a different story."

"Riptide," I grunted, obviously struggling to get out the words. "I'm in a hi-g bank now, and you can see what a tight circle I'm making. The ability to turn inside someone means life or death in a dogfight," I said, relaxing for a fraction of a second. But watch this!" The throat mike partially distorted the message.

In an effort to impress the shipboard personnel with an even smaller circle, I reached down and threw the switch labelled, 'combat flap.' Gripping the stick hard enough to draw the skin taut across my knuckles, I succeeded in squeezing another g out of the aircraft.

"Check out that maneuver deck-apes," the soldiers yelled in the background.

"They're jumping up and down as the rows of green and red lights on the aircraft bend back onto themselves," the General assured me.

"Riptide," I called, sounding like a man with a bad head-cold. "The Peregrine Falcon pilots swear they can take on two Zeros for breakfast and a destroyer for lunch."

"Not on their best day," the Captain zinged back.

Breaking out of the turn, I steered *Dolly* toward the Ryukyu Islands.

Seven hops in one day may not be a record for a utility pilot, but it certainly made me want to crawl into a bunk for an extended night's sleep.

Chapter 9

Asian Knights

The next morning I brought the KR-2 Sandpiper back to *Sky Dragon.*

Restless after a good night's sleep, I walked aft to watch the sea birds soaring lazily near the playful porpoises.

Since it was the early part of the day, I expected to be alone on the fantail and was surprised to find an aviation radioman standing there taking pictures. He had his back to me.

"Do you always spend your mornings here?" I asked.

"I'm just fidgety, Debuchi-san, he answered, recognizing my voice. "This convoy seems big to me," he said scanning the horizon. "But it's only a dot compared to the mighty armadas the West will be able to muster.

"Yesterday, Sakamoto said that the West was going to make the Japanese seem like cruel, vicious people to counteract the foreign visitor's impression of a polite, gentle, and family-oriented society."

I turned to face Inspector Ibuse as he showed up balancing a cup of tea on a rattan tray. "What's the first name of that Private Agi I hear mentioned on the radio?"

"Mallory, he's more of a librarian than a soldier," Ibuse said. "He's from Gifu, a town two hundred miles southwest of Tokyo; it's famous for the manufacture of paper hats, fans, lanterns, and umbrellas. He claims his mother was smitten with a Westerner named Mallory. The Englishman came to purchase Gifu's paper-based products which sell better in the British Isles than the toy samurai swords purchased in such large numbers by the Americans.

"And speaking of samurai. The more aggressive Western nations chose to minimize their own long history of conquests over the last two hundred years by calling attention to Japan's feudal period and the group of fighting men referred to as samurai."

"I'm a descendant of the mighty samurai," a light-bearded sailor joining us insisted, managing to ruin the image of a fighting man by offering to share a capful of almonds.

"If the truth be known, only a tiny percent of us has any ancestors that were samurai," I commented to the little group.

"After hearing Sakamoto's lectures I'm ready to throw the Western armies out of Asia," the aviation radioman said, pulling in his stomach.

"Weren't the knights the samauri's counterpart in Europe?" Ibuse asked, cracking an almond to savor its penetrating scent.

"The knights were mounted soldiers serving under a feudal superior. The old adage, *Way of the Warrior*, applied to the European knights as well as the samurai," I assured them, pretending to have a sword in my hand.

"What did they do?" the radioman asked, ducking under my thrust.

"During wartime, the knights made their living by plundering the villages and castles of the enemy," I responded, knocking the Inspector's tea cup off the tray with my flailing around.

"Was there anything else the European knights did besides fight?" the inquisitive radioman asked, shaking out a canvas flight-deck shoe splattered with tea.

"*Hai.* They were the tax collectors. And very efficient ones at that." I demonstrated their technique by drawing a hand across my throat.

The radioman picked up the broken cup when Inspector Geki Ibuse gave him one of his chilling stares. "My oldest sister told me she heard that the samurai were very polite," he said, bowing deeply in mock tribute.

"Extremely so," I said, pretending to draw a business card out of my pocket. "There had to be an introduction and an exchange of background information before combat."

Ibuse and I left the stern of the ship at the same time. He had to get back to *Ikeda*, and I was looking forward to taking the Sandpiper on a combined test flight and two-hour trip to an Okinawan air base.

Reading over the maintenance yellow sheets twenty minutes before launch time, I noticed the torn fabric on the upper wing had been repaired. This was my lucky day, I thought, noting the sign-off signature of the best mechanic in the air group. From past encounters, I had this vivid picture of Rikichi Nogi imprinted on my mind: sweaty, weary, with a dirty rag hanging out of his back pocket, trudging through the hanger bay on his way to fix another mechanical problem.

Nothing here I can't handle, I figured as I initialed the trouble sheet.

"Good luck, Debuchi-san," Aviation Machinist Mate First Class Nogi remarked, standing off to one side looking pleased.

"What are his chances of coming back?" I heard a deck hand ask the eight-year veteran in the battle to keep naval aircraft flying.

"About fifty-fifty," Nogi replied. "But, on the bright side, he couldn't have picked a better day for taking that final journey through the Torii in the sky. Look at that rainbow to the east."

"Blossoms bring storms, so to speak," the deck hand observed, taking note of the mechanic's cheerful expression that forecast trouble. "I saw him give you a dirty look when you printed 'taxicab' in the salt residue on the nose of the aircraft."

"I received another good report on you, Nogi," the flight deck chief said, showing up at the end of the conversation. "The assistant maintenance officer told me you're the hardest working aviation machinist mate he's ever known."

"Thanks," Nogi muttered, taking the first ladder down to the hanger deck.

Out of curiousity, I followed him.

Once out of sight of the chief line mechanic, he pulled a long, dirty rag out of his shirt and stuffed one end of it into his back pocket. Checking his schedule, he turned into hanger bay 1.

Seeing no one around the water fountain, Nogi splashed some water on his face and rubbed in a dab of grease from his dungaree shirt pocket.

Making sure the rag hung to the floor, he slowly walked past the weapons storage area. When the ordnance officer spotted him, Nogi's steps faltered and the back of his hand went to his forehead to wipe off the beads of water. Bowing slightly toward the officer as if even this small gesture was too tiring, the enterprising mechanic made a quarter turn to give him a good view of the dirty rag. Then with an air of resignation, he dragged himself toward his next assignment.

"What a hard worker," the personnel officer said, watching Nogi from the other side of the hanger bay. "I wonder if he knows what clean clothes even smell like."

Picking up speed once he was out of sight, Rikichi Nogi headed for his bunk. As long as he stayed away from the maintenance chief in hanger bay 3, he'd be able to catch a lot of sack time, I thought. Apparently, he felt himself entitled to all the sleep he could get, having grown up in Hakodae, a fishing port where everbody labored from dawn to dusk. The town has prided itself on hard work since the eighteen century.

Climbing into the cockpit, I reflected on my last discussion with Captain Naifu. The man was forty years of age and rigid in his attitude toward those junior to him. He insisted that I take a more assertive approach to flying an airplane.

I was surprised at the number of sailors watching from the outer edges of the flight deck. Maybe word had leaked out that I was a pretty hot pilot. I"ll just give them a little show, I decided when I went to full power.

With everything looking good in the cockpit, I waited for the green lights, arrayed in a circular pattern, to come on--the signal I was clear for take off. Hold it, I told myself, realizing my seat was not adjusted properly after I unsuccessfully tried to see the end of the flight deck over the instrument panel.

Taking time to spin the knob elevating the pilot's seat brought a blast from the Captain.

"Get airborne, you mallet head," Naifu screamed.

Quickly giving the knob one last turn, I watched the launching officer shake his head in frustration.

Releasing the brakes, I kept my audience in mind as I scooted down the five-hundred-foot flight deck. Playing the role of the fearless naval aviator, I squared my shoulders and attempted to plant my head firmly against the headrest.

Unfortunately, the last turn of the seat-adjusting knob had squashed my head against the canopy, forcing it into a ten degree tilt.

What is that?" Naifu shrieked at Kuni, his air operations officer. "Is he falling asleep on take off? This is not the way my aviators normally handle themselves," he said, turning to Kimiko Hattori.

The air base, on the Island of Okinawa, received word of my impending arrival. In the distance, the storm clouds goose-stepped away from the latest atmospheric display from the north--the erratic spotlights dimmed and the drum rolls went silent. With only five more days left in the month, November's merry-making and ear-splitting toasts had already become stale news.

To feed the public's insatiable desire for fresh thrills, Miss Cumulus Cloud swept in from Southeast Asia on the back of a gale. Using her ample contours and rain-driven transportation, she cut in front of several whispy clouds that were quietly waiting for December's contest to start.

I entered an inlet on the southwest side of the island, turned at a spot near the shrines and temples along the waterfront, and shot over to Naha, the capital city, where the big Tsuboya ceramic pottery center was located.

Subsequent to a quick air tour of the sixty mile long island, a piece of territory that resembled a crumpled paper dragon, I headed back over the inlet and landed at the Naha Naval Air Station.

After I changed into white, knee-high stockings, with matching shoes, shorts, belt, and a short sleeve shirt, I entered the lounge. I became suspicious when Shuji Genda, a member of the illustrious "Four Ghosts," accosted me, then he tempered the mood by suggesting we split a pot of green tea.

Trying not to stare at his eyebrows, the ends of which swept up like the tips of a pagoda roof, and his mouth with its permanent half-smile, I hesitated for a moment. This was not an order but an invitation. Shrugging my shoulders, I decided to be polite.

The usually filled and boisterous lounge presented no seating problems for us. Genda, carrying a stack of messages handed to him by the duty-officer, led the way past four pilots playing bridge and two officers from the maintenance department locked into a chess game.

"I'll get the tea, Lieutenant," I offered, conscious of the difference in rank. Maybe it's about the "Trademark Killer," I thought while hurrying to the serving table. Genda looks awfully serious.

"Sit down, Debuchi-san," Shuji Genda ordered, pulling out a wicker chair. "I want to tell you a story about something that nearly destroyed my overly competitive family," he said, after thanking me for the tea.

This is going to be boring, I thought, picking up a dark-colored orange from the fruit tray.

"My father and his younger brother," Genda said, staring at the top of my head, "were among the first to get civilian pilot lessons, incidentally, in an old French biplane." I peeled the orange and said a quick prayer for divine intervention.

"My father and uncle entered every airmail flying contest they could find," Genda said, not sure he had my full attention.

So what, I thought, my father's in television and my Uncle Masao's an ice skater. "Go on," I said mechanically, working hard to keep my eyelids fully open.

"Between airmail contests they entered air races and flew sightseers from farm pastures," Lt. Genda added, hoping his audience of one was absorbing this information.

Who cares, I wondered, playing with a chopstick, but keeping what I hoped was a look of interest on my face.

"The main part of this story concerns the airmail race from Iwaki to Ube," Shuji said, raising his voice to make an impression on me. "A distance of nine hundred miles."

I moved a small section of orange towards my mouth after tearing it into small pieces with my chopsticks.

"They were so intent on beating each other," Genda said, embarrassing himself by talking too loud, "that they flew through a rainstorm, with my father crashing one hundred miles short of the designated city and my uncle twenty miles further along.

"Were they killed?" I asked hopefully, figuring the story would end there.

"No! But the point is; if they had cooperated, my father entering some races and my uncle others, there would not have been the direct competition that almost did them in. My uncle still carries the scars, and my father has a permanent limp."

"What's that!" I yelped, after biting into the orange. My face became so scrunched up that my eyes closed and I could feel my white, tropical cap tilt.

"That's a Seville orange. It's very sour and is normally used for preservatives," Shuji smiled. "Your action with the orange proves my point. The idea is to think about the consequences, plan, and use the experience of others. You're going to need thousands of hours in the air before you can call yourself 'Emperor of the Skies.'"

"Did your relatives take your advice?" I asked, gulping down tea to dilute the bitter taste.

"No, they did something better. They formed an aerobatic team called the 'Genda Circus.' That forced them to cooperate, and from that day on they enjoyed each other's company."

"Are you asking me to be a replacement for one of the 'Four Ghosts,' sir?"

"No! I'm letting you know you'll never get permanently assigned to a combat squadron, especially one that has a distinguished record. We don't need someone around here who climbs into a cockpit without a thought in his head. And stop calling the instrument panel a dashboard; you're not driving one of your family's fancy sports cars.

"And one more thing. Although you're a skillful enough aviator when you put your mind to it, you still haven't developed the killer instinct a fighter pilot must have."

Glad that Genda's lecture was over, I got up from the table when he dismissed me with a nod. After staying just long enough to give a polite thank you in my best theatrical voice, I exited in a hurry.

"Don't forget your chopsticks," Shuji Genda shouted at me.

Reversing course after almost bumping into an oriental brass urn, I grabbed the the utensils and put them back in their carrying case, bowed, and made an unsuccessful attempt to look humble. "I keep a spare in the glove compartment of the plane," I said, linking the unsolicited information together with a goodbye.

Chapter 10

The Four Ghosts

"Any word yet on the murders?" Jun asked as he squeezed in a piece of unsolicited information about three navy policemen passing through.

"No. But murder, or not, we want to be up on deck within the hour," the Professor said. "A navy Zero squadron operating out of Naha heard about the mini-airshow put on by the army plane and intends to top it with their Four Ghosts."

"'Four Ghosts!' Is that a prediction? We've got a departed soul from that Achi dive bomb aboard already."

"No. They claim the Zeroes disappear while you're watching them perform."

"*This*, I gotta see," Jun said, "I'll even push away one of the two small dishes of noodles I big-dealed from the duty-cook."

"Captain Ohira will make an announcement over the loudspeaker. But in the meantime, back to oil," the Professor suggested to get their minds off the killings. "Oil is called the lifeblood of modern civilization. That is a paradox when you consider all the human blood lost to obtain that black, slippery substance.

"One of the most profitable oil fields was acquired by the Dutch over the bodies of the dead Indonesians. Thirty years later, with the help of the Dutch army and secret police, it's producing 65,000 barrels a day."

* * *

The final inspection was underway on the four Zeroes. They were painted an off-color white, carefully chosen to blend into a sky presently sprinkled with puffy white clouds.

I went over to see if there were any last minute instructions.

"This particular shade will be difficult to see from below. It's designed to be obscure even on a bright day," Ghost Leader said, responding to the flight mechanic's question about the plane's color.

"Commander, your team is called the 'Four Ghosts,' and yet this plane is a very solid object," I said, banging on the side of the aircraft to prove my point.

53

"We deal in illusion. The eye prefers to follow a straight line," Ghost Leader informed me, keeping his hand level as he moved it from left to right. "And in that split second before the brain switches to a new path, we accomplish our disappearing act."

"It sounds eerie."

"Did you put in new flares and the chemicals for generating smoke?" he asked the mechanic.

"Yes, sir. Each plane is fully equipped," the mechanic vowed. "Why does Emi-san call his plane the Red-Crowned Crane?"

"Because he had his helmet dyed red and feels he's rare and endangered."

Ghost Leader used the typical Japanese palm down gesture to beckon over a pilot with an interesting past. He had been assumed dead and placed in a rubber bag after a fiery takeoff crash five years ago. "Listen, Ito, stay in closer from now on. Make believe you're just an extra coat of paint on my wing."

"Team leader, I'll be in so snug, you'll see the brush strokes."

"You're looking better every day," he said with exaggeration to the man who had spent four years having thirty percent of his skin replaced. "What was the name of the hospital that did the reconstruction work?"

"St. Lukes," Kenji Ito said, flexing the hands that had miraculously escaped the flames. "I was lucky to have Mariko as my nurse. She married me later on, scars and all."

"Here comes Genda," Ghost Leader said quietly. "He flies a tight left wing but was late firing flares during the last airshow. I need one more pilot. Anybody seen the slotman?"

"*Hai,*" Genda replied, "I saw him over by the benjo ditch a moment ago. Oh, here comes the old complainer."

Walking over, with the speed normally associated with breaking in a new pair of shoes, Emi joined the team and remarked how easy their job was. "You have only one plane to watch. While I," he said, "back in the slot, have to watch all three."

"We'll buy you a plaque someday Emi-san, but in the meantime, we're putting on a show for the fleet spearheading the effort to free Asia," Ghost Leader announced. "Debuchi here, staged an exhibition in the army's Ki-43 yesterday, but we'll upstage that act with the navy's best."

Emi looked at me as if I were some kind of traitor for flying the Peregrine Falcon.

"Any changes?" Genda asked.

"The code word will stay the same. When I say 'vanish,' release the smoke-generating button, count to five, and engage it again. Let's go," he ordered as he turned and waved them towards their aircraft.

"Debuchi-san," the Lieutenant Commander ordered. "Get out to the fleet, lay down a chemical screen, and stay out of our way."

Within minutes, the four pilots had their engines started, had made quick power checks, and were headed toward the runway--taxiing in the same formation they used in the air.

Ghost Leader, using his gloved fist, motioned his right-hand wingman to move in closer.

Hearing me call in my position, Ghost Leader reminded me they'd let me have thirty seconds lead time.

"*Hai,*" I said, intending to go full throttle while they idled back after their climb out was completed.

Turning onto the runway, Ghost Leader took a quick look to both sides, checked the rearview mirror for Slots position, added power with his left hand and held his right one high. As the four engines wound up to an ear-splitting roar, he swung his hand down with the fingers pointing forward, alerting the flight to get off their brakes without a vocal command.

"Tower," he said. "Four Ghosts rolling."

Ghost Leader, *Genda's Circus, Green Pastures, and the Red-Crowned Crane* accelerated to lift-off speed without breaking formation. Clear of the runway, Genda quickly moved under the leader's left wing, Ito tucked himself beneath the right one, and Emi maneuvered into the slot in back of, and below, Ghost Leader.

I flew under, and shot past, the throttled-back flight at maximum power.

This is home, I thought, as I opened the canopy to draw in a little nourishment from the wind. It's the perfect vantage point to watch cloud-born floral displays continuously rearrange and water themselves. I felt sorry for those who were forced to stand on solid earth guessing what sort of day Mother Nature had in store for them.

I'd rather climb up to see for myself what mood she's in.

I was the opposite of my friend Tomi. I had the cooperative mentality of a wolf: a deep-rooted enjoyment in hunting with the pack.

Ten miles out, Ghost Leader adjusted the valve so the smoke would be ejected at a twenty degree upward angle, then radioed. "Riptide, this is Ghost Leader with four, ready to entertain."

"Ghost Leader from Riptide. We welcome you, and give you the sky above our fleet as your stage."

The light mist I dispersed from the external tank on the squadron's blue and yellow utility aircraft was still in the air when the Four Ghosts arrived.

Thick streams of colored smoke appeared behind and slightly above their shadowy outlines as the four aircraft burst out of the vapor-laden sky. Roaring across the convoy, Ghost Leader hit the flare button to distract the audience, disengaged the smoke generator, and yanked the plane into a steep climbing turn to get behind the smoke screen. I imagined there were oohs and ahhs down below when the four smoke trails stopped.

"The planes are gone," *Ikeda's* skipper called out over the radio, mystified. "No! There they are. Gone again! No! Now I see them; I must have blinked my eyes. Scary!"

Similar comments were heard in the background as he keyed the mike.

Ghost Leader pulled the aircraft around for another run. Everything seemed to be going as programed. I crossed over and laid down a misty vapor at the proper time. The team was flying tight, and the mechanical equipment was working.

After establishing a steady altitude and course with the smoke spewing out of the trailing edge of the wings, the leader called, "vanish," cut-off the tinted smoke and pulled the aircraft into a loop as they entered the neutral-colored mist. When he re-igniting the smoke generator at the end of a slow count to five, I knew that the spectators on the ships would visualize the broken space in the colored haze, combined with the hard to see aircraft, as a disappearance.

At the top of the vertical circle, Ghost Leader called, "vanish," cut off the smoke generator, and rolled the aircraft right-side up to keep it from completing the down side of the loop. I assumed the deception was even more dramatic at the higher altitude.

They had better ring down the curtain after one more, or the audience will catch on, I thought. Always leave your audience wanting more. Ghost Leader took the team down in a shallow dive to accustom the spectators to a long, solid line. Passing through the haze left by my blue and yellow plane, he suddenly leveled off, yelled "vanish," and immediately went into a steep bank.

"Riptide, this is Ghost Leader. Returning from the land of lost souls." He flew inverted over Emi's red helmet while taking his four plane formation on a low altitude flyby before departing the area.

"Ghost Leader, from Riptide. I don't know how you do it, but I swear you left this world for a few seconds during the show."

As the Ghost team turned and headed for Vietnam to do their next show, I ducked into a long chain of clouds stretching out towards Japan in the opposite direction. I had a short but familiar destination in mind.

I've chalked up plenty of hours ferrying Zeroes whenever I'm not doing these routine jobs that anybody can do. But I still can't seem to get orders to a combat squadron, just because the instructors have labelled me as too carefree, non-aggressive, uninspiring, and indifferent.

The assignment officer has completely ignored my excellent marks for airmanship.

* * *

Kaine said, "I don't see that little blue and yellow aircraft."

"You better not lean against the signal flag storage bin," *Ikeda's* second class signalman warned, "I've got to open the door to the cabinet."

"How about the business world? Did Japan have any important events?" he inquired, changing the subject. "Excuse me, I've got to reach the halyard to put up a new set of signal flags."

"In 1911, almost fifty years after its enactment, America finally cancelled all the provisions of that unequal trade treaty we talked about previously," the Professor said.

"America had a fifty year patent so to speak," Kaine volunteered.

"But that's not the end of it. The Webb-Henry Alien Land Act was passed in California--it excluded the Japanese from buying land."

"My dad is interested in buying overseas property to raise goldfish," the Signalman said with pride. "And I'm going to be the family's land appraiser.

"Didn't a war start about this time?" Kaine asked getting back in the conversation.

"*Hai,* 1914 brought with it the 'Great War,' to borrow a European phrase."

"Were the Europeans prepared for war?"

"War with Germany presented the biggest prize of all--the possibility of taking the oil rights along the Baghdad railroad in Iraq from Germany's Deutsche Bank. France believed the Allies could beat Germany easily and also take possession of the lucrative Bayer Aspirin trademark.

"The reason I'm giving you a lot of information on France, Kaine-san, involves the Far East. France drafted a hundred thousand Vietnamese to labor in her munitions factories."

57

"What areas did Germany excel in?" Kaine asked.

"Germany was ahead in photo optics, electrical application and chemicals. Leica was on the verge of a real breakthrough in mass-produced quality cameras--this was a chance for the Allies to cut into that lead.

"But it would be hard to work up any enthusiasm for Germany's aristocrats. Their leader, Kaiser Wilhelm, was always ranting and raving about the yellow menace."

"I wonder what happened to that blue and yellow plane" Kaine pondered again, seemingly obsessed with its disappearance. "Maybe he was forced to ditch.

* * *

Far from having vanished--in less than an hour I had selected the air corridor on the eastern side of the island and had flown over Shuri, Okinawa's capital in the last century.

After receiving permission to reenter the Navy's airspace, I called, "Naha tower from Utility Seven One Six. Have you in sight. Request landing instructions. Destination, Mitsubishi modification line."

"Utility Seven One Six from Naha tower. Runway twenty-one, ten knot crosswind, watch for an airport vehicle waiting to cross the landing strip after you're safely out of the way."

A large number of fishing vessels dominated the view off my right side as I flew over the harbor.

The minute I landed and rolled past the brightly-colored vehicle, it scooted out on the runway. Must be on an awfully important mission, I thought, watching the little truck dart behind me to take a short cut to the hanger area.

"Utility Seven One Six from Tower. Turn off at the third exit and proceed straight ahead to the Mitsubishi hanger."

"Hai," I replied, having already spotted the distinctive triple red diamond emblem of the corporation.

Looking off to the starboard side, I saw an aviation machinist mate stumble off the service vehicle, apparently overly-anxious to guide me into the proper spot.

To my surprise, the flight mechanic that was directing me had hair a foot longer than regulation.

What's going on, I wondered. I haven't been at sea that long.

The shock continued as I climbed down from the plane to face a stiff-bodied mechanic, with hands on hips, just waiting to chew me out.

"Is that the best you can do?" said a feminine voice, that was anything but angry.

"Yukiko! I must be dreaming," I exclaimed, as the little bundle of beauty and energy leaped into my arms, almost before the men in the area had a chance to turn their backs, pretending not to notice.

"I've missed you," I murmured tenderly. "I wish this period of unrest in Asia was over, so we can get back to some sort of normal life."

"Me too," she purred playfully. "But let's enjoy whatever time we have together now." She put her tiny feet down.

"I have a couple of hours," I said, pulling off my flight gloves and helmet.

"I don't," she said, the mist in her eyelashes made her dancing cinnamon-colored eyes seem enormous.

"How is your family?" I asked politely, holding her at arms length to admire her. Her skin reminded me of a full moon on a clear midsummer night.

"They're okay. My dad is thinking of selling five acres of his land," Yukiko confided. "Is it true you were transferred off the carrier?" she asked, not aware of her habit of changing subjects without warning.

"*Hai*," I answered, surprised. "Boy, news sure travels fast on the bamboo telegraph."

"Well, even though we're not married, the navy wives invite me to their luncheon meetings," she told me, her eyebrow arched in amusement.

"I better watch myself," I said, wondering if that was a hint.

"Most people expect you to be Ghost Leader someday,"she fibbed, looking pleased. "I've made up a joke poem about your new nickname."

"Tell me."

"No. I'm saving it for the proper time," she said, looking secretive, then changed the subject. "Do you remember that history professor? I think his name was Michi Sakamoto. The one who used to talk about perceptions and perspectives all the time."

"Yes, I do. I missed a baseball practice to hear one of his lectures my third year in college."

"My girl friend Miiko told me she heard that Sakamoto said there may be a big operation soon to expel the Western occupation forces from the Far East."

"There's something brewing, but I don't know when or where," I said dodging the subject. "There are a huge number of Western countries lined up, ready to smash our economic game plan."

"The craving for a fat pocketbook casts a suspicious-looking shadow on the motives of both the Eastern and the Western politicians."

"You're probably right, my high-spirited butterfly, but let's not take time to discuss it now."

Ever so gracefully, Yukiko, using her right hand like an artist's brush, drew me toward the bench next to the shrubbery that formed a natural fence line.

When I was comfortably seated on the flat stone bench. Yukiko brought and served me green tea taken from the line mechanics supplies. She used all the formality inherent in a proper tea ceremony.

Sitting close together, we thought of the times we enjoyed the approach of night with only the dim light from a stone lantern, fireflies, and shadows for company--before the threat of hostilies with the West became so apparent.

Taking her hand, I grew serious for a moment. "Yukiko dear, I don't know if there'll be war, or how much destruction it will cause our homeland. But somebody has to get the ball rolling or Asia will never be free."

"I understand," she said, thinking this was not to be a very romantic conversation. "The morning radio programs have been bringing people in from neutral countries. Those nations who aren't consumed by racism and jealousy are sympathetic with our position. But I can't help worrying about you."

"Don't fret for me, sweetpea. Whatever happens. I have known the affection of a beautiful and talented woman. Not all men are so lucky. Where would you like to go?"

"Sweetpea. Boy, are you old-fashioned. But nice old-fashioned," she said giving me a big hug. "Kiyo. Do you remember when we put up a poetry scroll on that old pine tree next to West Tokyo's biggest department store?"

"I've had that locked in my memory bank ever since," I admitted.

"Do you recall when we went back to see if it was still there?" she asked.

"Sure," I said filling in the first part. "Getting off the train, we wove our way through the crowds that were headed for a holiday sale on winter clothing at Echigoy's. At that time of year, men were wearing everything from stripped blazers and woolen suits to the more traditional garb. The women, from warm dresses, slack suits and reefer coats with pleated backs to embroidered kimonos."

"Smiles came as we turned the corner on the east side of the store," she said. "The tree was still there, looking very fragile with a dozen scrolls hanging from its branches."

"We ran from scroll to scroll, as I remember it, hastily searching for our very own piece of poetry."

"'Here it is!' you shouted, making the people in front of the department store laugh."

Hurrying over to my side, she had grabbed the scroll and read the little poem aloud.

"And as was their custom, nearby shoppers stopped and listened. Many had read the poem before."

"To honor the other amateur poets, we read and commented on a half dozen scrolls pinned to the trees."

"I wonder how many people saw and made remarks about our poem?" Yukiko asked, hesitantly.

"Six months ago, we spoke what was in our hearts. I wouldn't change a word. Would you?" I asked, affectionately.

"No. We put it back on the tree," she replied with tears in her eyes.

I got up from the bench.

"I'll meet you out by the front gate," Yukiko told me. "I want to get into something more appealing than this working uniform."

I sat back down open-mouthed.

"Mechanic-san," she cried, looking inside the hanger with Mitsubishi's triple red diamond emblem over the entrance. "I'll leave the work clothes on the bench outside the restroom," she said to the machinist mate sprawled out on the wing of an aircraft. Pointing to the little building next to the hanger, she rushed off.

"Are you bewildered, Debuchi-san?" the aviation machinist mate asked, climbing down off the wing and coming out to greet me.

"To say the least--but happy."

"She arranged it with Captain Kitano," he confessed. "Who, I understand, was the officer-in-charge of the flight school when you went through."

"Yes, and it's just like him to go for something like this," I said. "But I'm here to look at the Zero with a modified wing tip, to see if it has been completed."

"It's right inside the hanger."

"I'll take a quick check."

"Mitsubishi blunted the wing tips." he said, putting his hand on the square portion.

"*Hai.* I see," I said, not believing they were changed enough to affect the aerobatic team. "How do I get to the front gate?"

"It's only two blocks from here. Just follow the concrete walkway."

"Thanks, I'm off. See you in a couple of hours."

"I'll be right here at the hanger all afternoon."

Before I'd gone a block, I spotted Yukiko in her Western garb, a beige suit with pearl buttons, red shoes, hat, gloves, and bag.

"Where to?" I asked, joining her.

"There's a nice little coffee shop within walking distance."

"Coffee, instead of tea," I teased.

"I thought it would be different," she said, deciding to carry her warm, tan broadcloth coat when the temperature climbed.

"Who did you bribe to pull that trick on me?"

"Nobody. Captain Kitano said he remembered you," Yukiko insisted, passing by a store specializing in tailor-made uniforms and squadron decals.

"Hmmm!" I said, stepping aside for a Buddist Nun dressed in a dark gray gown vigorously cooling herself with an ivory-handled fan.

"Wasn't your profession one of the earliest to adopt Western attire?"

"Yes, nurses and women who lived in the great seacoast cities started wearing Western clothes many years ago. Except on holidays, weddings, and other special occasions, of course. "

"Sakamoto told me that Americans still believe Japanese women live in kimonos and follow men around like little puppy dogs."

"Their ideas come from that embarrassing and falsely portrayed Western opera, *Madame Butterfly*," she assured me, wrinkling up her nose at the thought. "Why do you have *Mitsubishi Melody* chalked on the nose of your aircraft?"

"The Four Ghosts deal in illusion and drama, it just seemed like a good name," I said with a twinkle in my eye. "I could change it to *Yukiko's Yo-Yo's*, or, maybe, *Yukiko's Yahoos.*"

"Don't you dare," she warned me, pausing in the doorway to the coffee shop to cover her intensity.

"Cho, a Korean pilot, has *Seoul Mate* on his plane."

"I don't have any idea what that means," Yukiko giggled. "But for some reason I like it."

Taking off our shoes and putting on slippers, we followed a waitress in a blue and white uniform to our table.

Yukiko placed her hand in mine. "Since I've come all this way to visit you, promise you'll find your way to Nagasaki to see me."

"I promise. But I don't think I can get there before spring. There's going to be a lot going on in the next few months."

"Everybody here is expecting war. It doesn't look like the European and American armies will leave Asia peaceably."

"King-Emperor George VI says that their occupation armies are going to stay."

Why is it," Yukiko wanted to know, "that the Europeans have armies in Asia, when we don't have any in Europe?"

I left the question unanswered.

"The navy wives refer to you as a wolf," Yukiko said with an impish smile.

"Why?"

"Because of those penetrating eyes that seem to bore straight into the bone marrow," she said, gently closing my eyelids with the tips of her fingers. "It brings back primordial memories of some dark and forbidden forest."

"It's true that I'm more of a social animal. Unlike Tomi who likes to operate alone. Did the wives warn you about a wolf at your door?"

"Don't gulp down your food." she countered as I put a chopstick full of rice to my mouth. Yukiko stayed quiet as she looked deep into my eyes. She said they were dark like a summer storm.

I wanted them to reveal the dangerous side of combat flying. I wished I'd seen action against the international squadron in China or in one of the air battles with the Russians.

"What's with this Tripartite Pact?" She asked with one of her lightning fast subject changes.

I softened my eyes and held only hers in my vision. "We also want a pact with Russia. Every treaty we sign gets one more white nation off our backs. It's not a military alliance. We are not members of what the Western papers call the Axis."

"I would hope not, Kiyo dear. In Nagasaki we make short shrift of anyone spouting the Nazi line. I have to get back. The captain booked a seat for me on a military transport. Kiyo, will you wait at the tower with me?"

"Unless there's a full moon,"

"What's that got to do with it?"

"I turn into wolfman. Remember?"

She took her finger and made a slash in the air. "Chalk one up for you."

I called for the waitress before telling Yukiko, "I wish I was going to Nagasaki with you."

"Ghosts can show up anywhere."

63

"Even in bedrooms?"

"Only when they're asked," she retaliated with a smile.

The stroll to the air station through a secluded park was punctuated with numerous passionate hugs and kisses. Our last embrace was so fierce that I almost lifted her off the ground.

By the time we got to her plane, there wasn't much opportunity for a long goodbye. I helped Yukiko up the little ladder to the passenger door and squeezed her hand one last time before moving off the step.

I walked slowly into the dim light as the plane pulled out of its parking spot. I hoped that she wouldn't join the armed services nursing corps when war between the Asians and Westerners started.

During the first part of my trip to Miyako-Jima, I pulled out the monthly magazine titled *Speed* from the leg pocket of my flight suit. It featured articles on aviation and motor cars. The lead story claimed Japan had thirty-five civilian airfields when the West stopped the flow of aviation fuel.

Glancing down occasionally at the magazine in my lap, I took note of the places I might have seen if I'd had a job with the Japan Air Transport Company. Tientsin, Chungking, Swatow, Amoy, and Hankow in China were possibilities. As an alternative, I might have been on an inter-island route in the Philippines or perhaps the Mukden-Hsinking route in Manchukuo. For a change of pace I could have gone to Vientiane in Laos, Hue in Vietnam, or Angkor in Cambodia. Japan Air Transport flew to all of them.

I skip-read through the article on commercial airfields until I came to Hiroshima and Kobe. Although Hiroshima had the better passenger facilities, Kobe, besides being convenient for me, listed the nearby aviation radio beacon JXO at Osaka as an added inducement for aviators.

I started paying closer attention to my dead reckoning navigation technique when the commercial radio beacon at Naha faded out.

Maybe I'll fly over the *Ikeda Maru* on my way to the Miyako-Jima Air Base, I thought, smiling when I realized I'd be able to catch Professor Sakamoto's lectures whenever I got within range of the Iris frequency.

Chapter 11

Amfac

I took the heel of my hand and banged it on the auxiliary receiver to bring out the sound. My cousin's voice came through clearly.

"When will the West stop conquering other nations to use for their own benefit?"

"Not until they're threatened physically. It reminds me of that old Japanese children's story, *The Flying Farmer.* The farmer, in his greed to get more ducks, if you'll remember the tale from your own childhood, kept increasing the size of his homemade trap. Finally, one day, he snared so many ducks they were able to fly off with both the net and the frightened farmer."

"That turned out to be nothing but a bad dream."

"*Hai.* But according to the story, it scared the farmer so much he never took away a duck's freedom again."

The Professor hasn't given the troops the required shot of adrenaline needed to become first-class fighting men, I thought. He should put some good old jingoism and hyperbole into his speeches or he'll never be able to rally them. "Hoping to obtain equality in world affairs," I heard him say after I turned up the volume. "Thailand and Japan declared war on Germany in the naive belief that Asians would be treated with respect after the successful conclusion of the war. This was not a very bright move, but the lesson sunk in."

"What part did we play in World War One?"

"Japan disbatched Kaba class destroyers for duty in the Mediterranean area and convoyed Australian troopships."

That remark caused me to recall one of the older students in my last year in college. He'd been a gunner's mate on one of the Mediterranean destroyers. That man could disrupt the classroom just by describing, in vivid terms, the low-cut dresses worn by the voluptuous, Celtic women from the poorer regions of France. They were known as courtesans in the ports along the Moroccan coast. I stopped reminiscing and went back to listening to the radio and Sakamoto.

"Our country was involved in military action against the

65

German installations in the Marianas, Carolines, and Marshall islands. In addition, Japan's military units forced German and Austro-Hungarians out of Tsingtao, China. These hostile acts against Germany came back to haunt us later on. The Nazis are backing one of the Chinese warlords in our present battle on the mainland. German officers have been seen in an advisory capacity. By the way, the blue and white campaign ribbon you see on some of the older servicemen denotes their participation in the war against Germany.

"Even Thailand sent an expeditionary force to France."

"A big war like that must have caused a lot of misery." I thought.

"All enemies are labelled evil and hungry for war. By the way, that hasn't changed much. America spends seven times as much on war production as we do. But guess who gets the blame for being militaristic?

"The United States is building a giant complex for the military brass in Washington. It's so big it would be an embarrassment to the old Prussian Army clique."

I thought he sounded sad.

* * *

One hundred and ninety miles later, Miyako-Jima was close enough to identify. It looked big compared to tiny Kikai-Shima.

This should be great sight-seeing, I thought. Miyako-Jima was famous for its Sand Mountain beach resort and its natural diving platforms along the cliffs.

I was in the middle of a turn around the lighthouse in preparation for landing when I recalled that Mariko Ito was based at Miyako-Jima. Having heard Kenji complain about his inability to get in touch with her, I figured I better inform her of his concern.

After taxiing in and parking the plane at the far end of the tarmac, I strolled over to the admin building. Her name was on the bulletin board adjacent to the entrance and I immediately called the appropriate office.

"I'd like to speak to Mariko Ito, please. This is Kiyo Debuchi, a navy aviator. She'll remember me,"

"Just a moment," the person on the other end said, going off the line.

66

"Kiyo-san?"

"Hai?"

"This is Shiroko," came a voice I've heard many times before. "You're a friend of hers?" she said, accusingly.

"That's right. I saw Kenji Ito at Naha, and he seemed worried about Mariko." I started to say more but was interrupted.

"There's a little tea house six blocks north of the main gate. Can you meet me there?"

"I guess so," I said. "But we'll have to do it right away."

"I'm leaving now," she said.

I beat her to the tea house. I watched the small, trim-figured Shiroko in a white linen suit coming through the door, looking for me.

"Over here," I called.

"It's great to see you. I thought you were in Yulin?" I said as she took a seat.

"No. I'm a civilian working for the navy, remember. More often than not, you'll find me at a desk at the entrance to some nurses' quarters."

"I see," I said, wanting to tell her that the light-colored suit, black silk blouse open at the neck, and silver bracelet combination went well together.

"How do you like the place?"

"Outstanding, there are no habu snakes like some parts of the Ryukyu Islands."

"I know what you mean; I just came from Okinawa."

"We've got a giant problem," she informed me, softening the comment with her laughing, dark eyes.

"On the contrary," I assured her. "Kenji looked good. He told me to tell Mariko that he loves her. The telephone service has been chaotic the last few weeks."

"If I tell you something, you must promise not to reveal it to Ken."

"She has a boy friend?"

"No."

"Sick."

"No."

"Okay. I promise."

"Mariko only stayed here overnight. She's on her way to the hospital ship, *Whispering Wind*--at sea."

"Kenji Ito will have a hemorrhage.

"Not if you don't tell him. Like my own job here, it's not a permanent obligation."

Where is your home base?"

"The Judge Advocate General's office in Atsugi."

"Are you ill?" I asked. "You look kind of pale."

"It's nothing; I just had a scary incident happen to me this morning. I met a an officer in civilian clothes who said he was from the transport *Ikeda Maru*."

"That's scary?"

"Hai," Shiroko said. "This man, who called himself an army police Inspector, had sadistic eyes. They still haunt me. If his disposition fits his looks, I feel sorry for the men on the *Ikeda Maru*."

"Shiroko-san, what can I tell Ken?"

"Just tell him she's on temporary assignment," Shiroko Daizen said as if she was explaining it to a small child. "She's in good health and looks forward to seeing him."

"You don't think I should mention the ship, huh?"

"There's no need to. Unless he asks."

"He'll never think of asking that question. Will I see you if I get back this way again?"

"No. I'll be leaving in a few days for Yulin."

I thought about those menacing black eyes Shiroko mentioned while listening to the Iris frequency later in my temporary quarters. Sakamoto was speaking.

"The European War was good for America. For the first time it was able to drop the title of debtor nation.

"Using something called the 'Alien Property Act,' it seized the prosperous German Hackfield and Company in Hawaii and renamed it American Factors. It's more often referred to by its nickname, *Amfac*. The United States also grabbed seven billion dollars from one of the German Banking families."

"Talk about how to be a victorious Japanese soldier, and knock off the history stuff," I complained to the world.

"By joining the war, America's movers and shakers had free access to German patents. Especially valuable were the inventions to improve commercial radio reception."

68

Chapter 12

Engine Fire

After leaving Miyako-Jima, we worked our way through a network of cauliflower-shaped clouds. I was part of a flight of three Mitsubishi attack bombers on a secret mission. The naval command seems to think utility pilots are skilled enough to tackle anything but a permanent spot in a combat squadron.

I'd been about to climb into the blue and yellow special when they cancelled my flight plan and directed me to pinch hit for a pilot who had turned up sick.

It was mid-afternoon and I was restless. These cigar-shaped aircraft each carried more than two thousands pounds of classified material.

I queried my bombardier-navigator on our position.

"We're in the East China Sea. Twenty miles from the targeted area, Debuchi-san," he replied, smiling at the idea of having two utility pilots assigned to the same plane. Second Class Petty Officer Segawa had also gotten shanghaied in from the utility squadron for this important mission, and was as mystified as the rest of us about the purpose of the flight. Two airman had been pulled off the normal ten man complement because the plane was three hundred pounds overweight.

No one, including the flight leader, knew the contents of the cargo. It had been put aboard and closely guarded by federal officials until the aircraft had gotten airborne. The only instructions given the crew were: latitude, longitude, and release altitude.

"I figure it's a special mine set to activate after the convoy clears the area," the top turret operator said over the intercom.

"Maybe it's a rush order of spinach and broccoli for the fleet," the starboard waist gunner chipped in.

"With such strict requirements on height and location, I figure it's a new type of weapon," Akira Segawa, my copilot offered. His intense, black licorice-colored eyes and prominent cheek-bones were shielded by large sun glasses, a hallmark of the squadron's flight crews. His mouth was crinkled up with laughter, masking a wiry figure primed for action.

"Whatever it is, I want all turrets manned and the radioman at his station," I ordered, pushing my sunglasses up higher. "We're well within range of Royal Air Force planes stationed in Hong Kong.

"Three minutes to release point," the bombardier-navigator advised.

"Big Dipper flight from Big Dipper leader. Commence let down to two hundred feet. Debuchi, take the number two spot. Stay in loose trail."

"Test fire your guns," I commanded, not liking the large buildup of clouds to the south where enemy fighters could be hiding. "Sing out if you spot an aircraft. We're going to be vulnerable to enemy attack at low altitude."

Reports of successful test-firings came in rapidly from the nose, tail, waist, and dorsal gunners.

Because we were carrying a 2,300 pound load, I was prepared to change the fuel/air ratio to full rich at the slightest hint of trouble from the two Kasei fourteen cylinder radial engines.

My concentration was interrupted by an explosion on the surface of the water. "Hang in there, bombardier," I said, getting the aircraft back on heading when I realized it was just a bolt of lightning to the south of us.

"Bomb bay doors open; thirty seconds to release point," the bombardier-navigator announced.

Keeping a firm grip on the control wheel, I readied myself for a drastic change in aircraft attitude.

"That port engine overheat light flickered again," Segawa said, running a hand over his short, expressive face, his jaw muscles tensed.

"It'll turn out to be a short in the sensing element," I assured him, gripping the wheel even tighter. Any loss of power during these critical maneuvers, I thought, and we'd wind up swimming.

"Ten seconds!" the bombardier announced as a convoy destroyer came into view.

"Fire on number two engine!" the top turrent operator shouted.

The horizon tilted dramatically as I banked away from the crippled engine.

"Five seconds!"

I leveled out.

"Drop point!" Flight Leader's bombardier called.

The sudden discharge of twenty three hundred pounds coupled with the loss of one engine flung the bomber skyward into a climb perilously close to stall. I fought off the approaching loss of control and kept the wing from dropping towards the wrong side. If we turned in the direction of the dead engine, our families would receive notice of our demise.

"Toss out the ammo and anything else that's not absolutely essential for maintaining flight," I ordered, readjusting my sunglasses.

"Check-in, Big Dipper flight," Flight Leader instructed.

I fought to gain altitude foot by foot as the plane lightened up.

"Big Dipper Three One Two. Still trying to catch my breath," I reported.

"All aircraft climb up to cruising altitude," Flight Leader commanded. "I'm going to take a look at our prodigy. There was no detonation."

I've got to remember to clean my sunglasses one of these days, I thought, straining to see out the side window.

"There they are," the nose gunner said, excitedly. "Three of them at eleven o'clock."

"They're painted red with six feet or so sticking out of the water," my copilot announced, trying his best to focus in with the plane bouncing around. He had his binoculars trained on them.

"Can you tell what they are?" I asked anxiously.

"They're mail buoys," Flight Leader announced, astonished at the sight. "They had us go to all this trouble just to drop mail to the fleet."

"It's only the ships second day at sea. There must be another reason."

"Some of the draftees have been aboard ship in Sasebo harbor for the last two weeks," the nose gunner said. "With no mail and no liberty."

"I guess that's what they mean by hurry up and wait," the radioman contributed.

"As little as a personal letter weighs, there should be thousands of them addressed to the Malayan convoy," I guessed, turning the plane towards Miyako-Jima. "I wonder why they kept the mail drop a secret?" I mumbled.

"I don't know," Segawa muttered, "but a letter to Inspector Ibuse containing a clue to the Trademark Killer's identity would sure improve morale aboard the *Ikeda Maru.*"

"I've got the Iris frequency tuned in for diversion," I said, after spotting more ships on the horizon.

"What did Sakamoto say?" my copilot asked, readjusting his earphones to hear better.

"He said something about standing on a tennis court that had been used by the 1936 Olympic stars."

"The signals cleared up," Segawa noted, "the Professor's voice is coming through loud and sharp."

"**Japan became the third largest maritime nation and Japanese chemists liberated Japan's textile dyeing industry**

71

from foreign dependence,"

Kaine: "What happened to the racial equality we hoped for?"

"Great Britain and Australia killed the measure at the Paris Peace Conference."

With just a few days to go before the fleet launches assault boats on its practice mission, I thought. The Professor's going to have to rack his brain to find a way to keep the crew interested in history. Jun Kaine was still asking questions.

"Coming back to the Pacific for a moment. Would buying the Philippines have been practical?"

"It would have improved the economic outlook for both the Filipino people and the twenty thousand Japanese living there."

"Didn't I read somewhere that we sold and installed four hundred Shirano textile looms in the Philippines?"

"*Hai*. They went into operation about three years ago. We also opened a branch bank in Manila when Japan's sales to the Filipinos hit the 13,000,000 pesos a year mark."

The signal faded somewhat, but that didn't stop my sharp-eared copilot from hearing it. "Toys and silk helped Japan establish a very satisfactory trade balance in African territory," he repeated.

Approaching Miyako's air strip, I had the radioman shut off the auxiliary receiver while I concentrated on our single-engine predicament.

Segawa wrote down the performance figures on the good engine.

"Let's hope the Miyako-Jima supply depot has a new one available," I said. "We've got to get back to Naha by midnight."

"My father worked for Mitsui during the years the Professor was talking about," the top gunner informed us.

"Radio, from pilot," I commanded. "Call Miyoka-Jima and tell them we'll need a new MK4E Kasei engine."

"Who's that wealthy American capitalist J.P. Morgan that was mentioned on the radio?" the waist gunner asked.

"According to Sakamoto," I said. "Morgan's the American that refused to meet with Japanese stock market genius, Tokushichi Nomura. The same Nomura who purchased a rubber plantation in Borneo, had valuable properties in Sumatra, and had a securities office in Manhattan."

If I had stayed with the Fujimoto Billbroker securities firm," Akira Segawa said, "instead of joining the navy, maybe I'd be in New York right now. They opened an office there right after I left."

"You're not the only one that had anything to do with Osaka, the business capital of Japan," the top gunner said, "I had a part-time job as a messenger with the Osaka Stock Exchange."

"I've got the tower frequency on primary," my radioman informed me.

"If I blow this landing," I commented to Akira Segawa, "my next assignment is liable to be with an air ambulance squadron in China."

"Ask for a new copilot if you go," Segawa shuddered.

"I've got Miyako-Jima in sight," I announced as the flat, irregular-shaped island came into view.

I gently banked the aircraft to the left and put the nose on the centerline. The landing was smooth; the attack bomber was running low on fuel.

Before we got to the parking area, I was notified that the air station wouldn't have a replacement engine for two weeks.

I spun the aircraft around and headed for the aviation fuel pits.

The top turret got in one last word on Osaka. "In 1918, the Matsushita family's father parlayed his idea for a new type of electrical socket into a fortune. You've heard of Panasonic."

"Who hasn't," I said, signaling for the mechanic to stop refueling.

"What's going on?" my copilot asked when I gunned the engine.

"I'm not staying here for two weeks," I told him. "We're supposed to deliver this plane on time."

I positioned the aircraft on the end of the runway and revved up the left-hand engine to full power.

"This plane weighs l5,000 pounds empty," Segawa warned, his short inky-black hair standing on end. "It needs both engines to operate with any sort of safety factor."

"We have a light fuel load. Don't worry about it.

With only half the normal horsepower available, I started the take off roll, breaking free of the ground just before the end of the runway became a consideration.

We're overtaking a Nakajima air ambulance at your eleven o'clock," Segawa cautioned just as we got airborne.

I tilted the plane's right wing enough to avoid the little medical evac, but lost altitude and narrowly missed crashing into the maintanance shack.

The copilot figured he'd have to tone down this escapade when he wrote his sister Mariko.

After a shaky climbout, I changed my mind and brought the plane safely back to the island. Let somebody else worry about the engine, I decided.

The crew tied down the aircraft and stood by for new orders. Segawa went to get something to eat.

I noticed plenty of Zeroes on the tarmac. Maybe I can take a local flight in one of them, I thought, even though I'm not assigned to a fighter squadron.

Fifteen minutes later, after gaining permission and finding out the ground crew had the day off, I pulled the chocks from under the wheels of one of Silent Storm's land-based aircraft and tossed them to the side.

Placing my fingers in the hand-hold on the fuselage and my flight boot in the lower step, I propelled myself with artistic grace to the non-slip surface of the Zero's wing.. An unnecessarily dramatic maneuver, but soul-satisfying.

Sitting in the parking area waiting for the engine to warm up, I looked over the take off check list.

tailhook	up
arm/safe switch	safe
compressed air gun-charger	off
flaps	set for take off
wing fold	down and locked
fuel gauge	full
oxygen cylinder	full
hydraulic pressure	normal range
ignition	both
RPM	checked
mixture	rich

I was glad this model was equipped with balanced ailerons and geared tabs. It made for better high-speed handling charactoristics.

With everything under control, I adjusted the cockpit temperature to a cooler position and raced for the runway, ready to make like a frog on a hot lily pad.

Halfway to the paved landing strip, I found myself squirming in the pilot's seat trying to get comfortable.

Aware that my shorts were now twisted around my rump like a pretzel, I pulled off to the side of the taxiway. My effort to straighten out the wrinkled garment, by grabbing a fistful of underwear mixed in with tugging and raising myself off the seat at the same time failed.

"Four One Five, do you need a mechanic?" queried the control tower.

"No," I replied, wriggling in an effort to smooth out the preshrunk, cotton-knit B.V.D. undershorts I had bought in Thailand from a Singapore source. The salesman had said, "no bunching, creeping or bulging."

"It's just a cockpit problem," I assured them. "I'll be ready in a minute.

Thank God, I thought, I didn't buy that Vitalis sixty-second hair cream for men. I was rather proud of myself for making the correct decision. But getting back to my immediate problem, rotating my butt to the left and pulling the cloth to the right didn't seem to be the answer. Sliding down in the cushioned seat only made it worse.

Disgusted, I relaxed and unzipped the front of the flight suit to get at the offending object. Reaching in to pull the shorts into line, I was interrupted by the tower again.

"Four one Five, do you want us to call one of your squadron pilots?"

"Absolutely not!" I answered somewhat panickly, groping for a piece of material. "I'll be squared away any second now."

I tried coiling up like a snake while scissoring my legs, which proved unsuccessful. "I'll never get to be a fighter pilot if I can't even defeat a pair of shorts," I moaned.

It might work better if I stood up in the cockpit, I thought. But with all this groping inside the flight suit, it might be misunderstood.

After one more hip wiggle against the armrest, I was forced to take a breather.

Opening up the canopy triggered off more comments from the tower. "Shut up!" I yelled, while sneaking down the side of the aircraft away from the observation tower.

I skipped around on one foot, completely oblivious to my surroundings. For the next phase of the battle, I jerked the zipper all the way down, thrust my hand in and yanked at the obstinate underwear's leg openings. Receiving conflicting signals, the cloth crept up as fast as I could straighten it out. Hiding behind the plane, I snatched at the elastic band. Success! I had managed to twist hard enough to bring the fly opening around to the front.

Unfortunately, when I threw my hands up in celebration of my victory over the textile industry, *Wen Kami*, the sinister Japanese apparition, decided to enter the contest. The fabric rose up, the elastic rotated with a mind of its own, and I was quickly back to square one.

With my plan unraveled, and unable to pull the long undershirt out of the way to get at the replusive shorts. I yanked off my flight suit in frustration, and tore at the detested cotton fabric until it was in shreds.

"Excuse me Debuchi-san. Can we be of any help?" a familiar voice asked innocently.

Coming out of my fogbank, I turned to see three enlisted men from

Silent Storm standing not twenty-five feet from me. Emi, the slot man for the Four Ghosts, had a smirk on his face that would have gotten him the death penalty if he was being sentenced by a court martial.

"Where did you guys come from?" I asked, my face lighting up like a midnight bonfire.

"I took the crew out for a ride a couple of hours ago. Not needing much runway for the KR-2 putt putt, I set it down on the other end of the airstrip, the veteran Zero pilot volunteered. "Seeing a squadron plane off the taxiway, I parked the little biwing and ran right over to offer my help."

"You know how these tropics are," I lied. "A colony of ants crawled inside my flight suit and I couldn't get them out."

"Aren't first class petty officers allowed to visit women in the comfort houses, sir?" the ordnanceman asked, having watched my antics for the last five minutes.

"*Hai.* No. Nevermind, shipmate. It was just a matter of me getting rid of a few insects."

"With all due respect, Debuchi-san, I don't know when I've seen a better strip show. And I've been to Shanghai," the aviation technician said, testing the limits of my good nature.

" The tower's sending a truck out for us," Emi reported to get me off the hook. " Do you have to go back to the compound for anything?"

"No," I answered, getting back into my flight suit, *sans* underwear, a french expression for without, that a linquist like myself enjoys tossing around.

"You're going back to *Sky Dragon* in the KR-2 with us," Emi informed me. "Silent Storm has borrowed your services from the utility squadron. We're desperately short of pilots."

I told the driver of the Mazda three-wheeled truck to tow the Zero back to the hanger, and strolled over to join the Sandpiper crew. Segawa could stay with the bomber.

Chapter 13
CAG

Sky Dragon received a steady stream of up-to-the-minute information.

Its Combat Air Patrol pilot--in this case, me--was strapped in and ready to go. The plane was fueled, armed, and had a flight deck cleared for action.

The radioman I had made friends with back on the stern of the ship climbed up on the wing.

"You had better look at this before I take it up to the Captain," he said, handing me the communique from the radio shack.

One glance and I knew I was in for trouble.

"Did you read it?" I asked.

"Hai. Is it true you've never landed a Zero on a carrier?"

"An inconsequential detail. I'll see to it that the Captain gets the message. I need to talk to him anyway. Thank you."

"You had better do it right away," he said sliding down the wing to the deck.

The words coming into my earphones, relayed by a reconnaissance aircraft, had me keyed-up. "Enemy plane fifty miles southwest of fleet." The second transmission, "Probable Australian Hudson bomber," doubled my easily aroused anticipation.

"Debuchi, this is the Captain speaking. Prepare to launch."

"Yes sir, Captain," I said as he turned the ship into the wind.

The Commander of the Air Group, normally referred to as CAG, was the pilot responsible for all the aircraft aboard. He waved at me as he proceeded towards the bow. Not knowing of the foul-up, I'm sure he assumed the training command had used combat aircraft to check me out on carrier landings.

Nervously, I folded and refolded the communiqué given to me by the radioman.

"Launch the Combat Air Patrol," the Captain ordered.

I tossed the doubled up message to Aviation Machinist Mate Nogi, but as fate would have it was blown over the side by the prop wash.

"Silent Storm Four One One, rolling," I cried exuberantly.

Chapter 14

Grilled

I could picture Captain Naifu looking up at the sky with narrowed eyes, his hopes of commanding the newer and larger aircraft carrier, *Dark Cloud,* getting slimmer by the moment. He growled into the mike. "When you get back, I'm thinking of sending you to Taiwan in the KR-2 air-taxi. Gunner's Mate Toshi Kikuchi from the *Ikeda Maru* may be summoned to a meeting with Hiko Daizen's father, a member of the House of Representatives."

I was uneasy over this opportunity to track down a British Hudson bomber. If I failed to find the snooper or if I made a mistake when I brought the Zero in for a carrier landing, the possibility of getting permanent orders to a combat squadron would be non-existent.

A head cold when my training squadron got to the carrier phase, combined with a slip-up in paperwork, enabled me to obtain my wings without any carrier landings in a combat plane.

How big a deal could it be, I wondered, trying to cheer myself up. Hundreds of fighter pilots have performed thousands of carrier landings in the Zero over the last few years. And besides, Air Operations Officer Commander Kuni will be there to talk me down.

This model has unusual handling charactoristics, I thought after trying a wing-over. The small external fuel tank under each wing, in place of the larger centerline tank which most Zeroes carry, lets the plane roll faster.

Taking time out from watching the colored rings around the shadow of my aircraft on the clouds below. I spotted a medium-sized aircraft ducking into a cloud bank.

A Lockheed Hudson bomber had many guns and its crew would fight savagely for the King-Emperor. If I wasn't careful, I'd have 50 cal. machine gun bullets for dinner.

I blocked the doomsday imagery out of my mind, and reminded myself of the injustices done to Asia by the Europeans. Keeping that thought in mind, I raced over to be in position to catch the dangerous intruder whenever it left its place of concealment.

The aircraft engine, under my heavy-handed control, throbbed, sputtered, and backfired, before settling in at the higher rpm. Without orders to initiate hostile action, I decided all I could do was give the bomber crew a good scare. Just enough to send it running back to base.

Keeping the Zero on the outer edge of the large cloud mass, I mentally prepared myself for a brush with death. I had to stage a near-miss and pull out of range before the gun turret had time to track me.

A shift in wind direction, and the clouds ended up not much bigger than the cotton stuffed in an aspirin bottle. With my adversary out into the open, I roared in, determined to scare the living wits out of the aircrew--and I succeeded far beyond my wildest dreams. First, by missing the vertical stabilizer with my left wing by inches. Then by tearing off the antenna wire running from the top of the tail to the cockpit with my right. That hazardous snoop will do no more communicating, I thought, pleased with myself.

Wait! Something was wrong, I realized as my nerves began to calm down. A Hudson has twin tails, but I remembered seeing only one. Perhaps it was a Bristol Blenheim, a single-tailed British bomber. Turning for another look, but staying out of range of the bomber's guns, I never saw the triangle insignia until I was nearly all the way around.

Impossible, I thought. No Dutch bomber would be traveling in that direction. Moving in closer for a better look, I saw raised fists and angry faces at the side-windows of the aircraft.

Side-windows! That *is* strange, I thought. Shifting my eyes to the area above the windows, I was confronted with a clear view of the heart-stopping lettering, KLM Royal Dutch Airlines.

Banking hard to the right, I left the area at top speed, praying no one saw the identifying marks on my aircraft. This was as embarrassing as the time I missed the bag passing second base.

Serves them right, I thought, trying hard to convince myself. I'll bet there are businessmen aboard that aircraft from the Rothchild family, Royal Dutch-Shell, or maybe even the Standard Oil Corporation.

I'd wager money they're out here to offer support to the Royal Dutch Army in its efforts to keep the refinery profits out of the hands of the rightful recipients, the Indonesians.

Unable to come to terms with the adrenaline rush, I did a series of loops and rolls to reduce the stress from the unfortunate occurrence with the airliner. Still apprehensive but conscious that the afternoon was almost gone, I headed back towards the convoy.

I could feel my heart rate slowly return to normal.

Since navigation was not going to be a problem on such a short flight, I didn't bother to take my abacus out of the glove compartment.

Oops, to please those aviation zealots, I suppose I should call it a navigation kit. Anyway, you can't help but stumble onto a fleet of that size if you head in its general direction.

While I didn't like having to admit it, after I found the faint lights of the fleet, I'd have to hurry in order to make my landing before dusk.

I spotted the ten-thousand ton vessel and its destroyer escorts right after the heavy cruiser *Painted Vail* came into view. I took a deep breath, adjusted my throat mike and spoke from deep within my diaphram.

"*Sky Dragon*, this is Silent Storm Four One One," I announced in a voice that any actor would be proud of.

"*Hai,* Four One One, this is the Air Operations Officer. Follow my directions to the letter," he said, failing in his effort to duplicate my speech pattern. "Do not deviate. Understand?"

"*Hai, hai,*" I said, breathing hard, but happy to hear Commander Kuni's soothing voice.

"You're already in position for a straight in approach. Keep it coming. Start your let down."

"*Tadachi ni,*" I replied.

"Lower your flaps."

"Flaps down." I said, catching a glimpse of the red and white stripes on the dangerous rear slope of the flight deck.

"Lower your landing gear."

"Gear down," I said, searching for the indicator lights that stayed off when the wheels were up, amber in transition, and green when they were extended and secured in place with a metal pin.

"Four One One, I expect to hear down and locked."

"Hold on a minute. I'm only showing one green light on the dashboard."

"The starboard landing gear is still up," Naifu remarked through the background noise.

"Four One One, climb out of the traffic pattern and get both wheels down," Kuni ordered. "*Normally*, Debuchi, aviators refer to the area where the gauges are located as an instrument panel, not dashboard. It isn't a car."

"*Tadachi ni,*" I said, flustered, but enough in control to keep my voice modulated.

Increasing power, I climbed high over the carrier and had just started a series of hi-g maneuvers when I felt or heard a loud rip. Quickly leveling off, I gave it a visual check, thankful that the upper surfaces of the Zero were all observable from the cockpit. I noted nothing wrong, until I saw the tear in the left flap which was undoubtedly caused by my forgetting to raise the flaps before I applied hi-g forces. Although this was an embarrassing episode for an experienced pilot like me, I tried looking on the bright side. There were probably scrapes on the underside of the wing from that unfortunate encounter with that Dutch passenger plane anyway.

I stared at the starboard landing gear indicator on the instrument panel. A hi-g turn to the left--another rip, and the green light still wouldn't come on, a shallow climb rolling from side to side still showed one gear up.

In desperation, I applied negative g's. As my body rose off the seat and pushed against the shoulder straps, the engine quit. Why didn't I think of that, I cringed. The Sakae 21 engine has a tendency to cut out in negative-gravity pushovers.

The euphoria of weightlessness prevented me from noticing the flickering amber light. By the time positive g forces brought a halt to my mental trip to Nirvana and the engine went back to normal operation, I was greeted by a steady green light.

"*Sky Dragon*, I have two down and locked," I announced in a voice more suited to the stage.

"Four One One," Air Operations Officer Kuni responded, worried about the approach of nightfall. "Start your descent."

"*Tadachi ni,*" I said, pulling off power and angling for the stern of the ship.

Monitoring my airspeed, I waited for the call to drop flaps. When it came, I slammed the lever down sharply, and called out, "Flaps down" in what I thought was a cool and professional manner, happy that the tear hadn't fouled up the flap extension.

"Drop your tailhook," the Air Operations Officer commanded.

"Tailhook down," I said, pulling the lever that released the rear latch on a four-foot long metal rod.

From the deck of the *Midnight Star*, in the process of rigging its breeches buoy to send him to the Sky *Dragon*, Gunner's Mate First Class Kikuchi should be able to see the tail hook dangling below the aircraft, its grooved tip positioned to catch a wire.

"Do you have me in sight?" Air Ops demanded.

"If you're the one with a paper lantern in each hand, *hai,*" I answered, adding a little levity to break the tension.

"Keep your wings level. Watch the lanterns as an indication of whether you're too high or too low," Kuni instructed, going along with the humor, even though in reality it was a bank of lights that kept the pilot on the correct glide-slope.

"*Hai, hai,*" I reported, my eyes straining to keep the lights in view.

"Ease off power. You're too high. This is no different from landing on a runway, except you have to hit a designated spot while the ship's moving up, down, and sideways."

"Thanks a lot," I mumbled, painfully aware that I'd be past the last wire before I got halfway up the deck.

"Put the power back on! Keep those wings level! Pay attention to the lanterns!"

I was more worried about reaction time. The Zero's speed at touch down is much higher than the little biwing passenger plane I had flown aboard.

"When you're over the ship's ramp, and if you're at the right height, speed, and angle, I'll holler, Cut! And in case you've forgotten, that means pull off the power. Remember, if you miss all six arresting wires there are twenty-five planes parked on the flight deck in front of you."

Super, especially on a carrier that only has a 514-foot flight deck, I thought, as I battled to level the wings and maintain a steady glide angle.

"You're high! You're high!"

Won't this ever be over ? I agonized, my hand stiffening from gripping the control stick so tightly.

"Cut!" the Ops Officer hollered, as I passed over the red and white stripes to take my first crack at landing on a carrier in a hot plane.

"Holy Torii," Ops cried as the underneath of the starboard wing came into view. "One of your external fuel tanks has broken loose."

I dove for the teakwood deck--slamming into it with enough momentum to send the aircraft's unshackled fuel tank bouncing up the deck. The tailhook floated over the first, second, and third wires, before the God in charge of drunks and beginner's luck took over. The plane drifted back down, passing the fourth, the fifth, then, with only a few feet to go, dropped low enough to snag the number 6 wire just as I added power thinking I was going to have to take it around for another try.

The wire hummed and stretched against the increasing amount of traction being applied to it, but unfortunately, it failed to stop my runaway fighter plane which was racing towards the nearest Achi dive bomber. I was a flammable dart headed for its unintended target.

I broke out in a cold sweat.

Knowing it was too late to apply the brakes effectively even with the power off, I sat transfixed, watching the high speed propeller whirl savagely. This out of control teriyaki knife was poised to chop the parked aircraft into small bits.

When the dozen or so planes straight ahead of me loomed larger than Mount Fujiyama, I shut off the engine, pulled my seat belt as tight as I could, and waited for the inevitable carnage.

Air Boss Kuni stepped into the breech. Under his direction, a large net made from strips of heavy canvas sprang up, entangling my aircraft in its web before the plane and I were able to self-destruct.

Smudged-cheeked Nogi, raced out to aid the flight deck mechanic who had been felled by the run-away fuel tank.

"CAG," the Captain cried, "this will become one of the all time great sea stories." He looked relieved when the aviation machinist mate was able to get up on his feet. "But who's going to believe it?"

"That's what makes a good sailor's yarn, Captain," CAG said, knowing he would no longer have been in line for promotion if I had crashed into the parked aircraft or the sailor had been seriously injured.

"Debuchi, you're going to take Gunner Kikuchi to Taiwan. He's been granted emergency leave." Captain Naifu promised. "Later on, we'll think about getting you transferred to a bicycle brigade."

"Yes sir!" I responded, helmet in hand, running nervous fingers through my soggy head of hair before leaving the cockpit.

In preparation for using the chair and pulley system to deliver its passenger, the destroyer *Midnight Star* fired two lines towards the *Sky Dragon* .

"What did you do yesterday?" I asked Gunner Kikuchi, hoping to take his mind off the carrier launch into the darkening sky.

"I went to the ship's library. The acting-librarian is sure unique-looking. There's absolutely no arch in his eyebrows and he has lots of freckles on his arms. But what a memory. He's sure a storehouse of information.

"How did he come by his knowledge?" I asked, as the green circle lit up.

"Private Agi worked for the Sasebo library," Gunner informed me after we were safely on our way. "When he had the evening shift, he'd browse through the translated American newspapers to pass away the hours. The *New York Times* is considered America's official publication."

"What did he learn of interest?" I asked, impressed with the part about a ship's library that had a cedar ceiling with alternate light and dark colored squares and intricate patterns on the teakwood decking. They were reminders of the days when you had to pay to get aboard.

"Naval affairs and politics were closely linked," Toshio commented accusingly. "Britain's navy insisted that no treaty be signed that promoted freedom of the seas."

"I heard that once before. Why?"

"Since Britain owned all the seas and oceans, it felt a treaty was a waste of time."

"They ought to put a padlock on Great Britain," I said.

"I'm trying to picture the British Isles with a giant chain link fence around it," Gunner remarked with a big grin. "In the meantime, U.S. presidents continued to reject independence for the Philippines because of commercial interests. The American Governor General appointed by the President believed in Anglo-Saxon rule."

"When did they figure on giving them independence?"

"The U.S. finally set a date when they realized that Japan was strong enough to support a Filipino try for freedom," he commented, disturbed by the racket coming from the Sandpiper's washing machine-like engine.

"How else do you guys pass the time away on the *Ikeda Maru?*" I asked when I had the Sandpiper on the right heading for Northern Taiwan.

"The best way to kill time is to attend one of Professor Sakamoto's lectures," Gunner's Mate Toshio Kikuchi replied.

"The lectures that are being broadcast?"

"Hai. Using a discussion format, he's telling us about the last five-hundred years of Japanese history. He hopes to be finished by the time we reach Malaya. He thinks we'll be better fighters if we know the true story."

"What were they talking about when you left?" I asked, adjusting the 150 hp engine's throttle for cruise speed.

"Events during the 1920s. Didn't I hear someone refer to you as *the dreamer?*"

"Hai. That moniker was hung on me while I was playing baseball."

"That's my favorite sports event. What position did you play?"

"I was a utility infielder," I replied, leaning forward to probe for something interesting on the instrument panel. This flight would take over an hour.

"Being a utility infielder sounds like you had more fun than the employees Sakamoto talked about roller skating from loom to loom in the cotton mills. It was one of the tricks that enabled Japan to win the competition with Anglo-India's textile industries."

Going through a cloud formation that reminded me of a sagging string of popcorn, Gunner Kikuchi saw the flash reflected off the clouds from the exhaust stacks.

"What do we do in case of fire?" he asked, nervously tugging at the ends of his eyebrows, his nose wrinkling in silent interrogation.

"That chest chute you're wearing will take care of you. The parachute is packed so that it springs out of its canvas covering whenever the pins securing it are pulled," I said, pointing to it. "Don't worry about leaving the aircraft--I'll push you out the door."

"Okay," Kikuchi said, checking the two large spring-loaded clips fastening the chute to his harness. Looking over at me, he asked why I only had only one side of my parachute clipped to the harness?

"I'll buckle it in a moment," I pleaded. "We've got a ways to go yet."

Forty minutes after leaving *Sky Dragon,* I searched my mind for some memorable event to pass away the time. One of the best, I said, beginning the story, took place at Biwa Lake when I was on leave after flight school. I had gone out in a rowboat with Suzu, the style-conscious daughter of a Kobe woman from the Moga generation. After an hour or so of rowing in circles, as I remembered it, she grabbed me by the ears in a tender fashion, pulled me close, lifted up her chin, poked out her lower lip invitingly, and whispered in a husky voice, "If you're too shy to start this little game, then I'll do it for you."

I got a good look at her as we drifted through a narrow stretch of illumination from the concession stand. She had painted nails, bright-red lipstick, rouged cheeks and a permanent wave that showed-off her coal-black hair to good advantage. If an American audience from *Madame Butterfly* could have seen that girl in action, I thought, they'd have gotten a truer picture of Japan.

I grabbed her, perhaps a little too enthusiastically. Her skin was as soft as the down on a baby duck. That's when I found out there was nothing but a pleasing personality under that dress. "Like any lover," I said to Gunner, "I panicked. Lost my balance in that treacherous rowboat and ended up dumping us in the water."

Toshi didn't bother to comment on my tale.

After another ten minutes of politics from First Class Gunner's Mate Kikuchi, I broke in to ask. "Did they ever talk about aviation?"

"*Hai.* As a matter of fact, they did. In World War One, Japanese pilots flying for the Allied cause, operating from the seaplane tender *Wakamiya,* sank a German torpedo boat off the coast of China."

"Anymore?"

"Before the war came to a close, Japanese army pilots had flown over ninety missions.

"Have you ever been to Taiwan?"

"No."

"I'll give you a quick tour; there's plenty of moonlight. Look to your left. That's Yu Shan, Taiwan's tallest mountain. It's over thirteen thousand feet high.

"Above eight thousand feet it's all conifer forests. As we descend you'll notice cedars, junipers, and maples.

"What's that?"

We were down in the subtropical level at three thousand feet where the evergreens include camphor and other laurels.

"It looks like tropical jungles now."

"With bamboo and palm trees mixed in.

"We're now at the mangrove forest level and I'm heading for an air station about ten miles from the capital. We won't have time on this trip, but someday you must visit Butterfly Valley, a famous tourist attraction."

"Any wild creatures on the island?"

"Fox, bears, monkeys, and wild boar."

I aimed the plane for the lights on the eastern side of Taiwan's northernmost harbor. "That's the City of Taipei on your side," I said, dipping the wing so Kikuchi could see the capital.

With the Naval Air Station in view, I yawned and reached across my chest to put the map away.

"What's that?" Kikuchi cried, his eyes terror-stricken as he watched a white mass unfold from my chest."

Because the chute had been cocked at an angle, my sleeve caught the release pin.

I struggled to keep the billowing silk from interfering with my view of the runway..

Grab the parachute!" I hollered, feeling through the slippery, white material for the control stick.

Two pairs of hands--one pulling yards of shiny silk towards the right seat, the other desperately trying to get through the folds, lent itself to some spectacular zooms, dives and hairpin turns.

"Aircraft in falling leaf pattern, this is Chilung tower," the air controller reported, spotting the lights of the little biwing aircraft in the distance. "No aerobatics are permitted over the air station. What's your call sign?"

"Chilung tower, from *Sky Dragon* Air Taxi," I said, using both hands to take a swipe at the control stick through the pile of soft and sleek fabric. "Experiencing carburetor icing problems. Will have it under control momentarily."

"Should I bail out?" Kikuchi yelled, unable to see outside because of the pile of silk.

"No! Just keep pulling the chute over to your side."

Kikuchi unbuckled his seat belt and started stuffing the silkworm's handiwork under his rear end.

I unsnapped the remaining clip on my chute harness. "Take it! The chute's only partially deployed."

Grabbing hold of the canvas container to keep the rest of the chute from flowing out, Kikuchi placed it in his lap and rested his arms on top of it.

Bent as far to the left as I could get, with my head scrunched against the side window, I fought to keep the runway in view. Gunner threw up his arm to protect his face, just before I banged the plane down hard enough to jerk the unbuckled Kikuchi against the instrument panel.

"Are you okay?" I hollered, taxiing the passenger plane towards the administration building.

"Just a bump on the forehead. No permanent damage," Kikuchi said. "Are there any more planes going back to the carrier? I noticed three other KR-2s on the way to the parking area. Maybe one of them could give me a ride."

"Somebody must have put out the word on our arrival," I said. "I see two women standing under the ramp lights, ready to greet us."

But it was a wide-bodied duty officer who first met the aircraft. He squinted his burnt sugar-colored eyes as he motioned for the medics when he saw blood on the petty officer's forehead.

Kikuchi reached into his jacket for the telephone number NHK radio had sent him.

I draped my coat over my arm--it was a quite comfortable, 60 degrees.

"That injured sailor's the one we're looking for," the instigator of my fertilizer disaster whispered to her companion. "Did someone mention blood?" she said raising her voice. "I'll get a nurse."

"It's nothing," I shrugged, speaking for Gunner Kikuchi. "But I've got high blood pressure just looking at the welcoming committee," I said, winking at Shiroko.

"That's too bad," the smaller one said in a strong, musical-sounding soprano. "I work for the security section of the medical complex in Yulin. And won't be of much help to you."

87

"I'll make an effort to fly over your place whenever I'm within range of Yulin's air station," I said, as if I had the responsibility for making out the flight schedule. "As you know, I'm Navy Aviation Pilot Kiyo Debuchi, and this is Toshi Kikuchi."

"I'm Shiroko Daizen and this is Ruriko Hattori. We're here to take Gunner's Mate Kikuchi to the radio station."

Shiroko shook her head, indicating I was to keep this meeting on an official level.

"Follow me, Kikuchi-san," Ruriko said in a scratchy voice that bordered on a tickle. "Would you like to come along with us, Debuchi-san?"

"Yes. If I get to sit between you."

She looked at Shiroko, and lifted her eyebrows in despair. "Does the name Daizen ring any bells with either one of you?"

"No. It's a common name," Gunner said.

I had forgotten that Hiko had been Shiroko's brother. As we walked toward the transportation, I thought about Ruriko, this modernly dressed woman with the startling black eyes and scratchy voice who had once entertained me for two hours with anecodotes about the feminine side of Japanese history.

Ruriko Hattori had urged me to keep the true picture of Japan firmly planted in my mind wherever I went. She said I must never forget my heritage: the land of ceremony, with large modern hotels co-mingled with the more traditional structures of the past. Kite-flying alongside baseball, tennis, gold, and super-luxurious trains whizzing through ancient rural areas. And pretty women like Ruriko, I added to myself.

The five mile trip to NHK's temporary radio station was completed in minimum time due to the Ruriko's familiarity with the area.

"Wait a minute. Are you by any chance related to Corporal Hiko Daizen?" Toshi Kikuchi asked as we walked through the door of the tiny transmitting station.

"Yes," Shiroko confessed. "He was my brother. And I'd like to have more information on his death."

Having arranged Gunner's visit, with the help of station manager Kubo and Representative Daizen, Ruriko acted like she was in charge once we were inside NHK's broadcast studio.

At the designated hour, Ruriko, although she was not a permanent employee of the station, was permitted to interview the guest on the late evening show.

"Gunner's Mate Kikuchi, I know you can't devulge the location of your ship, but we understand there's a serial killer aboard your vessel."

"I don't know anything about a serial killer," Gunner said.

"Wasn't a body found in the boiler room with the killer's bayonet left as a calling card?"

"Hai," Kikuchi said uncomfortably. "but I'm here in Taiwan because of a family emergency."

"You're a constituent of Representative Daizen, who just happens to be Shiroko's father. He'd like to be filled in on the details of the murder. The military is stonewalling, and he feels the people have a right to know."

Kikuchi felt trapped. He didn't want to antagonize a legislator, but on the other hand, he was a career sailor and had his future to think about.

"The slaying of Corporal Hiko Daizen was in the newspapers," Ruriko prompted him.

"Hai," Gunner replied hesitantly.

"Killed with a bayonet?"

"Hai."

"He left his trademark," Ruriko indicated. "He's a Trademark Killer," she said, pleased with her play on words.

"Ummmm," Kikuchi mumbled. He hadn't gotten used to a term that sounded like a commercial logo.

"Wasn't the Yokohama victim a corporal? And wasn't he found stabbed to death?"

Kikuchi wasn't able to lie before a radio audience. *"Hai,"* he said hesitantly.

"With a bayonet?"

"Possibly."

And didn't Corporal Kono receive a threatening letter?"

"I think so."

"Shortly after he was promoted to that rank?" NHK's headline-seeking male reporter asked, although it wasn't his interview.

"He received word of his advancement the day before he got the warning." Gunner Kikuchi said, grabbing the arms of the chair for support.

Doesn't that sound like the serial killer's out to get newly appointed corporals?" the amateur crime beat reporter for NHK asked.

"I don't know," Kikuchi said, squirming in his seat uncomfortably.

The station manager cut in. "Were any privates or lance corporals singled out for destruction by the ship's crazed knifer?"

"Not that I know of."

"It's time for the armed forces to home in on this menace to our gallant servicemen," Ruriko said, amidst the chorus of agreement coming from the station employees.

"I guess you're right," Kikuchi said, throughly cowed by the intiminating manner of Ruriko and the NHK reporters.

Shiroko, her brunette hair swept up on the sides and worn long down the back over an eye-catching Chinese white silk jacket embroidered with black dragons, walked over toward him.

Once outside of NHK's building, reporters from the outlying radio stations crowded around us.

"Your cough sounds better," Ruriko said loudly, playing a hunch.

The newspaper reporters scattered when they heard the word "cough."

"Can I buy you dinner?" Kikuchi asked when the news media disappeared. "How about some Western food for a change of pace? All I've been eating is navy chow prepared by the troopship's cooks."

We stayed overnight.

Chapter 15

Dutch MP

On the return flight from Taiwan, Gunner was nervous and talkative. He told me a story about the ship's library.

"When I originally went there," he said, "to find out what American reporters were saying about the Japanese, Private Second Class Agi, in charge of the place, had me pegged as a comic book reader.

"When I told him I preferred more serious books, Agi countered by asking me to hand him the stack of unsorted magazines piled up in front of the desk.

"There was an interesting article in one of the glossy publications I turned over to him. It even had a map showing the location of Japanese -owned areas in the Philippines--amounting to one-fifth of the cultivated land in Davao province." Gunner seemed to have finished his story. He didn't say anything for a few minutes.

"What else did you find out?" I asked.

"Japanese imports to the United States were running over five hundred million dollars a year."

"Did this fabulous soldier-librarian tell you about the Japanese airmen who flew for France in the *Escadrilles des Cigognes?*"

"No!" Kikuchi mumbled the name, having problems with the pronunciation. "What's that?"

"The Stork Squadron, " I said, not expecting to be topped.

"He did say that a nursing supervisor at Nagasaki Municipal Hospital took care of a Japanese pilot who was badly wounded flying a French Nieuport fighter plane in World War One. She believed the French awarded him the *Croix de Guerre* with citations."

"And the *Legion d'Honneur,* " I added, determined to have the last word on aviation topics.

"Any overseas investing?" I asked, changing the subject back.

"While we were buying ninety percent of the stock in the largest cotton mill in the United States, America's J.P. Morgan made a large loan to fascist Benito Mussolini."

He should have loaned it to me, I thought.

Tired of Kikuchi's stories, I told him about my trip to the Dutch military-controlled Indonesian Islands last year when I flew a Japanese business leader to a meeting. I was probably selected for the mission because of my linguistic degree with a minor in Dutch.

* * *

I had dinner in the home of a Major Dirk Van Mook, of the Dutch Army Airforce. I deliberately spoke hesitantly to him, and stumbled over the words whenever I talked.

After the meal, the Major got ready for his once-a-week military police duty. The blond, blue-eyed, barrel-chested, teutonic warrior took one last look in the mirror to check out the fit of his privately purchased whipcord uniform. The gray-green cloth was a little darker than government issue, but it went well with his black, knee-high boots. After all, he and his fellow officers represented Queen Wilhelmina in this part of the world and he wanted to look his best.

Van Mook decided to wear the Foreign Legion-type Kepi, with its tall, flat, round top, and stiff visor etched with blue piping. Most Dutch officers had switched over to the softer caps with a lower silhouette.

Believing I knew very little of the language, he spoke carefully and gestured frequently, "Do you want to come with me?"

I paused as if I was searching for the right words. "Yes, thank you for asking."

We departed after he sent a salute towards the bedroom where the Queen's picture hung. She was Commander of the Armed Forces with the power to promote or demote him.

He was proud of his Queen. Her military forces controlled 1,000,000 square miles of territory in the Far East; that's equivalent to one-fourth the size of the United States.

Striding through the nearly deserted streets of Jakarta gave him a feeling of tremendous power. One word from him and Indonesians died. It was also in his perogative to let them live for minor infractions, if they treated him with all the respect due a white man.

"Power is more addictive than gambling or alcohol," Van Mook whispered, watching an Indonesian scramble to get out of his way. "Let others strive for money and opiates,' he rationalized, patting his 9 mm Belgium automatic pistol nestled in its black holster. "The power to kill without penalty is more seductive than wealth or drugs."

Hurriedly we went from bar to bar. Once the call, "Five minutes to lights out, prepare to turn into your bunks," sounded, Van Mook told me he was pleased to see them emptied of armed forces personnel as he swept through the eastern side of the city.

"No dissenters the nights you're on watch," said the bartender-owner of the high-priced, dingy-looking, money-making hole-in-the-wall that passed for a saloon. The local bar was at the center of the city and was the last stop for the MP patrols.

"Just like a graveyard when you're in command, Major," the duty-sergeant reported, frowning when he looked over in my direction. "I checked the west side of town," he said. "Do you want us to chase the locals out of the bars tonight?"

"No!" Van Mook said sharply. "Let the bartenders make some money off of them. A hangover helps them get through their twelve hour work day."

"There's trouble in the Chinese seaports again, Major," the Sergeant reported. "That's nothing new, though. I remember when a couple of dozen Chinese students were shot by the British police in Shanghai. Then in an additional show of force, French and British Marines bayoneted hundreds."

"If the Dutch in the East Indies had been sent to police those 'unequal trade treaties' instead of the British, Van Mook said menacingly, "there'd be a lot less turmoil from those coolies, and a lot more work."

"Not a bad idea," the sergeant agreed. "The Dutch oil companies are heavily involved in China right along with Britain and the United States. Can I ask you a question, Major?"

"Sure, go ahead," Van Mook said, giving the bartender a blistering stare that promised him a short and miserable life if he didn't get a free drink up on the counter immediately.

Nervously, the bartender unlocked the cabinet where he kept the unwatered liquor and poured Dirk a generous shot.

"Do we maintain law and order in Guiana?"

"With the help of the United States we do. Lawyer-politician President Roosevelt, he has Anglo-Dutch blood, bowed to the wishes of Queen Wilhelmina and sent three thousand of his soldiers there to keep it from declaring its freedom. That will allow our Dutch Empire to maintain control over a valuable piece of South American territory for another two decades or so. Guiana is prized real estate--it can grow two crops a year from its fertile soil."

"Outstanding!" the sergeant said with glee. "That'll keep those sorehead original inhabitants who refer to it as a police state in line. The South Americans call it 'Suriname' instead of its European name."

"Did the Americans have an army in China during the last decade?"

the bartender asked.

"They sure did," Van Mook assured him. "In addition to the 15th Infantry regiment garrisoned in Shanghai, America had aircraft, over four thousand marines and a number of light tanks in Tientsin, plus field artillery and mortors. To complete its military posture, the U.S. built an airfield for the American Army just outside of the city."

"When will the West relinquish their hated special extra-territorial rights in China?" the sergeant said in a disparaging way.

"Don't knock the North Americans. They support us in our rule over Indonesia's Asian population. The Japanese don't," he insisted, looking over angrily in my direction.

"In fact, the Japanese did away with British rule in Ningpo, one of the earliest unequal treaty ports a couple of months ago. Isn't that right, Debuchi?"

"Hai," I agreed. "Before Japan took up the Asian cause, the Western military had control of all the important Chinese ports."

The Sergeant glared at me."It's been four years since the Chinese Communists declared war on Japan, but do they have the necessary motivation to defeat the capitalist Japanese?"

"No," Dirk Van Mook said. "Somehow we've got to get all the white nations into the battle."

The bartender decided to enter the conversation when the drink wiped the scowl off the Major's face. "I had a guy in here that said a Dutch aviator told him the German-Chinese Eurasia Aviation Corporation was bringing in ammunition for Chiang Kai-shek's Nationalist army."

"Would you mind answering another question, sir?" the Sarge asked when nobody bothered to comment.

"Make it quick."

"The sailors who come in contact with North Americans claim the Yankees think the Japanese believe Hirohito is a diety. Do you know anything about that?"

"The Americans go off half-cocked whenever they think it benefits themselves," Van Mook said, giving me an understanding smile. He snarled at the craven bartender when he didn't put the bottle up on the bar. "I'll bet they didn't say anything about the old Emperor of Russia who many Russians believed received his dictorial powers from God. Or Great Britain's King-Emperor who God appointed head of the Anglian Church, according to the believers."

"Do you happen to know," the Sergeant asked, attempting to imitate Van Mook's snarl when he received his free drink, "whether or not the

94

Japanese businessmen here in the East Indies get mixed up in politics?"

"They'd better not," Van Mook answered, pounding his fist on the bar. "It's bad enough that they have that Oriental Development Company in operation. By giving the Indonesians positions in management, they're teaching them to be disrespectful of us. We had enough trouble taking over this area in the first place. It's forty-six times the size of the Netherlands. It took us thirty-five years to complete the conquest and now the Japanese businessmen are trying to take advantage of our generous and peaceful nature by causing trouble."

"Thirty-five years is a hell of a long time for our army to stay focused," the Sergeant said, stating something that was self-evident.

"We Dutch were the first to use flat-bottomed landing craft," Van Mook said, pointing out the modern tactics necessary for victory.

"Did that win the war for us?"

"The destruction of rice paddies was used as a combat weapon," Van Mook volunteered. "At the conclusion of the conquest, we were angry enough to cut the residents out of all judical rights and to draft them into compulsory labor. The average yearly dividend over a period of two centuries for the Dutch investors in favor with the Netherland's Royal House has been eighteen percent."

"That's better than winning a lottery." the Sergeant notified the bar tender.

"It hasn't been easy, even with an army and navy permanently stationed here. We had to break up a try for independence by hauling off 25,000 Indonesian freedom-fighters. This forced us into running a police state."

"But we're in pretty good shape, now," the bartender said.

"Things would be perfect if it wasn't for the Japanese," Van Mook said, talking fast so I wouldn't catch the drift. "Those Oriental misfits managed to expand their economy even while we were shipping out tons of sugar, spices, coffee, etc. from the Indies with compulsory labor and the advantage of a monopoly."

"Thanks for the information, Major. See you next week. It's always a pleasure serving with you," the Sergeant uttered respectfully, backing out the door when he saw the officer in charge of the MP's reach over the bar to get another bottle of whiskey.

* * *

"And for a finale," I told Gunner. "A Dutch private drove us back to the Major's abode in a 1924 Spyker roadster." That figured. The company that made the car just happened to enjoy the Queen's patronage.

"We're eight hundred miles north of the Indonesian Islands, with only a few days remaining before our training mission begins in Hainan," Kikuchi offered, fidgeting with his safety belt.

"It feels more like three weeks," I conceded. "And surely like a century to the Chinese forced into the illegal trading agreement that Sakamoto talks about."

"Any contract signed and kept in place by the threat of military force is illegal, according to what Agi told me. This lawless arrangement allowed foreign companies to buy at one-fifth the cost to Chinese merchants. Ironically, Japan sold three items for every two the U.S. did."

"Was anybody listening to the Asians plea for freedom?" I asked.

"No. A trade war raged throughout the world, according to what Agi read from a translated *New York Times*. Did you hear that part of the discussion?" Gunner asked.

"Is that the article where they condemned Japan for unfair competition and America led the retalitory group by adding anywhere from a five to two hundred percent tax on Japanese imports?"

"Hai."

"How does Agi remember all that stuff?" I queried, looking at the fuel gauge.

"He has a photographic memory," Gunner Kikuchi said grinning, "including the retention of numbers. Just to give you an example: When Japanese trade with Asia increased another twelve percent, Europe believed it could not compete in the Pacific without the backing of the military."

"I can't believe it," I told him, then turned to ask if he looked forward to the Malayan campaign.

"Somewhat. The soldier-librarian told us that Japan had no friends among the agressive Western nations. It was also competing against Germany in optics, microscopes, cameras, and binoculars."

"Was the competition tough?" I asked, wondering why I didn't get an answer to my Malayan question.

"Germany produced high quality instruments, chemicals, and pharmaceutical supplies at a reasonable price," Kikuchi disclosed, taking out his handkerchief to wipe his forehead.

I reached under the seat for my box lunch. A cabbage and white horseradish dinner would be nice, I thought, served on black lacquer dishes, topped off with dumplings wrapped in noddles.

Chapter 16

Television & War

If I thought landing aboard the carrier without blowing both tires would bring congratulations from Kikuchi--I was disappointed.

Yeoman Nitta came hurrying over. He was under orders from Inspector Ibuse to find out what happened at NHK.

"Did you listen to Sakamoto's radio discussion last night?" I asked in an effort to distract him.

"No, but I did learn from Agi that electronics and textiles were hot selling items. An American fan sold for three times the price of a Japanese electrical one, and you could buy Japanese textiles in Lancaster, England for less than the textiles made in Lancaster."

"I'll catch you later," I said. "I've got to work the kinks out."

I walked to the catwalk through the drizzly, overcast morning--the damp atmosphere suited my mood. I've got to finalize my plans for getting aggressive, I thought,

I'll just stay out here, I decided, sitting cross-legged on the wet surface, humming a mournful song. "The thick overcast is depressing," I said to no one in particular. "Like harbor fog, it brings forth images of impending destruction. Let those fool soldiers inside waste their energy doing calisthenics and talking about the past."

I snapped out of it

In the old workout compartment, oblivious to my troubles, Aviation Machinist Mate Nogi was getting his morning's exercise alongside a mustached sailor. The wood paneled room didn't remind me much of a gymnasium.

"What are you doing here, Debuchi-san?" Nogi hollered.

"Stiff. I had a tiresome flight. What are you discussing.?"

Nitta joined the group, mixing up his exercise routine with slashes and jabs while shadow boxing.

Nogi removed the junk from his pocket that was impeding his effort to bend over.

I gave a slight bow to the chief ordnanceman, whose son was the youngest official in Sumitomo's banking system.

"Bending at the waist, first to the right and then the left, I looked around for an aviator to talk to.

Yeoman Nitta started running in place. "Has there been any change in the draftees attitude concerning combat because of Sakamoto's talks?" I asked him. "Regretfully, I must report I haven't noticed any."

"Maybe a spark will ignite when the Professor speaks about the current year," he said, trying to appear optimistic.

"If Western gunboats patrol Asian rivers, shouldn't Asian gunboats patrol the Mississippi River in America?" Nogi offered in a sudden burst of logic. "And also the Thames River In England, the Loire River in France, and the Lower Rhine in the Netherlands.?"

"The idea of fairness and equal treatment would shock them," I said with a tight little grin, ducking one of the Yeoman's exuberant punches.

Sakamoto suspects our military and naval messages are being intercepted and decrypted by the King-Emperor's forces."

"Although my wife's a graduate of Ryukoku University and likes to think of herself as progressive," a commissioned pilot from the Aichi dive bombing squadron inserted, apparently tired of foreign affairs, "she objects to the newer Western dress and hair styles and doesn't wear bathing suits or paint her toenails like the Moga girls."

"What's that snapping noise?" I asked, not interested in hair styles.

"Maybe it's the lotus buds opening up," Nogi answered, winking at the chief ordnanceman.

"Isn't Ryukoku an old University?" Nitta asked when he paused for breath.

"*Hai,* it's been around about three hundred years, I believe."

"What do you think would satisfy the influential and political forces in Washington?" Nogi asked in a serious tone of voice.

"Total surrender of the trade market or allowing certain American corporations to invest in our more successful companies," I answered, watching Nitta tear a hole in the punching bag.

"Who championed the bombing approach?" Nogi wondered, still portraying the innocent act.

"One of the hardline conservative's favorites was General Billy Mitchell," I said. "Mitchell believed in white dominance."

"Did this compassionate philosopher have anything else to say?"

"Definitely," I said. "But people all over the world were looking for answers. 'The Great Depression' had the United States and Europe scrambling for survival. Mitchell thought it was legitimate for the West to control Asian territory like Java, Singapore, China, and New Guinea. He likes the idea of whites being the ruling class."

"We made out?"

"As Japan's trade increased, the West's trade fell to less than fifty percent of pre-depression value," Nitta said, looking around for Agi to confirm it. "He's not here!"

"He's aboard the *Ikeda Maru,* remember?" Nogi commented. " And he probably knows the exact percent for each country."

"How does he do that?"

"I don't know, but he said that the Japanese used Keynesian economics before the name was even known in Japan. He said that seven percent growth per year was achieved with it."

"What did the West do about it?" Nogi asked, raising his five foot two inch frame off the deck.

"They applied tariffs, quotas, and preferences aimed at the Japanese and forced us to lean towards a system of cartels," Nitta answered. "And Japan operated the largest nitrogen fertilizer plant in Asia," he said, pride showing in his voice. "Diesel engines were produced and rayon production initiated."

"Are you ready for battle? Debuchi-san?" somebody hollored.

"My father's against it. He figures he'll lose his position as one of the television pioneers if the West ever gets an opportunity to shut down our factories."

"Was your dad eager to take the lead in electronics?"

"He was all set to televise the 1940 Olympic games right up until the time they got cancelled because of the war in Europe."

Feeling loose again, I left to take the unglamorous KR-2 back to Southern Taiwan.

Chapter 17

Hong Kong Hijinks

Going through the Taiwan straits, I kept China off my right wing until I spotted a large residential area on the two hundred mile long island to my left. Taking up a southerly heading over the city of Tainan, I flew down the coastline to complete the final fifty miles.

I hadn't even finished my lunch at Kaohslung airfield before a wild rumor reached me. They were hunting for the pilot that had gotten through flight school without receiving any carrier landings in a combat plane. The Sandpiper was not considered a combat aircraft.

A junior officer in the chain of command at the Atsugi Naval Air Station was chosen to be the scapegoat, and I was going to have to testify against him at his court-martial.

This was a no-win situation. As the aviator most directly involved, I grabbed an unassigned Zero and taxied out for Vietnam's Vidhya airbase-- on the pretense of delivering parts for a crippled aircraft.

After receiving tower clearance for *Gossamer Wings*, and using only my finger tips, I felt my way along the throttle notch until I found the spot that brought the desired response. Not incurring any resistance, I gently fondled *Gossamer's* fuel control. Rapidly picking up speed, she plunged headlong down the asphalt path to hedonistic delight.

In an effort to prolong the rhythmic pleasure the rippled airstrip supplied, I caressed her pitch-down trim control.

The end of the runway came up too fast. Unable to hold back any longer. I gave her a final squeeze, and shoved the throttle full forward, severing the ethereal connection between earthbound drudgery and heavenly rapture.

Arm in arm we soared into the sky together in search of an airway made of thick, creamy clouds.

With a sheepish grin on my face, after having one of my more enjoyable takeoffs, I settled down for a long hop. The Zero, specifically built for extended flight, provided ample room for stretching.

I placed my feet flat on the cockpit floor within easy reach of the rudder pedals. The control stick was between my legs just inches from my kneecaps, a comfortable distance for the length of my arms even when I put my elbows on the arm rests.

Knowing I might see combat within the next couple of weeks, I took a critical look at the controls. Fuel mixture, throttle, and drop tank release levers were within easy reach of my left hand. The radio equipment and seat adjustment were the only items on the opposite side-- which meant my right hand was always free to operate the control stick.

The artifical horizon, turn and bank indicator, and magnetic compass occupied the center slot directly in front of me. Air speed and altimeter were mounted slightly to the left and under the gyro-stabilized, man-made skyline.

The two machine guns were chargable by hand. Their breeches extended back into the cockpit just above the instrument panel. As a safety measure the cannon master switch was placed under the panel so it couldn't be accidently tripped, but it was still reachable without the pilot having to move his shoulders forward.

With Taiwan twenty miles to the rear, an inbound, early model, army Ki-27 Fire Dragon began a turn towards me, then flew on. Flying in an open cockpit with a scarf wrapped around his neck did give him a romantic touch, I had to admit. It was reminiscent of the Japanese pilots who flew with the French in World War One.

Weather wasn't a problem. The sky resembled a quiet lake, with a few whispy clouds circling aimlessly like fingerling trout searching for food.

I set the autopilot on a heading of 240 degrees, then relaxed. Contentment was a warm sun shining through the canopy. The heat caused my skin to glisten like a golden-colored cough drop. Contentment was a dark instrument panel that signified the plane's history of hydraulic tantrums was over.

I got out the area map and jotted down two emergency landing sites along the route. The first possibility was the British International Airport in Hong Kong, and the second was the Qionghai military airfield in Hainan, two hundred miles further to the south.

Two hours into the flight, I noticed the oil temperature gauge reading slightly higher than normal; but regardless of that irritant, the relationship between my playmate and myself remained beneath the red-hot zone until I passed abreast of Hong Kong.

Menacingly, *Gossamer Wings'* engine temperature crossed into the dangerous area. I held my breath and lovingly pushed the mixture control to full rich to soothe her. It wasn't enough. Something had broken the mystical bond between us. My ladylove was rejecting me. Fifty miles out of Hong Kong I was forced to admit that our relationship was going to end before Qionghai airfield was in sight. *Gossamer's* anger was rapidly coming to a boil.

I felt like a suitor after his first argument. Glancing over my left shoulder, I saw that the fire extinguisher read full. Just double checking, I thought prudently, knowing I had looked at it on preflight, along with the flotation bags in the wings.

I hoped that Hong Kong tower still had translaters available. Due to the West's embargo on fuel, Greater Japan Airlines hadn't flown from there for several months.

Twenty-five miles out, with the oil temperature inching deeper into the red, I pushed the older-model helmet back from my high forehead and decided I could wait no longer. "Bird Mountain Tower from Treehouse Nine One One. Declaring an emergency, request landing instructions," I radioed, not trusting my English at this critical phase. I hadn't had much of a chance to converse in it lately. I tried a port-pidgen dialect picked up from foreign visitors along the waterfront in Yokohama.

"Treehouse Nine One One, this is Bird Mountain tower. Caught only part of your transmission, old chap. Something about a landing, I believe. If it's an emergency, you are cleared immediately. Wind south, southwest at ten knots. A translater is on his way. If it's not an emergency, you have an Imperial Airways airliner from London and a KLM Royal Dutch DC-2 ahead of you."

About the only words I caught were KLM and wind south, south west at ten knots. Spotting the Dutch DC-2, I kept the last of *Gossamer Wings'* fast-fading passions alive by using only gentle movements of the control stick to pull in behind the Netherlands' cargo plane. The translater broke in as I maneuvered to stay in back of the slower aircraft.

"Treehouse Nine One One, from Bird Mountain Tower. Do you have an emergency?" the translater asked in a clipped and authoritative manner.

"Hai! Hai! from Nine One One," I called, ready to yank off my goggles if the new ventilating holes around the rims failed to keep them from fogging up at the lower altitudes.

"Bring it straight in, Nine One One, I'm clearing a path for you--KLM Two Two and Imperial Airways Four Five, take it around."

The tower operators were still admiring the classic lines of the late model Zero as the fighter plane's wheels touched the surface of the runway, as tenderly as a tear-stained kiss from a Romeo to his Juliet.

I applied steady pressure on the hand-brake and turned off at the second taxi exit. Throwing open the canopy, I grabbed the fire extinguisher and jumped to the ground. Taking a screw driver from my flight suit pocket, and feeling like an unwelcome intruder, I bent down and opened the lower section of the engine cowling, keeping the fire extinguisher handy.

The engine was red hot, but not on fire, I noted, relieved. Obtaining a new engine would have been next to impossible.

Spotting the clogged oil filter inlet as I turned my head to straighten up, I reached into the opening and yanked out a tangled mass of leaves, acorns, and twigs that might have once been a bird's nest. Best never to mention I missed it on the preflight, hurrying to get out of Taiwan. I had enough trouble on my hands because of the carrier-landing fiasco.

A lorry full of police and Royal Canadian Riflemen surrounded the aircraft. I was under arrest for not having filed a flight plan.

Unfortunately, the British still used flogging in Hong Kong and Singapore as a punishment for stealing, regardless of the age of the transgressor. And one could make a case that I stole the Zero. Hong Kong was subject to British Empire law.

There were no words, just an aburpt motion by the big, impatient, Canadian Sergeant for me to get into the second lorry, this one driven by a uniformed Anglo-commanded Indian who gave me a friendly smile.

Both being Asians, the Indian and I frowned as we passed a giant portrait of King-Emperor George VI.

A British civilian and an officer were waiting for me at the steps of the control tower. As the lorries pulled up, they hurried over to me. The civilian translater, wearing a regal mustache worthy of the empire, asked me in fairly good Japanese, "What are you doing in Hong Kong without an authorized flight plan?"

"I'm Naval Aviation Pilot First Class, Kiyo Debuchi, flying aircraft parts to Vidhya. My engine malfunctioned, forcing me to declare an emergency."

"This is Mr. Aston Sinclair," the translater said, nodding towards the over-retirement-age, Royal Air Force Warrant Officer wearing the order of the British Empire, a Malayan occupation ribbon, and awards for heroism in England's war against China.

"He's in charge of airbase security," the translater relayed. "We'll send a crew out to check the accuracy of your statement. In the meantime we have a spare room in the control tower reserved for visiting pilots. The sergeant will escort you there. You're confined to that room. Your aircraft will be towed to a smaller tarmac and kept under guard."

"Why am I getting such a hard time?" I asked. "I spotted a Ki-43 Peregrine Falcon on the flight line as we drove up here."

"That belongs to an army first lieutenant. Unlike you, he filed a flight plan."

I shrugged and followed the sergeant and translater to a small room on the ground floor.

"You don't happen to know what that lettering is on the Peregrine Falcon, do you?" I inquired, trying my best to keep from grinning.

"*Dolly Madison II*. Your countryman has a bloody poor sense of humor," the translator volunteered in Japanese overlaid with a cockney accent. "A few strokes of the cat-o-nine tails would cure him of that."

"This area is heavily patrolled," the Sergeant informed me. "You'll be shot if you leave your living space before I obtain confirmation from Tokyo. I'll have your meals sent over from the mess hall."

I thanked the two men as they departed for their normal duties. I won't be able to see their military fortifications at this rate, I thought, but I might as well try since I'm here.

The room had one small bed, dresser, chair, and a wash basin which included a bar of lifebouy soap compliments of the omnipresent British Lever Brothers. While rumaging through the three-drawer dresser, instead of the towel I was searching for, I came across a pair of Kershaw binoculars stashed way back in the bottom drawer.

I couldn't believe my good luck. They were Royal Navy binoculars left behind by some careless aviator. Must have had a helluva hangover to forget these great glasses, I thought, borrowing a term from my waterfront days.

I felt overextended, but if I was going to accomplish anything, I didn't dare spare the time for a seventh inning stretch.

After one miscue in the corridor outside my room, I located the entrance to the operating section. I took off my shoes and crept up the stairs. Opening the door a crack, I spotted a large radio transmitter just to my right. Slipping in quietly, I squeezed into the narrow space between the transmitter and the observation tower's glass enclosure. Fortunately, there was four and a half feet of wood between the glass and the floor. It should be enough for me to hide behind.

From this vantage point, I could not be seen by the tower operators yet had a good view of Hong Kong and some of the surrounding area.

Crouched down, I placed pencil and paper on the floor within easy reach and aimed the binoculars out of the glass enclosure to the west.

Starting at the south side of the huge Coca Cola sign, I panned from left to right. Stopping to focus in on command headquarters, I wrote down the names of the six battalion flags lined up under the Union Jack. The battalions were evenly divided between Canadians, Indians, and the British. Further over to the right were the flags of the artillery and engineers.

I hastily tied a hankerchief over my nose to keep from coughing when the smoke from the tower operators' cigarettes slowly drifted my way. I tried to keep my mind occupied by watching an Imperial Airways aircraft take off and couldn't help but wonder if the airport terminal wasn't one of the main reasons for keeping this Chinese territory out of the hands of its rightful owner.

When the blond-haired civilian tower operator banged on the side of the transmitter I was hiding behind, my nerves jumped to attention.

As long as they don't need to open the access door on this side, I'll be okay, I prayed optimistically, wrinkling a nose already well-supplied with creases.

I breathed easier when I heard the man make a comment to his fellow tower operator while walking back to his console. "It's bloody well working okay now. Must be a loose wire."

Putting the binoculars back on the ledge, I swept the area. Bullseye! I spotted the large antenna and the row of fortifications on the western perimeter. Barbed wire, gun emplacements, and ammo dumps. The pathways between the strongholds came into view as I watched the soldiers carrying supplies back and forth.

It was important for me to leave Hong Kong with as much information as possible, especially the antenna location for the large electronic eavesdropping station that Britain had constructed to listen in on Asian military and diplomatic frequencies five years ago. By the size of it, I guessed the King-Emperor knew every move the Japanese navy made.

I wondered if they knew about the 'Trademark Killer.'

Waiting too long before going back to my assigned room turned out to be a mistake. I had stretched my luck too far. I heard soldiers hollering back and forth to one another. Somebody must have come in with my meal and discovered me gone.

Crouching lower, I hoped they wouldn't think of searching for me in the glass-enclosed observation tower. Sneaking a look over the sill, I saw soldiers spreading out in all directions.

The tower was suddenly very quiet. Apparently, everyone had been asked to participate in the search before darkness set in. I leaned on one hand in an attempt to look around the corner of the transmitter and fell with a noisy thud. Frightened, I lay still. No sound. Taking a chance, and keeping a bent-over profile, I looked around the observation platform.

Finding it empty, I stuffed the notes inside my shirt pocket, and tiptoed to the door. Hearing no one on the other side, I quietly descended the stairs and went into my room.

After pushing the food tray under the bed, I opened the window, and hollered out in fractured English, "What's all the excitement about?"

The Sergeant ran over with the translater in tow. "Where have you been?" he screamed when I made my appearance known.

"Nowhere," I said to the translator. "I was just trying to catch a nap."

"Gorblimey! That coolie who brought in his food was right," the mustached translater relayed.

"Come with me," the Canadian sergeant commanded. "You're going to jail. You screwed up. We were about to let you leave. Tokyo says you're on an authorized supply mission. We found aircraft parts behind the pilot's seat. I did get the impression that your superiors are anxious to get their hands on you."

They took me to the southeast side of the air base where they had a military brig.

With little ceremony they placed me in a cell and left. The lockup next to me was empty, but I still couldn't make out the silhouette of the person on the other side of the unoccupied one.

Over at the Murray Parade Ground, the British were playing their National anthem on territory that didn't belong to them, an arrogant expression of the white man's contempt for Chinese sovereignty.

A feminine voice whispered. "Are you Japanese?"

"Hai," I said softly. "Who are you?"

"My name's Hisako Bayar. Before you arrived my only company was a Chichak lizard who spent most of his time upside down on the ceiling."

Shortly after midnight we heard British voices approaching.

The civilian was dressed in a light gray single-breasted business suit with pleated trousers and a solid-colored dark brown tie. He was lking fast.

"I've got to catch a plane within the next hour. We'll question them in ore. Did you search the Mongolian's suitcase and his seabag?"

Yes sir. I understand this trip has been authorized by the Whitehall Offices."

top priority."

Hisako Bayar and I were forced onto an Imperial Airways transport owned by BOAC, which I believed stood for the British Overseas Airways Corporation.

Out in the early morning light, I got my first good look at my traveling companion. She was tall and voluptuous. But her most appealing quality was a high-cheekboned, sunny face with the darkest, smoldering eyes I've ever seen. She was bare-legged and bare-armed, but somehow still managed to appear regal.

I guessed she was a couple of years older than me.

A miniature flag, consisting of a dark blue cross embossed on a light blue field, with the obligatory British Union Jack sewn in the upper left-hand corner, was mounted outside the plane over the pilot's compartment. Someone removed it and placed it in the navigator's kit as we approached the aircraft.

A messenger ran alongside as we taxied out, yelling something about a tower operator claiming he had found binoculars and some footprints in the dust behind the spare transmitter.

"They'll make you pay for that transgression," Hisako whispered, hanging on to her luggage.

"The bee stings hardest when you're already crying," I said, after the entrance door was closed, cutting off the outsider's voice. I marvelled at the efficiently sound-insulated interior.

The four engine biplane, capable of holding forty-five passengers, got airborne.

To pass the time, I asked Hisako what part of Mongolia she was from.

"I lived in a grass-covered valley in the mountainous part of the country, north of the capital city."

"Do you support the present government in the Peoples Republic of Mongolia?"

"I'm no communist. But Mongolia is one of the world's oldest countries, and I do love the terrain, even the arid parts, including the Gobi desert."

"Where did they pick you up?"

"In front of the British Hong Kong Club at the corner of Wyndham Street and Queen's Road. I don't have a passport."

We hadn't been told our destination, but wherever it was, it took a long time before I was able to identify the southern coast of Vietnam out of one of the large passenger windows. Later, as dawn broke, I spotted a bunch of little dots off the Malayan coast.

"Do you know the names of those tiny islands, the ones those small ships with the large antennas are sailing away from," Miss Bayar asked, not sure if she saw their shadowy outlines correctly.

"No. I don't. But the British patrol craft are sure operating far out from Malaya."

"Do you see that channel up ahead?"

"Hai."

"If I'm not mistaken, that's where a freighter and an ocean liner were sunk by British mines."

Finally, we flew past the Pan American Clipper parked at the floating docks at Singapore's seaplane base and headed for the airport built especially for British Imperial Airways.

As we came in for a landing, I noted the magnificant stucco estate in the suburbs belonging to the owner of a multi-million dollar tin enterprise. I also spotted dozens of American built Brewster Buffalo fighter planes circling overhead and Lockheed Hudson bombers fanning out over the water in rigid search patterns.

It was still daylight when we were herded off the aircraft and loaded into a waiting South African-made, armoured reconnaissance car, driven by an Australian soldier.

"Hisako," I whispered.

"Yes."

"There are thousands of Japanese living in Singapore, and a couple of them have plantations on the Malayan coastline. Hopefully, I can contact someone in the Japanese section along what's called the Middle Road area."

"You can bet they're being watched night and day, if they're not locked up," she said.

A Scottish officer dressed in a white mess jacket, kilt, black hose with red trimming, and brass-buckled patent-leather pumps passed by. He was on his way to the officer's club, I assumed.

I took it for granted that the Ango-Saxon-looking man in civilian clothes riding with us was a member of the British secret police.

"Are you Chinese?" he asked Hisako.

"No. I'm from the Peoples Republic of Mongolia."

"Do you know who that is?" he asked, pointing to a statue of a white man in front of the Victoria Memorial Hall.

"Yes," she said with revulsion. "That's Sir Stamford Raffles, the European most responsible for Malayans losing their freedom."

"Young lady, you wouldn't last very long under my authority. I enforce the laws of King-Emperor George the Sixth wholeheartedly," he said threateningly. "But to get on with pleasanter topics. We have an establishment about a mile down the road where we turn out over six thousand tires and twenty thousand tennis shoes per day."

"Do you have the market cornered?" I asked.

"No, we would have a bigger share if it wasn't for the Japs," he spat out, glaring at me.

"How about bicycles?" I asked, innocently.

"Don't you mention bicycles to me," he groaned. "Your country sold thousands of them to the Malayans, cheating Britain's manufacturers out of one of their most profitable items."

"All I see are foreign policemen and light-colored faces," Hisako said. "Where do the Malayans live?"

"They're all bunched together in thatch-roofed houses built on stilts in the seedier section of town." He then turned to me. "In case your countrymen start any trouble, those American-built planes you saw today will cut them to pieces. They're superior to any aircraft your country can produce."

"We only know how to copy," I said with a sigh, letting my chin sag. "I wish we could build a first-rate product, but it's hopeless," I agreed sadly, lying through my teeth. Or to put it more succinctly, if he knew what I was doing, he'd call it apple-polishing. I know it as grinding sesame seeds--demonstrating my favorite idiom by pressing my fist in a circular manner against my palm.

Hisako looked at me with her eyebrows raised while she stifled the impulse to burst out laughing.

"That looks like a fun place," she said, pointing to the Coconut Grove nightclub.

"You can't go in there," he said. "We have a color bar."

I thought she was going to hit him. Her eyes glowed like the embers from a dying campfire.

The recon vehicle paused outside the large metal gates at Fort Canning as if it was genuflecting. This was Imperialist Britain's crown jewel of the Far East. A cannon went off signalling the noon hour.

We continued on, then stopped in front of a run-down hotel.

We're putting you up in a two-bedroom suite recently vacated by an American rubber plantation consultant. It's well guarded. so don't try any funny business."

There was a knock on the apartment door soon after we got settled in.

I opened it and stared at a Thailand sailor. "What can I do for you?" I asked, pleasantly.

"I'm three apartments down the hall. The British are holding me prisoner for the politicans in Paris," replied the slim bluejacket with pencil-thin eyebrows and piercing stare. "My ship was engaged in a naval battle with the French. It was sunk by gunfire and I ended up being captured. My country was trying to get back the land that was taken from us by the French army."

"Come on in," I said.

Another knock.

This time it was a Malayan servant with a tray full of food. "Take particular note of the wooden bowl with the lid on it," he said in broken Madarin that was clear enough for Hisako to understand. "By the way, there's a German Jew in the next apartment."

"What'd he say about the bowl?" I asked when he departed.

In answer to my question she picked up the lacquered lid. The bowl contained a brown-colored liquid.

"It's dye, my linguistic hero," Hisako said playfully, putting the lid back on.

We divided up the baked prawns wrapped in coconut leaves and steeped in coconut milk, then proceeded to demolish a large dish of wafer-thin pancakes. Some contained diced radish; others had cabbage, shrimp, crab or chicken filling. There was also sago pudding and peanut sauce in separate bowls.

"What do you make of the dye?" the Thailand sailor asked, taking another pancake and a cup of Benkulen tea.

"It will enable us to darken up our skin," I said. "As you know, the Malayans are brown-skinned, have dark eyes, and are short in stature with wavy to straight hair."

"All three of us have the right-colored eyes," Hisako Bayar pointed out as she tried a dab of the brown substance on her forearm.

"Come to think of it," I said. "We can get by just the way we are. This is a cosmopolitan city, even though the British subjects think white skin is the only acceptable shade."

Hisako grabbed a sheet off the bed and headed for the bathroom with the bowl of dye in her hand.

"What's this?" she demanded, cracking open the door and sticking her hand out with a box in it.

"Lux soap," I read. "Britain's Lever Brothers have their tentacles everywhere."

Ten minutes later she was marching down the stairs with the tinted sheet drapped over one arm.

The Thai sailor and I had to rush to the railing at the head of the stairs to keep her in sight.

The guard approached as she neared the entrance door.

"What is a good-looking Englishman like yourself doing keeping Asians captive?" she asked in passable English.

"There's a possibility you and those two sailors are spies. As for the German Jew, the British Empire is not accepting any Jewish immigrants."

"That sounds like the head of the state-run Anglican church talking," Hisako said, without a trace of a smile and only a hint of the Shanghai accent acquired from the place she had learned a smattering of English.

"I suppose you're some sort of Buddist or Confucist," he said angrily.

"It's none of your business what I am. But I can tell you this much. We don't have a government-sponsored diety like you do."

What happened to the charm, I wondered.

"The Communist Chinese will be on our side if Japan attacks," the guard said.

"I don't know about the Chinese Communist, but your country encourages the use of India-grown opium, and triples its profits by selling and taxing it in Malaya."

The guard was furious and had his back to us when he raised his hand to slap Hisako. "You must be an offspring of Genghis Khan," he shouted.

While the guards eyes were still on Miss Bayar, the Thailand sailor crept forward and wacked him a good one on the back of the head with the heavy food tray. "That's for taking land from Thailand's southern border," he grunted.

Right behind him and breathing heavily, the Jewish civilian grabbed the sentry's keys and carefully opened the door to the outside.

We spread out, The German Jew said he'd stop at the Synagogue on Bencoolen Street before finding his way to Shanghai then on to Japan. Hisako Bayar headed for an international telephone center, and I wanted to see as much of Singapore's defenses as I could in the shortest possible time. I stole a canvas-covered Hillman light utility truck and went to the highest point on the island, the five-hundred-and-eighty-foot hill known as Tin Mountain, where I scribbled down the location of the reservoir on the northeast slope.

For some reason, the haunting image of the nearby ford motor plant stuck in my mind as I drove toward Johore Strait. Upon arriving at the waterway, I looked past a white-tailed sea eagle to take note of the causeway's 3,000 foot length. It was intact, unguarded, and consisted of a wide road, a two-track railway, and a pipe for fresh water. From there I drove slowly to the civilian airfield so as not to attract attention. The Hadley Page airliner was still there. The crew was probably drunk somewhere in town.

Hisako had said she'd find her own way back.

I had no trouble starting the engines and managed to spot the location of all four of Singapore's military airfields as I left the island, headed for Canton per Hisako's suggestion. It was an easy plane to fly and I quickly reached the nearest cloud cover before the fighters got airborne.

Upon entering Canton, I followed Hisako's advice, and made my way to the city's world-famous cabaret. This sophisticated establishment had gold-colored draperies, black rugs, white-leather booths, and its own radio station. It attracted people from the exotic regions of Mongolia, Manchukuo, and the Western regions of Russia--as well as an assortment of adventurers from China, Japan and the Western seafaring nations.

Finding the entrance was easy. Honoring an earlier custom, the building had been constructed facing south. It was thought to be more healthful that way.

Before entering the dining room, I bought some jade earrings at the duty-free store located in the lobby. I ignored the ivory carvings and lacquerware even though it was being offered at bargain prices.

Jade earrings made an excellent gift no matter what city you happened to find yourself in.

The waiter welcomed me with a nod and the all purpose expression, "tsin-tsin," then placed me in a booth by the window facing the left bank of the Pearl River.

I surveyed my immediate area. A couple sitting across the narrow aisle from me caught my eye.

I wondered what the stern-looking man with the elegantly-dressed woman was talking about so intently. She was facing away from me.

I received two quick shocks. The first was discovering that the woman was Hisako Bayar. The second occurred ten minutes later, when a white women, sporting a pillbox hat that left her red hair peeking out from under it, walked in. I knew her.

I jumped up. "What brings you to this lovely city, Jane?" I asked.

"We're headed for Shanghai. I haven't seen you since Hawaii," she allowed, handing me her black polo coat.

"Please sit here," I begged.

"That Asian lady with the thick, black hair brushed high up on her head has on an expensive outfit," Jane murmured. "She's wearing a silk dress with a Mandarin collar and a sable wrap."

I pretended that Hisako and I hadn't eaten rice from the same pot, so to speak, but I continued to eavesdrop on her conversation. I wondered how she had arrived ahead of me and was curious about her companion. Jane started to speak, then grew silent when she caught the intensity of the woman in the adjacent booth.

"Dimitri," the female object of Jane's scrutiny cooed to her escort, a bulky Caucasian with hooded-eyes. "Thanks for getting me out of Singapore so rapidly. The British were giving me a hard time."

"It's even worse in Rangoon, Burma, he said, "the British consider any person without white skin of lesser value than a paper lantern."

"I wish America would side with the Oriental countries instead of the European," Hisako said. "Mongolia has a vital role to play in the Far East," she insisted, pushing the menu out to arm's length. "It's important for the Asian countries to unite against the whites. Surely, as a Russian Jew living in Harbin, Manchukuo, you can sympathize with that idea.

"Speaking of conflicts," the waiter interrupted, bringing a sharp retort from Dimitri. "Hong Kong radio is accusing Japan of sending a fighter pilot under false pretenses to spy on British fortifications, and they're hoping mad."

"The British army doesn't belong here anyway!" Hisako claimed before getting to her next question. "Is the West in position for a direct invasion of Japan?"

"This sounds like an Asian International Conference," the heavy-accented man observed. "But look at this, Hisako," he said, spreading out a map in front of the beautiful Oriental woman.

"I'll bet he's KGB," I whispered to Jane.

"Before we get into the map, Dimitri," Hisako said. "I want to thank you for this lovely sable jacket. I didn't expect any payment for the information I gave you."

"It's nothing that any red-blooded Russian man wouldn't do for someone as captivating as you. Providing he was willing to stay in the frozen north for weeks on end, was an expert shot, and happened to be a friend of the best furrier in the business."

"You certainly went to a lot of trouble to keep me warm," she said, tapping with her satin shoes.

"I did have some help from a Japanese sailor," Dimitri admitted. "That robust paper-shuffler was superb with a knife, and even managed to pay his share of the Siberian hunting trip by earning his way. He could skin a sable quicker than a surgeon makes an incision."

"Shifting through the information I gave you should have kept you busy for months," Hisako commented with her finger pointed at the map he was holding. Her almond eyes showed no emotion.

"Does your family still raise horses?" Dimitri asked.

"Yes," she said, "I miss them terribly."

"I heard you were quite a rider," he said, meaning it as a compliment.

"I loved it," she said. "I still picture myself going at full gallop, hair flying in the wind, feet jammed into the stirrups, racing over the wilder sections of the Mongolian countryside."

"I would have liked to have seen that," he said.

"That man is up to something," Jane commented before bringing up a new topic. "When I stopped in Yokohama two years ago with my dad, I expected to see a teeming mass of people in kimonos and getas."

"Americans who have not traveled to the Far East are misinformed," I assured her. "I don't wish to be too critical of the United States, but your government wants to pretend the rural people represent the whole country. I went with a *Moga* during my sophmore year in college. She was much more typical of the city and coastal residents."

"What's a *Moga?*"

"You call them flappers, or jazz girls," I said with a mischievious glint in my eye.

Hisako caught my eye and winked, then checked out Jane, who had on a dark green Celanese rayon dress with puffed sleeves and a low neckline. She also wore white Cossack boots.

"How about the Fiji Islands?" the Mongolian lady inquired, shifting her eyes from Jane back to Dimitri.

I hoped my dark-blue, high-collared service dress uniform with its single row of brass buttons still looked pressed after having been in my seabag for awhile.

I figured any discrepancies in the appearance of my tunic and trousers would be more than offset by the red stripe on my right sleeve, awarded for good conduct, and of course my pilot's rating badge and wings.

I rubbed my black, western shoes on the back of my pant legs to increase the shine.

"The Fiji's sound rather romantic to me," Hisako said in a teasing tone. "Dimitri, do you but any chance happen to know anyone who could get a navy pilot transferred into a fighter squadron. He has a dead-end job right now and needs a boost in morale to make him more aggressive."

If it's important to you, I could talk to the naval commander in SE Asia. He's quartered in Vietnam. I got to know him when I enlisted his help in my effort to find a new home for the Jewish refugees from Europe.

"The British will probably draft Fiji Islanders," the waiter, claiming to be an ex-merchant mariner, volunteered as he served the shark fin soup.

"True," Dimitri agreed irritably, moving on to the next segment. "And the Gilbert chain, which the islanders wish to call Kiribti, is where the fourteen-square-mile island of Tawara and the British flag are located."

"It's only two hundred miles from the Marshall Islands where Japan has large agriculture holdings, but even more worrisome is Europe's stranglehold on the Far East," the Oriental beauty noted.

"Yes, and we've only talked about a portion of Europe's conquests," Dimitri informed her. "From the communist viewpoint, the whole southeast quadrant on the approach to Japan is either under or threatened by Western Empire control."

"How does that affect your department?"

"It'll certainly make my job much easier. China will be ripe for conversion to communism if a capitalistic country like Japan is removed from the picture."

"The West can't ever take control of Canton again, can they? Which reminds me. How are your wife and children?"

"I wouldn't bet on it," Dimitri replied, ignoring the last part of the question. "It was only four years ago that United States sailors from the heavy cruiser *Augusta* equipped with rifles and steel helmets, marched down the main streets of Shanghai as if they owned them. And hundreds of Scottish Highlanders in battle dress complete with menacing looks, drilled in the heart of the city to intimidate the citizens of that cosmopolitan city. British police were everywhere."

"Speaking of odd couples," Jane said, placing her darker hand, thanks to the California sun, on top of mine. "We couldn't do this in the states," she said, squeezing my fingers together, "Interracial touching is frowned on."

"So I've heard," I said, interested in this delightful Westerner's background. "Where, exactly, do you live?"

"Poway. Not far from father's factory in the northern section of San Diego county. Do you know where San Diego is?"

"It's a big naval base in Southern California," I replied, finally

115

remembering what her tantalizing green-eyes reminded me of--spearment candy. My childhood weakness. I just might fall in love, I thought.

"East is East, and West is West, and never the twain shall meet. At least, according to Rudyard Kipling. Except of course, in Hawaii," Jane said playfully, referring to our meeting in Honolulu six months previously. I had been in civilian clothes visiting relatives, and Jane was on a trip with her father, Poway Aircraft Company's chairman of the board.

"Dad was afraid I was going to stow away on that beautiful ocean liner, *Asamu Maru*. It was headed for Yokohama, Kobe, Shanghai, and Hong Kong, before returning again to Hawaii."

"The Harley-Davison motorcycle representative was probably aboard it," I said in an attempt to show the commercial ties between our two countries and bring the topic back to safe ground. "He made frequent trips from San Francisco to Yokohama.

"The N.Y.K. lines had an outstanding six-week ocean cruise package before the fuel shortage," I said diplomatically, not mentioning the fact that U.S. opposition was the reason the liners could no longer make the trip.

"No need to worry," Jane said, nervously pulling on her golden necklace. "Someday you'll be able to get all the oil you need. The Western monopoly won't last forever."

"In the meantime," I said, "your country is crushing the life's blood out of us. Is that fair?"

"Washington power politics," she said, sounding like her father, "has nothing in common with the subject of fairness, Kiyo. They'll keep whatever the've taken by force. And continuously make plans to get what they don't already have."

"I know the Dutch military controls the Indonesian oil fields."

"It's the survival of the fittest. The fight to get oil was always a mismatch. The heavyweights against the weaker nations. Britain fought three wars against Burma to take over that nation and its oil fields. Burma had already reached a production figure of seventy thousand barrels a year.

"After the English seized permanent control, the King-Emperor put up an additional three thousand oil derricks."

Having heard a rumor that people from the mainland were sent to Honolulu to pick up the names and addresses of Japanese-Americans living there to take back to Washington, I tried a delicate question.

"What were you doing in Hawaii? Vacation?"

"Yes," Jane said evasively, moving her suede handbag to the center of the table. "I was with my father. I hope you didn't think we were doing something underhanded? In America, you're innocent until proven guilty."

"And the guilty always get caught," I said with a smile.

"Let's take a walk outside before we have our tea," she suggested. "We could visit the new Wuhan-Canton railroad station."

We hadn't walked far down the narrow, crowded streets before deciding to take rest on a curved stone bench next to the Pearl River.

We gazed at the riverboats jamming the waterway.

"Have you ever flown the A5M?" Jane asked, without appearing to care.

I had to keep in mind that her father was head of an aircraft company and could use information about the planes slotted flaps, flush-mounted panels and warped wing.

"That's an older model," I said, looking indignant. Could I get away with asking her how big her father's aircraft plant is, I wondered.

"My father never fell for the American government's line about the Japanese being a bunch of imitators without the intelligence to come up with new ideas," Jane said, speaking carefully.

"We strive to keep up with the times," I said, trying to appear humble.

"As a noncommissioned officer, I guess they won't let you fly the latest aircraft," she said sympathetically, playing to my ego.

"I've flown the army's Ki-43, the Pergrine Falcon, the best fighter in the world," I blurted out before I could stop myself. "But, how about you, Jane? Don't you get tired of living in the boondocks with the fear of losing out to the larger aircraft companies?"

"No," she countered, displaying a coquettish pout. "My dad's company has a big contract for building army bombers, and we're on our way to becoming a nationally respected corporation."

"Bombers, eh. Those little single-engine jobs, I imagine," I teased, captivated with her.

"No, four-engine ones, thousands of them."

"I'm glad for you," I fibbed, getting up and reaching for her hand.

"In honor of your Izu Peninsula Tea Grower's lobbyist in Washington, I'd like a cup of tea now," Jane said, earrings bouncing.

"Tea sounds wonderful," I said, hypnotized by her sultry-green eyes. Was I getting in too deep? I wondered. But it didn't really matter. I was leaving in the morning. The naval district had swapped in the Hadley Page passenger plane for *Gossamer Wings.*

A hundred miles from the Red Bamboo restaurant, I was intercepted by two white Zeroes from *Sky Dragon*. The one on my right had *Ghost Leader* painted on its nose and the other had *Green Pastures.*

Well at least I'm surrounded by the best, I thought. Those are Silent Storm aircraft.

After dipping the noses of their aircraft in a chivalrous bow to *Gossamer Wings,* Ken Ito, the pilot in 412 and Ghost Leader flying 415 pointed towards the northeast, letting me know I was to report back to my air base immediately.

That's the second time I've seen the name, *Green Pastures,* I realized. Does it have anything to do with Sub Lieutenant Ito's conversion to Christianity because he had received emergency treatment at St. Luke's hospital? I thought it was a tall-tale when somebody told me that in gratitude for the life-saving care he received, he had picked two words from the second line in the twenty-third psalm: "he maketh me to lie down in green pastures," to paint on the nose cowling of his plane.

Maybe Ito saw possibilities in belonging to a Westerner's religion. Perhaps he was thinking of going into politics later on. Worshipping someone who rose from the dead had given precedent for Chicago's deceased Christians to get up from the grave and vote.

Banking to the left and flying under Ito's aircraft, I headed in a northeasterly direction for Southern Taiwan.

I turned on the radio to *Ikeda's* Iris frequency and heard a gaggle of voices. Michi Sakamoto was speaking.

"Slow down. You, there on the far left, in the front row. Go ahead, what have you experienced?"

"In China, peasants were kicked, punched, and bayoneted by Western soldiers."

"Over there in the corner by the steam tables."

"In Burma, the citizens have to bring whatever the Englishmen requests on the double, or get cuffed in the head."

"The sailor standing behind the fourth row."

"In Malaya, they are beaten for the slightest infraction of colonial rules. British-held territory in Borneo is run like a feudal estate with the workers treated like slaves."

"Does anybody have information on the islands further out?" Sakamoto asked, telling Kaine to copy down the replies.

"In the Gilbert Islands, Including *Tawara*, British trading companies are the law," someone shouted far from the microphone.

"Here's a couple of items for you to remember when you go into combat," Sakamoto offered. "In the Philippines, Filipinos are called niggers and monkeys on official American documents.

"Isn't the Philippines going to get its independence in 1946? A voice that I recognized as Agi's asked.

"The Philippines threatened to throw in with Japan if America didn't set a date for independence. But that promised freedom is five years away, and the American plantation owners make too much money to give it up unless there's a lot of loopholes in the treaty."

"Isn't America siding with the British Empire?" the belligerent Kato bellowed.

The American leaders are jealous of the British Empire, and want to sit at the same dinner table in case the King-Emperor leaves some crumbs for them. Even with the Philippines, Wake, Midway, Hawaii, and Alaska garrisoned by American troops--the United States still feels inferior to the great European Empires like France and Britain."

I wondered whether his talks would help those men get through the very perilous events in the coming months. Sometimes knowing why you're facing danger, gives you the strength to hold up even under the most adverse conditions.

I kept looking for Kaohslung Air Base.

Chapter 18

Cry all Night

My buddy Segawa had returned from Miyako-Jima and woke me up before the sun was high in the sky. "We're invited to a radio show," he informed me.

"It's early?" I complained.

"*Hai*. And it's a glorious morning for either touring the city or having a beer."

"I've been jumping around so much, I lost track of what day it is."

"It's Friday. And hurry up or we'll miss the next couple of street cars."

"Let's eat in town," I said, heading for the shower.

According to the greeter at the radio station, NHK was about to encounter its stiffest competition since this home entertainment feature was first introduced to Japan in 1925. The newest broadcast facility, NWR, was in Taiwan interviewing people, hoping to find the voice that would cut into NHK's dominate position on the airways.

As we approached our seats in the front row, I saw a familiar face.

At times, Ruriko Hattori's eyes resembled black pearls, especially when she was in a sultry mood. However, she did flash her devilish but infrequent smile at me before I said, "I thought you worked for NHK?"

I applied for the femme fatale role in 'Cry All Night,' a new soap opera that NWR hoped would boost their ratings."

I tried to think of an appropriate comment concerning America's envolement with Britain's Lever Brothers, the manufacturer of most of the toilet articles advertised on America's daytime radio shows, but I failed to come up with anything. It seemed like a reasonable thought to me that Western troops held onto land in the Pacific side of the world to please Unilever, the owner of 250 British and Dutch companies worldwide.

Kimiko had suggested her sister volunteer to take care of wounded soldiers at one of the local hospitals. But Ruriko did not see a bunch of hard-working doctors and shot-up patients as helping out her cause.

120

Instead of a reading for a role in 'Cry All Night,' Ruriko Hattori, feeling assertive in her green-wool dress, cherry-colored belt and Western-style shoes, suggested she be allowed to interview members of the armed forces. "I spoke to a colonel in the audience just back from China," she said.

The easygoing, gentle-eyed, program manager, Takiji Kubo, was reluctant to step into a new arena. But he liked her style, even though he considered her voice wrong for the part in 'Cry All Night.'

"Is anyone from Iwaki?" he asked, speaking to the audience from a spot just in front of me. "That's where our home studio is located."

"I was born and raised in Fukui on the other side of the island from Iwaki," an exhibitionist hollered out.

"Fukui, isn't that where the botanical gardens are located?" Kubo asked with a tight smile.

"*Hai,* plus the Fujishima shrine, and nearby, the Maruoka castle. But most people know the city because of its connection with the silk trade ever since the tenth century."

Kubo looked over toward Ruriko. "Didn't you interview Gunner's Mate Kikuchi about the Trademark Killer?"

"Yes, I did. That was an exclusive."

Straightening out his narrow-stripped, Wembly necktie to cover up his nervousness, Kubo agreed to cancel the fifteen minute cooking class that was slated for the next time spot.

That's a break for her, I thought. There'll be lots of housewives listening in. "Oh! What a beautiful tie," Ruriko commented to Kubo, darting a glance in my direction.

"I purchased it on the *Empress of Britain* a couple of years ago," he smiled, pleased that she noticed it. "The Canadian Pacific liners used to make regular trips to Japan."

Flattery, pretended shyness, and a come-hither smile had the writers believing she would follow the script they were quickly putting together for her. She should be an actress, I thought, and would be if it paid more. Besides, after Satomi, her oldest sister, married that Norwegian sailor last year, she needs something out of the ordinary to boost her ego.

One hour and a change of clothes later, Ruriko read over the questions she was to ask Regimental Commander, Colonel Oka. "Incredibly dull," she stopped by to tell me. "It needs a dash of pepper to liven it up."

Station manager Kubo was pleased with the way Ruriko eased her

121

way through Oka's family and professional background. "Now it's time for her to praise the Colonel and tell him how much the people appreciate the job he and his men are doing for their country," he confided to the audience.

After getting him to remove his single-breasted overcoat and rushing past the opening chit-chat, Ruriko Hattori took the plunge. "Colonel," she asked, wanting to penetrate behind those clear, pitch-black eyes that seemed overly large for his small body. "I understand you took leave in Thailand recently. Could you give us your impressions of that country?"

"I wasn't aware that anybody knew I went to Thailand," Colonel Oka said, fiddling nervously with the red stripe on his trousers. "I'll be glad to give you my recollections," he offered, exhibiting a readiness to switch subjects if it appeared to be a trap. "Like ourselves, Thailand was a victim of the Western unequal trade treaties, and is presently making strong verbal attacks against Western imperialism."

"How did Thailand vote on the Manchurian question in the League of Nations?" she asked, tapping her Congo-brown suede shoes in cadence with the Colonel's speech pattern. The leather should have felt good. It was a little cold this time of year for getas.

"Thailand and Poland abstained, then voted against any sanctions being applied to Japan," he replied, trying to judge by those startling dark eyes what her real motive was.

"Is communism a threat in Thailand?" she asked, reacting to the hesitancy in his voice.

"Communism is of concern everywhere," Oka responded heatedly, now that he was on safe ground. International communism is a major threat to our way of life. Countries interested in stopping this menace should swap intelligence information and share successful control methods."

Before she could short-circuit him, the Colonel went on.

"By popular usage, the title, Communism International, has been shortened to Comintern, and I consider Anti-Comintern a calling."

"Stepping away from communism for a moment, Colonel," Ruriko hastily interjected. "Are airline routes a big priority with the West?"

"*Hai,*" Col. Oka replied, "Britain's Imperial Airways is the leader, and the rest are scrambling to catch up. Pan Am outmaneuvered Germany's Lufthansa Airlines and managed to get a forty-five percent share of the Chinese National Aviation Corporation, a monopoly."

"Did airline and military expansion stop there?" Ruriko asked, using her hand to smooth out a wrinkle in her kimona. She thought it best to wear the white one with a red lining, the traditional November color, while interviewing the conservative-leaning army colonel.

"No," Oka replied, buttoning and unbuttoning the top fastener on his tunic. "When I asked her, she, I mean," Oka said flustered.

Was that allusion to a female a slip of the tongue? Or were you, perhaps, thinking of Thailand?"

"I'm a little nervous. This is my first time on radio."

"We're near the end. A personal question if you don't mind, Colonel Oka?"

"Go ahead. But stay away from my trip to Thailand."

"Your bio says your father's name is Tadashi Kondo. Is that correct?"

"I married Kumiko Oka. Her mother and father had no sons--so to carry on the family name, as is customary, I took her surname."

"How about your own family?"

"I have two brothers."

With Kubo waving frantically. Ruriko decided she had better ask questions on the original reason for having him as a guest. "Were you stationed in China for very long Colonel?"

"I go back to the time when Chang Kai-shek and his Third Corps rid Peking of subversives.

"Europe at that time had control of China's power levers, and because the West wouldn't allow any Chinese soldiers within fifteen miles of China's major seaports, the country became known as a sub-colony. The standard European colony had more control over its destiny than China did."

"How was China manipulated?"

"Real power resided in Shanghai, the fourth largest city in the world. Whoever governed Shanghai, governed China, and by having control of Shanghai's International Settlement's Municipal Council, the West was able to do just that."

"Didn't it require lots of money to govern Shanghai?"

"*Hai.* And the Municipal Council had plenty. They sold licenses to rickshaw drivers and opium dealers at exorbitant prices."

"How long before the Europeans lose control?"

"It won't happen overnight. Twenty-four German officers led by General Von Falklusen trained elements of the Chinese army antagonistic to Japan."

"Our time is about up Colonel. We managed to stray from the main topic. We can have you back another time to talk about that ancient and honorable country," Ruriko informed him. "I'm sorry I made you uncomfortable by discussing your trip to Thailand."

Maybe he had a girl friend there, I speculated to Segawa, placing it in the back of my mind for future reference.

"I appreciated this chance to get some of these things off my chest," Colonel Oka responded. "Unless my Commanding General objects, I'll take you up on the invitation."

Switching off the microphone, Ruriko led the army officer out of the broadcasting area to where Kubo and I were anxiously awaiting them.

As soon as the door closed behind Oka, the jubilant station manager rushed to get out the good news. "We have a winner. Calls commenting on the Sino-Japanese war have been pouring in, along with those wanting more information on airlines and world-wide communism."

"Give me another fifteen minutes of air time and I'll interview an international trade expert from Tokyo to tie this all together," Ruriko Hattori pleaded, spotting an opening to enhance her status at the station.

"You've got it! I'll delay the daytime quiz show," Kubo proclaimed, before he decided how he was going to explain it to Chiiko, who was anxious to show off her new red gabardine suit and rayon stockings to the studio audience. "We may be onto something big."

Ruriko nodded in agreement and praised his leadership. She pointed to a gentleman from the audience--obviously a plant.

"Professor Sano," she said, "received a doctor's degree for his work on the upcoming battle for commercial air routes and its effects on trade."

There was one more task to complete before starting the interview, Ruriko decided, as she sat down and picked up the phone to call Representative Daizen's office. She said she wanted to thank him for his help in getting the interview with Gunner Kikuchi.

Fascinated with her style, my friend Segawa and I decided to stay and watch.

Ruriko walked over and checked the height of the big overhead mike in case she needed to change it. She waved off the station manager when he walked toward Chiiko Sukuri.

"Radio fans," she announced before Kuba had a chance to ask Sukuri to take the time slot. "Welcome to the second broadcast of, 'Not Afraid to Say It,' the hard-hitting program that brings you controversial opinions from people in high places. Colonel Oka gave us some straight talk on communism. Now, we'll hear from Professor Sano, an Osaka University specialist on international trade." Ruriko Hattori spoke with relief, as the station manager escorted a slim man dressed in a pale-blue suit and black felt vest trimmed with white piping past the tight-mouthed Chiiko to the guest chair. He deposited the little boy with him in the first row.

"Good day, Professor," Ruriko said after a brief introduction. "First, let me say that Osaka is an excellent place for a university. The city is one of our most important commercial centers.

" I asked you on the phone yesterday if there were any recent developments to restrict international investments. Do you have anything to share with our radio listeners?"

'Thank you for having me on the show, Hattori-san," Professor Sano said.

"Colonel Oka," Ruriko said, impatiently tapping her gold tassel earring. "told my radio listeners that a path was now open for a string of American naval stations that will allow U.S. warships to operate, with the necessary base support, all the way from the United States to Macao, China," she said, looking for an explosive comment.

She got it. "And Macao is controlled by the Portuguese army," Sano said, shaking his head in a disheartened fashion.

"What is Japan's biggest advantage, Professor?" Ruriko asked, watching Sano's son fool with the brim on his circular hat. He was dressed in a short-sleeve shirt, shorts, knee-high socks, and sneakers.

"Japanese salesmen are persistent. No sale is too small," he suggested, removing the blue-banded, black Panama hat from his lap when the heat from the lights made him uncomfortable.

"Don't you have three sons?"

"Hai, I hope my wife has a daughter next time. For no family is complete without a little girl to celebrate Doll's Day with."

"Our successful trade negotiations with the rest of the world doesn't help our relations with the West, does it?" Ruriko asked.

"The bitterest pill for the West to swallow was when Japan increased its favorable trade balance with the white-oriented countries like Australia, New Zealand, Canada, and the United States."

I wondered if his candid statements would cause him problems with his fellow members on the university's faculty.

"What advantage does the West have over us?" Ruriko said. Her tone suggested she already knew the answer.

"Control of raw materials," Sano said automatically, not seeing any danger in this question. "The great empires of the West, using their ability to cut off the flow of vital supplies, can strangle our economy,"

"You sound pessimistic, Professor." she stated, "The country must be in pretty good shape if a college instructor like yourself can afford to purchase imported Seersucker suits and Nettleton loafers.

She's right, I thought, remembering I had spotted black-lacquered getas with colorful velvet thongs, patent-leather slip-ons, silk plaid ones from Vietnam, and even brown and white American saddle shoes while walking to my seat.

"There is a very real possibility that the white nations," Sano said, "will take over the rest of the Far East just by keeping the supply of raw materials bottled up."

"This is the stuff my audience wants to hear," Ruriko said, rubbing her hands together. "What can the little guy do?"

"Support the measures already taken," he replied, treading into perilous waters, especially our army's decision to run the communists out of the territory of Manchuria, giving it the opportunity to become the independent country of Manchukuo."

"But the colonial Western powers and some elements in China, especially the communist, are seething. Was it worth it?"

"What is freedom worth? You have to start somewhere, even if it gives the British a propaganda tool."

"We have five minutes of air time left, Professor. Tell us something about one of our more belligerent rivals."

"Australia acts like a European nation."

"Are they a danger to us?" she inquired.

Noting the Ainu from northern Japan sitting in the third row, dressed in a beautifully decorated green silk robe and traditional headband, I wondered whether Ruriko had invited him to the show.

"Hai, like all industrial countries," Sano said, "Australia is aware of the huge amount of money to be made by obtaining control of the more valuable air routes. Japan is in a period of rapid development, and Australia does her best to slow down Japanese imports to preserve her market for Britain. The attempt has not been successful--Australia continues to complain about aggressive Japanese trading south of the equator."

"I see our times up. We wish to thank Professor Sano for taking a break from his busy schedule to bring us information we all should be aware of. Comments can be directed to the NWR Radio Station at the address given at the beginning and end of the program. This is your hostess, Ruriko Hattori, reminding you to sneeze only once."

"What does she mean?" I asked, turning to the older woman sitting next to me.

"To sneeze just once means someone is speaking highly of you. To sneeze twice, means someone is speaking ill of you," she said, somewhat

126

surprised that I didn't know that.

I bowed my head to show my thanks.

"Hattori San," Takiji called in a loud voice, meeting her at the half-way point from his office, "Two minutes into your program and I knew we'd have to hire someone to answer the extra phone calls."

"We're tackling subjects we've been hiding from. If you give me the leeway, I'll bring you some real controversial topics."

"I don't know if I can give a woman that much responsibility."

"Don't go soft on me. And don't fall for that right-wing stuff. Japan had its first woman pilot in 1922. Women direct traffic; they are pearl divers, teachers, priests, commercial artist, airline stewardess, librarians, business managers, and at the top of the pyramid, the Sun Goddess."

"Okay," the manager said, somewhat cowed. "We'll give it a try. Two days a week. Tuesday and Thursday." He followed that remark with a warning, "I want no statements that will get us thrown off the air."

"You know I wouldn't do that," Ruriko assured him, attempting to look innocent.

Chapter 19

Chinese Donneybrook

The dictionary defines Donneybrook as a scene of many fights--and China in the 1930s was the perfect example. Western countries, having gotten what they wanted, began reducing their direct military involvement, while Japan, on the other hand, seeing its influence dwindling, increased its military efforts. China, weakened after years of exploitation by the West, was in no position to offer an organized and cohesive resistance.

Segawa and I took Colonel Oka out for a drink and a friendly chat at the nearest bar. I hoped to get some information from him on foreign aircraft flying in China.

"How do you see the current situation, Colonel?"

"With the increasingly belligerent tone coming out of the Western capitals, I'm apprehensive. No matter how large our armed forces, the cold hard facts present a gloomy picture. The most the Independent countries of the Far East can hope for is the combined strength of Japan, Thailand, Manchukuo, parts of China, and the patriots in the occupied Asian countries. If our prayers aren't answered, standing up against the giants of the West will turn out to be a disaster."

"What do we have in common with Thailand?" I asked.

"We are Thailand's number one trading partner, both countries are conservative in nature, have been reasonably close for a century, have been victims of Western threats, and are anti-communist."

"I can see why we should work together to clear Europe's occupation forces out of Asia," I sputtered. "It'll prevent the Westerners from completing their plan for conquering the rest of us."

"Why doesn't New Zealand's Royal Airforce and Navy join us in this fight to free Asia?" Segawa asked, paying more attention to his drink than the answer.

"I don't know! Bigotry, I guess. We sure could use their fighting spirit. New Zealand has come a long way--especially in the field of economic control, self-defense, and recently, almost complete independence. The final step will include scheduling foreign events without Britain's approval.

"With all the sailors in the Pacific, it's a good time to own a place selling Nippon beer," Segawa said, looking to the practical side.

"A good bar fight will give you more information about the reflexes and tenacity of a potential combatant than a hundred incidental meetings," I reported with a far-away look in my eye, "Shanghai is the place to be if you want to acquire secret data. There, you can always find a Chinese lady, dressed alluringly in a Cheong-sam, willing to find an answer to any question you think worth paying for."

"You say Cheong-sam with a certain amount of pleasure in your voice, " Colonel Oka noted. "Did you do some private research?" he said as we got up to leave.

"No, but I'm a big admirer of the high-collar, beautifully embroided Chinese dress, especially the black one with a slit running down the length of the leg." I said huskily to an attentive audience.

"Isn't the slit the same length on all Cheong-sams?" Segawa asked, waiting for an answer like it was the most important question on earth.

"The height of the collar and the length of the slit change from year to year." I told him as we headed for a street car.

Because of a tip intelligence had received about an American plane manufacturer and his daughter having been seen in Shanghai's International Settlement, I was given the use of one of the twelve pre-production models of the speedy Ki-45 Dragon Killer to check out the rumor.

I rather liked visiting China. We had a Chinatown in Kobe, my hometown, and it's been rumored my family had Chinese ancestors in its family tree. I suppose that is a possibility; in 200 B. C., a Chinese Emperor sent an expedition to Japan.

Coming in from the north, I flew over Cathay, the ancient name for the part of China laying north of China's longest and most important waterway, the Yangtze River. A minute later I was crossing the Whangpoo River and into the city.

I had made it to Shanghai from Taiwan including the landing, parking and a phone call, all in less than two hours. Furthermore, I was elated when I found out the California visitors turned out to be the Howells. For a modest fee I obtained their whereabouts and telephone number.

Jane and I got off the streetcar to walk on the Woosung River bridge then grabbed a rickshaw for the rest of the trip. I couldn't resist pointing out the sign in a park that had been patrolled by the British police: Dogs and Chinese keep off the grass. I got out of the rickshaw and trashed it.

That evening Jane and I found ourselves in the Golden Peacock Nightclub, a place where you're sure to meet other foreign travelers.

Bumping into a Caucasian missionary as we entered the doorway, I steered Jane Howell to one side of an ornamental bronze gong before asking where her dad was at this time of night.

"It's no secret. He's meeting with a representative from a South Bend, Indiana company that manufactures aircraft Instruments."

"This is a business trip?"

"Yes, I came along to keep the wives entertained. Dad's lost since mom died." She paused long enough to reach over and rap the Chinese gong with her knuckles. We both enjoyed its hollow, vibrant sound.

The band was playing "China Night," a Japanese song that was very popular in Peking, and I was pulling out a chair for Jane at an empty table near the side booths when a man with the unlikely nickname of Manchuria roared into the place. He looked around until he saw someone from the Japanese armed forces. Then, cheered on by a bunch of American marines wearing Honduras and Siberian campaign ribbons, he walked over and knocked the Japanese sailor off the bar stool.

The bartender was able to break up the fight easily when it became apparent that not many Manchukuons were going to line up on the side of this man calling himself Manchuria. Most seemed ready to go to the aid of an Asian with a good industrial track record.

Once the atmosphere became combative, a drunken Dutch aviator rose unsteadily to his feet. Proudly displaying his Bronze Cross medal with its bold-faced inscription: FAITHFUL TO QUEEN AND FATHERLAND, the spokesman for the Teutonics announced he and his men were going to wipe up the bar with any yellow skin who didn't side with the West.

"First, talk to me," a deep voice coming from the bowels of the earth rumbled across the room, followed by a gigantic-sized soldier that got down from his seat three bar stools to the left of the Dutchman. "My name is Major Gegan Sukebator," he said, his raven eyes blazing and decidedly dangerous. To emphasize his point, he moved his left shoulder forward so the Manchukuon patch was plainly visible. Other soldiers and airmen from the newly formed country came forward, together with their Japanese counterparts, to join him. It was one more sign that the Far East was breaking free of white domination.

The Dutch aviators were bewildered and scared. Always before, the Asians had backed down, knowing the ferocity of the British police and the hell-hole conditions of the British Shanghai jails. The Golden Peacock was one of a limited number of Shanghai night clubs where soldiers and sailors from all races could mix on equal terms. Normally, the Westerners stayed in settlements which barred Orientals from entering.

On the river waterways, American gunboats like the *Panay* considered themselves top-dog. And any family-owned Chinese rivercraft that didn't show the proper respect was pushed out of the way. The smaller of the two American pilots watching the proceedings got so excited, his whispered voice became loud enough for the Manchukuons to hear. "They won't be so tough when we hit them with our strategic bombers," the blonde man said with drunken glee,

"You know as well as I do," the larger one remarked, "it's a good day when we come within a half a mile of the target."

"That's to our advantage." the heavier one retorted, laughing. "Think of all the coolies we can get, *accidentally....*"

What he said about the inaccuracy of the Norten bombsight made the Manchukuon's blood run cold and my face whiten, for we knew our cities would be targeted in a war with the West.

I heard three Caucasians, discussing the old-line companies that had made their money in opium, ask the king-sized Major to sit at their table for a moment. They appeared intrigued by the Manchukuon's attitude,

Gegan Sukebator pulled up a chair. His big hands and friendly smile looked out of place next to His Majesty's croquet players. The dark-haired British subject slid his delicate hands under a paper napkin to avoid comparison and introduced himself as Woodward from Jardines.

"What can I get you to drink, Major?" Cyril Brown, the light-haired American from Russell and Company asked.

"I'll have Mandarin tea with a sprig of cinnamon, if you'd be kind enough to go to the bar and get it for me."

"Certainly," Brown said, walking a few feet from the table before telling a Chinese waiter to fill the order. Cyril knew the Westerners had an ace in-the-hole. Franklin Delano Roosevelt's maternal relative, Warren Delano, had been a partner in Russell and Company founded in 1824. With branches in the Chinese bayonet ports, where its partners acted as American consuls, the American company was as influential and affluent as the British East India Company.

"Major, we noticed you sticking up for the Japanese. Don't you hate them?" Johnson, the fat Englishman representing Swain Company, asked.

"For freeing the territory, providing an atmosphere for industrial growth, and offering to help keep communism out? Hardly."

"But the Japanese are nothing but a bunch of conquerors," Woodward announced.

"Compared to whom? Iceland or Switzerland?" Sukebator asked, looking him straight in the eye. "Tell me, what is an Englishman doing on the board of an agency that dictates the rules for seven million Asians in Shanghai and indirectly all of China?"

"But those little yellow. . .," Johnson began out of habit before he could stop himself."

Putting one of his huge hands on Johnson's arm and squeezing until he saw the first signs of tears, Sukebator's whisper sounded like a fog horn issuing its ghostly warnings on a stormy night. "Careful now, there's very little difference in skin color between me and that Chinese waiter your friend just ordered a drink from."

"Let's be watchful with our comments," Woodward suggested to his friend. "Asians vary enormously in their coloring."

"Mr. Woodward, do you work in that big Jardin and Swire's building, the one that looks like a palace?" Gegan asked.

"Here's your drink Major," Brown said, interrupting Woodward's reply.

"Thank you, but I asked you to get it," Sukebator said, giving it to the table on his left. "I saw you hiding behind that American airman while the waiter got it."

"That's what Coolies are. . ."

"Mr. Brown, Cyril, I believe, " Gegan Sukebator said, cutting him off. "I suggest you choose a different way of expressing yourself in the future?"

"Yes! Certainly, I see what you mean--I'll be right back."

"Aren't there a lot of Japanese moving into Manchuria, I mean, Manchukuo?" Woodward asked.

"Yes! In contrast to England and America, our immigration policy does not bar Asians from becoming citizens, or establishing a place of residence if they work there."

"But you are Asians?"

"Very perceptive, Mr. Johnson," Gegan said with a hint of contempt in his voice, He raised his glass in mock salute, catching the eye of a beautiful woman lifting her glass in agreement.

"Good luck with your job at Swain Company," Sukebator said half-heartedly while getting up. "There's a lady I must meet."

"Good luck to you, too, Major," Johnson said, watching him head for a booth where a knockout of a woman was sitting by herself. "Look at those two Dutch pilots in the booth next to her," he remarked to Brown. "They're wearing survival knives. Do they expect to crash-land in here?"

My God, I thought as the Manchukuon approached the table. In this light, her skin is the color of a new born fawn.

I lost the rest of the thought, when my dinner companion gave me a friendly kick with her black patent leather shoes for staring too long at the gorgeous female.

"She looked over here like she knew you," Jane commented.

"It's a long story," I said.

"Don't you feel out of place in civilian clothes?" she asked.

"No," I said. "There are over thirty thousand Japanese civilians in the area."

"Do you know anything about the China National Aviation Corporation?"

"Not much."

"It's a sudsidiary of America's Curtis-Wright Company."

I should've known that, I thought, they make aircraft engines.

Ignoring the death stares from the two Dutchmen, the Manchukuon Major, using a Chinese dialect from the northern regions, his voice taking on a softer tone, said. "Good evening, lovely lady. My name is Gegan Sukebator. I couldn't help but notice that you seemed to be in agreement with the way I handled the Englishmen. Do you mind if I sit down?"

"Please do, Major," she said in Manchu, seemingly enveloped in his deep resonant voice. "But why so formal. My name is Bayar, Hisako Bayar. It's nice to meet someone who has the guts to put those arrogant Europeans in their place. I have a dear friend from your country. He lives in Harbin."

"Please call me Gegan," he said, his dark eyes drinking in a face encircled with masses of coal-black hair and tiny ears adorned with black pearl earrings. "As a mixture of Manchu and Mongolian, I consider myself an Asian more than I do any particular culture."

"You remind me of the massive trees in the forest of my childhood," she said, admiringly. "I'm also the offspring of several races. But like you, I carry a minimum of tribal baggage."

"America calls Manchukuo a puppet state," Jane remarked.

"That's wrong," I told her, buffeted by several conversations. An all-Manchurian convention in Mukden named Henry Pu-yi as their president. There were Chinese elements who saw the advantage of having a prosperous nation next door to provide an expanded market place for Chinese goods.

"Who were you with earlier today?" I asked.

"Don't be jealous. I was with a representative from the British-American Tobacco Company."

"Is that the outfit that has a four-story brick building down on Waterfront Avenue?"

"Yes."

"Was he charming?"

"He took me to Hangchow to see the city that Marco Polo visited, but managed to spoil it by griping continuously about his company being squeezed out of Manchuria."

"Sounds dull."

"I heard that Russia has established an Oriental Bureau for its Communist International Organization here in Shanghai."

"It was founded in Moscow. They advocate violent revolution. But the local office won't cause any future problems. We closed them up."

He admires her, I thought, when I saw Gegan reach over as if he was going to touch Hisako Bayar. But before his giant hand came in contact, he drew it back. It's likely he remembered, that like a baby Sika deer, it's best in the long run to gently extend your hand, and let the wild creature come to you.

Chapter 20

The Ruriko Show

A night flight got me back to Taiwan in time to join Segawa at the studio. Ruriko Hattori introduced the first guest on her early morning show.

She thinks her immediate goal is being met, I thought, when she confidently raised a hand to her thick, black hair.

"The program will be broadcast three days a week if this time slot works out," Ruriko said, adjusting the angle of her guest's chair so it faced the microphone.

"I can't believe it," I whispered to Segawa. "That looks like Van Mook sitting in front of us." This is going to be a busy day, I thought.

"My next guest" she began, looking towards the petite woman with the short hair teased into small curls, "is about to become the focus of a controversial subject. What is the role of women today in combat? Miiko Arishima works in the accounting and records department at Nagasaki Municipal Hospital. And although not a nurse herself, she has been authorized to speak on their behalf.

"Arishima-san, welcome to the show," Ruriko said, waving her hand towards the chair.

"I am honored to be on your show," Miiko said, standing rigidly in a frosty-blue chiffon dress, an embroidered hankerchief folded into a triangle worn at the neck. It was the lastest fashion craze from the port cities.

"Is my information correct, that you want to see women assigned to the air ambulance service as flight members.?"

"*Hai,*" Miiko answered, rubbing her hands nervously together. She sat down, not looking at the microphone, "Men like my boy friend, Jun Kaine, recently promoted to lance corporal," she said proudly, placing her dark blue shoulder bag down by her seat, "may need skilled medical care in the forward combat zones in a hurry, and the majority of nurses at our hospital think women should be part of that team."

"But surely," Ruriko Hattori countered, "working in a municipal hospital is a service to your country."

"It's a city hospital with civilian patients, and some of the nurses want to take care of wounded servicemen."

"But if our country attempts to free Asia by military means," Ruriko remarked, looking for a knockout punch, "nurses might end up on the front lines in Malaya, Burma, or some other insect-infected place."

"According to your previous guest, Colonel Oka, we will not be breaking new ground. He said he saw marching, uniformed Thailand women, wearing Western-style shoes sturdy enough for long hikes, and skirts that he called short. They were probably two or three inches below the knees," Miiko surmised, fiddling with her ornamental hairpin.

"Suppose they get injured," Ruriko remarked, looking horrified. "I certainly wouldn't want to go to a hospital in a plain khaki skirt. I'd be mortified."

"What if Britain bombs Japan? We'll all be on the front lines anyway," Miiko advised.

"I don't think any military man wants to bomb civilians."

"How about the politicians?" the bookkeeper asked in her soft Kyoto accent. "The British Empire has a poor record on protecting civilians of another race."

"What about a hospital ship? The *Whispering Wind* for instance," Ruriko offered. "They not only tend the wounded but have decent living quarters. Hopefully a fancy stateroom with stewards running from room to room. The nurses don't want to bunk down in some old temporary shack on the mainland do they?"

"If I had my way, there would be no wars," Miiko said, looking unhappy. "But men are being shot and someone has to take care of them."

"They have medical battalions for that."

"The corpsman are fine for emergency first aid and stretcher work, but they don't have the training for air evacuation duty. Their job is to keep the injured alive while moving them to more sophisticated forms of medical help."

"I'll bet your boyfriend disagrees with you on this subject."

"He does. But he's smart enough to realize that not all Japanese women live in kimonos, not all wear sandals, and not all shy away from a challenge," Miiko said, with a bite in her voice. "You, for instance."

"I must admit," Ruriko said candidly. "We are not always what the Western movies portray us to be."

"My mother, playing the role of the timid housewife, puts the back of her hand up to her mouth like she's hiding from the world, then gives my father, who's a pharmacist, his allowance."

"Don't you just love it?" Ruriko said turning off the mike and signaling for the station manager to fill in. "My father claimed to be the boss at home when talking to associates. But in the house I noticed my mother was the final authority on the things that count in life: investments, education, servants, furnishings, and the children."

"What woman, during the dangerous medieval period, came up with the idea of making the man seem important, by standing aside to let him go through the door first," Miiko wondered gleefully. "All the time, figuring if some bandit was lurking behind the entrance, it was going to be the male who got hit over the head."

"Better yet," Ruriko giggled. "Westerners think we're second-class citizens for putting up with that chivalrous act. If it was left up to me. I'd have given the originator a medal."

"It has some resemblance to a man in the U.S. staying on the gutter side when walking with a woman," Miiko bellowed, tears of laughter streaming down her face.

"Let's get back to the subject of women in combat," Ruriko said turning the mike back on in a happy frame of mind.

A half-hour break, a rush to the dressing room, and Ruriko Hattori reappeared, dragging a peace advocate into the studio. Her program had become an instant hit and people within walking distance began filling up the station auditorium. For her remaining guests she had changed into a flaring black-velvet skirt, white blouse, and broadcloth jacket with big pockets.

"Sugano-san, welcome to the Ruriko Show," she said after introducing the man dressed in a Hawaiian shirt, a bush jacket, and slacks.

"Thank you," Akito Sugano said. "And congratulations on the program's new title. You're mighty popular and deserve the recognition," he said, with a bow reserved for the rich and famous.

"Don't you have a son in the navy?" she asked.

"I wonder if he ever runs a comb through his hair?" Segawa said to me, uncharitably.

"Yes, I have a boy at sea," the mild-looking, puffy-eyed Sugano replied, his voice tinged with unhappiness.

"Are the peace movement's objections to the Sino-Japanese war something new, Sugano-san?"

"No! Like the U.S. reaction to their war against the Filipinos--from the very onset there was never any enthusiasm among the Japanese people for the war in China. And now that it's dragged on from a matter of months to years, it's become decidedly unpopular."

"Go on," she allowed, obviously glad his remarks were controversial.

"I pushed the pro-Jewish policy which received government sanction

137

three years ago," he claimed, trying a wink, pleased when she didn't frown. "I'm happy to announce that racial equality and racial harmony are still being stressed."

They never seem to stick to the subject, I thought.

Ruriko made an effort to get him back on track. "Didn't Japan want China to join in a greater Asian collaboration? In effect a commonwealth?"

"*Hai!* But the idea is impractical as long as there's opposition from the West. Besides, the Chinese Communist want no part of it," Sugano assured her. "That's a beautiful outfit you're wearing," he added.

She was not moved by his compliment. "Will the West do everything it can to stay out of war in the Pacific?"

"No! Going to war has many advantages for big time manipulators," he proclaimed, moving his chair closer to hers. "First they freeze the enemy's assets and then find a way to use them. Second, they no longer have to pay the debts they ran up with that country. Third, they can use the enemy's patents without having to pay a license fee. All three are big ticket items. Maybe getting out of China would prevent the West from taking that step."

"Do you think Roosevelt is convinced that Japan wants to force all European troops out of Asia?" Ruriko asked, looking at the clock for help. "More to the point. Wouldn't China be pleased to see all foreign armies and navies returned to their own country?"

"*Hai* to all those questions," he replied with a smile that came off lopsided.

"I'm reading now from a Toyko newspaper. It says that America is still supplying arms and munitions to Chang Kai-shek and his German advisors," Ruriko said, tucking in her skirt when his eyes lingered there. "Why did we ever think America's Neutrality Act would be adhered to, when Britain's King-Emperor was lobbying against it?"

"Wishful thinking! That's why it's so important to have peace. My group campaigned four years ago to find a solution. America used a loophole in the Neutrality Act even before they dropped the pretense of remaining on the sidelines," he declared, leering openly. "Mark my words. Much of the equipment shipped by America will end up in communist hands."

"What has your group found out about the battle on the mainland?" she asked, placing a hand protectively on the neckline of her dress.

"I hardly know where to start," Saguno confessed, seemingly more interested in the questioner than the question. "A segment of the ten thousand Japanese soldiers garrisoned in China under the terms of a treaty concluded in 1901 after the Boxer Rebellion, clashed with troops serving under a local leader at a rail junction on the southern outskirts of Peking.

"Casualties mounted, innocent people were killed. Aircraft with Chinese insignia attempted to bomb Japanese warships in the river at Shanghai, hit the city instead, inflicting thirteen hundred casualties. Target errors were also committed by the Japanese Army Command going after a power plant in Chunking."

"An article by James R. Young, in a March l, 194l, issue of an American newsletter called *Vital Speeches,*" Ruriko pointed out, "says that American-built planes bombed Chunking, wiping out parts of the city. Japan doesn't use American planes."

"It's a mess," Sugano admitted. "I remember when a Chinese Hawk aircraft accidently released its bombs over an international zone in 1937."

"Your group wants to bring home all Japanese military forces?"

"Hai."

"What did your group say about the British having troops in Shangtung province one year after the war started in Europe?"

"We had no comment."

"How about when Wang Ching-wei landed a Chinese army on the coast of Fukien Province to fight the forces of Chiang Kai-shek?"

"No comment."

"I know I wasn't unhappy," Ruriko said, eyes blazing, "when we bombed the munitions highway to Russia at Lanchow. Speaking of hostility, how do you stop the communist or the West from taking over control of China?"

"We sit down with them and make them see the benefits of cooperation."

"And you think that men like Churchill, or Claire Chennault, a friend of the confidential advisor to the Central Trust Company of China are just going to disappear?" she said, amazed at his lack of experience with power-brokers. "In case you've forgotten, Chennault's that American fighter pilot who was given ten times his retirement pay to set up a mercenary foreign airforce."

"Oh, you're talking about the `Flying Tigers.' We realize their objective is fighting for money, not principle."

"When Chennault stopped in Japan before going on to China, he was surprised when the police didn't prevent him from taking photographs or care about his presence," she pointed out. "That's how little he knew about our country. "For God's sake, he was doubly surprised to find out we had a democratic government, a convenient, modern transportation system and large department stores. An up-to-date communication network only further confused him."

"My organization wrote a letter to the American President, reminding him of the time when his fledgling country condemned England for hiring mercenaries to crush the American try for freedom," Sugano reported. "'Instead of upholding your country's previous ideals, Mr. President,' I wrote, 'you mimic the worst features of the British Empire.'"

"Did you also mention that two Negroes were put to death by blow torches in Mississippi by a white mob?" Ruriko asked, watching him blanch at the term 'blow torch.' "And the state of Georgia still has chain gangs, and Delaware has flogging.

"Here's a late-breaking news bulletin," she said, motioning Sugano to be quiet. "Two hours ago, a Manchukuon Manchu Airline captain reportedly saw a fighter plane carrying the red, white and blue markings of the Royal Netherlands Airforce escorting a Dutch KLM commercial aircraft out of Jarkarta headed for Hong Kong."

She turned back to Sugano for an answer to her question.

"No!" he said. "We do not want to get into the internal affairs of the American hemisphere."

"Why not?" Ruriko asked. "America was so jealous of the booming Japanese stock market that they put pressure on Peru to slap quotas on Japanese goods. I consider that interferring in the internal affairs of another country."

"Our intention is to stay away from the balance of trade arguments."

"How about the British killing a dozen people and wounding thirty more after landing Royal Marines, when Trinidad, an island in the American hemisphere, showed signed of independence?"

"I have no comment on that," he said, slumping further in his chair.

The little whimp, Ruriko mouthed to the audience, toying with her green cotton-rope necklace and bracelet. "Closer to home then. I take it you were pleased when our elections resulted in defeat of a cabinet more favorable to increased expeditures for defense."

"*Hai!* But nothing changed. On the ground, a full-scale war between the Japanese and Chinese soldiers aligned with either the communist or white nations spread throughout northern China. Japan dispatched three army divisions to the mainland."

"One thing has changed," she commented, her scratchy voice in tune with her irritation. "American ambitions for the expansion of its economic interest in Asia are being destroyed, Sugano-san," she said, getting ready to close out this part of the program. "It's been very informative having you on the show--but waiting in the wings is Lieutenant Torajiro Ibara, recently attached to the naval district where a foreign gunboat was sunk."

Easing the peace advocate out of the chair, she quickly replaced him with firm-jawed, short-haired Ibara, garbed in a dark blue service dress uniform, complete with a brass-buckled leather belt worn over the tunic. After a brief introduction, Ruriko launched into what she thought was the most important question of the day.

"Did the naval district give orders to bomb an American gunboat on the Yangtze River?"

"No!"

I listened closely. Although I was new to the navy at the time, I remembered the incident.

"What were the consequences?"

"The naval district relieved the pilots who did the bombing, higher command followed up by replacing the Admiral in charge, and I was reassigned to Atsugi."

"What else was done?"

"Japan sent a formal note of apology," he said, sitting tall in his chair, "and paid indemnity for sinking the warship."

"Could it happen again?"

"I suppose it's possible as long as America keeps its navy patrolling Chinese riverways," the officer confessed. "But to reduce the chance of error, the Japanese high command issued instructions to exercise the greatest caution in the future, even at the sacrifice of strategic advantage."

"Is it true that Japanese troops are withdrawn from areas in China, whenever that sector is no longer threatened by European and American war supplies to hostile forces?"

"Absolutely."

"Has any headway been made with the disarmament question?" Ruriko slashed in, hoping to put him on the spot.

"Over the objections of the navy, the Prime Minister once suggested doing away with the main implements of overseas warfare: the battleship and the aircraft carrier," Ibara replied, removing his glasses. "The West saw this as an anti-colonialist move, which it was, and wanted nothing to do with it.

"Britain found the very idea of losing those intiminating weapons appalling; her warships continually patrol the high seas to keep her occupied countries in line.

"Since China was not an economic threat, Chinese errors are forgiven. France, Britain, and America were angry with Japan because they could no longer collect China's custom fees and set the rates. Although the U.S. was siding with certain political factions in China, it practiced discrimination against the Chinese at home."

Ruriko's radio program triggered off several heated discussions among the audience after her closing remarks. The provocative subjects had caused tempers to flair at the slightest hint of disagreement.

"You guys don't know what you're talking about," said a navy cook, on track to reach Sumo wrestling porportions. His comment irritated the people around them.

"Go back to your pots and pans, stew-burner," a sailor said, interrupting his conversation with a soldier who was showing him how to put a net over a steel helmet for camouflage.

"Let's get a beer at the Bronze Lion," Segawa said, handing me my pea coat.

"I'd rather go to a low-down sleezy joint for a change."

"Why do you have a winter coat with you when we're going to the tropics?"

"I've been in the navy long enough to know that orders to the equator today might easily turn out to be Northern Siberian tomorrow."

The broken sign over the Green Beetle's scarred door reminded me of a lighthouse on a rocky shoal. A warning to the inexperienced that an ill-advised maneuver brings on destructive consequences.

"How about Stalin's men flying against the Japanese?" A tipsy sailor proclaimed as he staggered in the entrance ahead of us. "I hear the Russians gave four hundred aircraft to a Chinese warlord."

The interior hadn't changed much since my last visit. The same dirty mirror flanked by the same bartender still wearing a sailor's white hat upside down. It was my kind of establishment, I thought, smoothing out the torn up leather on the bar stool.

"One important mission has been accomplished," the civilian peace advocate from Ruriko's program said as we surveyed the crowded rathole. "The American 15th regiment was finally withdrawn from China.

"The majority of China's coastal cities are now free from Western intrusion," he added quickly, keeping a shaky hold over the discussion.

"Why not strike directly at the British Islands?" the fat navy cook inquired, waving his fisted hand to a disinterested gathering.

"There's about sixteen carriers in the combined fleets of Britain and America," a yeoman responded, attempting to appear knowledgeable, but coming across slurred and unsteady.

"Our aircraft carriers can whip em," the cook said, easing his way toward a 'B' girl.

"Then why does America's Admiral Leahy say the United States is so superior in aircraft carriers that there is no need for additional tonnage?"

"Our job is to free the colonies, not send aircraft carriers to Europe."

"Are you a Christian?" the peace advocate asked the tipsy sailor ordering a Nippon beer.

"No, why?" the machinest mate inquired, frowning.

"Japan was praised by the Far East Jewish newspaper, *Jewish Life.* Japan recognized Zionism as a legitimate Jewish goal."

"That won't make many points with the hard-line Christian elements in Europe and America."

We looked for an empty table when the servicemen at the bar began shouting.

"Does the U.S. ever elect a military leader as president?" the cook asked the civilian when the bar girl rebuffed him.

"Why does that belly-robber care?" a comfort woman complained to her new companion. "He should be asking somebody how not to overcook rice."

"When an American general becomes president," Sugano replied, smiling sickly at the woman's remark. "It's called the democratic system. When a Japanese general becomes prime minister, it's a military plot."

A shore patrolman came in, scowled and announced, "All damage controlmen, report to your duty stations immediately."

"What is a damage control crew?" the woman asked.

"Just what it sounds like," the shore patrolman snapped. "Men who are assigned to repair crews when the ship is in imminent danger."

"You better check the Comfort Houses," a soldier suggested.

"What are Comfort Houses?" asked a seaman, who must have spent most of his young life in a rice paddy in the foothills of the Japanese Alps.

"It's a place where women serve more than tea," an five hashmark chief replied, not wanting to overload the young sailor's brain with too much information.

"There's a ship in trouble," rippled through the crowd.

The man I saw Van Mook with was sitting alone at a table.

"Ho," I yelled, greeting him.

His return salutation was in Dutch.

Using my rusty Dutch, I asked him if he was with Major Van Mook.

"Yes. Van Mook went back to his room," he said, testily. "Join me, please."

Segawa and I pulled up chairs. "Why are you so mad?" I asked, ignoring the threat of violent activity behind me.

"I have the misfortune to be a servant to that power-mad, egotistical Dutchman, Van Mook."

"You don't have to be a servant," Segawa said, while we watched a sailor remove his face from the floorboards. The heavily tatooed coxswain who shoved it there was still standing over him.

"Every Indonesian is drafted for work, not only in Java, but throughout Indonesia. Using the army as executioners, the Dutch wield an iron hand."

"How big are the Indies?" I asked, my voice almost drown out by the angry shouts coming from the next table.

"About three times the size of Texas, the state that America is always bragging about."

"And Texas is twice the size of Japan," I submitted, more interested in keeping track of the ugly seaman getting up from his chair.

"How would you like it if you had to take orders from an arrogant European. Especially one who spends his time resting his feet on a veranda railing."

"Not much," we admitted.

"He told me that if anybody tried to give Indonesia its independence, they would have Van Mook to deal with. He believes the first Dutchmen who came to the fertile islands knew how to handle Asians, and intends to follow in their footsteps.

"Later, he said, 'Take that frown off your face. And if you think we'll let the Japanese take over these islands and free you, you're wrong. Now, get out my award for attending Princess Juliana's wedding. We're celebrating Queen Wilhelmina's birthday. And don't forget to dust her portrait.'"

"That's quite a story," Segawa said.

We left the sad-looking Hassan, and almost made it to the entrance before the barroom full of hostile men exploded.

I blocked a fist with my forearm and Segawa got in one good punch while we hastily half-slid, half-fell out of the doorway and headed back to the base for a continuation of the mornings celebration.

144

Chapter 21

Party Time

Happy birthday songs were sung, red rice thrown, and joke poems recited --all part of the Southern Taiwan Air Base celebration. This festive air was a welcome break from the thought of the upcoming confrontation.

Each mess table was in an undeclared contest to shout *Kamai* the loudest. The traditional "bottoms up" after a birthday name was announced left a bunch of sore-throated, red-faced participants. The first two names were toasted with saké, the rest with water, for the base commander was not going to let the men overindulge after a quick check came up with fourteen men with birthdays during the final two weeks of November.

Leaning over during the eleventh toast, I asked Segawa if he'd like to be stationed in Thailand.

He nodded in the affirmative, sneaking another glass of saké.

Pausing to yell, *Kampai*, I continued. "According to Tomi, an army buddy of mine who has flown with the Royal Thailand Airforce, their fighter planes are on the alert to prevent any further French or British incursion. Roosevelt has endorsed the King-Emperor's plan to invade Thailand. In fact, I've got a letter from a Thai student he gave me to read."

"What type aircraft are they flying?" Segawa asked, as he watched an airman search out members from his own squadron.

"I'll check and see if it's mentioned. Better yet, why don't I just read it," I suggested, pulling it out of my pocket.

"`Dear Kiyo,' Tom writes, 'I hope everything's okay with you. Say hello to Yukiko for me, please. I have a steady girlfriend and attend Buddist services regularly, which shouldn't suprise you. I still get kidded about my youthful looks, but I must be getting older. I had my appendix removed last summer.

"'Things are warming up in this section of the Far East. The British are sending out patrols along the border in preparation for a preemptive strike. England and France already have a piece of Thailand territory the size of California under their military control, and the Thais intend to get it back. But like our country, they're going to stay neutral in the European War.'"

I ducked as a piece of artichoke sailed by hitting an Aichi dive

145

bomber pilot in the forehead.

"' I was having fun dodging around some marshmellow-shaped clouds,' Tomi writes, 'when I saw a pair of Thailand Ki-43 Peregrine Falcons get jumped from behind by two British fighters. Taking advantage of the space-eating capabilities of the Falcon, especially in a climb, they pushed the throttles to the max and showed their tail lights to the Brewster Buffaloes trying to close the gap. In desperation, the British shot while still out of range.

"'You could almost hear them wondering why their superior aircraft couldn't catch the Peregrine Falcons, and why the Thai weren't spinning out at those altitudes.'"

"Go on, don't quit now," Segawa urged, eluding a swing from a paper umbrella.

Juggling a pair of chopsticks, eating rice, stopping for an occasional *Kampai*, and trying to read the letter was stretching my capabilities. "'As tbey approached 30,000 feet,'" I read. 'the Falcon engines had to operate with reduced horsepower due to the thin air, but the British fighters were in worst shape. At 33,000 feet the Brewster Buffalo had reached its maximum ceiling and the British pilots lost their ability to control the aircraft. The two Thai fighter planes climbed another thousand feet, turned on their gun cameras, rolled over, pitched down, and moved in for the kill with the speed of a runaway avalanche,'" I read excitedly, plunging my hand towards the floor. "'They brought their 7.7 mm guns to bear on those stubby little American-built fighter planes until the British planes turned away from the Thailand border.

"'I did suggest to the commanding officer that they replace the 7.7 with the larger l2.7 mm machine gun in the newer models. With that modification, I predict the Peregrine Falcon will have plenty of aces if war with the West comes to the Pacific.'" I stopped reading after scanning through the rest of the letter. "That's all there is about the air encounter."

"Watch it," Segawa warned. "The pilots at the far table are adding red rice to their paper airplanes for ballast."

"I'll be ready," I countered, placing my chopsticks together and filling the crease with bits of turnip.

"Nothing's going to top that snowball fight the aviators had at the Officer's Club in Yokosuka last year, Segawa said, holding up his bowl to use as a shield. "Remember that episode?"

"Hai! But that squadron bash we had at Atsugi wasn't too shabby

either. Pelting the Dragon Slayer squadron commanding officer with salad when he tried to give a speech was far above and beyond the call of duty.

"You said a warrant officer, two sheets to the wind, shouted, 'Boring!' just before someone got hit with a tomato that ricocheted off Sub Lieutenant Ito's shoulder."

"It might have died down, if that Haunted House Zero pilot hadn't yelled, `You throw tomatoes just like you shoot,'" I said excitedly.

"Some lieutenant complained when you kept referring to an engine cowling as a hood?"

"What a jerk."

"On the downside, you were sent to a utility squadron two months later. You don't suppose there was any connection, do you?" an Aichi pilot asked, turning to his friend on a more serious note. "As much as Thailand wants the Western military out of Asia, it behooves her to move carefully, and draw back if things don't go right."

"A free Asia will be to her advantage, won't it?" exclaimed a torpedo plane pilot, whose haircut must have been done by a barber using a dull-bladed lawn mower.

"The idea of some Asian country willing to go on the same fight card with the Western heavyweights should impress Thailand." I offered, using Professor's Sakamoto's favorite phraseology. "Japan is Thailand's major trading partner."

"He said that Thailand is fully aware that Japan's unemployment rate is thirteen points below the West, and knows Japan spends a lot less on its military and more on education than Western countries do."

"One more *Kampai!* then let's go to the band concert on the parade ground," Segawa suggested.

"My sister Hatako would enjoy that," I pointed out. "As soon as the music starts, she's up and moving."

On the way out of the mess hall, our path was blocked by a large Okinawan who had drunk a little too much saké. He was dressed in a green and yellow-streaked uniform, with a water-filled saucer on his head.

"You cannot leave the party, until the water evaporates," proclaimed the brawny sailor with crossed arms, imitating *Kappa*, a powerful mythical creature.

Segawa nudged me, "His power is gone if he loses that water."

"Do you know him?" I asked in a conspirator's whisper.

"Hai, it's the senior enlisted man from the Haunted House squadron," he whispered back.

"I know him. He's susceptible to flattery. Watch this," I cautioned in a hushed voice.

"Chief, you can't hide your charm," I told him in an ingratiating tone of voice. "Every man aboard this air station would sacrifice his first-born son for a chance to serve under your leadership. The experience would provide an honorable memory to cherish in one's old age."

The first-born son was too much for him. Deeply moved, he gave a bow reserved for royalty. Before the last drop of water hit the deck, Segawa and I scrambled past him and tore out the door.

"By the way," Segawa said looking at me when we walked past an older-modeled aircraft from *Sky Dragon*. "You're to report to the duty officer for a new assignment involving that plane.

* * *

It wasn't even lunchtime yet when I found myself cruising an area east of the convoy in a carrier-based Mitshubishi A5M2b, model 22 fighter plane, the forerunner of the A6M Zero. It was slated to go to the Atsugi historic museum someday. An ensign piloting an A5M in 1937 had become the first navy ace.

Sky Dragon had been one of the three carriers launching aircraft during that battle. Ghost Leader had flown an earlier version of the aircraft against the Russian and Mongolian Communist invading Manchukuo.

I waved my scarf at a passing MT-I Manchu transport. Its large passenger windows made identification easy. I moved in closer. It's probably returning to Manchukuo from a flight to China, I thought. I assumed it was the plane that had radioed a warning about the Dutch Army Air Force escorting airliners.

I noticed a European airliner with a fighter plane hovering nearby a short time later. I stayed far enough away so as not to appear as a threat and was surprised when the Curtis Hawk broke off and headed in my direction.

I tightened my chin strap, pulled down my goggles and opened up the canopy, automatically converting the plane into an airborne convertible.

Spotting my older-styled navy fighter with its antique open cockpit design, the escort decided to take a closer look. His Curtis Hawk was equipped with split flaps and a radial air-cooled engine. Its three-bladed prop was a technological improvement over the A5M's two-bladed one. It also had three 30 cal. and one 50 cal. electrically fired machine guns, and a speed of 280 mph.

I caught the name on the side of the cockpit, Major Van Mook.

I stuck my arms out of the cockpit, where glass normally would be, to highlight the inferiority of Asian-built products. No need to let a potential enemy know the outer edge of the wing was deliberately warped to delay the occurrence of a stall. No reason for the Dutchman to learn that the split flaps on the American-built Curtis 75 were there by courtesy of a Japanese patent.

The Curtis pilot would also be unaware that the A5M had streamlined fasteners on its removable panels, was flush riveted, had a jettisonable landing gear system, and a watertight fuselage.

When he pulled up alongside, I pointed to the Curtis Hawk and gave it a thumbs up. After Van Mook shook his head up and down in total accord, I pointed to my aircraft and gave it a thumbs down--prompting the Dutchman to show his agreement by putting his hand to his head in despair.

I shook my head from side to side and made circular motions with my hand indicating the landing gear was not retractable. Van Mook held his nose to show his disapproval. Putting the plane in a gentle bank, I turned away from the Hawk 75 and headed for home.

"Jakarta Base, from Bull Whip Three Two."

"Bull Whip Three Two, this is Jakarta Base, go ahead."

"No problem," Dirk Van Mook proudly reported to the Netherlands military. "If the Queen decides to go to war against Japan, the skirmish will be over in a hurry. The plane I just intercepted will fall apart under combat conditions."

It would be nice, I fantasized, if the band met me to celebrate the artistic performance I had just put on. My aquaintance with the Dutch language had allowed me to get the gist of Van Mook's report.

Taking off my helmet for a moment to enjoy the first sprinkles from a dark cloud that had turned wet, I pulled the canopy closed after getting a breath of ozone from a receding electrical storm,

I started humming, which soon escalated into song. The closed interior of an A5M, with rain splattering against the glass, provided better acoutics than a shower stall.

Keeping my eyes at half-mast to compliment my sleepy-sounding voice, I threw my head back, and belted out Yukiko's favorite song.

The upcoming war, the convoy, and the thunderstorm, were completely forgotten by the time I reached the second stanza.

But down below, things were not so merry. A Japanese oil tanker was steaming towards home. It was riding high, its fuel compartments empty.

The band was assembled on the flight deck to play their second concert of the day, not to applaud my bloodless victory.

I wiped the light drizzle off my face.

"Not all English mothers and fathers will be thrilled about the prospect of their sons fighting on foreign soil for the sake of the King-Emperor," said Nogi, anxious to share information with me since I had no malfunctions to report. I guessed he was talking about the upcoming showdown as he assisted me out of the cockpit.

"Those who control the most territory by military force manage to put the blame on us," he said between fits of coughing, which caused the band master to lower his baton 'til the noise died down.

"It's a case of the Global Empire's lion calling the Asian house cat vicious," I said.

"According to Sakamoto, the Nazis have some unforgivable traits: an anti-capitalistic attitude, aiding a warlord on the mainland, and Hitler's obsession with Jews," the veteran aviation mechanic said, speaking low enough that the band lieutenant did not look his way. "But from the European and American point of view, Germany's high productivity record combined with an ability to sell to foreign markets, it's early entry into the field of television, and an expeditious start in establishing airline routes for companies like Lufthansa did much to alienate it from those countries.

"I don't like what Germany's doing either," the ordnanceman opening up the A5M's gun ports said. Part of his attention was focused on the band's tune up routine. The sprinkles had stopped. All signs of rain were fading.

"It is easy, of course, to place all the blame on one power-happy individual, and let the other domineering politicians off scott-free," I countered, flinching, as the bugler let out a blast.

"Should we hold the Westerners accountable for all the troubles in the Far East?" the mechanic asked, disappointed that the band's first number was nothing but a standard martial piece by John Philip Sousa.

"No," I said feeling philosophical. "Life doesn't work that way. Just as the relationship of living organisms in the ocean are incredibly complex, so are the interactions between human beings and cultures."

"In other words, tell the whole story?" he asserted.

"Contrary to Western newspaper articles, Japan's main weapons have been her salesmen, not her military. But in order to be a first class economic power you need machined products. We were the second biggest user of ball bearings until Germany cut off our supply coming out of Sweden."

"That hit us in the pocketbook," Nogi volunteered.

"Did we cut into anybody else's trade?" the mechanic asked, attempting to prolong the conversation between coughing spells and listening to the band play a Stephen Foster number.

"To the guillotine with the yellow ingrates, for taking trade away from the French in the New Hebrides," the ordanceman announced loudly,

I tapped my foot as the band finally swung into a jazz number.

"Does Britain feel threatened?"

We won't be invading an independent Malaya, but a Malaya conquered and ruled by a European nation who presides over one-quarter of the earth."

"Weren't there other Europeans who tried to conquer the world?" the mechanic asked, looking around to see what his fellow sailors were up to.

"The Roman Empire with their slogan, 'sweet and fitting it is to die for the fatherland,' and later, France's Emperor Napoleon made a try. But the British Empire beat them all. It has eleven million square miles--over four times the size of the mighty Caesar's legacy. It's so big, that the 1941 New York World Telegraph's Almanac, starts out with the British Empire, then lists the rest of the world's countries under *other*. No nation has been so aggressive in battle, and so powerful for so long. This is a government that uses flogging and burns down villages as punishment."

While the men listened to the band, I picked up the cat.

"Any more problems?" Nogi asked, touching the cat as if it were a link to home.

"Does the cat have a name?"

"Combat, the aviation mechanic replied, reading from a tag on the collar. We're going to transfer her to the *Ikeda Maru*.

"I've been meaning to ask you. When are you going to make chief petty officer? You've been a first class petty officer for sometime now."

"I don't know," I said with a discouraged shrug of my shoulders.

151

Chapter 22

Flight Deck Drill

I was surprised to find Inspector Ibuse aboard *Sky Dragon* again.

"Where's Yeoman Nitta?" I asked.

"I'm handling this problem personally. Come down to the briefing room when you get changed."

I'd heard that the scary-looking Inspector had graduated at the top of his class and had been described as a real brain. It was rumored your chances of getting away with a crime when Geki was on your trail were about the same as a cockroach making it across a bare kitchen floor before being spotted by a housewife.

I knocked on the door of his temporary quarters.

"Come in," Ibuse said in a voice more suited to a funeral director.

"You wanted to see me?" I asked.

"The navy has ordered me to fly to the Taiwan Coast Guard station tomorrow morning, and Captain Naifu says you're to take me."

I couldn't think of anything to say.

"By the way," he said. "Have you ever had a passenger that brings cokes everywhere he goes?"

"Nothing comes to mind right now," I said. "Why?"

"I can't think straight," he said. "I've been listening to Sakamoto so much, my brain's rattled."

"What's he been saying?"

"He says combat was, and is, an honorable art for man. If it's done for freedom, not oppression."

"In the modern world," I said, "destroying a country's navy, merchant marine, and airforce leaves your enemy helpless. If he doesn't give up, it matters not.

"For a certain age group and personality, combat is invigorating. There are men who drive race cars, some walk tightropes, some wish to be policemen in the dangerous sections of town, and others choose the armed forces for risks."

"But, although Sakamoto said he wasn't the military type," Ibuse relayed, "he did claim that being prepared to defend one's country can be stimulating, and does fill an important niche in the nation's overall needs."

"I'm not necessarily disagreeing with him, counselor, but for the

152

sake of argument, is chivalry practical in war?"

"You can win a war without targeting the civilian population," the lawyer insisted.

In actuality, Ibuse was feeling depressed. He knew his chances of making JAG someday were slim. Whenever he prosecuted a case, the court-martial panel had a hard time separating him from the defendant. In fact, last year, a youthful-looking and handsome second lieutenant was tried and found guilty for a particularly hideous rape. The presiding officer, numbed by all the testimony, banged down the gravel with extra force, and sentenced Geki to five years in the stockade before correcting himself.

"Is Sakamoto being pressured by anyone to accelerate his information sessions?"

"*Hai.* The Admiral's aide mentions it a couple of times a day. He insists the men aren't motivated yet. In fact, he was against the original idea. He wants to do it the old fashioned way, with patriotic speeches."

"The aide's pressuring me too," Ibuse said. "To find the assailant before Prime Minister Tojo sends out a personal representative."

"Now that the Professor's down to the final couple of years, what were the major events in 1938?"

"President Roosevelt does not consider Japanese-Americans as true Americans. His biased articles in the Macon Daily Telegraph in 1925 on the undesirability of mingling Asian and European blood demonstrated this. He wished to exclude Japanese citizens to prevent mixing of the two races." The Inspector's eyes were as dark as a row of bowling balls and worried.

"Was trouble in Europe avoidable in 1939?" I asked.

"They were operating with a hidden agenda. The most desirable aviation routes, potential automobile sales, and the projected multi-billion electronic industry were the unstated reasons behind the desire to knock out the competition."

"How about the big European money-makers like opium, chocolate, and oil?"

"You can add one more. Soap! Britain's Unilever is one of the oldest and most powerful corporations in the Pacific. It owns the Lever Brothers soap company."

"Doesn't oil still dominate?"

"British Petroleum is not to be trifled with."

"Is British Petroleum the one they refer to as BP, the company with the yellow and green pennant?"

"*Hai.* It owns the Kuwait Oil Company and is cozy with America's Standard Oil."

"What frightens you?" I asked, seeing his apprehensive look.

"We can only hope that the Gold Dust Enterprise will confine itself to sinking ships and shooting down aircraft in the Pacific."

"You don't sound very hopeful."

"The Western strategists are fascinated with the wood and paper partitioning in Japanese homes, and talk continually about bombing them from American bases in the Pacific. Even Siberian airfields are being considered for an American strike."

"Doesn't anybody aboard ship ever talk about women and sports?"

"Kaine suggested talking about one of his seven sisters, or the female-dominated society in his hometown, but nobody wanted to listen.

"As for sports, Sakamoto informed us that Japan held the upper hand in the Olympic swimming events nine years ago and won a Gold Medal in the Women's 200 meter breaststroke four years later. Golf and skiing were just becoming popular."

"Far East?" I inquired, prior to taking a breath.

"Asian investment in the Philippines was viewed with alarm by the Americans, especially the Japanese owned B.B.B. brewery in Manila."

"See you tomorrow morning," I told him. "Right now I've got a flight deck drill I have to participate in."

Plane number 411 was part of a large group of aircraft assigned to the flight deck demonstration. I noticed torpedo planes on my right and left wings and fighters fore and aft.

The idea, as I understood it, was to run as many combat planes as possible through the flight deck. Planes would be coming up the elevators onto the flight deck as space was cleared.

The deck-spotters and aircraft-handlers had worked through the night, perfecting a smooth transition from hanger deck to flight deck. Everything revolved around the forward elevator. With that lift running smoothly, planes could be launched and more planes brought up from the hanger deck in a continuous cycle.

"Captain Naifu wants this to go perfectly," Air Boss Kuni told the men gathered together for a last minute briefing. "He promised he could cycle fifty aircraft through a simulated launch without a hitch. The admiral's staff aboard the *Ikeda Maru* will be tuned into our shipboard frequency. We'll be broadcasting as if this practice session was the real thing. Only don't anybody take off. Instead, taxi to the forward elevator, and we'll send you down to the hanger deck. Follow the director to either the center or rear elevator and we'll cycle you back up."

"Sir, you said the forward elevator was the key. Why?" Nogi asked, facing me so his smudged-cheek showed.

"Because if it gets jammed," Kuni said, "it'll prevent the movement of aircraft throughout the ship. The entire cycle will be disrupted, and I'm here to tell you that will make the Captain very unhappy."

"Why is this drill so important?" he asked.

"For one thing, the admiral makes out his fitness reports on all the commanding officers this month. For another, he has a bet with the skipper of the *Ikeda Maru.*

"There's the call to man your aircraft. Let's do it!"

I followed the tired-looking Aviation Machinist Mate Nogi like a robot. I moved from spot to spot with precision, surprising everybody who knew I was from Utility Squadron Five and had little experience with flight deck operations.

When the twelfth aircraft started down, I was taxied ahead until the engine cowling and starboard wing tip hung over the forward elevator opening.

"The progress is even better than expected," Captain Naifu said over the bullhorn. "Keep it up. All our planning and drill sessions are paying off."

Proud of my role, I reached down to open up an air vent.

Unfortunately, this brought my joyous world to an abrupt halt. Directors, plane-handlers and Captain Naifu started screaming at me to close the valve and shut-off the engine.

What valve? I wondered, fearfully conscious of the chasm just beneath the tottering nose of the plane as the big canvas flotation bags poured out of each wingtip. Crawling out of the cockpit, though tempting, might provide enough movement to tumble the aircraft into the opening.

"Make sure he's on the first landing craft into Malaya," Captain Naifu howled.

"That could happen to anybody, Captain," I apologized. "I just happened to pull the wrong knob."

Nogi hacked and stabbed at the canvas in a hopeless effort to deflate the flotation bags. Temporarily defeated, he put chocks under the wheels and hung on the port wing to keep the plane from toppling into the hole.

Waiting until the elevator rose and stayed flush with the flight deck, he reached under the nose of the aircraft to attach a tow line. Unfortunately, his timing coincided with my panicky efforts to shut off the flow of air to the flotation bags. Instead of the bag collapsing, an oil cooler door flew open, knocking Rikichi Nogi flat

After watching the still unconscious body of the sailor being carried off to sickbay, one by one the flight deck crew began finding emergency items to take care of in other parts of the ship.

"Debuchi," came that dreaded voice simulating the boom from a bass drum. "Why do you hate me? Is it due to the fact that I can look down on your scrawny little head from up here? Or is it because you'll never obtain a promotion under my command? Or possibly because I think you're an incompetent, ugly, useless, mealy-mouthed slug?"

"No, Captain. I think you're doing your job."

"Every night, Debuchi, I dream of you being shot down by enemy fighter planes," Captain Naifu said, with a touch of pleasure in his voice. "The plane explodes before it hits the water. No one looks for the occupant."

"I know you're joking, Captain." Receiving no answer, I climbed out of the cockpit and walked dejectedly across an empty flight deck, with only the wind acknowledging my presence. At least something is willing to make contact with me, I thought, attempting to dress up that sad episode poetically.

When I had time to mull over the incident. I came to an unsettling conclusion. In my recollection of the unfortunate event, my fingers had only brushed the top of that flotation bag button as I reached for the knob next to it. What if Trademark was afraid I could identify him, and had the solenoid reset to a point where even the tiniest amount of pressure would energize it--Crashing down onto the hanger deck would have probably killed me.

Chapter 23

Map Trouble

Disheartened, ordered by the squadron skipper to depart for Taiwan immediately, I left my life jacket hanging open and parachute harness unbuckled while I made my way to the flight deck at a pace more in harmony with a slow motion movie. I knew Captain Naifu was anxious to get rid of me or more formally stated, have me fly Inspector Ibuse to the Tainan Coast Guard Station.

It was still dark when I arrived on deck; the crew had finished pre-flighting the KR-2 Sandpiper and had installed the army investigator in the rear seat.

"The plane looks more like a homing pigeon mistakenly tossed into the ranks of its enemies--the hawks and eagles," the smart-alec Ibuse commented as I got ready for another flight in the little 150 hp biplane.

"It's all ready to go, birdman," the flightline crewman said, emphasizing the title, birdman.

"How many years have you been in the navy, sailor?" I inquired, ready to chew him out.

"Twenty-two! And I'm an old shipmate of Captain Naifu's."

"Naifu. Doesn't that mean knife," I countered, with a dramatic flair to my voice.

"My humble apologies for not mentioning that fact sooner, Debuchi-san," he smirked. "But I think you'll find before this trip's over, the knife will have cut you down to size."

"Oh!" I mumbled, deflated, then nodded to Ibuse.

Looking wistfully at the snow-white Zeros surrounding me, I climbed into the cockpit, sighed and reached for the shoulder harness. The Tokyo Gas & Electrical company product just didn't radiate the same assurance of twentieth century flight that the Mitsubishi products did.

Not wanting to make any mistakes, I tightened my life vest and went over the check off list carefully. Trim tabs in take-off position. Throttle friction lever tight. Mixture in full-rich. Carburetor heat in cold. Fuel level booster pump on. Flaps, ten degrees down. A quick glance at the left and right magneto, before placing the ignition switch in the both position, and finally, check to see that my chest chute was connected to the harness.

"Debuchi," a familiar voice shrieked, cutting through my earphones like a razor."Are you going to sit there all day? The torpedo, dive bombers, and fighters would like to do something besides gulp up fuel."

That's right, I remembered, signaling the flight deck officer I was ready, the air taxi is the first plane to be launched.

I released the brakes, pushed the throttle forward, and moved to the centerline as the green circle illuminated. Even at max power, I had a hard time playing the gallant warrior with the engine noise more in the range of a farm tractor than a call to challenge the skies.

Although it didn't sound as airworthy, the ugly duckling with its double wings and light load lifted off the deck in less space than its larger horsepower contempories.

Recalling my near disasterous turn into the ship's bridge on a previous take off, I climbed straight ahead, refusing to look either right or left.

"This plane sure smells stuffy," the hard-to-please Inspector complained.

"Probably from sitting in the hot sun," I said. Looking three times to be sure I had the right knob, I opened the ventilation door, and held my breath in case anything went wrong.

When no unforeseen consquences from this latest act appeared, I leveled off at six thousand feet and adjusted the throttle for cruise speed.

With the routine chores completed, I grabbed the Far East chart out of the map case and hastily scribbled in some alternative routes.

I leaned back and thought about the plane itself. I knew it was used as an air ambulance in China, was flown by the Coast Guard out of Tainan, and was rumored to be part of the Taiwanese Volunteer forces.

Sick and tired of flying the KR-2, I turned north, figuring on asking what the Coast Guard thought of the plane--if I couldn't find out what the inspector was up to.

"Sir, what business do you have in Taiwan?"

"The Manchukuons presently have a Coast Guard detachment on temporary duty at Tainan and both of our victims had previously been stationed there. They also have had assignments in Manchukuo. I'm going to see if there's any connection."

"Weather shouldn't be a problem in the southwest portion of the island," I told my passenger. "Those clouds that resemble a pile of white pillows thrown haphazardly across a blue bedspread are to the north."

"You are something more the poet than the pilot, I think," Ibuse said.

Once I had the Taiwan coastline and its tiny airfield at Tainan in sight, I began my descent. When I passed through two thousand feet I was joined by a Ki-27 Fire Dragon with an unfamiliar insignia and something written on its side.

Taking a closer look, I saw *Defense of the Homeland, Anto Providence,* printed on the fuselage.

After eliminating me as a communist threat, the Fire Dragon pilot pointed at Tainan airfield.

As I passed over the shoreline, I noticed two pontoon-equipped KRs anchored to a buoy. The Fire Dragon aviator wagged his wings and flew on.

"Tainan tower, this is *Sky Dragon's* air taxi, It's hazy at low altitude and I've never landed here before; I had better use my head lights."

"I assume you mean landing lights?" the tower operator snickered.

Easy on the controls, I reminded myself flaring out for the final phase of the landing. At forty knots, not much can go wrong. I hummed, dropping the nose to get rid of the last ten feet of altitude.

"He just dove into the runway!" the tower operator claimed to an onlooker. "Look at that bounce! That's some sort of record."

"You've got your mike keyed," I cautioned him.

Fighting to keep from oscillating in the wind gusts, I put in a little right bank on the second bounce.

"Now he's landing on one wheel", a second air controller injected.

"Tainan tower, from *Sky Dragon* Air Taxi, your runway's a little bumpy," I insisted, banking to the left after dismissing the idea that an aircraft could cry out in pain.

"Stay calm," the tower operator wailed. "The medics and fireman have manned their vehicles as a precaution."

I gave a shout of joy equivalent to a trumpet blast when I managed to keep the KR-2 on the runway after blowing both tires. This hadn't been one of my better days.

"Don't move," the tower ordered, "we'll send someone out to get you."

"I'll need a tire jack," I advised as smoke trickled out of the ruptured rubber disks. "Apparently these tires have seen too many landings."

"Yeh, all in one day," the air controller said.

Even before I had the engine shut off, the plane was swarming with rifle-carrying men wearing foreign-looking uniforms. Manchukuons, I hoped.

Ordering us out of the plane with gestures, the soldiers looked closely at my reddish-brown hair and dark, chocolate-colored eyes, amidst a lot of chattering, pointing and head shaking.

Finally, in poor Japanese, the honcho asked for my authority to be at this locale. If I understood it right, they were afraid I was a communist spy masquerading as a Japanese pilot.

"That's a Japanese aircraft!" I said, looking back at the plane.

"The Communist Chinese and Mongolians have captured four or five of these aircraft," the head soldier said in fractured Japanese. "We also fly it. You will wait with us until an army interpreter shows up. He's expecting an Inspector Ibuse."

"That's Warrant Officer Ibuse behind me. Can I go down to the Coast Guard headquarters?" I asked, using a combination of sign language and broken Manchu, "while I'm waiting for the Inspector to complete his business?"

The soldier with the sergeant stripes nodded yes and assigned a private to stick with me until the major arrived.

With the private in tow, I spent two hours looking around the Coast Guard station facilities before the interpreter came on the scene.

My eyes opened wide as a car pulled up and a big major I thought I recognized from somewhere else came towards me.

His face resembled a piece of hastily repaired rare crystal: cracked, but not broken--damaged, but hauntingly attractive. The ideal features for a gentle giant, I thought, finally remembering him from the Shanghai night club. He had changed a lot in the last couple of days.

The voice, deep, pleasant, with a hint of earthquakes and volcanic activity about it, spoke in fluent Japanese. "I'm Major Gegan Sukebator," the large man said with a gracious smile. "To whom do I have the pleasure of speaking?"

"I'm Naval Air Pilot Debuchi, on an authorized flight from the aircraft carrier *Sky Dragon,*" I responded. "Can I get it filled up with premium gas?"

"We'll top off your fuel cells, with the standard 100 octane," Sukebator assured me. The tape on his face moved as he talked. "If you don't mind my saying so, Debuchi, that was some landing."

"Deliberately so. I'm flying a KR-2, and I understand your Coast Guard uses them."

"Have you spoken to the Coast Guard Commander yet?"

"No!" I said, hesitant about looking directly into his eyes, the color of which, like the Major's hair, reminded me of a bird--a raven, perhaps. "I've been down to the waterfront looking at the pontoon-equipped models."

"Let's go talk to him. I can only hang around for twenty minutes or so," Gegan said, starting for the Coast Guard building where the Commander's office was located.

"I have a young Japanese person with me," Major Sukebator warned the occupant as he cracked open the door.

"Tell him I'm not buying anything, Gegan," the Commander hastily answered.

"I've got a houseful of Japanese products already," Sukebator translated, his dark eyes lighting up with laughter.

"No danger. This one's a deep-water sailor," Gegan Sukebator said, pushing me into the office. "Meet Petty Officer First Class Debuchi from the carrier, *Sky Dragon*. I can vouch for his nationality but not his flying ability. This is the pilot that brought in the Inspector. I sent Ibuse to see the base personnel officer."

"Pleased to meet you, Commander," I said with the customary polite bow. "While I'm here, I thought I'd talk to someone about the KR-2."

"Sorry about that vendor crack. But at least once a week a Japanese salesman stops in here trying to sell me something," the powerful-looking Commander said, returning the bow from his seat. "What do you want to know?"

"I was just curious about the *Chidori-go* float planes," I said.

"We use them mostly against opium smugglers when we're back home. The British can no longer license and push drugs in Manchukuo like they do in Hong Kong, so they use small boats to drop off the illegal stuff. With over three hundred miles of beach to patrol, we could use more aircraft, but the fighter squadrons have priority right now," Sukebator interpreted, without missing a beat.

"We only use the landing gear model. Do the floats give you any trouble?" I asked, waiting for the translation.

"We have both wooden and metal ones," the Commander said, drumming his short chubby fingers on the desk to show the conversation was coming to an end." If your oufit is thinking of using this configuration, there's one minor problem. The water has to be reasonably calm. The float planes are KR-ls. When we use the KR-2s, like you're presently flying, it's to transport supplies and big-whigs."

"Thank you, Commander, I had better get back to my plane. I'm headed for Qionghai airfield in Hainan," I remarked when word came over the squawk box that my plane and passenger were ready.

"Good luck, and if Japan decides to free Asia from Europe's stranglehold, we'll do our part. And one more thing. The station will be billing your ship for the two tires."

Oh, no, I thought. Captain Naifu will have a hemorrhage.

I was really disappointed in Inspector Ibuse when he accepted a four engine seaplane pilot's offer to fly him back to the convoy.

Airborne again, I belatedly went to the area chart as my primary source of navigation. Hainan was my next stop. Unfortunately, with no autopilot, I discovered I had difficulty flying the plane and reading the map at the same time.

Putting the southern border of the aeronautical chart in my lap, and draping the other end over the instrument panel, I found the Island of Hainan and the coffee stain right on top of the control stick. Leaning over to look for Qionghai airfield on the map, I inadvertantly pushed the stick forward, sending the plane into a dive.

Hastily grabbing the controls to level off the plane, I managed to knock the chart to the cockpit floor. Using my foot in an attempt to flip it into my lap only pushed it between the rudder pedals. Bending over to pick it up, I cracked the bridge of my nose on the control column hard enough to draw blood.

Throughly frustrated, I took a deep breath and started all over again. Leaning over cautiously, keeping one hand on my nose and the other one free to retrieve the map of Southeast Asia, I got the inside tips of my index and middle fingers on its outer edge. It was too far away to get my thumb on it.

Slowly, carefully, I pulled the map towards myself. With only inches to go, the downward position of my head caused my nose to bleed profusely. Unbelievably, the chart slipped out of my grasp when I drew back my arm to wipe my nose on the sleeve of the flight suit.

Mad at the lack of cooperation between the aircraft and the recalcitrant map, I slammed the instrument panel, and was surprised and dismayed when all the warning lights came on--and stayed on. With bells ringing and alarms flashing, I concentrated on getting the aeronautical chart back. An idea burst in my overworked brain. I remembered seeing a movie comedian retrieve paper money from a sewer pipe by lowering a stick with a piece of gum on the end.

My luck had changed for the better--there was a package of gum in the right-hand pocket of my flight suit, along with a pack of cigarettes that I had intended to try someday.

This was the kind of gum you had to pry off your teeth. Putting all five sticks in my mouth, I chewed furiously, working in plenty of saliva to

162

make it one, big, gluey wad. When I had just the right consistency, I took a chopstick out of a zippered pocket and stuck the gooey substance on the end.

Yanking the plane out of a diving turn, I reached down and poked the long, Chinese-style chopstick over the top of the rudder pedal. Fortunately, the Gods of Good Fortune intervened, enabling me to hit a section of the geographical aide with the adhesive material on the first try.

Cautiously drawing the chart towards myself, smiling with self-satisfaction, I wasn't aware that *"Wen Kami,"* the invisible hostile being, had entered the picture. As one end of the map slid over the top of the foot lever its sticky surface adhered to its other half poking out from the bottom of the rudder pedal.

I was in a dilemma. If I pulled hard enough to separate the ends of the map, the gum might come loose, and I had already used up every piece.

I had no more gum, but I did have a pack of Dunhill cigarettes, and this was the time to try one. Keeping my right-hand on the control stick, I reached into my pocket with the left. Pulling out the cellophane-wrapped package, I alternated between opening the cigarette pack and flying the plane. After a nice, last minute maneuver that kept the plane from rolling over on its back, I managed to get a cigarette out.

Placing it in the left-hand corner of my mouth, in what I thought was reminiscent of a World War One fighter pilot, I was dismayed to find I had no matches. Unable to curse properly, for the Japanese language had no explosive swear words like the Anglo-Saxons, I hit the instrument panel again.

Thinking I heard a chuckle coming from the back of the aircraft, I twisted around but saw no one.

"There's always a way for an intelligent man to solve a problem," I said outloud. I had it! The emergency kit must have matches.

Loosening my shoulder harness and lap belt, I turned around to get at the packet. My knee bumped the control column, rolling the plane before I could react. The KR-2 was not built for aerobatics, so the cargo, along with my personal belongings were slung to one side, and the engine, suddenly shy of oil as it hit the inverted position, stopped running.

Flat on the floor, my nose bleeding, with less than six thousand feet between me and death, I scrambled back into the pilot's seat.

Playing it by the book, I fastened my harness and seat belt, put the mixture control to full rich, hit the primer a couple of times, hollered "all clear" out of habit in case anybody was near the prop, and punched the starter button.

When the engine was running smoothly, I took stock. My first task was to retrieve the map. "Why didn't I get it while I was on the floor?" I yelled in disbelief.

My luck wasn't all bad. The emergency kit had torn loose and ended up on top of the instrument panel within easy reach.

I took out another cigarette. The first one had split in two when I kneeled on it.

Pulling out a pack of matches from the emergency kit, I lit up and tried another pose. This time I tilted my chin at an angle I remembered the hero using in a silent film about a war-time pilot.

Determined now to get back to business; I parked the lit cigarette on the top of the instrument panel, unstrapped, got down on the floor and recovered the lost chart.

Finding myself forward of the control stick and sprawled on my stomach, I tried to get back in the pilot's seat before the plane rolled again.

Unfortunately, my shoulder hit the control column when I reached over my head for the cigarette. The Sandpiper zoomed upward, squashing my bloody nose against the seat and sending the lit cigarette rolling across the cockpit floor, where it teetered for a few seconds against the circuit breaker panel, before slipping under the right-hand passenger seat. A place where it was not unusual to find tiny pools of hydraulic fluid and oil.

"Air Taxi from Coast Guard Station," the radio squawked.

"Go ahead, Coast Guard. I copy."

"Utility Squadron Five requests your immediate return to Tainan."

Chapter 24

Flying Canoe

A Coast Guardsman met me before I exited the aircaft.

He climbed up on the wing and hollered. "You're to fill in for an injured seaplane copilot. The chief pilot instructed me to bring you to the seaplane ramp immediately."

"I can't fly a seaplane," I said getting into the three-wheeler for the short trip to the concrete slope at the edge of the shoreline.

"I'm Makio Bamen," the aviator in a black flight suit greeted me as we approached the four-engine marvel. "This is just a formality, Debuchi. Squadron doctrine calls for two pilots."

Ibuse stuck his head out of the plane's hatch. "I'm not going if he's at the controls."

"I've already told you, Inspector," Bamen said, "I'll be doing all the flying."

"How about the Sandpiper?"

"Another utility squadron pilot will see that it's ferried to Hainan after he picks up a complimentary message for the Army Chief of Staff from Dr. Abraham Kaufman, one of the Jewish leaders. Japan didn't close its doors to Jewish immigration, as Britain and America did.

"Captain," chief pilots on four-engine seaplanes like to be called captain, "has this flight been approved?"

"According to the directive from the naval district, we're going to deliver Inspector Ibuse to the *Ikeda Maru* before taking you to Canton, China as a replacement pilot for the Fourth Regiment's Air Ambulance Wing."

I strapped myself into the copilot's seat. "I appreciate the chance to learn something about a plane that carries such a large crew."

We taxied out from the seaplane ramp, headed for deeper water.

Finding a clear path, Makio Bamen pushed the four throttles forward and ordered full power from the flight engineer.

"How much room do you need to take off, Captain?" I asked, when the plane was still in the water after what seemed like an eternity.

"It depends on the surface wind. If we have large ripples or whitecaps we'll break loose of the surface in a hurry. But on a calm day like this, with a glassy sea, I'm going to have to coax it off."

Moving the control wheel back and forth at the right moment made the plane skip. At first, altitude was measured in inches, then finally, a big enough bounce broke it free of the ocean and sent it into the air.

"Sit back and relax, Debuchi-san. Your inflight meal will be served shortly. We have a small kitchen in a section of the hull just beneath our feet."

I was served spicy-glazed sardines, shrimp, and milk, followed almost immediately by rice crackers, soybean nuts, bean curd, and a dish of noodles on a lacquer tray.

"There's an awful lot of talk about fascism," the flight engineer said. "What's your impression of this political movement?"

"The Nazis met the desires of the middle class by supplying lots of parks, good transportation, medical care for all, strong defenses, and beautiful highways. But the country has only one political party, very parental in nature, no good for free-thinkers like us. You're not allowed to rock the boat."

"But politics isn't our biggest problem at the moment. The size of the Western armies are what worry me," I said. "The British Empire secured by Britain's Queen-Empress Victoria exceeds the wildest dreams of Napoleon, Caesar, Genghis Khan, Alexander the Great, or Theodore Roosevelt combined. Over one-fourth of the earth and the human race are controlled from Whitehall Palace in London."

Captain Bamen scowled. "Just the mention of Whitehall makes me angry."

I'd felt that way for a long time.

This airborne canoe duty is more like a pleasure cruise, I thought when Bamen said. "The Kawanishi flying-boat is superior to anything the West has. And to prove it, we're going to land it next to the *Ikeda.*"

"Riptide, this is Big Fish, twenty miles out with Army Judge Advocate Geki Ibuse aboard."

"Big Fish, from Riptide, the *Kaji Maru,* along with the other ships in her column, are moving northerly to give you enough landing space. The fleet is steaming at 15 knots, the *Ikeda Maru* will have a cargo net strung on the port side. We understand you practiced this maneuver off Taiwan's coast."

"No, from Big Fish. There wasn't time, but we believe Inspector Ibuse will be an excellent wing-walker even without the training," Captain Bamen assured them, running over his landing checklist.

"The seaplane's coming in!" Lance Corporal Kaine's voice came in through the auxiliary receiver. **"When the war started in Europe,"** Sakamoto said, **"Japan insisted on staying neutral, and has remained so."**

"At least the weather people had the sea-state right," Seaplane pilot Bamen said, throwing a switch that shut off the aux. radio to the cockpit. His eyes would be mere pin points from looking at the glare reflected off the calm waters.

"I'll bet you never visualized the ships being spread out over such a large area," I said.

"The idea is still the same, Debuchi-san," Bamen stressed. "Land in the path they've cleared through the middle of the convoy, taxi up next to the *Ideda Maru* and adjust our speed to the convoy's. Then, the Inspector walks to the end of the wing and jumps for the cargo net. Three simple steps.

"I'm not convinced its quite that simple," the methodical investigator said. "And neither would my wife Fujiko. On the other hand, my daughter Satsu would love it."

"Rip Tide from Big Fish, Ibuse says he'd be happy to fly in this comfortable four engine aircraft any day of the week."

"It's the world's fastest seaplane," the flight engineer bragged. "Two hundred and seventy mph."

"How's this flying metropolis going to stand up in combat?" I asked,

"This is a tough bird. The six fuel tanks in the hull have self-sealing capabilities, and each one is equipped with a carbon dioxide fire extinguisher system."

"What happens if the fuel tank takes too many hits?"

"The bilge pumps will transfer the fuel to an undamaged tank," the Kawanishi seaplane copilot said with pride. "In contrast to the macho fighter pilots, we're well-padded with armor. This plane can absorb the extra weight from the added metal easily."

Bamen managed to keep the wide-bodied, four-engine Kawanishi flying boat in the open lane as it touched down. The outboard pontoons kept the wings from dipping into the water.

When the plane was stabilized, I opened the canopy and stood up in the seat with my head and upper torso out of the plane.

I glanced back and saw the long vee in the water behind the aircraft collapse as the plane matched speed with the ship.

167

Looking up, I noticed my cousin Jun holding on to his position along the rail.

I swung my attention back to Ibuse, who was now on the wing of the 50,000 pound seaplane inching his way along. He apparently had forgotten to put on a life vest.

Halfway down the wing, the Inspector slipped to one knee on the sleek surface. Fully aware of the large number of ships heading in his direction, I knew he'd be in real trouble if he fell off. It would be almost impossible for him to avoid the dozens of ship's propellers cutting into the sea.

From my vantage point it looked like he had slipped a second time when the wing tip rose with the swell.

Geki Ibuse had gotten a line thrown from the *Ikeda Maru* tied around his waist and looked ready to jump for the cargo net whenever the wing passed back through a level position. The *Ikeda Maru*, being much larger, moved correspondingly less than the floating aircraft.

"Jump!" hollered the ship's sidewalk superintendents.

Inspector Ibuse froze for a second, then leaped.

Jun Kaine applauded enthusiastically when Ibuse managed to get a tenuous one-handed hold on the cargo net even though it was plastered against the ship's hull.

"Shake the net," someone hollered. "He can't get the fingers of his other hand under the ropes."

I watched the Inspector continue his climb up the webbing. Bosun's Mate Banno had managed to flip the cargo net out far enough for Ibuse to grab it with his unoccupied hand.

I heard a weak greeting coming from Ibuse to the men on the weather deck, followed by a screech of metal when he brushed aside the microphone.

Ikeda's Captain, with Professor Sakamoto right behind him, hurried over to meet the Inspector.

"Did you see those eyes on the Army Inspector, Corporal Kono?" a voice drifted down from the ship. "They're so dark you can't tell whether he even has pupils."

"You should talk about eyes," the Corporal countered. "Yours look like a pair of cast-iron skillets."

"Our job's done here," Bamen said, pulling away from the ship.

* * *

168

"The last time I was in China," Bamen offered as we approached the coastline, "there was something called the Japanese Central China Development Company. It was a spin-off from the Japanese North China Development Company."

"About that same period, Akron, Ohio, complained about Osaka cutting into their profitable rubber sales," the radioman said.

We landed in the inlet between Macao and Hong Kong and taxied up the Pearl river to the city of Canton.

I hired a two-wheeled rickshaw with a fold-down top for the two mile trip to the airfield. It was pulled by a Chinese man with powerful looking legs.

The rickshaw owner took off running, then slowed to a fast walk.

When we started to pass through a row of air ambulances at the air base, I jumped out, paid my fare and took a hasty look at the medical evacuation planes before walking the rest of way to the control tower. My copilot, Akira Segawa was waiting there for me. He was telling a Korean volunteer from the Wonsan Construction Battalion about the hazards of flying an air ambulance.

Chapter 25

Air Ambulance

I hung around the hanger at the auxiliary airbase outside of Canton, waiting for an assignment. Meanwhile, my ears were being bombarded by the arguing maintenance personnel surrounding me.

"When did war seem like the only alternative?" an ordnanceman trumpeted, wrinkling his nose at the chlorine odor left in the air from the cleanup activities.

"It was a three step procedure," an aviation radioman said, waving a burned-out power tube. "The first was when France agreed to allow Japan, Thailand, and Manchukuo to use Vietnam bases, including Cam Ranh Bay and Saigon.

"And the second?" a hydraulics specialist asked in a low-pitched voice.

"According to NWR radio, two days later the American administration restricted the amount of aviation fuel that could be purchased," the aviation mechanic said. "They required Japanese businesses to obtain a license from the United States government for each sale. That placed the normal everyday commercial transaction into the political arena," he continued, putting his foot up on a tool box. "Free trade went out the window. It meant our commercial airlines had to reduce their number of flight hours significantly."

"What did we do about it?" the ordnanceman asked, looking over my way.

I jumped in with the answer. "Following that incident, in order to neutralize as many Western nations as possible, we signed the 'Tripartite Pact' with Germany and Italy. The 'Tripartite Pact' does not include military cooperation between Japan and Germany. We insisted on staying neutral. We had every reason to believe we could also sign a treaty with Russia and the Portuguese armed forces in Macao.

"Why did America get so excited?" the mechanic asked, looking at me with the same friendliness one would give an unwanted bug. We would never send our armed forces to aid the anti-capitalistic Nazis."

"It was a terrific propaganda tool for Britain and America," I added, proud that I remembered the answer. "Even though the 'Tripartite Pact'

170

was not a military one, it gave the Allies something to exaggerate, right along with the 'Anti-Comintern Pact.' Without regard for reality, the United States linked Mussolini, Hitler, and Hirohito together as an unholy trio. Sometimes they'd drop Hirohito, and replace him with the Prime Minister."

"I'm trying to picture what's-his-name getting together with Hitler and Mussolini to discuss marine biology." the small-boned hydraulicsman confessed.

Rubber-booted crewman washed down the hanger deck with hoses-- splashing water around with little regard for those who had polished shoes or trousers legs jutting out into the targeted area.

An unearthy quiet descended over the hanger when a swashbuckling military police officer in a high-collared, striped-belted, dark blue uniform entered. His bright-colored outfit was highlighted by a red cap with a dressy white plume sticking above it.

He asked to see the pilot of the KR-2.

Before shifting around to get a better view of the colorful officer representing the Judge Advocate General's office, I searched through my guilty conscience for a possible misdeed.

"Warships filled the shipyards, and sailors became a familiar sight in downtown America," the radioman said, when conversation lagged.

"It's been my impression from reading," the mechanic said, staring into an empty oil can for inspiration, or more likely to keep his eyes from looking in the Judge Advocate's direction, "that America is unbeatable at turning out war material."

Standing over to one side, a shore patrolman accompaning the MP asked me. "Did you get a letter from the legislator representing your prefecture?"

"*Hai,*" I aknowledged. He had released a strongly worded letter to the press, assuring his constituents they'd find the killer and put an end to one of the most disgraceful episodes in the history of the armed forces. "He's up for election this year," I said, pausing to let someone else speak.

"My father happened to be on vacation in Haiphong when Hirohito visited there," the Korean carpenter said, laying his hammer on the edge of the stainless steel table.

"Whenever they talk about our head of state," I said to cover my nervousness, "the white supremacist never mention the large American crowds who line up along the street for hours just to catch a fleeting glimpse of England's King-Emperor, the symbol of the greatest empire the world has ever known."

"I still don't understand," the radioman grumbled, "why America is so enamored with a country that has one-quarter of the world under its thumb."

"My high school buddy," the hydraulicsman remarked," said America wants commercial control of the Marshalls, the Carolines, and Mariana Islands presently mandated to Japan."

"But we have lots of trade and tens of millions of yen invested there," the ordinanceman said, picking up the cover on a trash can to depose of a gun-cleaning rag.

"Who is Sakamoto referring to when he talks about the soapers?" the mechanic asked.

"They're the wheeler-dealers in Washington, so-named because of their slippery methods, and their ability to conceal any subject under a thick coat of lather," I explained. "They know that Japan is committed to fight for the lead in commercial aerial routes. Each landing site in Asia and the Pacific will be worth millions."

"Are you sure he didn't tack on that name, soapers," the radioman inquired, tongue-in-cheek, "because of the influence large soap manufactures like Lever Brothers have on governmental decisions?"

"What other opportunities would the United States secure if they go to war--besides getting more territory?" the aviation mechanic asked, his voice garbled by a mouthful of rice.

They will use the Alien Enemies Property Act," I replied. "The last time they applied it, they grabbed Germany's patents on the new money-making marvel, radio. This time around it will include television patents and near total control of the financial centers."

"By the way," the radioman said after answering the shore patrolman's question. "I think you'll find that Lever Brothers is part of the British-Dutch congolmerate called Unilever."

"You're probably right!" the mech granted with a look that froze the sailor in his tracks.

A bluejacket from Bangkok, who was standing next to me inserted, "My country tried to take on the French navy last year."

"France was too much for Thailand to handle until Japan got involved."

"This Asian show of independence was objected to by the American government," the Bangkok sailor said. "And relations between America and Thailand started downhill."

"The United States prefers to have Europeans or Americans in charge of Asian soil," the radioman said, while making final adjustments on a malfunctioning radio receiver.

"By the way," the navy policeman said before departing. "According to the tests completed by *Ikeda Maru's* sick bay personnel, the bayonet found in the library had dried blood on it. To confirm this, the alleged murder weapon will be sent to *Whispering Wind* for more detailed analysis."

When I heard the word "Canton" mentioned on the receiver, I requested the aviation radioman to stay on that frequency. Canton had Chinese Communist guerrilla bands that were left behind during Mao's long march. This might be a chance for my first air-evac mission.

* * *

"Canton Firebase, from Air Ambulance Five One," I said as I passed over the upper fork on the eastern section of the Pearl River. "Fifteen miles out, requesting instructions."

"Is that you, Debuchi-san?"

"Does your mother eat rice?"

"I thought I recognized your discordant voice. What are you doing out this way?" Canton Firebase inquired. "The last I heard, you were operating out of Taiwan."

"Aren't you the scholarly tower-flower today, Sumii, What's with this discordant? Why don't you just say inharmonious like everyone else?" I said, giving him a taste of oneupsmanship. "I have downtown Canton in sight."

"Head for the northwest section of the city and I'll pick you up from there. Do you have any late information on a lady named Hisako?"

"Negative," I answered, wishing I did.

When I motioned Medical Officer Hiro to take a seat closer to the front, I exposed my bare arm and a pair of embroidered dragons.

"Are those dragons on the inside of your sleeve regulation?" the medical officer asked, catching a glimpse of them as he moved forward.

"No. Before I became an aviator," I informed him, leveling out on a course of 350 degrees, "I wore them on the cuffs of my jumper. They've become a good luck charm."

"I'll bet you're tatooed. A mermaid?"

"No. A pair of wings, high up on my arm near the shoulder," I replied searching for the town's northwest outskirts. "You can't notice it unless I take my shirt off."

"I heard you refer to this plane as an *Aikoku-go* . I thought everybody was a flag-waving nationalist?" Eichii Hiro asked, gripping the sides of the seat.

"To honor those citizens who donated money to build this aircraft so the wounded could get back to our field hospitals faster, I use *Aikoku-go,* the honorable expression for patriotism every once in awhile."

"I've never flown in this type aircraft before, Debuchi-san. What can you tell me about it?"

"It's a high-wing monoplane with room for two pilots, a flight surgeon, or nurse, now that Miiko Arishima's suggestion has been taken seriously. We have oxygen, intravenous feeding, stretchers for two injured servicemen, and room for a couple of ambulatory patients on folding seats. It has a 460 hp engine with a top speed of 150 miles per hour if you're interested in the mechanical statistics.

"Speaking of nurses, who was that big nurse with the swaying, seductive walk that I saw you with last month in Yulin?"

Her name's Atsu. Isn't she pretty?" the flight surgeon said. "Her smile has all the qualities of warm toast with a dab of butter in the middle," Hiro said enthusiastically. "Since we're into hot subjects. What can you do if we have a patient burning up with fever?"

"I have both temperature and ventilation controls here in the front cockpit. Relax now, Doc, I'm crossing the northwest section of Canton, our rendevous point."

"Air Ambulance Five One from Canton Airbase. If you're driving a funny looking plane with red crosses on it, I've got you in sight."

"Anymore smart remarks and you may need the services of this aircraft yourself, wiseguy."

"Come left ten degrees, your objective is a large, level pasture two miles ahead. You can't miss it. It's one of the few green spots left because of the draught."

"I've got it in sight," I radioed when I saw a bright-colored panel stretched out in the form of a cross.

"Hai, Canton out."

I shut the radio off, wanting to concentrate more fully on the delicate job at hand. When using a pasture for a landing field there's always the chance of a hole or mound to trick the unwary. Chances are it had been a rice field previously and might still be soft.

After clearing the last tree, I picked a spot to the left of an air ambulance awaiting clearance to take off. Keeping my eyes wide open to see as much of the unfamiliar terrain as possible, I rapidly lost altitude by side-slipping the aircraft. Observing no obstacles ahead, I quickly leveled the wings and made a jarring but satisfactory three point landing, allowing the doctor to release his breath and take his white knuckled fingers out from under the seatpan.

Rolling to a gentle stop through the softening action of the four inch brownish grass, I cut the engine as soldiers carrying stretchers poured out from the edges of the meadow.

Herding two heavily bandaged men and carrying two more on stretchers, six riflemen guarding the ambulance platoon crossed the open field, while two more kept watch for communist guerrillas.

Moving rapidly, the corporal grabbed two empty litters from the plane with the assistance of copilot Segawa and the medical officer, then quickly handed in the wounded-laden stretchers.

I heard a bullet riccochet off the engine cowling before seeing the riflemen drop to their knees to return fire. I wished now I hadn't cut the engine to keep the prop wash from interfering with the patient transfer. I pushed the copilot out the door into the unusually warm temperatures of southern China.

I turned my head just in time to see the other air ambulance take a direct hit from a communist mortar shell. Pieces of the prominent red cross markings were scattered like pellets from a shotgun shell.

A Chinese rifle squad leader from Wang Ching-wei's forces standing on the other side of the field had heard the shell whistle over his head. Wei's Nanking government had signed a peace treaty with the Japanese the previous year and weren't pleased with this communist tactic.

Detecting signs of activity to his left, a Wei soldier flushed out the three man mortar crew with a hand grenade. As the communists ran through a clear spot to get to an area of thick shrubbery, they came under attack again from the rifle squad firing from a prone position on the edge of the clearing. They shot with an accuracy normally reserved for the rifle range.

The squad leader rushed out to where a communist soldier still showed some signs of life. He looked down with revulsion.

"Sorry," the young communist advisor from Stalingrad said, looking up with pain in his eyes. "We thought they were bringing in weapons. We know the Japanese want to die for their emperor."

"You have done an injustice to the Chinese belief in fair play," the rifle squad leader spit out angrily.

"Excuse me, Sergeant," flight surgeon Hiro requested, easing him aside to examine the young communist soldier.

"Take good care of him," the sergeant ordered.

"Too late, Sarge," Hiro told him as the last pulse beat faded away.

"Your men are good shots. He was hit three times in the upper part of the body."

"Anger can do that," the sergeant said, not bothering to lower his voice as other communist forces on the perimeter opened fire.

Grumbling he'd never get to see the Tam river again, the site of his boyhood home on the outskirts of Kawasaki, my copilot, head down, raced to the front of the plane--ready to pull the prop through and roll out of the way if the engine didn't kick over right away. His help wasn't needed. The power plant was still warm, and the aircraft roared back to life immediately.

He had finished his prayers to the seven-hundred year old Daishi temple and was halfway through the opening before a bullet hit the doorway over his head. Pulling his legs inside as he dove into the copilot's seat, he managed to get buckled in despite the jerky movements of the aircraft.

"Hold on to your patients, Doc, we're rolling," I hollered, as I increased power. The ground no longer felt smooth as the air ambulance pounded over its surface in a hurry to leave the area.

Jamming his feet up against the stretcher to keep his patients from rolling out, the wide-eyed flight surgeon held on tightly with both hands to the oscillating intravenous bottle.

Both ambulatory patients swayed with the motion of the aircraft. The soldier with his arm in a sling sat upright, while the more heavily bandaged one kept his head bowed.

Manuvering around the tallest clumps of withered grass, I went to full power. Now the turf became our enemy, slowing down the aircraft as it attempted to reach takeoff speed.

When we hit a bare spot, I eased the plane off the surface, leaving behind the burned out remains of our counterpart.

The doctor, expecting a steep climbout, was appalled when I headed right for the grove of pines, seemingly without concern. At the last moment, having gained enough momentum, I pulled back on the stick and converted speed into height, climbing at an angle that cleared the obstacles with nearly a foot to spare.

"Watch for enemy aircraft," I warned the passengers--alerting them with a voice that sounded like a file on metal. "Dutch, British, and American merceneries have formed something they call the International Squadron and roam the skies in Western planes looking to pick up some easy money."

"They wouldn't shoot down an unarmed air ambulance with red

crosses painted on it, would they?" Doctor Hiro gasped.

"Yes, they would," I assured him. "and for justification they'll claim the Japanese put red crosses on everything."

"They get a bonus for every plane they shoot down," Segawa added, mumbling something about his wife and two school-age children. "And since they don't have the acceleration or turn capability to dogfight with the Navy's Zero or the Army's Ki-27 Fire Dragons, they look for easy prey.

"You're talking about the Flying Tigers, aren't you?"

"No, they haven't started flying in this area yet. They'll replace the Italians, who've had a hundred and fifty planes and pilots in action against our forces for years."

"If the International Squadron gets paid for shooting down aircraft," the doctor wondered, "how truthful do you think their victory claims are?"

"It depends on the size of their home mortgage, how many kids they have, and the amount of money in the bank," I guessed.

"Most of them are just mavericks from the military with a maverick's idea of what's right and wrong," my copilot said, twisting around to look out the starboard side. "I don't think any of them pretend to be straight arrows."

"You mentioned the Dutch?" the doctor said, surprised at the mention of that nationality.

"Yes, they get $500.00 per month salary, plus $1,000.00 for every plane they shoot down, and an additional bonus for missions completed. All paid in gold."

After we had flown for twenty minutes without trouble, the talk took on a more cheerful note, until Segawa called out, "An I-16 Abu fighter, three o'clock high, he hasn't seen us yet."

Already at low altitude, I dropped even further. Low enough for the prop wash to leave ripples on the watery surface of the rice paddies, causing the flight surgeon to stop in the middle of a joke and go back to white knuckle flying.

"Why did you ever become a flight surgeon if you're so uncomfortable in the air?" my copilot asked, when the doctor stopped halfway through a sentence.

"It was a new occupation and we were given early promotions. I was promised a job at the Atsugi Aviation Research Laboratory," Hiro replied, observing Segawa tune in the base frequency.

"That I-16 has spotted us now," Segawa warned. "With this crate's top speed we're not going to outrun any fighter planes."

"Isn't the I-16, Russian? Is it any good?" the flight surgeon asked nervously.

"Yes! The Soviets are supporting certain warlords with squadrons of fighters, bombers, and ground personnel. The I-16 held the world speed record a couple of years ago. It carries machine guns and 20 mm cannon."

"What's the Russians game?'

"They don't want Japan to have a say on the mainland, because China would then remain capitalist. Somewhere down the line, they'll cut off military aid to everybody in China but the communist leaders."

"I find the whole thing confusing," Hiro said. "Germany is training Chinese ground forces, and Italy has a big role in flying against Japan."

"It's amazing what politics and greed will do," I chuckled.

"Is our position hopeless?" flight surgeon Hiro asked nervously. "I can see the fighter now, off to the right, er, starboard side."

"We might have a chance if I can get him down to low airspeed," I remarked, wishing I had a been able to practice more with Ghost Leader. "The Russian I-16 has a stability problem when it accelerates too rapidly."

Hugging the ground, I tracked the Abu fighter in the rear view mirror as it maneuvered to get into firing range. Switching from flying over farmland to maneuvering around the erratic turns of a wide, muddy river, I flew the air ambulance dangerously close to the tall shrubbery lining the stream banks on the southern side--occasionally skidding far enough, using the new tip-toe matic rudder pedals, to narrowly miss the large warehouses to the north.

The I-16 pilot, no doubt, had cut his teeth over the bloody battlegrounds in Spain, and was now determined not to let this easy victory get away from him. Keeping the air ambulance in sight, he executed a sharp turn, ending up behind us.

"He's on our tail," Segawa warned, throwing in a comment about his insurance policy.

"Drop the gear and flaps," I ordered, pulling back on the throttle after rubbing one of my embroided dragons for good luck.

Flying the I-16 at such critically low airspeed had the Soviet pilot at a disadvantage. He's probably charging his guns and putting his eye to the gunsight right now, I thought.

"Air Ambulance," came the electrifying call from Black Magic Two One Five, "I have the I-16 in sight; hang on," Tomi announced, following a series of fast-paced "hisses" on the emergency frequency.

Spotting the highly maneuverable Ki-27 Fire Dragon, the Soviet pilot in a moment of panic, knowing this was not a movie where the mounted Cossacks were going to come over the horizon in the nick of time, ignored the manufacturer's warning. Rapidly accelerating from low speed, he stalled out the left wing. Fighting to regain control, he saw his last glimpse of planet earth before slamming into one of Macao's taller buildings, as a flock of birds scrambled away from the Russian's mistake.

"Black Magic Two One Five from Air Ambulance Five. Splash one! Thanks for your timely help, Tomi."

"Air Ambulance Five from Black Magic. Hsss, nice flying, Kiyo. I'm not going to take credit for that one. Best wishes to your patients."

"There's a lot of static on the radio," the flight surgeon conjectured.

"No," I informed him, chuckling. "Sometimes, the pilot of Two One Five sounds just like a jungle cat."

"That was a great piece of piloting," the doctor said, congratulating me. "You should be in a combat squadron. Maybe fighters."

"Thanks, Doctor," I said without blushing. "That's my intention."

"Where do we go from here?"

"Hainan."

"Air Ambulance, I'll take a look around to see if any of the three dozen or so aircraft from the International Squadron are in the area," Black Magic said, as he began climbing in a wide spiral pattern to cover the greatest amount of territory.

"There's one," he announced. "No," he decided, after coming in for a closer look. "It's a German Junker from the Chinese-German Eurasian Aviation Corporation. If it wasn't a civilian plane, I'd knock it out of the sky.

"Here we go. Just like I figured, there's a British Gloster Gladiator headed towards you, probably being directed from spotters on the ground."

I knew that when Black Magic 215 located the enemy aircraft, any housefly that happened to be trapped inside his canopy would have noted characteristics in the pilot normally associated with a feline species. Thick hair, every bit as dark and shiny as a black panther's, standing on end. Ears wiggling in anticipation, then laid back close to the skull. Chestnut-brown eyes, with the gold tint of a predator, narrowly focused.

"I'll have to get him quick," Tomi reminded us before throwing the arming switch and gunsight on. "Even though the Gladiator's an older biwing aircraft, a South African got twenty enemy kills over Europe in one of them last year."

He would have to nullify the Gladiator's ability to make a tight turn, a characteristic of its double wing configuration, by using the Fire

Dragon's superior rate of climb and acceleration.

"I've spotted the colors of the International Squadron, whose pilots all came from Western countries, most of whom had occupation troops in Asia," Tomi radioed. "It'll give me the impetus to slash at the Gladiator with my 7.7mm machine guns until he's out of action.

"The Teutonic nightmare keeps trying to get on the inside but I'll keep him out of firing range by initiating a climb. He's frustrated now and letting the thought of a bonus interfere with his better judgement.

"I've got an opportunity for a head-on shot at the Gladiator," Tomi said excitedly, "and am pouring machine gun fire into the opening between his engine hub and cowling. Lead and hot steel should be shattering the moving parts in the radial engine, reducing it to a metal junkyard framed with smoke.

"The biwing fighter is struggling to make it to land, but it's still a hundred yards from shore. It's crashing into the flood-swollen and raging silt-laden river. He'll never make it out alive," Black Magic 215 reported, departing for home base.

"The Westerners don't wear water survival gear over China," I murmured with a superior feeling, patting my life jacket.

Chapter 26

The Clock is Ticking

Flight Surgeon Hiro talked me into dialing in the Iris frequency.

The Professor was broadcasting from a land-based site. The practice amphibious landing had already occurred.

It sounded like Sakamoto had let Private Second Class Agi give some examples of his phenomenal memory.

"**The economic war was still in full swing,**" he lectured, sounding more like a salesman than librarian. "**The Japanese were selling bicycle tires for seven cents each, typewriters at twelve dollars, bicycles at five dollars and automobiles at three hundred, including transportations costs at West African ports.**"

He's incredible, I thought.

"I wish he'd give some up-to-date info," Hiro complained.

"**While Japan was selling microscopes in Boston for two dollars,**" the reference librarian made known. "**Its American competition was charging seven dollars and fifty cents for the same power of magnification.**"

"**America's toothbrush was four times as expensive as a Japanese one in my hometown.**" someone with a Korean accent managed to say.

"**What did President Roosevelt do about it?**" Jun asked.

"**Washington was filled with Anglophiles in 1941, the leading one being the President,**" Michi Sakamoto cut in. "**These men were unable to forget their tribal background. Caught between the freedom of the new world and the nostalgic pull of the old, they chose to talk about one, and actively support the other.**

"**Two very important items occurred last year that are not given enough credence,**" Sakamoto said solemnly. "**The United States did not listen when the British Ambassador to Tokyo said that** he could just as impressively make a case for Japan in China as against it.

"Japan signed a treaty with the coastal region of China and Wang Ching-wei became President," he announced, sounding amused at the murmers of surprise circulating throughout the group. "We hope this prevents the West from reasserting their stranglehold on Chinese seaports."

"The famous *Atlantic Charter*," the man with the Korean ancestry chipped in, "that was signed by Churchill and Roosevelt, said in part, 'Great Britain and the United States wish to see the sovereign rights and self-government restored to those who have been forcibly deprived of it.' Did they? No. Instead, the two leaders agreed that restoring forcibly deprived rights wouldn't pertain to any of the nations Great Britain, France, America, or the Netherlands had conquered."

"Can you tune the radio in to get a clearer signal?" Hiro asked,

"*Hai, hai,*" I said. reaching for the knob. He was pleased when I told him that since Hainan was only about twenty miles off the mainland of China. We had spent very little time over water.

"We'll talk exclusively about the present year, 1941," Sakamoto said, coming through clear as a bell. "Some of you have been part of these discussions since we began talking about Japan's trading accomplishments in the 1400s, and are rapidly getting updated."

Judging by his next words, someone evidently interrupted Professor Sakamoto long enough to give him a fistful of messages.

"I'll share some of this information with you," he said. "This one is from the Captain of the *Kuji Maru*. Thank you for giving the men of this convoy the motivation that will enable us to fight for Asian freedom with a display of tenacity and skill that's unavailable to the Western conquerors.

"From *Midnight Star*: Due to Professor Sakamoto efforts, we'll go into battle knowing our cause is just, and our enemies formidable.

"Aware that the alternative to war is the complete domination of Asia by the Western forces, the *Painted Veil* is anxious to use its big guns against the military forces of the Global Empire.

"Having listened to many of Professor Sakamoto's discussions, *Sky Dragon's* aviators are prepared to spearhead the honorable attempt to drive the British forces from Malaya."

"I must confess, I don't feel motivated yet," the flight surgeon said. "How about you?"

This was a tough one for me to handle, so I decided to fall back on patriotism. "I'm trained for combat," I said, "and look forward to fighting for my country."

"One of the earlier events this year," Michi said when he finished with the messages, **"was Thailand's successful attempt to get Xandong Island, situated in the Meekong River, out of French hands. And Japanese marines replaced the British Royal Navy on Liukung Island off the coast of Shantung, China.**

"According to a letter I got from home," Hiro said. "When Japan reduced the power of the French Army in Vietnam, America was deeply disturbed. But American Congresswoman Jeanette Rankin, apparently you can't fool that lady easily, wondered why the Roosevelt administration was so concerned about Asian soldiers being in Asian territory when they weren't distressed with Europe's occupation troops being there.

"Ironically," Dr. Hiro continued, "just as Jewish names were mentioned in connection with nuclear physics and the possibility of new weapons of mass destruction, Japanese Captain Inuzuka was receiving an inscribed gift for his service to the Jewish people. Seventeen thousand Jews found haven from the European holocaust when they slipped into the Japanese section of Shanghai and used it as an immigration locale."

"I can vouch for that. A couple of thousand Polish Jews made their way to Kobe when I was home on leave, and the people gave them a warm welcome" I said.

We went back to the radio and Sakamoto.

"America's already in bed with the British and French Empires. Together they have control of one-third of the world and most of its armaments. And in addition, ground has been broken for the huge pentagon complex for the military establishment in Washington, a building that makes the old Prussian mlitary command headquarters look like a play pen. This massive structure, more than one mile in circumference, will be devoted entirely to the art of war.

"The biggest problem for America in the Far East is not China but Vietnam," the Professor said, bringing the discussion back to Asia. **"With Japan able to take away the power of the French military, and talking about independence, it could easily turn the Far East into a hot-bed of nationalistic movements. Burma,**

Malaya, Indonesia, and the Philippines could get the idea that they have the power to reject the European-American occupation forces if they got help from an Asian country. Like some insidious disease, a taste of freedom would spread and lead to even more liberal demands. The United States will not back down on this issue. Japan has to depart Vietnam and leave the French soldiers in control. No conditions, no compromises."

The Sergeant Major called the group to attention and introduced the rear admiral to the Ira frequency listeners.

After thanking Professor Michi Sakamoto for chairing the discussion of events leading up to the present set of circumstances, the Admiral launched into his prepared speech. "Enroute to the practice amphibious exercise here in Hainan, you were given the opportunity to improve your knowledge of Japanese history and had something constructive to occupy your time.

The flight surgeon and I listened closely to the Admiral's words.

"Now that we've completed phase one, I'm going to give you an update on our mission.

"Five months ago, the Netherlands, Great Britain, and the United States imposed a trade embargo on Japan and froze all our assets. This blow to Japan's banking system, coupled with the country's dependence on trade, began a countdown for our very survival. The final blow came on the first of August when the Gold Dust Enterprise, as Sakamoto so aptly calls the European-American partnership, cut off all oil shipments to our country. Needless to say, the Japanese stock market dropped out of sight, and Japan was headed for national bankruptcy."

Hiro and I stayed silent.

"Japan is an industrial country with no oil resources of its own. We either import or close down the factories and throw our citizens out of work," the dynamic forty-eight year old amphibious specialist declared. "Trade is Japan's lifeblood. Without oil, our merchant fleet can't leave port, and the wheels of our great commercial ventures will stop.

"As the manufacturing plants shut their doors, the number of jobless will become intolerable, possibly leading to a takeover by Japan's Communist Party, or more likely, we'll become a satellite of the larger Western powers. For the first time since the British sent its occupation troops into our homeland in the 1800s, we are faced with a no-win situation. If we do nothing, we become a has-been nation. If we lash out to obtain oil and freedom for Asia, we face the wrath of a dozen or more Western nations.

"We have managed to get four white-controlled countries off our backs: Russia, Italy, Portugal, and Germany. We're not stupid; we know they'll join with the rest of the belligerent countries of the Western world when they get the chance. But at the moment, it reduces the odds.

"The choice is a clear one. Attempt to get the Western military out of Asia, and hope for an honorable peace settlement, or bow to every demand the European and American nations make.

"Normally, there would be an opportunity for success in such an endeavor, Japan could reasonably expect to take on England, France, and Holland in our own backyard and win some concessions.

"The fly in the oinment is the United States," the Admiral said with an unhappy tone in his voice. "America has given every indication it will back Europe's occupation forces if Japan tries to evict them.

"The U.S. military bases at Hawaii, Midway, Wake, Guam, and the Philippines will have to be neutralized long enough for the European armed forces to be evicted.

"Should the United States change its mind about using American lives to support the European colonial system in Asia, Japan will be able to free Asia and purchase oil, without the nightmare of having to fight off the American Goliath.

"Meanwhile, the clock is ticking, and the reserve supply of oil is being allocated to the defense department and those industries and shippers with the highest priorities."

The Admiral finished up with: "Your officers realize how much you soldiers looked forward to getting your feet on dry land. But your duty to prepare yourself for the upcoming confrontation is more important. The lessons learned in 'Operation Warmup' may save your life later on.

"If we successfully complete our Hainan training mission, and do it in the allotted time, you will be given a twenty-four hour pass in Yulin."

And I had Hainan in sight. Dr. Hiro leaned around me and made appropriate comments on the picturesque island. "It's got forrested mountains."

"Six thousand feet high," I said, checking my own altitude.

"How big is the island?"

One hundred and eighty miles long and one hundred and ten miles wide, with plenty of rainfall."

"Where are you headed?"

"Qionghai Airfield, it's in the foothills about half-way down the eastern side of the island."

Chapter 27

Dress Rehearsal

I flew along a narrow strip of sandy beach on northern Hainan's coastline waiting for my copilot's signal before turning inland.

"According to the chart we need to head for the interior whenever we spot palm trees," Segawa notified me. "But make sure we stay north of the tropical hardwood forests."

I started my descent when the palms came into view and stayed over the semi-tropical flora all the way into the airfield.

Thanks to Nakajima's new glare-reducing tinted glass, Akira Segawa spotted the twin-tailed aircraft that suddenly appeared in front of us in time for me to yank the air ambulance inside out getting away from it.

"Report him," suggested a scared Segawa. "I saw *Morning Breeze* written on its side as it went by."

"That's the long-range communications plane, owned by the NWR Radio Corporation," I said. "I'll chew him out when we get on the ground."

"Air Ambulance from Morning Breeze, sorry about cutting you out in the traffic pattern. I got distracted when the reporters searched through the frequency band to get an exclusive for their station. "

The asphalt landing strip that had been poured over the coarse native grass provided plenty of landing room even for larger aircraft.

I heard the noisy tree cicadas the moment we stepped out of the aircraft. Followed by a chattering Douc Langur monkey showing off its extremely long tail and bright yellow face.

A light-blue, Jungle Glory butterfly with huge, dark-blue borders on its wings landed on Akira Segawa's nose.

From the heavily vegetated area surrounding the field, a male dark-brown deer with horns resembling a rocking chair peered out at us.

I kicked at a heart-shaped shell, called a heart cockle, someone must had brought in from the beach.

I had the copilot move the aircraft as soon as we found a shady spot to park it under. Afterwards, we broke out the mosquito netting and the four-legged bamboo-framed cots in preparation for an overnight stay.

At dusk a dark-brown, white-throated owl appeared. It was in pursuit of the night-flying insects pouring out of the long, rough grass off the side of the runways.

Since I'd never done anything more out-doorsy than tripping over a clod of dirt at second base with the "Kabuki Kites," I felt uneasy.

Thankful that I was an aviator and wouldn't have to do this very often, I snuggled down for couple of hours sleep.

Rubbing the sleep out of my eyes, I attempted to listen to cousin Jun describe how the men and supplies landed safely on Hainan's sandy shores, and how Sergeant Major Hozumi had stood, legs spread wide, announcing in a voice loud enough to make the leaves tremble, "You clowns don't have to worry about the Malayan jungle," he had shouted. "The only way we'll ever get a foothold on one of the beaches is if the British can't stop laughing long enough to shoot straight."

Four Mitsubishi Zero fighters flying in diamond formation streaked across the sky at low altitude. Next, they climbed in a northerly direction, dove and flew back over the beach, splitting up to the north, east, south, and west, then continued on out of eyesight.

Everytime I see a Japanese fighter plane with a gleaming white paint job and its blazing red fireball, I thought, it sends a tingle up my spine.

"Did you see the motorized unit heading south from the port of Haikow?" Jun asked, "It should have been moving over the well-traveled maintenance roads used by the rubber workers and field managers."

"*Hai*," Segawa answered.

"When Sakamoto got a glimpse ot that first rubber tree, I wonder if he recalled his auditorium lecture on the history of Hainan," I said. "The Chinese had operated rubber plantations on the island until they became unprofitable. Japan took over Hainan's collapsed economy for fear of a French or communist takeover and rubber harvesting was resumed."

"He didn't forget to tell them Japan spends less on the military as a percentage of its budget than Thailand does," Jun said.

Segawa and I walked over to our parked aircraft at the edge of the grass. Behind us loomed an army Ki-43 Peregrine Falcon and a Ki-45.

Reaching into the compartment behind his seat in the air ambulance, Segawa removed a tent and lantern from the storage area.

Just as we had finished setting up a better shelter and installed the wind chimes at the entrance, the airbase duty officer came running over.

188

"Urgent telephone message for you, Debuchi-san."
What now, I thought, following him to the hastily constructed tower.

"Mushi, mushi," I said. "Debuchi speaking."
"Have you ever flown a Ki-45?" asked an authoritative voice.
"Hai," I said. "Recently."
"I want you to pick up Hisako Bayar at Canton. Use the Ki-45 for transportation. It'll take you less than two hours to get there."
"Why am I picking her up?" Time's getting kind of short for transporting civilians, I thought.
"I'm not at liberty to tell you that. Just obey orders. I can tell you its a request from Ruriko Hattori through the offices of Representative Daizen."
I went over for another look at the twin-place fighter plane, dubbed the Dragon Killer. I was joined by Ruriko from the communications plane, and she looked smug.
"Did you get a call from your superiors?" she asked.
"What about?"
"Aren't you supposed to bring Hisako here? The communications crew will be responsible for her once she's safely on the ground."
"I'm looking forward to seeing her again," I said. "I've had the pleasure of running into Hisako Bayar several times in the last week."
"Was she ever with a big Manchukuon Major from Harbin?"
"Hai. He's the one that had angry words with a couple of Dutch aviators."

* * *

Taxiing in, I saw my would-be passenger holding onto a little hand-held mirror while she brushed her hair.
"Miss Bayar?" I said jumping down off the wing, all smiles.
"Hello Kiyo" the exotic Mongolian called out. "If we keep meeting like this, people will talk."
"Being linked with a charming female boosts my standing in the navy. In fact, I'll volunteer to be your humble servant for the duration."
"Did you say that to the American girl I saw you with in Shanghai?"
I mumbled an answer.
"Thank you for coming to get me," she said so alluringly I almost bit

my tongue. "Are my long-sleeved Shantung silk blouse and dark slacks appropriate for the trip?"

"Hai, and I've got a flight jacket you can use," I stammered, admiring her poise and strikingly dark eyes.

"Just to the west of the airfield," she said, pointing with her right hand, "the cities have been subjected to bombing from a variety of war lords, the Russians, and the international squadron. There's a dozen hidden agendas within a three-hundred mile radius. Western-built aircraft dropped leaflets over Canton promising freedom. Which, I'll bet ten Mongolian ponies, they never give. All the French haven't left yet, either."

Fitting her into the parachute harness and life vest gave me time to admire her firm, rounded figure.

"You're all set, lovely lady. Let's go," I said, boosting her onto the cork walkway on the wing, then into the rear cockpit.

"Just a moment," she said noting the 30 caliber machine gun installed on a 270 degree swivel mount. "I used to go hunting with my dad. How do you load this gun?"

I pulled a foot or so of the cartridge belt of out of the ammo can and reluctantly showed her how to fit it into the firing chamber. "We won't have any need for it," I said, hoping she wouldn't shoot off the tail playing around with it. I was relieved when she didn't ask any questions about the iron ring sight--that made me think she wasn't serious.

Even though the twin-engine, 340 mph Ki-45 was not well-suited for carrying passenger baggage in the radio-gunner's seat, she didn't squawk when I crammed her luggage down in beside her.

"How many planes have you shot down?" Hisako asked.

"Never bothered counting them," I said, with downcast eyes.

"I like humility in a man," she said. "However, I haven't flown in a combat plane before, so keep me informed of what you're doing," Hisako suggested, apprehensive about this powerful-looking fighter plane, but not so jittery as to forget buckling the parachute to the harness.

"Tadachi ni," I assured her as the tower light cleared me for immediate takeoff.

"I'm easing the throttles open, not forcing them," I commented as the Dragon Killer picked up speed. "Now, I'm letting the plane take to the air on its own accord, instead of jerking it off the runway," I added as the aircraft tires began to float over the surface.

"It's airborne. But I'm not going to climb right away. Instead, I'll let the nose stay level for a few seconds to pick up some extra speed. Now, I'm pulling the stick gently back to maintain a ten degree climb. There are

190

no obstacles ahead of us."

"What was that?"

"Just the landing gear and flaps coming up," I assured her, having activated them much later than my preferred high-angle takeoff.

I found I had made a big mistake in making a right hand turnout to take up a southerly heading to Hainan. I thought the route over Shamian Island, a former white enclave for wealthy European businessmen, would keep me away from Hong Kong air space, and enable the pair of us to do a little sight-seeing at the same time. The trouble was, I had strayed too far into hostile territory.

"The minute we spot an enemy plane, I'm headed for the deck."

"The deck! Isn't this an army plane?" she asked, running a fingertip over my earlobe.

"I meant low altitude," I replied, twitching my ears like a wolf shaking off a pesky fly.

"You're a throwback on the evolutionary scale," Hisako said, amazed at my ability to move my ears.

"Hold on!" I said. "There's a foreign-looking aircraft, over by the Pearl river."

"Are you going to dive?" she asked anxiously.

"No, he's below us." I guessed it was a Dutch Brewster Buffalo from the International squadron, a substituted name to hide the fact that its just another tactic the Westerners use to keep control of the area.

"That low-flying pilot has spotted us. He'll be greedy for bonus money, He's climbing, with the belief he can make up any loss in the distance between us when he gets to altitude."

Losing a couple of miles in the climb, the stubby-looking American built aircraft, reportedly manufactured in Newark, New Jersey and assembled in Norristown, Pennsylvania, leveled off.

I didn't bother to tell her that the Netherland's pilot had already charged his guns and was staying at full normal power on the throttle quadrant, his combat speed held in reserve. He was too far from his home base to waste gas. He patiently waited for the distance to shrink.

Keeping the Dutch aircraft in my rear view mirror, I eased the throttle forward as the gap between us shortened. I managed to open up a couple of miles, then lost ground when the Dutch aviator decided to ignore the fuel requirements needed at higher speeds. "Well, I guess I'll have to do the same," I muttered, putting the throttle into the combat power detent when the Brewster Buffalo got uncomfortably close. "If I was alone," I said, in my best bravado voice. "I'd take a crack at him."

"The gaps widening again," I said louder, pulling back on the fuel control when the Dutchman seemed to lose interest.

"You should have shot him down!"

Me and my big mouth. I thought, the lady is a tigress. "You're sure?" I inquired, looking for an out.

"Stop playing around and get the creep," Hisako yelled at me. "Pretend I'm not here. Although, I'd prefer that you tell me what's happening."

"All right," I shouted back, trying to keep my voice from quavering. "First thing we have to do is turn around," I said, rolling the plane on its back and heading downhill into a split S. "This will point us in the opposite direction at a faster rate."

"I love it!" Hisaka hollered half-way through the maneuver.

With the built up momentum from the split S red-lining the aircraft, I closed the distance between us like a homesick dragonfly. I adjusted the illuminated gunsight, threw on the arming switch, charged the 50 caliber machine guns and kept her informed every step of the way.

"Turn on the gun camera if this plane has one," she said. "We'll have a picture of him being knocked out of the sky."

The Dragon Killer was in range and firing before the Brewster Buffalo could obtain altitude advantage, but my initial burst was a hurried up, nervous shot and did no vital damage. The Dutchman was apprised now of my tactics, and he slammed the throttle full forward again intending to bend the aircraft far enough around to place the iron ring and bead gunsight on his target.

"We have more horsepower and rate of climb," I informed her. "And have heavier, forward-firing weapons." I didn't mention the fact that I had no combat experience in the aircraft.

"Blow him apart!" Hisaka Bayar cried as we passed over Canton. "Ninety years ago," she said, "the French and British took over that city's government and set up a police state. The Chinese had to compensate the Europeans for France making war on Asia. It's Oriental payback time," she cried, temporarily losing her lady-like manner as she pulled back the charging handle on the swivel-mounted machine gun.

I skirted in and out of danger like a jittery pickpocket at a New Years sale. Finally, I got the reflector gunsight on the painted-over spot where a black-bordered orange triangle, the Dutch national insignia, should have been.

A quick burst with the 20 mms as the Buffalo started to loop in front of and over the top of the Ki-45 was not long enough to open holes in its unprotected fuel tanks.

Hisako said she caught a glimpse of the pilot and the olive drab upperside of his aircraft when it arced above the "Dragon Killer."

Thinking he had gotten away without an explosion and was now in position to make a diving turn, the Brewster aircraft rolled right-side up and straight into the furious fire of Miss Hisako Bayar. Disregarding the possible consequencies, the Mongolian hellcat had opened the cockpit canopy and shifted her safety belt around to its widest position. To brace herself against the wind, she had spread her legs and jammed her riding boots into brackets mounted on both sides of the inner fuselage.

"These footholds remind me of the stirrups on my favorite saddle," she yelled from a standing position. Unconcerned about her long, black hair flowing into the slipstream, the rider from the Mongolian plains shot at the dark-green, soft underbelly of the American-built fighter plane with a vengeance.

Smoke poured out of the intruder's cockpit, and he rapidly lost altitude. Ironically, another lady had been indirectly involved in that duel between east and west--the Dutch pilot was one of Queen Wilhelmina's airborne prison guards, a member of the military establishment that kept a million Indonesians under its control. A white soldier, thousands of miles from home, was about to find his final resting place in the continent he felt so superior to.

Pleased with the turn of events, and mad at myself for not being more aggressive, I flew on.

My slowness during the attack phase cost us a couple of bullet holes in the engine. I had to use the wobble pump, because the automatic mechanism for supplying fuel to the carburetors was shot up.

I should congratulate her, I thought, dejectedly. After all, she was the one who got the kill. I brought the twin-engined plane down to a landing at a barren auxiliary field near Qionghai air base.and taxied behind a half-finished shack.

Reaching up to help her out of the plane, I found I was too late. She had already jumped to the ground. "This calls for a good old fashioned Hainan celebration," I said, congratulating her.

"It's getting dark. Where are we headed?" she asked.

"To Qionghai airfield. It's about a six hour walk."

"How come we didn't land there?"

"The regiment will be using the space tomorrow and any planes in the air will be diverted to this field."

"How about borrowing a bicycle?" she asked spotting a half-dozen of them leaning against the temporary control tower.

That'll cut our travel time in half," I guessed, grabbing the bike with a bamboo basket attached. "Give me your bag. Some of these hills are steep."

"In that case you'd better save your breath," Hisako advised after selecting a bicycle and tossing the loops of her overnight bag and a large hooded jacket over the handlebars.

While passing through the final stand of buildings before we reached our destination, we found ourselves enchanted with the village's rustic houses, tiny market place, and nearby river.

Still full of adrenaline, we decided to stop and unwind. We purchased food and lots of saké at the local store, and commenced to celebrate.

Throughout the partying, hundreds of planes passed overhead enroute to practice targets in the southern half of the island. "It's nice to be in a place where you don't have to worry about a visit from Russian soldiers if your country doesn't adhere to the communist line," Hisako said, talking about her homeland while pouring herself another glass of saké.

Reluctantly waking up the next morning when a cat rubbed up against my face, I finally got up the strength to acknowledge that I was still alive. I felt chilly and wondered why I was lying on a rubber poncho. Searching around for a cover in the cool, early morning air, I stopped when I felt bare skin. That's me, I thought, with some misgivings. I lifted my right leg and peered at it from half-opened eyes. My hasty diagnosis was quickly confirmed--there were no trousers on it.

I moved my hands slowly past my thighs, then inched them up towards my stomach, Finally, I came into contact with something besides nudity. It had a silky feel, and was lying in a heap on my belly.

Turning hesitantly to my left, I chanced a quick glance and saw more bare skin. A hip protruded from the bottom section of a white, long-sleeved blouse. No slacks were visible.

Cautiously moving my head to survey the surroundings, I saw a group of shrubs and a house just behind them. *My God*, I thought, we're in somebody's back yard.

"Hisako," I whispered hoarsely, unable to speak louder without a bolt of lightning lifting my scalp. "We better get out of here in a hurry."

Groaning , she reached for the slacks she'd brought with her from Mongolia, pulling them over herself without ever becoming fully conscious.

194

"Let's go," I said, poking her in the ribs.

The jab brought a howl, and the slacks vibrated under the negative force.

A dog in the next yard barked.

"Not so loud," I pleaded, pushing the silk panties over towards her, while my mind pretended this was not happening.

I tried another poke to the ribs.

"Go away," she countered in a little girl's voice. "I'm too sick to go to school."

"Come on," I demanded pulling on my undershorts and trousers. "I wonder what the local newspapers will say about a navy pilot and his gunner caught sleeping nude in the backyard of a small village," I muttered.

"Come on," I repeated.

"It's not because I didn't do my homework last night, Mom," she said, rolling up into a tight ball. "I'm coming down with something."

Standing up, I looked down lovingly at this courageous girl, with her knees rammed against her chest, eyes closed tight, slacks lying across her bottom in a modest fashion. Turning towards the river, I noticed two bicycles in the water, with just the handlebars showing.

"What are those bicycles doing in the river?" I asked in a surprised voice.

"It seemed like a good idea last night," Hisako Bayar replied lazily. "You said they were dirty."

"You better get dressed, before the people who own that house come out," I ordered, mesmerized by the four empty saké bottles circling endlessly in tiny whirlpools.

Hearing sounds that seemed to be agreement and still in a state of mental confusion, I walked down to the river to retrieve the bicycles.

"Drinking saké without eating is dangerous," Hisako explained as she got into her clothes and came down to the river just as I was bringing out the second bicycle.

Shaking the bike to get the water off of it, I agreed with her wholeheartedly, unsure of what had occurred during the last five or six hours.

"Whatever happened, and I'm not confessing to anything," Hisako said, putting a hand to her mouth in imitation of a girl from the farm country, "I just wanted to let you know, Mongolian girls do not rush into romantic adventures without the proper courting."

"Hisako," I said taking her hand. "You're a wonderful, intelligent, beautiful woman. Someone who's caught up in the trials and tribulations of our times--in company with a man--who may not have looked after your welfare properly."

"It's not your fault, Kiyo. You're one of the good guys," she said, smiling at me. "Let's just start all over again."

We--and I like to think of "we" as a pair of romantic adventurers, had traveled only a short distance from the little village before we heard the clanking of tank treads on the move.

"I don't know if I should go where there's so many men," Hisako insisted, grabbing her hooded jacket after peeking through the shrubbery at Qionghai Airfield. "Especially naked ones, she laughed after thinking about the previous night.

"We're lucky, Hisako," I said, holding her tight. "There's your ride. *Morning Breeze* is parked not far from the brushy area to our left."

"I hate to leave you," she said, "but I'm anxious to find out about Ruriko's, 'Save the Children' campaign."

And I have to get back to my air ambulance," I said, kissing her lightly on the lips.

"Good bye, good friend," she said as she headed for the communication's aircraft--unsure of what sad song fate had composed for her.

The afternoon of that hectic day, I watched the curtain open on a strange group of actors.

"I'd have beaten him here," the private complained, "if Kaine," he pointed to the Lance Corporal, "hadn't taken that short cut."

"He glided across the rice shoots on those snow shoes?"

"They acted like flat-bottom boats," Jun Kaine said, proud of his innovation.

I made no comment but instead listened to the soldiers' chatter as additional units piled into the airfield.

"When you lay down your rifle during a rest period," Lance Corporal Jun Kaine said, repeating a story told to him by a soldier who had been on the semi-tropical island previously, "you're likely to find that the weapon has been taken over by a colony of insects during the short time you're relaxing."

I gathered there had been little sleep for the personnel of platoon 4 the first night ashore. Catching catnaps and making maximum use of the maintenance roads, the point men like my cousin had been the first to arrive.

With no motorized equipment from Haikow yet in sight, the infantryman decided to use the spare time to clean-up. Jun had already unpacked his clothes, and had removed his pen, paper, and toothbrush from its special container before locating his bar of soap. "Kaine's law," he insisted. "Whatever you're looking for in a knapsack is always on the bottom."

Stripping down, the men hung their clothes on the nearest tree and used the light drizzle in lieu of bath water. They were joined by a couple of dozen Burmese calling themselves "Thakins," a sarcastic reference to the name they were forced to call their British masters back home.

"This is more refreshing than a shower at the Young Men's Buddist Association," one of the soldiers from the Burma Nationalist Army said.

I knew there weren't too many active Thakins, the British had imprisoned anyone advocating freedom for Asia.

The bright-colored birds were forced to endure the sight of a multitude of skinny, chubby, knobby-kneed, light, dark, tall, short, and ridiculous-looking bodies attired in soap suds, racing around the area in their bare feet waiting for the next downpour to rinse them off.

"This is a lot better than the canvas buckets and empty gasoline drums we used when I was a private in the Nomonhan campaign against Soviet Russia and Communist Mongolia," Sergeant Ogata acknowledged, pretending he was a wealthy industrialist at a summer resort.

"What was your job in Nomonhan?" Kaine asked.

There was only about seventy people per square mile in Manchukuo at that time, including Mongols, Manchus, and Tunhus. And the country was pretty much surrounded by communist. Sgt Ogata admitted to being part of the force guarding the Southern Manchurian Railway.

Before they could say another word, the men from the great cities and farming areas of Japan found themselves standing under the driving rain. And typical of this latitude, five minuters later, with the help of a clear sky and warm sun, they had no need of a towel.

A tank-repair vehicle broke through the underbrush with an incredulous tankman on top holding his sides with laughter at the sight of all the exposed skin. He perched his goggles high on his head, and groped for his camera.

Geki Ibuse stepped out of the staff car with a frown on his face.

Hurridly getting dressed, the foot-soldiers rushed over to greet the officers, asking if there was any late news about Malaya.

According to the Mobile Unit Commander, the only news is bad news," the picture-taking tankman informed them. "The British have beefed up their Malayan occupation forces with Scottish and Anglo ruled Nepalese troops.

A long line of light tanks equipped with three man crews and 37 mm cannons pushed into the underbrush surrounding Qionghai.

Spotting platoon 4's personnel, the tank commander waved them over to a large clearing on the west end of the runway and climbed up on a tank equipped with a long, collapsable bridge.

"The bicycles you'll be issued," he said holding one up, "are the standard Japanese design sold around the world, including the thousands bought by Malayans. This little item, is the same model that members of the U.S. Congress said would ruin their economy. Each combat unit will have a repairman assigned to it, plus one roving repairman from headquarters brigade to fill in at critical times. Any questions?

"Over there to my left."

"Can we depend on this bike under jungle conditions?" asked the research librarian, wearing a khaki jacket, kidding himself that the ventilation flaps on it would be enough to keep him cool.

"This bicycle is tough, and won't rust out during the short time you'll be using it. It's extremely light, and spare parts are available in the villages.

"Any other questions? If not, starting with the truck on my left: get your bicycle checked for defects, then continue straight ahead to the truck with the canopy over it, for your food rations. The water vehicle is on your right, but with the amount of rain in the tropics, its just excess baggage. It won't go aboard the *Ikeda Maru* with us.

The mechanized infantry unit grabbed their cycles from the trucks and quickly adapted to driving on grass.

After signing his maintenance sheet and getting a meal of rice balls and miso soup, Jun Kaine walked over to stand under one of the large shade trees.

Hearing his name called, the Hachijo Island soldier spun around.

"*Ho!* Kaine-san," Sakamoto shouted. "I have someone with me I'd like you to meet. Lance Corporal Jun Kaine, this is the honorable Major Gegan Sukebator." He had already nodded in my direction.

"Glad to meet you, Lance Corporal Kaine," The giant soldier with the serious raven eyes and rose-colored skin said. "I've been assigned as an observer to your brigade by my government."

"That's great. I have a ton of questions for you Major-san." Kaine said with an appropriate bow. "But first, you'll probably want to look around and get more comfortable with the functions of this brigade."

"Why is everybody looking at me so funny?" he asked.

"You're wearing a German-style helmet like those worn by Chiang Kai-shek's Chinese Army," Kaine said with a smile.

"We had a Chinese deserter show up at headquarters. I must have grabbed his helmet by mistake."

"I'll get you a Japanese one," Jun laughingly promised him. He surmised that it had been a while since the major had been assigned field duty.

"What kind of manpower will we be facing if we challenge the West?" Sgt. Ogata asked, his poetic voice sounding strangely out of place.

"The number of military personnel on the side of the Teutonic power-brokers grows daily as they put pressure on all white nations to unite," Sakamoto answered.

"George the Sixth," I heard the Major say, "by the Grace of God, of the United Kingdom of Great Britain and Northern Ireland, Emperor of India, and his other Realms and Territories; King, Defender of the Faith, is proud and grateful that he has his Anglo-controlled forces ready to fight for the Global Empire in Asia."

"The maxi-empire of Britain and midi-empire of the United States are intent on scratching the mini-empire of Japan from the Oriental Independent list--but Japan, Thailand and Manchukuo are just as determined to have a free Asia," Sakamoto emphasized. "Japan's Prime Minister Hideki Tojo has previously been awarded Thailand's most prestigious decoration: The White Elephant."

"Have Sakamoto's motivation speeches turned you into a tiger yet?" Segawa asked me.

I hesitated. "Not yet, but I'm working on it."

"Our ace-in-the-hole is the nationalists in the occupied countries," the Professor said. "We have asked them to assist us in the task of driving the Western soldiers out of Southeast Asia.

"It'll be a tough fight." he stated, detaching the canteen from his belt. "Malaya, and its city of Singapore represent the Oriental centerpiece for the Global Empire. Britain has spent a fortune on Singapore's naval and air bases. Pschologically, the West can't afford to lose it."

"Any problem getting gas for the air ambulance while I was flying the Dragon Killer, Segawa?" I asked.

"No! They fueled it last night," my copilot assured me.

I stuck my head in the hatchway to see what a communications plane looked like on the inside.

"Ho?" Ruriko said, trying to find me in the dim light.

"It's Petty Officer First Class, Debuchi," I replied, like she didn't already know my voice. "What's a radio station doing on Hainan?"

"We're trying to scoop the 'Nightingale of Nanking' and NHK radio," the scratchy voice answered. She glanced nervously towards the cockpit as the pilot changed the prop pitch. "The army's still trying to hide something," she said, referring to the murders.

"Is that important?" I asked.

"We're trying to get an exclusive for NWR. The *Japanese Times* has just..."

"Is that the English language paper?" I interrupted.

"Hai. Last month they purchased the *Japanese Advertiser,* a Yokohama outfit that's been in business since 1890. The *Times* is looking forward to becoming a powerful force in the communications field."

"If you want to get ahead fast--get in television," I said from the doorway.

"That's too far in the future," Kubo, NWR's station manager complained, looking over Ruriko's shoulder

"My father got interested in TV way back in 1926," I told them. That's the year inventor Kenjiro Takayanagi created one of the world's first television shows by forming a Japanese written symbol on a cathode ray tube."

"How long before we can buy a set?" Kuba asked.

"In large numbers for a reasonable price within the next three or four years, I'd guess, unless the West keeps it all to themselves by using this war as an excuse to knock out our manufacturing capabilities. The amount of money and power that can be accumulated during those first five or six years of mass produced television sets is staggering. If the West takes over our country and prevents us from selling any TVs during the early years it will mean a fortune to the foreign, get-rich-quick tycoons.

"Good-bye and good luck," I yelled to Ruriko. Keeping my emotions in check, I winked at Hisako.

I bumped into Segawa as I departed the aircraft.

"I'd like to fly on ahead to Yulin so I'll have more time to spend with my sister Mariko in case she managed to get back to Yulin," the air ambulance copilot said.

"How am I going to get ahold of the plane in an emergency?" I asked, irritably. "My orders are to stay near the brigade."

"The historian said you could ride with them."

"Why should I do that?"

"If you do, I'll owe you one."

"If I give you permission. You'll have to stay in close touch with the naval station."

"I won't leave the base," Segawa promised.

"If I need the plane," I said. "I'll call the base duty officer from the van, and he can pass the word on to you. Get moving."

"Don't worry, Professor," Kaine said as I approached the pair. "We'll free Asia in time to get you back to more the peaceful pursuits of life--before you lose interest in that stone garden project of yours."

"I hope you get your wish," Sakamoto said. "Along with many other dry landscape hobbyists, I like the serenity and the feeling of reverence that comes with imitating the natural surroundings by using earthy materials. How do you spend your spare time, Kaine-san?"

"I grow tiny vegetables, breed miniature fish, and sell lilliputian cakes. There's a large market for them generated by the traditional tea ceremony put on once a year by the families who have dolls and doll houses handed down from generation to generation."

"You're on the right track, catering to the small fry," Sakamoto said. "That reminds me, in 1927, Japan gave the United States over fifty skillfully crafted dolls as a gesture of goodwill. They were nearly three feet tall and were attired in beautifully handsewn kimonos."

"Professor," I said. "I'll take you up on your kind offer to let me ride in the van so my copilot can spend some time with his sister in Yulin."

"The tank commander is looking our way, Debuchi," Lt. Sakamoto cautioned. "Since we're assigned to the armored battalion, we'd better get rolling. We'll be traveling in a personnel carrier for the first few miles."

I reluctantly climbed aboard the Nissan-built vehicle.

Having tanks, artillery, and machine gun units from brigade headquarters in the area gives the rifle companies a feeling of security in battle, I thought. However, I supposed the infantry would operate more like guerrilla raiders than a highly organized army. The standard military procedures wouldn't work when you are moving fast and taking advantage of local assistance.

"Did you see those snow-white navy Zeroes yesterday, Kaine-san?" I asked trying to show some interest.

"Hai, but my attachment has always been to the army's aircraft. A pilot who visited my high school on career indoctrination day flies an orange and tan Nakajimi Ki-27 with an outfit in Thailand. His eyes lit up like a candle in a dark room when he told us a story about one of his exploits against a communist aircraft."

"Is that the reason we're fighting a war in China, to keep it from going communist?" a private asked.

"That has a great deal to do with it, but it isn't the only reason," Sakamoto inserted from the front seat of the personnel carrier.

Platoon 4 personnel were ordered to pick up the pace as tactical aircraft made simulated dive bombing and straffing runs.

My luck wasn't running good. The truck stalled and wouldn't start, and my copilot had already taken off. The professor found room in another vehicle, but I ended up with a bicycle, tagging along with Kaine and Agi.

Jun Kaine rode slower than he normally would have to give me time to get my muscles in shape. I quickly grew tired of rice balls, chestnuts, and napping in fifteen minute segments. My biggest wish at the moment was for a candy bar.

After we moved out of the plantation area, the traveling became more difficult, the paths much narrower and steeper. There were more streams to cross, and the foliage was thicker.

A dummy mine went off on Kaine's left as we sat down for a short rest. Platoon 4 was only in loose contact with the brigade as they headed southward, so we ended up pushing our bikes more than we pedalled them.

I'd just gotten settled down and had made peace with the local six and eight legged creatures when orders to move on came through.

At the next water obstacle, the sergeant had them break off tree branches, assigning half the men to construct a makeshift bridge, while the other half used the left-over branches as a raft.

"Keep moving. Use nature to your advantage. Be innovative," the colonel ordered. Like a man possessed, and with a target time in mind, he set a pace that taxed the abilities of the infantry battalion.

Pushing a bike along a trail that was barely visible to the human eye, I tripped over the roots of a hardwood tree. From my sprawled out position on the ground, I spotted a King Cobra under a large red begonia. "A new species," I mumbled to the dirt lying beneath my nose. "A Red King Cobra?" On the left side of the trail I noticed a red outline in the shape of a heavy boot.

"Are you going to lie there all day, sky boy?" Hozumi asked in a reasonable tone, prepared to turn up the volume.

"I'm getting right up, Sergeant Major. Wait a minute. Maybe I struck my head. Everything's red."

"If you were a soldier, you'd know that a red haze in Hainan is not uncommon. It's caused by a layer of fine dust that allows only the red portion of the spectrum to filter through at this time of day."

"Thanks Sarge, I thought I had a concussion."

"This place is bad enough with its overabudance of the world's most persistant flies, bees, butterflies, spiders, termites, mosquitos, and moths. They constantly buzz, crawl, fly, and hop all over our bodies hunting for a food supply. Daily doses of quinine prevent malaria, and the shots we took will prevent bubonic plague and cholera. But layers of creams and lotions to discourage the myriad of other insects are a dismal failure. I've seen more injuries from slapping at flies and bees with foreign objects than we'll ever see from enemy bullets."

Jun Kaine pulled the oilcloth from around his 7.7 mm Nambu rifle to look for signs of water. Not finding any, he went on to check each of the ammo packs stored in the four pockets of his tunic. None showed indications of moisture. "The new lightweight khaki drill uniforms, designed for operations in humid climate, are a big improvement over the old ones," he said.

Agi, carrying his boots so they wouldn't get wet, had stepped on the thin, brittle outer-covering of a saddle-oyster shell coming ashore. Even while jumping in pain, Kaine commented that Mallory Agi had managed to grab one side of his knapsack to keep the umbrella from falling out.

"Watch where you're going!" Chief Banno warned.

"Sure, no problem." Kato, the navy landing trooper claimed, his eyes growing dark as a moonless night.

With sweat co-mingling with the rain drops on my face, I moved off the warm, well-trodden trail and confronted the darkness of the semi-tropical forest. Scarey bedtime stories came tumbling back to haunt me. A forest meant wild animals, snakes and poisonous plants.

Misery loves company so I moved out of the foliage and back on the trail as fast as my body would carry me. Most of the inductees had been born and raised in cities and were just as apprehensive as I was.

"Keep a lookout for signs of platoon 3's crew," Hozumi shouted up ahead "They started inland ahead of us to set up obstacles and act as the enemy."

I managed to keep up with the advancing columns.

One hundred meters down the way we ran into a stream. It was shallow enough for the infantry to wade over, but too rocky for the food, medical and ammo carts. The pseudo enemy had destroyed the only bridge leading over the stream. A private with a few semesters in forestry jumped forward with a specialized tool, and cut, stripped, and threw two medium-sized trees over a section of water that had the least number of rocks.

Platoon 4 personnel charged across the waterway, some wading and some going over the makeshift bridge assembled from the hastily laid tree trunks.

The natural roof provided by the moisture-laden forest should keep the sun from shining directly on the fast-moving troops, I thought. But it did little to relieve the hot, sticky feeling.

The sound of machine gun fire chattered from both the right and left flanks. Platoon 4 had allowed themselves to be ambushed.

Benjiro Ogata, the sergeant from platoon 3, whom the grapevine said was tougher than dried-out rice, screamed at the soldiers to stop bunching up. "If we had used live ammunition," he claimed. "we would have killed a couple dozen of you."

"Not me!" Chief Banno exclaimed, preening in his 1940s model landing trooper uniform, embellished with anchors on the left sleeve and helmet. A bandolier with a dozen pouches of ammo worn around his waist completed the image of a sea-going soldier.

Shouts up ahead sent Agi running to help out. Pulling up just in time, we saw a corporal laying at the bottom of a deep pit half-covered with leaves. "Platoon 3 has struck again." Kaine said before he realized it was no act.

There was no movement when we grabbed a skinny tree located on the rim of the hole and tilted it down into the pit.

Major Sukebator, anxious to participate in every aspect of the amphibious exercise, climbed down into the cavity.

It looks like your 'Trademark Killer' has struck again," he yelled. "There's a bayonet sticking out of his chest.

The rice balls I had eaten had turned to lead in my stomach, and the thoughts of getting some fruit from the tropical trees for variety flew out of my mind.

I grabbed the nearest soldier. Together we pulled the corpse out on the trail. We didn't remove the cross made out of two pieces of jagged wood that was stuck in the ground next to the dead infantryman.

"I'll pass the word along to the ambulance crew and Inspector Ibuse," Sergeant Major Hozumi said. "It's Corporal Kono."

The rest of us continued up the trail.

"Who's that big Major?" Agi whispered.

"His name is Sukebator. He's in the Manchukuo Army,"

"Is Sukebator a Manchurian name?"

"Not exclusively, it's also a very well known name in Mongolia."

"I'm glad he's along," Kaine laughed. "Both here and I hope in Malaya--just how big are you anyway?" he asked, turning in the direction of the Major while looking skyward.

"Six foot eight inches tall and I weigh two hundred and ninety-five pounds." the giant answered, making the leaves tremble in resonance with his comment. "If you're looking for credentials, I was heavyweight champion of the Manchukuon Army. But I'm not the big one in my family; I've got two brothers on the destroyer *Enchanted Shadow* that call me tiny. The navy threatens to use them as anchors if they get out of line."

"I don't mind telling you, I jumped through my skin when I first saw you," Agi informed him.

"You saw the cuts up close that came from a fight with a couple of Dutchmen," Sukebator said, as the sun broke through the trees lighting up a face resembling a piece of shattered crystal.

"What happened to them?"

"They're no longer with us. May God rest their souls."

"Tell me something about your country, Sukebator-san," Jun requested, moving behind the Major as he started down a little-used trail.

"Glad to," Sukebator allowed. "For a long time, China has wanted our territory, and referred to it as one of her providences. But from a practical point of view, Japan and Russia have had control since the early 1900s. Then recently your country kicked the communists out, and gave us our independence. Of course those countries who do not wish us to be free call it a puppet government.

"When the Manchurian territory received its new name, Manchukuo, it installed its first leader, and is in the process of building an army and airforce. In 1935," he said, pointing to a campaign ribbon, "I led a platoon of Manchukuons against the Chinese communist in Jehol providence. We are very proud of our new country."

"Doesn't Manchukuo have to do what Japan says?"

"The Manchus and Mongols are not going to be pushed around by any country, especially one that's not even part of the mainland," Sukebator assured him, pausing to let Jun catch up. "Your nation helped us to stay out of the grasp of the radical left, and for that we are grateful. We will listen to your advice when it's in our best interest."

"Is China giving you any trouble at the present time?"

"No, but the People's Republic of Mongolia and Soviet Russia will bear watching." he replied, putting some distance between the two of them with his long strides before he realized it. "The China situation is immensely complicated. There are still powerful traders in China dealing with their counterparts in Japan. The only people in China that have declared war on your country are the communists."

"How about Chiang Kai-shek's troops?" I puffed.

"Chiang and his Nationalist forces realize your problem is with European control of the coastline. His main concern is with the communists," Gegan informed him, looking between his arms from a tree branch he had rested his elbows on. "He knows you don't believe for a moment that you can take over the whole country, or even want to. Clandestine trade between Japan and China is active and beneficial to the wheeler-dealers on both sides. However, to keep the fat-cats in Washington happy, Chiang must walk a fine line. Obtaining money through America's Lend-Lease Act is very profitable."

"What was that?" Jun asked, hoping the giant would rest a while longer.

"Tree cicadas, a real strident species. I'll say one thing for your country, Kaine; it can sure stir up a hornet's nest. I've seen Germans, Italians, Soviets, Americans, British, and Frenchmen all contributing time, men, and money to defeating your nation."

"We're the first Asian country to take on the whites head to head," I said. "Asia has a lot riding on the outcome of this struggle. It means economic freedom for Asia's capitalist countries, or continued domination by the West, or worse yet, communism."

"I'm more bothered by the thought of good food," Kaine said. "I can taste my mother's Takara Mushi soup even in my sleep."

"What is Takara Mushi?" the Major asked.

"It's made from chicken broth, mushrooms, peas, shrimp, and pumpkin."

"Sounds pretty good. On the way here, I had some lemon-shrimp soup in Thailand that was outstanding," he smiled, remembering the aroma and citric-acid taste. "I hear motor traffic up ahead; we'd better get going."

"If you'll grab some fruit off that tree, Major-san, I'll break out the toasted sesame seeds and roasted eggplant prepared by our illustrious army cooks."

"You bet. We can't stop to catch them, but have you noticed there appears to be fish in every stream?"

"Yes, and I also noticed every bridge on this damn island has been blown up by personnel from platoon 3, like the one just ahead of us."

Sukebator, tearing an entire limb off a fruit tree framed by the red mist with lightning in the background, was an excellent photo opportunity for Agi and his ever-present camera, I thought.

Throwing some of the fruit to the Lance Corporal, Sukebator placed the thick branch, stripped of its foliage, across the creek.

"Hey," Kaine called, reaching down to pick up a bicycle someone had discarded in their haste to get through the jungle. "That branch is wide enough to ride across." We all jumped when the tiny dummy charge accompanied by a loud noise went off. "It was booby-trapped!" Jun noted, too late.

Cramming food to his mouth and taking giant strides, Gegan lifted me out of the stream when I managed to fall off the log. We took the narrow path which quickly turned into an old maintenance road. Gegan waved us on and promised to look us up when we teamed up with the main forces.

Pedaling furiously, Jun Kaine glanced behind long enough to toss the rest of the eggplant and sesame seeds in the Major's direction while shouting, "See you later."

Other members of platoon 4 converged onto the maintenance road both ahead and behind us. Moving swiftly now, I watched the soldiers throw fruit at each other while I munched on the dried food especially prepared for this practice ejection of European forces.

Expecting to reach Yulin by the first or second of December, platoon leaders urged their men to make all possible speed.

Spotting Sakamoto leaning out a window in the communications van, Kaine queried him on the battle strength of the British forces in Malaya.

"It looks as if the British will have nearly a three-to-one manpower advantage," Sakamoto replied, with a worried look on his face. "Believe me, if the Malayans don't help us, it will be a long, hard, ugly campaign."

"Why wouldn't the Malayans help us?" I asked.

"They may be afraid of British reprisals if we don't accomplish our goal. The English have executed resistant leaders in the past."

"What's our next move?"

"The platoons split up yesterday. Half went south on the Gulf of Tonkin side, and the rest of the troops and most of the light armor headed right down the center of the island."

Ibuse was not surprised to find out that I happened to be in the vicinity when the murdered body was found.

"Where are the girls?" Chief Banno asked, studying his map as if it would give him a clue.

Chapter 28

Fiat Fighters

I had talked Yukiko Yoshida into meeting me at the southern tip of Taiwan.
I had arranged a flight for her with a Utility Squadron Five buddy of mine
while I piloted an early model Zero on the three hour trip to the Island's
southernmost airfield. The plane was scheduled for modification, and
I planned to return in the squared-off wing-tipped Zero so it could be
tested under more realistic conditions in Hainan. This ferry trip out of a
field thirty miles north of Yulin would be my last assignment to Taiwan
before hostile fire commenced.

The possibility of deadly combat must have increased the libido, I
thought. I didn't exactly feel guilty about Hisako, just uncomfortable.
After all, I had never proposed to Yukiko. We were more like a comfortable
habit.

* * *

"How have you been?" I asked, speaking through the open window
when I found the rustic cabin she had rented.

From my vantage point I could only see her head.

"I tried that new electric train with the plush seats," she said. "It
goes much faster than the one I took the last time we were here."

"I can't stay long, I told her. "I've got to get back to Hainan."

"Is that right," Yukiko sighed, coming up to the window clad only in a
few wide strips of cloth that fell no farther than the tops of her knee
caps.

"That's a new type of happi coat, isn't it?" I asked, losing track of
the conversation.

"Maybe I'm trying for a new version of happi-ness," she replied,
eyebrows arched.

"That's a terrible pun, but I must see what's under the coat," I
climbed through the window and took slow, measured steps like a wolf
stalking its prey.

"Not so fast," Yukiko warned, backing up, using the same unhurried pattern as her pursuer. "You must plan your itinery to Hainan. You have no time to lose."

"Perhaps I spoke a little hastily," I granted, my fingertips finding nothing but thin air as she spun away from me.

"Don't chase me, future Ghost Leader," she protested, one panel of her coat sliding open to reveal more of the skin-coloring I adored. "I'm hunting for a pencil so we can plan your trip back."

"You said you had a joke poem for Ghosts?"

Pulling me down to the floor, she recited the verse in a husky voice.

"There was a pilot named Ghost,
   Who sent me flowers by post.
What do you do in return?
   For a bunch of dead ferns,
Can you make him live up to his boast?"

The mixture of the enigmatic verse and close proximity to her dropped my sleepy-sounding voice another octave. "Stay still a moment, Yukiko," I said, reaching for her. "I just want to see what kind of material the coat is made of."

"It's not finished yet," she said, standing up. "I haven't had a chance to sew the panels together. Besides, you sound like you need a nap. You shouldn't rush around exerting yourself."

"I'll take a nap if you'll join me," I promised, thinking I had her trapped.

"I might, if you didn't have to make out that flight plan," she purred, her cinnamon eyes taking on a mischievous look.

"All right," I said gracefully, knowing when I was defeated. "I'll stay till tomorrow morning."

With that announcement, Yukiko found a reason for looking at the bottom edge of one of the cloth strips. "I don't remember how much I hemmed," she said, slowly pulling it up to her eyes for a closer look.

"I don't care," I babbled watching her right side become gradually unveiled from calf to thigh to waist to breast to neck. Not waiting for an answer, I tackled her around the knees in a cushy movement that ended up with our bodies entwined on the padded floor. Lifting her in my arms, I duck-walked over to a pile of softer bedding, falling into the fluffy material, encountering little or no resistance.

Indeed, looking at it from *Wen Kumi*, northern Japan's evil spirit in charge of temptations, point of view, you could say she helped.

"Do you want to play doctor, nurse?" I asked between lingering kisses.

"Do you have a field of expertice you're particularly interested in?" Yukiko murmured.

"I specialize in annual physicals," I bragged, kissing the tip of her nose.

"How much are your fees?" she whispered tickling my ear. "Do I have to make an appointment?"

"I'm always available where you're concerned, sweet one. No charge. But I have to warn you, my examination technique has not yet been approved by the medical board."

"Ghosts do carry stethoscopes, don't they?" Yukiko asked shyly.

"You'll find this phantom to be the standard variety, honey," I answered in the same half-serious tone, while pulling her tightly to me.

* * *

November was just about gone by the time I had brought the squared-wing Zero back to the hastily constructed airfield just ahead of the fast-moving army.

Segawa met me with the air ambulance and orders to stay with the medic unit until further notice.

Moving away from the air-evac plane, the copilot and I strolled over to look at at a pre-production model of an army Ki-44 Devil-Queller.

What a beautiful fighter plane," Segawa pointed out. " I heard that a Nakajima test pilot took it out to 400 mph and climbed to 35,000 feet in under five minutes."

"It's got a powerplant that was designed to be installed on a bomber," I threw in.

Ten thousand feet above us, two Fire Dragon fighters roared off at full power toward the Chinese coastline.

A radioman in the communications van hastily fine-tuned his receiver to the air squadron's frequency and plugged it into the loudspeaker. I heard Tomi in Black Magic Two One Five say, "Do you have the bogies in sight?"

"Two One Five, from Two One Six," said the answering pilot. "We've got a mixed bag below us. Three Italian Breda fighter planes escorting a German-built Heinkel bomber, all pretending to be Chinese aircraft."

"I'll bet two yen the bomber pilot is either American or Australian," Black Magic Two One Five wagered.

"You're on," Two One Six countered. "My guess is Russian or Italian."

"If we swat those low-flying birds," Two One Five warned, "the one sitting up on the perch will have us in its sights."

"If we had someone at a higher altitude we could take them all out," Two One Six declared. "

Tired of warming the bench. I intended to demonstrate to my teammates what a big league prospect can do.

"My buddy Tomi can use some help," I hollered, racing for the hot new plane.

"You can't do that," Segawa screamed. "There's only seven of them in existence, and you've never flown one before."

"I've piloted plenty of Nakajima aircraft," I shouted, vaulting up on the wing and into the cockpit. This was my chance to get rid of the faint-hearted label that had been wrongly hung on me.

"You'll spend the rest of your life in the brig," Segawa warned. "At a minimum you'll never get promoted to chief petty officer.

I found I had a hard time seeing over the front of the big engine.

Segawa shook his head, and with the assistance of a curious mechanic pulled the prop through a couple of times.

With both external and internal batteries on line I hit the starter button.

The engine coughed and sputtered even though the temperature gauge was registering seventy degrees.

Hitting the button again, I got a cloud of smoke and a deep-seated roar--I was in business.

"Hainan Tower, this is Devil-Queller Seven One Six, taking off on an emergency," I said, rolling past the communications plane on my left.

Closing the two piece canopy, I sat up straight, applied power and hit the runway at high speed in anticipation of a short field climb out.

Pulling back hard on the stick, I yanked the plane up at an angle that drove my head and shoulders deep into the backrest. That'll show them the aggressive side of my nature, I thought.

"Just like a Tokyo night club," I heard Tomi say. "Sensory pleasures await the bold."

Having reached maximum speed at level flight, the Black Magic fighters dove on the escorts. Thinking they had the Fire Dragons in a vulnerable position, the rest of the Italian fighters committed themselves.

The mixture of pleasurable anticipation and terror knotted my stomach as I drove the massive-engined Devil Queller to a commanding altitude. I procrastinated too long closing the space separating me from the two Breda fighters. A burst of fiery-red steel from the 7.7 mm and 12.7 mm guns of *Dolly* reduced the lead Italian aircraft to a trail of smoke, and forced a hastily parachuting occupant to abandon the other one.

I had the Nazi-built Heinkle in my gunsight as it came within range, but was deprived of the victory, when the *Dolly Madison* special blew the bomber's port engine into a cascading mass of valves, seals, rocker arms, and safety wire. Five crew members, the normal complement for a twin engine Heinkle, quickly scrambled out before the fire spread.

Tomi rolled his aircraft in a manner more in keeping with a tumbleweed than a precision maneuver.

Suckered into believing he had caused Tomi's Ki-27 to go out of control, the veteran Italian fighter pilot took his eyes off the fluttering aircraft to look for another target.

Hoping the plane could take the strain, I tightened my stomach and leg muscles and started into a hi-g turn--intending to finish off the Italian pilot with the aircraft markings that showed he had been part of the team that flew at 440 mph to break the world's speed record back in 1934.

I relaxed stick pressure too soon, and lost the target to Tomi's wingman. Concerned now, because the dogfight had taken me deep into Chinese territory. I started a gentle, wide-sweeping turn to head back to Hainan. I expected high praises from the Black Magic pilots for my timely entrance into battle.

"Next time you might try a few more g's when you're fighting," Tomi's wingman said.

I had struck out again.

Four Fiat fighters lying in wait for me pulled off an all-pro squeeze play. They were powered by 840 hp air-cooled radial engines and flown by Mussolini's *Legionarias,* all aces from the Spanish Civil War. The cockpit talk between the Italian pilots was picked up and relayed by the communications van. Devil Queller's demise was brief, deadly, and unpleasant according to their chatter.

"Tuonare Due, aeroporto Giapponese, tocco. From Thunder Two, "Japanese aircraft at one o'clock," the air station translater said.

"Preparare!" Tuonare Due. "Attacco!"

"Get ready, from Thunder Two," relayed the interpreter, followed by, "Attack!"

Taking advantage of their numbers and altitude, they decended on me.

212

When I failed to react quickly enough, each Fiat fired a long burst from its twin l2.7 mm machine guns into my aircraft, then departed under full throttle.

This had been a four hit shutout.

"Tuonare Due from Tuonare Uno, "Excellente," was the final transmission before the Fiat volunteers joined up.

"I don't think that needs any translation," the interpreter said, sounding worried about me.

With my right hand and control stick covered with blood, unable to think clearly, and too weak to bail out, I fought to get the powerful-looking aircraft and its shot-up engine under control.

In rapid sequence, the oil overheat light came on, the engine lubricant evaporated, and the final chapter of Devil Queller Seven One Six was being written. Squinting in an attempt to see through the blood-streaked goggles, oblivious to the smell of burning rubber and superheated metal, I struggled to keep the fatally wounded aircraft from diving straight into the ground.

The rice field to my left looked shallow, and if everything went right, I hoped to bring the plane down without a catastrophic ending. After a quick debate with myself on whether or not to try flaps, I reached over and pushed the flap handle down. So far, so good.

Terror played tricks with my technique and my blood-soaked hand slipped forward on the control stick, tossing me downward at a critical juncture in the flare-out stage of the landing. In the frantic few seconds it took me to grasp the stick with my left hand, and with no extra power to recover, I stared at an untimely death.

The aircraft's nose slammed into the rice paddy, smashed through the watery vegetation , hit a dirt mound, flipped over, and came to rest upside-down amidst a cloud of steam and churning water.

Shaking, I nearly pushed the harness release button before having second thoughts. In the absence of restraints, I'd end up in a heap, still inverted, without room to maneuver. Better take this slow, I thought, finding it hard to concentrate with the blood rushing to my head. One step at a time. First, I'll bang on the canopy. Because of the crash, it might have a weak spot.

Using my fist, I hit the glass hard in an attempt to break it loose. Again and again I pounded on the side of the glass enclosure. Realizing the possibility of water leaking through the air vents, I increased the number of blows in proportion to the amount of dampness I felt at the top of my head. The cloth helmet was acting like a sponge.

Gasoline fumes added to my woes. I opened my hand when the knuckles became too lacerated and raw to take any more punishment. Wincing, I slammed my palm against the canopy--until it too, became nothing but a crippled handicap.

Rejecting the sight of my torn up glove, I took a deep breath and tried the impossible with my left. First the fist, then the palm, until, covered with blood and gore, it became no more useful in forcing open the cockpit canopy than its counterpart.

Ignoring the excruiating pain in my hands, and the moisture that had reached my eyebrows, I fumbled past the holstered 9 mm automatic pistol, the shoulder wound, the belt of amunition, and the parachute harness, until I found my survival knife. Grasping the handle of the knife between my wrists, I, in agonizingly small steps, worked the hilt into my mouth. Keeping the knife in place by anchoring it with my forearms, I pried savagely at the compound between glass and metal until I was exhausted.

Trembling with excertion. I used the tips of my thumbs, the only part of my hands not hurting, to release the latching mechanism on the safety harness.

Squirming around in the enclosed confinement until I no longer resembled a piece of U-shaped dough, I ended up sideways to the dash board--my booted feet rested against the glass structure.

Wiggling my toes in nervous anticipation, I took another deep breath and forced myself to relax. When the tension on my aching muscles had eased somewhat, I drew my knees back to my chest for leverage and gave a vicious kick to the side panel.

The metal strips ripped loose and the glassed-in framework fell off into six inches of water and rice shoots.

I climbed out, wet, but elated.

Overhead, the Fiat *pilotas* performed a series of snap rolls to shake off the adreniline overdose.

At the end of their third roll, my receiver suddenly came to life. "Two Fiats at three o'clock level!" That sounded like Ghost Leader. "How did you get here?" I yelled into the mike before I saw the external fuel tanks.

There was no acknowledgement of my transmission and my transmitter indicator light never came on.

The Fiats tighten up their combat formation. They must have gotten the word in some Hong Kong bar that Japanese naval aviators flying Mitsubishi Zeros were a handful for even the most skillful European fighter pilot.

"Although the Fiats were built in Italy and flown by Italian pilots," Ghost Leader announced, "they're carrying the insignia of the International Squadron to keep up the pretense of remaining neutral."

I mimicked the steps the Silent Storm aviators were taking to prepare themselves for battle. Reflector gunsight on, arm/safe switch to arm, then grasp the knife handle-shaped throttle switch to release the firing lever for the 7.7 mm weapons..

I reached into the recesses on top of the instrument panel pretending to manually charge the two machine guns, then the two 20mm cannon, which would be charged electrically.

"Silent Storm flight, get rid of your drop tanks," Ghost Leader ordered. He would be adjusting his gunsight to compensate for the amount of sunlight streaming in the cockpit.

When I saw the ejected eighty-seven gallon tanks leave the aircraft, I tugged at my left glove out of habit.

Ghost Leader's two wingman flew as a synchronized pair. That was probably *Genda Circus* in 414 going high, and *Wako,* paid for by public donations, and named after the fifteenth century pirates who practiced democracy, going low.

My eyes, resembling nature's most successful predator, blazed with anger at the arrogance of the European mercenaries. I looked at the Devil Queller's useless gunsight, frustrated that one of Mussolini's Fiats wasn't drifting into my electronic crosshairs.

"Watch out, Ghost Leader!" demanded *Wako* to his superior. "We're both after the same aircraft."

"Go after the three in the clouds, *Genda,*" he commanded.

I watched *Genda's Circus* pour 20 mm shells into a Fiat fighter's exposed belly, while he simultanously twisted his aircraft around for a follow-up shot. Before he got into a new firing position, the Fiat blew up, sending a steady stream of debris heading back to earth.

The engine and parts of the main frame fell closest to me with a loud splash, the pilot's seat and oxygen tank somewhat further away.

I had to walk a short distance before I recognized the next group of fallen objects as a scorched flight jacket, shattered goggles and a map case.

Bits of hair and slivers of skin, I knew, would drift with the wind, and would drop to the ground at a later time.

Next time, this could easily be me, I thought. Unless I learn how to be a winner.

I couldn't spot the Zeros. I guessed they had left the area. I assumed the remaining two Italian aviators had departed for their Chinese airbase. Mussolini's mechanics, upon greeting the Fiats' return, were sure to be unhappy at seeing half the morning launch wiped out.

Wait! The Zeros had done a 360 degee turn. I turned up the radio full volume and raced up the nearest hill in the direction the Fiats had taken.

I could see the airfield from my higher vantage site.

To the horror of the Italian pilots touching down on the runway, believing they were home free, the Silent Storm aircraft reappeared in the opening phase of a strafing run. Their twin 7.7 mm machine guns chatted softly as they probed for the target. The louder, deeper-voiced cannons joined in, making it a deadly quartet. The lead Fiat, attempting to get airborne again, was the first to get hit by *Wako's* exploding 20 mm shells, sending the Legionaire spinning into the path of his sidekick. The destructive force generated by the blasted aircraft gave birth to a tangled mass of fire, smoldering rubber, scalding hydraulic fluid and burning bodies.

"If the Italians want to pretend to be Chinese, they better learn the language, instead of speaking in their native tongue over the air," *Wako* commented as I returned to the Ki-44.

"I suppose the Facist hope the so-called yellow race will kill each other off," Ghost Leader radioed.

My receiver was working fine, but I had no transmitter.

The Zeros must have spotted my downed aircraft, because one of them peeled off and flew directly overhead wagging his wings. He then steered toward a stream to the south of me. I took his down-river heading as an indication of the direction I should travel to get to Japanese lines.

My walk to friendly territory took an hour--and transportation to the coast and hence to Hainan was fast. I rejoined my surprised copilot the following day. He was sure I had been killed.

December I, I94I

"Jump in," Sakamoto said, reaching out a hand from inside the communications van. Once again I had been talked into letting Segawa proceed to Yulin alone.

"Thanks," I said, managing to get aboard by using my bandaged hands before the clumsy vehicle pulled out.

"With nobody shooting at us, this should be a quick trip" Mallory Agi stated, He took a seat behind the professor as the caravan led by a six-wheeled staff car picked up speed.

216

Our final plunge down the central part of Hainan, eating army food and learning to ford rivers would be something to shout about later on, providing we finish the last twenty miles with Kaine doing the driving.

"Speaking of speed. Knowing that Japan was going to stay neutral in the European conflict," Sakamoto said, grabbing for a handhold after a particularly hard bump,

"Your favorite Western bureaucracy, the Department of Omissions," Agi declared. "left out vital information about the tremendous build up of Soviet arms and manpower hundreds of miles behind the battlelines. The new Russian factories are turning out tanks, aircraft, rocket barrage equipment, artillery, and munitions of every type in staggering amounts."

The biggest delay on the road south happened when two amubulances managed to run into each other on a wide-open highway. "All Tokyo taxi drivers should be banned from driving any vehicle in places where there are no narrow streets or stop signs to impede their race car attitude," Private Agi suggested between periodic lurches

Fidgety and tired of the subject matter, I was lucky enough to find an accommodating motorcycle driver when he pulled up alongside the van.

With a hurried goodbye to the discussion group, I jumped into the sidecar. After a breathtaking ride, we reached the southern tip of the island much quicker than the rest of the convoy.

"Drop me off here," I told the driver when I spotted a directional sign to Ya Xian. I can find transportation the last few miles to Yulin.

Grabbing my knapsack, I dug out Shiroko's address, and headed for the little beach resort. I entered the tourist spot almost before I could work up a sweat.

Not finding her at home, I relaxed on the sandy beach for a couple of hours recharging my batteries for the upcoming confrontation in Malaya. There wasn't much time left before the shooting started.

When I got to the outskirts of Yulin, I phoned Segawa.

"Your new duty station will be in Vietnam," he informed me. "Your transportation will be arranged by the harbor master."

"I'll be ready," I said, elated.

"Women are running your life, Debuchi. You went on a trip to Shanghai because of Jane Howell and now scuttlebutt says that Hisako Bayar arranged this latest transfer."

"I don't think Hisako has that kind of power," I said, hanging up.

It was another two hours before the communications van arrived. I followed their procession through the main street of the port city down to the water front.

Lance Corporal Kaine drove the van past the hospital ship *Whispering Wind* docked at pier 3 and parked it at pier 4 where the *Ikeda Maru's* cargo handlers were standing.

The army band, dressed in their white summer uniforms with red caps and red shoulder boards, wore shiny black leather pouches on the hip just for the occasion. They had been playing all morning and the martial musicians showed signs of fatique.

Hiding behind the band, a nervous Atsu Ogata waited for her Uncle Benjiro to appear. When Sergeant Ogata came into view she stepped out into the roadway.

"Take over Corporal," he ordered, after he spotted his kin in a mid-calf length khaki tropical uniform with big pockets, scarf, silver buckled belt, and black calico scuffles. The restrained steps he took to close the distance between them, displayed his wish to adhere to all the ancient and charming dignity of the rural farmers--but it did seem peculiar to those from the coastal areas.

Atsu was not so inhibited. She came on the run, then suddenly stopped, bowed and moved forward slowly to give him a big hug. "I'm so glad to see you," his rosy-cheeked niece said with a smile. But when he seemed uncomfortable with the thought of touching in public, she dropped her hands.

He bowed his head a number of times in a nervous manner, pleading with his eyes for Astu to understand how much seeing her meant to him.

Do you have to rejoin your platoon right away?" Atsu asked.

"Not until tomorrow," Benjiro Ogata replied, knowing his corporal would fill in for him.

"Where are you going for the next few hours, Professor?" Kaine asked, after they placed their gear aboard the *Ikeda Maru*.

"I thought I'd take a tour of Yulin's naval facilities," Sakamoto replied, rubbing the sore spots caused by the less than comfortable army vehicles. "Why don't you guys come with me?"

I decided to tag along. I needed a new pair of skivvies to replace my shredded ones.

"Don't Spain, Finland, and Italy also have troops shoulder to shoulder with their Nazis compatriots?" Jun asked, squinting his eyes to block out the sun, trying to remember what it was like to be cold.

"Yes, and not acknowledging the immense build-up of the Russian Army," Agi said, while bending his head back in an effort to see the top of the crane, "allowed the American side of the Atlantic to say their armed forces were needed to stop the Nazis. This was a major requirement to justify America's shooting war in the Atlantic."

"You're absolutely right, Agi-san, and meanwhile, Japan scrambled to find a source of oil, but has had no luck, because the tentacles of the British Global Empire reach everywhere," Michi Sakamoto explained, turning into a small-boat repair shop. "In order to survive, Japan will have to face Britain on the battlefield."

"The Burmese have oil fields," Agi proposed, stumbling over a pipe wrench. "But purchasing their oil means a fight with the British in Malaya, Hong Kong, and Singapore." he stammered, putting a hand out to grab a stanchion. "With Britain out of the way, Burma can profit from the sale of its oil, and Japan will have a source for this vital fluid."

Two navy policemen, distinctive in appearance because of the single-row, brass-buttoned tunics, coupled with shoulder boards depicting the judge advocate's office, directed them away from critical work areas. Shore patrolmen positioned further down the street kept traffic flowing.

"Did you know Ambassador Grew notified Roosevelt that an oil embargo would lead to war?" Sakamoto asked, unable to hear Kaine's comment. "Grew's message was received, but produced no results. The power-politicians gave no indication of their disapproval of an oil embargo even if it forced Japan to attack."

"No, that's news to me," Agi countered. "But I heard the dollar-a-year men are now distributed throughout Washington. The bureaucracy is no longer the stable, go-slow institution that keeps hot-heads from bringing on a crisis situation.

"Power was funneled into the hands of those with the most influence with the President," Michi said, curious enough about the welding process to stand and watch a shipfitter use a torch on a broken spar.

Kaine spoke up promptly. "America's seven thousand miles away."

Sakamoto, shading his eyes as he stepped out of the repair shop, nodded in agreement. "You're right. However, the American Strategic Bombers--the B-I7 Flying Fortress, and the B-24 Liberators were designed to overcome that disadvantage. And now, they have a full scale mock-up of the B-29 Super Fortress."

"Miiko!" Jun squeaked in a loud voice as we entered the retail store.

A pretty, diminutive woman in high-heels with a wide black belt pulled tight around her waist, quickly placed a hand to her mouth. She turned around, both embarrassed and pleased at the look of astonishment on the soldier's face, as he rushed towards her.

The daily routine of the store was interrupted as the armed forces customers and employees paused to watch the eager soldier hurry to greet the glowing lady.

Kaine, not concerned about his culture's distaste for public displays of affection, hugged the loveable Miiko as she ducked her head self-consciously.

"I'm so glad to see you, Jun dear," Miiko whispered, her face a bright pink.

After saying, "hello," Sakamoto acknowledged Jun Kaine's introductions. All of us were charmed by Miiko's soft Kyoto accent. Michi finished with, "We'll see you later; don't forget briefing at ten tomorrow," then he pulled the rest of his team into another sector of the store, leaving the two of them to pursue their unexpected rendezuous.

By evening, I had received my written orders to report to the Silent Storm squadron at Vidhya Air Base. I hoped that would entitle me to have painted, not chalked, *Mitsubishi Melody* on the nose of the aircraft, and as a bonus, maybe my name stenciled in under the canopy.

My transportation to a forward airfield in Vietnam turned out to be the *Ikeda*. In the meantime I was hanging out with the discussion group on the dock. The communications van would shortly be loaded aboard.

"Where's Kaine?" the motorcycle trooper inquired, taking the opportunity to wipe off his wind visor while he pretended not to be staring at the king-sized Manchukuon coming toward the van.

"Is it true, Japanese officers eat, drink and participate in sports with the enlisted men?" Major Sukebator asked. "I hope so, because I've been assigned as liaison for the Manchukuon volunteers."

"*Hai!* And not only that, they spend off-duty time with them and become a substitute family member," Sakamoto allowed. "The officers listen to their men, and are expected to lend a helping hand whenever they have problems."

The army band, on their way to the ship after completing a special jazz session for the general and his staff, stopped when they saw a group of soldiers and a bewildered-looking aviator sitting on foldup chairs in animated and almost heated conversation.

"America seems determined to maneuver Japan into making the first move," Agi said. "For all of Churchill's and Roosevelt's pre-war speeches about the red menace, Asia's deeply felt concerns about communism are being disregarded by America's Secretary of State."

"Japan is extremely nervous about the possibility of China turning communist," Sakamoto disclosed, motioning for the band members to join them. "There are communes right here in Hainan. China, once it settles its internal strife, should be able to reject both the Western and Japanese quasi-control of her homeland, and take her rightful place as an honorable and ancient civilization. She has been badly mistreated by all parties. Because of the interference in her internal affairs, and the inability to see China for anything but a market place, the world has been cutoff from the counseling of a country with a civilization stretching back over four thousand years."

The motorcycle trooper could no longer contain himself. "I don't see how this regiment can inflict much damage on the Global Empire. From what I've seen, our army appears to be made up of men who carry parasols, matched luggage, and snowshoes. There's even, I understand, a sailor going aboard the *Ikeda Maru* with his peacoat laid out in case the temperature drops below ninety degrees. To say nothing of an aircraft carrier that shoots up tomato crates and a wild rumor on the fighter plane frequency about a female aerial gunner."

"That reminds me, Professor," Kaine said, moving around a saxaphone-carrying corporal. "Last year I heard a group of sailors, back from shore leave in Mexico, talking about articles they read in United States newspapers that said Japan is a totalitarian state."

"Definitely not. It's too difficult in a culture like ours for any one person to accumulate enough power to duplicate the one-man rule associated with Western nations. Our democracratic government is still functioning. The Japanese industrialist do not kowtow before Prime Minister Tojo. Calling us militaristic is not only wrong but counterproductive," Michi said, angrily. "As you probably heard, in Japan, you can't take a walk around the block without obtaining a consensus. Just to give you an idea how the power is split, there were seven million votes for the Labor Party this year.

"America is already in an undeclared war on the Atlantic side of the world," Sakamoto exclaimed, standing up to lean on the back of his chair, "and is supplying military hardware to England and Holland's occupation forces in the Pacific."

"Speaking of war," the lieutenant from the military band commented, running a finger inside his tight collar like a schoolboy to relieve his nervousness. "Can this attack on the occupation forces be called off?" he asked looking towards Sakamoto.

The group leaned forward to hear the professor's answer.

"The destruction of the American fleet can be. But not the Malayan endeavor. We are fearful of the United States and would give a great deal to keep her out of the war.

"Can't some sort of compromise be reached, Professor?" "Isn't there any way to keep them out?"

"We believe that Anglophiles, Admiral Stark and General Marshall urged the administration to back Britain if Japan tries to get the British occupation forces out of the Orient. This information has been widely disseminated throughout Asia. Our leaders are very concerned. Apparently, only Asians will ever be asked to leave Asian territory by the United States, certainly not Europeans or Americans. Japan would be willing to withdraw her troops from China if the United States would do likewise in the Philippines."

Sakamoto passed out copies of several American magazines with articles that discussed the fire-bombing of Japan. "If you'll notice," he said. "They even go so far as to show possible routes from Siberia, the Philippines, the Aleution Islands, and the British Colonies. Apparently, they expect any hostility with Japan to be concluded within a few months."

An MP, wearing a white band on his helmet for night duty, told the motorcyclist to move on. Taking maximum advantage of his heavy boots, the trooper started the engine with one kick.

"Here's a late-breaking announcement from Hong Kong," the radioman said rushing out of the van. "Britain's King-Emperor declares a state of emergency in Malaya and has put the country on a war footing."

"Will the convoy be traveling in dangerous waters now that Britain is ready for battle?" Gegan asked, turning towards the MP.

"You can expect Western military action at any time. The United States had already warned Britain that Japan will be moving against His Royal Majesty's occupation troops in the Far East."

"Any news on the family fight in Europe, Professor?" the motorcyclist asked, gunning the engine.

"The high-water mark was reached in the European War when the

Romanian, German, Hungarian, and Italian troops were stopped on the outskirts of Moscow after suffering massive losses, and Soviet Russia has taken the offensive with renewed vigor. A United German/Finnish army has been contained, and Bulgarian, Czechoslovakian, Polish, Scandinavian and Spanish volunteers to the Nazis army--particularly those in the SS regiments --are no longer the major threat to the Allies they once appeared.

"The Russian military will be on the move again as the coldest part of the year approaches," explained a captain in the tank troop, sitting with legs spread apart, wearing spurs given to him by his father, a former cavalryman. "Although America is sending land-lease material to Communist Russia, it is only a drop in the bucket compared to the enormous Red Army requirements; however, the new Soviet war factories are able to handle the load. And we will not stop shipments of war materials to Russia via Vladivostok. We don't want to aid the Nazis."

"Can we get to Malaya before America hits Japan with B-l7s?" shipboard librarian Agi asked, feeling left out with so many others participating.

"It will be close," Sakamoto stressed. "Roosevelt has floated a suggestion to his cabinet to find out their reaction to a sneak attack on Japan. Leaks to the press have been initiated to get the response to an offensive war from the Philippines. More communiques have come from America on the ease of setting Japanese cities on fire, with no mention of the danger to children. It is our understanding that incendiary bombs are on their way for the Strategic Bombing Squadrons based in Luzon."

"How long are you going to be staying outside the van, Lieutenant?" the MP asked. "There are men sleeping nearby."

"Not long, Sergeant," Sakamoto assured him.

"Why this desire to burn cities?" Gegan asked.

"From day one, the political thinking has been not to beat Japan's army, navy and airforce," Michi inserted, before the MP could say anything more. "It wants to prevent a new generation of super salesmen from operating long enough for their 'soapers' to get a piece of the action. Britain is also in favor of ravaging the cities."

"Japan has been very careful about her neutrality," Agi advised, turning towards the band which now occupied half the semi-circle to his left. "It turned down the German offer to join the Axis side in the war in l939, and again this year. Even though we are rejecting the fascist side, there have been no offers from the Allied leaders. War would not have come between anybody but the Global Empire and Japan if the West hadn't applied an economic stranglehold. Japan is well aware of the armed might of the West."

"Professor, even though we're anti-Nazis, we're also anti-communist. Give us some more information on Russia," Agi urged.

"The U.S.S.R. has already introduced the best battle tank in the war. With all due respect to our tank forces," Professor Sakamoto said applogetically, conscious of the fact that a tank corps captain was still in the group. "The T-34 is in mass production and is making its presence felt on the European front. The Soviets established a battlefield combination far superior to anything Gold Dust or the Nazis have access to when it combined the T-34 tank, the new M-3l rocket launcher, and the heavily armored and heavily armed Sturmovik ground attack aircraft--some of which may be flown by women."

"Which is the more devastating, the plane or the women?" I wanted to know.

"I just hope we never have to find out," Sakamoto said with a smile. "Although there will be many gigantic battles and much suffering on Soviet soil still ahead for the Russian people, the United States citizens reading their newspaper this morning should have realized that the ultimate outcome in Europe has already been decided.

'If someone had ever cut Great Britain's oil sources off," Gegan remarked out of nowhere. "They'd have used their military forces immediately to obtain a supply. Like Japan, England is an island depending on trade for its very survival."

"This talk is cancelled because of darkness," Sakamoto exaggerated. "You," he declared, looking at Agi, "have kept us talking all afternoon. It's dinner time." At which point I took off.

"We can't blame Kaine for keeping us from missing a meal. He isn't with us."

"I suspect he slipped off somewhere with Miiko," Sukebator remarked.

I'd try finding Shiroko early in the morning.

Chapter 29

Ya Xian Beach

December 2, 1941
Standing on the warm sand, Jun Kaine smiled. "Hiding a girl as pretty as you in a navy town was not an easy thing to do, especially one wearing a crinkly, organdy-colored, cotton dress.

Miiko blushed.

"You're wearing Getas with your Western attire!" the teen-aged looking Kaine said, surprised at the thought.

"What could be more appropriate for hot weather, than these wooden breeze-catchers. Open-toed, open-heeled, open-sides, and I'm wearing the thicker style to keep me out of the mud when it rains."

"I thought you seemed taller," he remarked, standing close to her.

"Why are you wearing those diagonally wrapped cloth strips between your knees and ankles? Puttees I think you call them," the amber-eyed, woman asked, finding her bare legs and thigh-high hemline more suitable for the warmer climate. "Extra fabric seems out of place with a tropical uniform," she kidded him. "Don't want to show your bare legs, huh?"

"It's wonderful to have the chance to be with you, Miiko," Jun said, ignoring the good-natured comment, "but I must admit, you're the last person I expected to see on this island. How did you do it?"

"I was flown here in a blue and yellow utility plane. I have to be back by the 5th of December. Transportation for civilians will be difficult to arrange after that date."

"Did I embarrass you by my enthusiastic greeting in the store, yesterday?" Jun Kaine asked, concerned about her feelings.

"Not really. You'd be surprised at how fast old customs are dying out.. Especially along the coast. Besides, we've been watching films from all over the world for years now. It's just the older generation and the rural people who still have trouble adapting."

225

"What were you doing at the Yulin Naval Base?"

"I'm giving a three day course at the base hospital on an accounting system that Tokyo University has been using. This is my second day; I'll leave tomorrow afternoon."

"They brought you all the way to Hainan just to give a lecture?"

"I'm also doing a favor for a legal officer attached to the naval district in southern Japan. He gave me a personal message to pass along to someone named Shiroko Daizen in the security department."

"I wonder why it wasn't mailed?"

"The addressee is somewhat garbled and since Shiroko comes under the judge advocate general's command, the legal officer assigned her the job of figuring out who to give it to.

"Where are you staying?"

"Over at the nurses' quarters. I'm sleeping in Mariko's old room, she's a nurse rumored to be stationed on a hospital ship."

"How did you manage that?"

"Her girl friend, Atsu, suggested it," Miiko said. "Atsu has an uncle aboard the *Ikeda Maru*. Sergeant Ogata. Do you know him?"

"He's not in my platoon--but I got acquainted with him when he surprised us with a bubble bath."

"That sounds like a wild ship. You must tell me about it some time."

"How did you hear about Ya Xian?"

"An off-duty nurse told me about it. And as you can see, Ya Xian is a popular resort less than ten miles up the coast on a first-class highway," Miiko said proudly. "And since I had access to Mariko's 1937 Datsun...." she mumbled, looking away from him.

"Miiko dear, I was happy to suggest we spend time walking in the sand when we were viewing the moon in Yulin last night," he said. "After you informed me that you had keys to a car. That wasn't a hint, was it?"

"You brought up the subject without my prompting," she replied with a hand to her mouth. "But I did say I had to be back early," she said, speaking between her fingers.

"That was quite an assortment of vehicles in the lot where the car was parked," Jun said, "I was surprised to see a Mitsubishi bus, a Honda racing car, an old Toyota A-l, and a Nissan Motor Company truck all in one place. "How does one get gas around here?"

"We're only a short boat trip from China. Enterprising Chinese merchants ferry fuel over to the island in exchange for rubber all the time

"That short, pleasant drive along the coastline, coupled with the joy of finding no one at Ya Xai beach, has put me in a mood for some foolishness," Kaine whispered.

"There's a stream over to your left for drinking water, Miiko pointed out, as she grabbed two large towels from the back seat and ran for a minature sand dune formed by nature's deft hand.

"I'll be the girl who needs rescuing. Like the ones you see in those French Foreign Legion films," she informed him from her spot on top of the sand hill.

"I'm on my way," he announced, kicking off his shoes.

"Halfway up, he was pelted with one of Miiko's wooden clogs. "Not yet. I want to relax and enjoy the sun," she said, pulling the towel over herself and throwing the other sandal at him.

She giggled.

"How can you enjoy the sun if you have something over you?" Jun Kaine teased.

"Take this!" she said, tossing him an extra towel. "I'll show you."

Bewildered, he caught it and looked at her for instructions.

Petite Miiko, completely covered by the huge bath towel, seemed to be doing something underneath it, he thought, watching the absorbent cloth move in an irregular pattern.

"It's more enjoyable if you get the sun a little at a time," she said, as she pushed her dress out from under the cloth covering her.

"Well, I guess it wouldn't hurt to get down to my underwear," Jun said. But after removing his shirt, trousers, and puttees, he discovered a slight problem. The towel barely stretched from his chin to his knees. Any movement and he was out in the open.

"I see why the army makes you guys wear those cloth wrappings. It's to cover your shin bones," Miiko advised him, sticking a shapely leg out from her improvised cotton tent for his inspection.

"Did you feel the earth shake with my desire for you?" Kaine pleaded like a sailor on a weekend pass.

"What a coincidence, Jun dear. I thought I felt this pile of sand move. Apparently I have a good imagination."

"I'm just beginning to realize that, my Queen of sand and sea."

"Did you know your eyes are the color of coffee with just a dash of cream?" she murmured, looking down at him from the short distance separating them.

He was saved from answering when a small brassiere went flying through the air. I can't believe this is my Miiko, Jun thought, throwing his undershirt to the four winds.

"It feels so nice to have the sun on my naked body," Miiko said, lifting up the side of the towel to block Kaine's view, while still allowing the sun's rays to shine on her.

"You did say naked," he mumbled, reaching down to remove his shorts.

A sharp gust of wind flipped the bottom end of Miiko's towel off her body. Reaching up to help her, he found himself with more flesh than cloth. "I've got it, I've got it," she assured him, yanking the towel down around her.

What a sexy body, he marveled, getting a long enough look to form an opinion before she could get her barrier in place.

Raising the towel again to let the sun in on the side away from him, Miiko felt the first dreadful rumble from the bowels of the earth. She dropped her bath cloth in fright as the ground moved enough to roll her down the two foot high sand embankment. Bumping up against Jun, she fought for a piece of his towel to hide under.

He put his arms around her as the beach continued to shake. Nudging, kissing, and rolling up against each other accelerated the exploring process.

With each sway, excitement mounted.

The rocks behind them groaned, the sea tilted and their fervor for each other grew.

Miiko dug her nails into his shoulders, trying to hold on as the earth's bucking bronco continued its unrelenting oscillations in its role as grand champion.

"Suppose there's a Tsunami?" he panted, when the earth rolled Miiko on her back.

"Who cares, you darling fool," she cried, reaching for him. "These may be our last moments."

The world heaved, the bodies surged.

The earth took a minute to rest, but not the two entwined inhabitants on Ya Xian's lonely beach. Their efforts grew more frantic and rythmatic. Except for the moans and husky whisperings of the lovers throw together by mother nature, the strip of sand was deadly quiet, like the lull before the storm.

"Gentle, dozo, Jun dear," Mikko asked in hushed tones. "You're as inexperienced with the ultimate act of love as me."

As the two lovers in their wild ecstasy stepped up to the highest sensuous peak, eager to fall into the peaceful valley on the other side of the summit, mother nature struck again. This time with a vengeance. The pair was tossed and turned, united in pleasure so complete that tears as well as laughter permeated the internal pulsations screaming for biological release.

It was over. Miiko and Jun lay quietly, hand-in-hand, listening to an earth returning to its more passive state.

"At least we didn't get one of those deadly Tsunami's," Kaine uttered lazily, his heartbeat coming back to normal.

"Maybe the earth didn't, but I'm not sure about me," Miiko suggested, her soft Kyoto accent more noticeable. "What is the exact definition of Tsunami anyway?"

"Harbor wave," he answered, smiling over at her. "I think it's caused by a seaquake. This quake apparently originated further inland."

"I noticed how much more muscle you have since your bicycle trip down through Hainan," the little dark-haired beauty said, shyly.

"I lost four pounds on that trip," he said proudly. " And I might have lost another pound a few minutes ago," he joked.

"You mean from the earthquake, or..."

"Mostly or!"

"I see," she murmured, pleased. "I understand now where you got the nickname 'Buzz Saw,'" she kidded.

"Miiko Arishima!" he proclaimed, in a serious tone, taking her hand in both of his.

"What!" she asked, startled by the formality, her breathing picking up a pace just after she had it under control.

"I want you to marry me."

"Oh," she said, coming unglued. "That's wonderful, but could we save it until after the war, please. I want to have children, but not while there's any fighting going on."

"All right," he said, disappointed. "But anytime you change your mind, and I'm in the vicinity, we'll get married, okay?"

"Yes, Jun dear, and now we'd better start back," she said, tenderly.

* * *

"This is a beautiful beach," Shiroko said as we came around a sand dune.

"Somebody forgot their towels," I said picking one up. "Since we have something to dry ourselves with, it's a good excuse for going swimming in the buff," I said with a grin that would make a Cheshire cat envious.

"I can't do that. Besides, your hands are still bandaged."

"I do believe your ears are turning the color of our national bird, the flamingo, at the thought of skinny dipping."

"I'm due back at the base," Shiroko said, tugging on my hand.

I got her back to the nurses' compound just as a man dressed in army work clothes with a mosquito net over his cap and smelling of moth balls approached.

She relieved the civilian woman at the desk and I stayed around to chat awhile longer.

The soldier with a piece of dark netting covering his face set down his tool box in front of Shiroko's desk.

"I'm here to repair the sink in room 212." he said, obviously unprepared for an encounter with such a beautiful woman.

"There's only one nurse in the building," Shiroko, the duty house mother informed him, swirling her shoulder length hair. She had about as much chance of disguising herself as an efficient, drab, hard-working functionary by putting a frown on her face as a hi-octane speedboat had of qualifying as a canoe by placing a paddle aboard. "I'll tell her you're coming," she said, reaching for the phone to call Atsu, who had left the ship while it was docked.

"Here's the master key," Shiroko said, after checking the maintenance sheet to see if it was a legitimate complaint.

"Thank you, pretty lady," he said, adjusting the dark glasses and floppy hat that had covered most of his features. He hurried to the stairway.

"He's up at the top of the stairs already," Shiroko said. "I recognize that squeaky board."

She picked up the phone on the first ring. "There's a man up here!" Atsu hollered.

"Don't be frightened. He's a repairman. Sent here to fix the sink in room 212."

"I hope it doesn't disrupt my schedule," Atsu said. "That lovely Miiko creature hasn't packed up her gear yet."

A blood-curdling scream raced down the stairs and slammed against my eardrums.

"I'm looking through the gates of a blacked out hell," came the yell from the upper story.

I hesitated, an old habit of mine.

When Shiroko made a move to get up, I took off to try a sacrifice bunt.

'You came from a family of traitors," he was shouting as I started up the steep staircase. 'But you won't live long enough to pass on those genes."

Halfway up the steps, I saw the razor-sharp bayonet slash through the air.

Bleeding profusely, Atsu was not going to go down without a fight. Grabbing a vase, she broke it and went for his eyes.

He suffered a scalp wound fending off the porcelain receptacle, "I'm going to do more than just kill you," he snarled, blood trickling into his brow. "You're nothing but a piece of trash."

Lips split, eyes terrified, her hair flying, Atsu used her knee followed by a shoulder lunge at his neck. It didn't bowl him over, but the impact jarred the bayonet loose.

Waving his hands around like paws clawing at the air, he lost the initative for a second.

My assault knocked him to the floor with me on top, leaving him few alternatives but to kick his legs wildly and bite like a savage dog at my shoulder and neck. During the struggle, the intruder managed to grab a fistful of my short hair. He pulled my head down as he raised his own off the floor.

The pain of our colliding skulls arched my body enough for him to roll out from underneath. "I've got you now," he cried, his cruel, dry eyes in vivid contrast to the tear-stained ones of the woman lying next to me.

We both scrambled for the bayonet stuck in the floor like a macabre cross.

I grabbed the weapon as we rolled under a wide-open window and wasted a few seconds getting a good grip on the handle. Unfortunately, that moment of hesitation allowed him the opportunity to jump through the opening. I didn't follow him; I hollered down to Shiroko to summon medical aid.

"Shiroko quizzed me while I waited for the ambulance personnel and the station police to arrive before I went back downstairs. "How bad is she hurt? Did you get him?"

"She's badly injured, and he was too fast for me," I said, knowing full well if I hadn't been so squeamish, I could have performed a service to society by using the bayonet on him.

Miiko made a sudden appearance, nodded at me and waved at the pretty woman on the duty desk as she approached. "Is your name, Shiroko?"

"Hai," she answered, running her quivering finger down the roster sheet. "But it'll be a few minutes before you can go up to your room.. You're Miiko Arishima, an overnight guest. Is that right?"

"Hai, and I have a piece of correspondence for you," Miiko said pulling it out of her purse and handing it to Shiroko. "The navy wants you to make contact with an army representative aboard the *Ikeda Maru.* The name on the envelope doesn't make sense, but it might be the nickname of a member of the band.

"It can't be very important if it didn't go by Teletype," Shiroko said, unaware that she had routinely tossed it into one of the routing bins .

I left for the harbor and arrived at the ship in time to catch a partial night's sleep. I tossed and turned. Would I recognize the assailant, by the husky shape of his body, if I saw him again?

Chapter 30

Fire Room

On the morning of December 3, 1941, I stood on the quarterdeck with Sakamoto to watch the stragglers come aboard.

"What's so special about today?" I asked.

"It's becoming more difficult each day to cancel any plans to neutralize the American fleet," Sakamoto claimed, sitting next to a pile of personal belongings. "If America would stay true to her own heritage and stopped backing the British Empire in Asia, there would still be time to divert our six carriers and put them to better use out here in the Far East."

"What did you do last night?"

Sakamoto frowned. "I was listening to a U.S. State Department's report that said Japan was headed for national bankruptcy and may be driven into an aggressive move."

"Secretary of the Navy Frank Knox stated that war with Japan was inevitable," Sgt. Ogata said, laying his matching luggage down by the duffle bags.

"Suitcases! Do you expect to be housed in a Malayan hotel?" I asked with a broad smile.

"We're civilized where I come from," he jested, placing his hands on the luggage while unsuccessfully projecting a haughty air.

Believing the major had inside information, an off-duty shore patrolman pitched in to help Sukebator with his belongings.

"Will Japan strike without a declaration of war?" Gegan asked, grabbing his bag after the second class petty officer collapsed under its weight.

"*Hai*. Against military targets," Sakamoto replied. "The likely possibility of a B-17 first strike from the planes based in the Philippines has everyone in the planning department on edge. Undeclared wars have been the norm for Westerners in the Far East for some time."

"Reports are circulating among the Allied radio networks that Japanese transports have been seen heading south along the China coast," Gegan Sukebator said, throwing the huge bag over his shoulder like a ten pound sack of flour.

"That will alarm the Western Colonialist," Sakamoto said. "Any threat to British or Dutch occupation forces will be seen as a menace to American occupation forces in the Philippines."

"Anything new, Professor?" Kaine asked, appearing at the top of the gangplank, dragging along a duffle bag with one hand and waving sayonara to Miiko, standing on the dock in her breeze-catchers and tangerine dress.

"Our schedule has been moved up; *Ikeda's* leaving Yulin harbor within the hour. We'll critique the Hainan operation at sea."

As the vessel pulled away from its moorings, Miiko, her light brown eyes filled with tears, departed for the nurses quarters to grab the rest of her gear and catch a ride to the air base.

Major Sukebator headed for his stateroom, seemingly reluctant to tear his eyes away from the harbor and its associated activities.

With only four days to go before all hell broke loose, even the ship's laundrymen were taking an active interest in news from the control center. The latest word indicated that diplomatic discussions with Washington were hopeless. The United States was still negotiating for the King-Emperor. Japan's desire to be flexible was being ignored.

"They're still talking politics," the assistant laundryman grumbled, watching the *Kuji Maru* take up her position on the starboard side as the military transports left the harbor.

"I almost missed the ship," Kaine informed me, noting that Quartermaster Kato, Librarian Agi, and the burly Yeoman Nitta had returned before him.

Pleased by my cousin's friendly tone, I assumed I had been accepted into the soldiers' inner circle.

"I've got some disturbing news," Inspector Geki Ibuse said calling Michi Sakamoto and myself over to one side. "It looks like newly promoted corporals are still in danger from the serial killer.

"I find that hard to believe," Michi said.

"All three bayoneted men from this ship had recently obtained that rank. And according to Debuchi here, nurse Atsu Ogata was stabbed yesterday while we were ashore."

"But nurses don't use the corporal designation," Sakamoto said, believing his scholarly logic would destroy the theory.

"Her second cousin was promoted to corporal a week ago," Ibuse said with a superior air. "Sergeant Ogata is brokenhearted over his niece."

The ship was jammed full. I was issued a cot and was once again assigned to the anchor chain compartment.

Sakamoto was handed a message as he left the mess deck. I tagged along. "A prominent non-Japanese Oriental told Congresswoman Jeanette

Rankin that the situation was serious," he read out loud. "And Japan has but two choices: Go to war or submit to economic slavery for the rest of its existence."

"I'll bet the U.S. is still finding underhanded ways to make money during this time of tension," Agi chuckled, joining us.

"*Hai.* A few months ago, Japanese ships had to give up $4,000,000 worth of silk to the American military before they were allowed to leave port.

"Here's what I was talking about yesterday. The British War Cabinet makes it official, and the United States doesn't object. The words in the 'Atlantic Charter' mean freedom for those countries under an enemy's rule, not King-Emperor George VI's military-controlled colonies. Queen Wilhelmia also exempted the foreign land occupied by her Dutch armies."

"Why are you looking so sad, Debuchi?" Agi asked. "We'll be sailing in a southerly direction for awhile before we turn toward the Malay peninsula."

"I was just thinking," I said with a sigh. "Roosevelt had lunch with former King-Emperor Edward VII and the Duchess of Windsor but didn't invite Hirohito, Carlos Romulo, or for that matter any of the freedom leaders from the Solomon Islands."

"Who's Carlos Romulo?" Kaine asked.

"A top-notch Filipino reporter," I said, as we stood staring at Hainan Island for no particular reason, "who believes the Indonesian nationalists are willing to help the Japanese should they try to free the islands from the Dutch army."

"Roosevelt let Churchill know he would not declare war, but instead, would make war," Sakamoto said, putting his hand on Kaine's shoulder to steady himself. "And it looks like he'll get his way. There is a subtle distinction here. He would not fire the first shot, but will make sure a first shot is fired."

"Churchill notified the two Canadian battalions occupying Hong Kong to fight house to house if war comes," Sukebator remarked when he returned to the quarterdeck. "They have little regard for human life."

"Pocketbook issues," Kaine said for about the hundredth time.

"Let's sum up the military situation," Michi said looking at his followers.

"Besides the strategic bombers, the United States can muster over one hundred fighter planes in the Philippines," Agi said. "Plus twelve twin - engine bombers, eight attack, and thirty navy patrol bombers."

"The Royal Air Force has visited the Philippine Islands," Kaine superimposed, "to obtain information for their possible use by British and Dutch aircraft."

"The Dutch occupation army stationed in Indonesia," Lt. Sakamoto said, giving a last minute summary of the battle forces, "has over two hundred aircraft of all types, including four squadrons of fighter planes in its inventory.

"In naval combat tonnage, the Gold Dust Enterprise has a three-to-one advantage over the Orientals." Michi continued to sum it up. "The British forces stationed in the Indian Ocean have completed the naval and warplane encirclement of the remaining free Asian nations."

"What's happening in Washington?" Sakamoto asked the navigation officer as he passed by us on his way from Captain Ohira's cabin.

"The emergency powers of the president allow him to make law by agency appointment," the commander answered.

"Churchill and Roosevelt are on an equal footing now," Sakamoto said. "They have more destructive firepower at their fingertips than Attila the Hun had in his wildest fantasy."

"What's an Attila the Hun?" Jun Kaine asked, looking for the least crowded passageway.

"Nevermind. But remember this," Sakamoto warned. "While the United States is making plans to bomb Asian countries like Japan and Manchukuo, Japan is still determined to evict the Western Imperial Forces and push for a free Asia.

"Aren't the Aleutians, Alaska, and Hawaii part of the United States, Professor?"

"No, Kaine-san," Sakamoto replied. "They are foreign territories that were taken over by the white race. None of them have been offered statehood status."

"How about the Philippines?"

"The Filipinos aren't automatically considered U.S. citizens."

"Professor," Agi said, relaying a message. "Kato wants to know if Japan has had much success against the communists in China?"

"Somewhat. We did manage to bomb the communist headquarters in Shensi providence last August. But with America aiding the warlords, it's slow going.

"Engineering Officer Hasi asked me to stop by his cabin," Lt. Sakamoto said, turning to me. "Want to come along?"

"You bet," I said.

I was right behind him when Sakamoto rapped on the engineer's door.

"Come in," the bespectacled machinery boss answered, looking up

236

from his desk long enough to return a polite nod.

"You've no doubt heard that we have an airman aboard," Michi said. "I brought Naval Air Pilot First Class Kiyo Debuchi with me."

"Hai, I've heard the rumor. It's an honor to meet someone with such a distinquished occupation."

Seeing the engineer up close for the first time, I was struck by how representitive he was of the typical Japanese male; dark hair, dark eyes, slim build--and shorter, on average, than our Western counterparts.

"And I am honored to meet an officer with such heavy responsibilities."

"You're from Kyushu?" the Professor asked. The engineer's stateroom, with everything in its proper place, made me feel guilty when I thought of my anchor room sleeping quarters. My clothes were strewn along the anchor chain.

"Presently. I was born in Miyazaki, a hundred miles from Kagoshima, your hometown, Professor. My parents moved north to Yokohama early in my life."

"What is Yokohama like? I've never been there."

"We like to brag about our beautiful public buildings, which the opposition party calls 'pork barrel.' It has clean beaches and wide streets. The city is extremely prosperous, and it has a large Chinese community. In fact, this uniform was made by one of the Chinese tailor shops," he said, rubbing a hand down the sleeve of his suit.

"Did you play marbles and hide-and-seek in Yokohama when you were a kid?" Michi asked. He had been thinking of his childhood lately.

"Oh, sure."

"How large a city is it?"

"About 400,000 people," Hasi guessed, pointing to the chairs before taking his seat behind the desk. "Thank you for coming, Professor; I wanted to ask you about the events leading up to the formation of this convoy. The ones you've been discussing with the crew and troops since we departed Sasebo."

"Hai. Anything I can help you with?" the Professor asked, always happy to share information.

"First of all. Have you heard anything new about our murderer?"

"No, not a thing."

"The men seem to enjoy your talks," Hasi said, prefacing his request with a compliment. "And I was wondering if you would take time to hold a session down in either the fire room or the engine room. The 'black gang,' as we're known to the topside sailors, don't spend much time on deck and it's too noisy for good radio reception."

"Certainly, we can do it right now if you desire."

"That would be fine. I understand you've been telling the story chronologically, starting with the original trade with China. What period would you like to talk about?"

"I'll give them a brief overview."

"Would you give me an example?" the engineer asked sitting up straight to give the answer his full attention. "Would you like some tea-flavored ice cream?" he inquired, holding up a couple of dishes of the cold substance before Sakamoto could reply. "My sister Natsuko had it stored in the galley's refrigeration room before we left Sasebo."

"Yes, on the ice cream," Sakamoto said for both of us, reaching for the special treat. "And to answer your question--Japan," he began, "having emerged from the depression quicker than most, gobbled up market-places from the West like a shopper on a two-for-one sale. Western Chambers of Commerce tried a variety of schemes to reduce the phenomenal growth of the Japanese economic boom."

"I'm told you deal in perceptions, omissions, and background information?" the Engineer declared, spitting out his questions like a man used to receiving definitive answers.

"*Hai*. For instance, America, while technically not a monarchy, was enamored with royalty," Michi said, while I shoveled in three spoonfuls of ice cream.

"Omissions? Hasi asked. He placed his hand near the intercom button. "I'm expecting a call from the chief watertender," he informed us.

"When the West writes about Japan, they never forget to mention Imperial Japan, or the Imperial army," Michi said, as I placed my hands on my temples to rub away a sharp pain in my forehead from eating the icy-cold, dairy product too fast.

"But when writing about Australia, they rarely use the correct titles: Australia Imperial Forces, Royal Academy, Commander-in-Chief of the Imperial Forces of Australia, the Imperial Service Club in Sydney, or the Royal Australian Navy."

"I get the idea," Hasi said, holding his hand up for silence as a fire room update came through.

"'Ill-gotten gains' was the term applied to foreign lands occupied by the Japanese--and 'civilizing' for the Western countries occupying someone else's territory," the Professor said when the man in charge of the engineering department dropped his hand. "America's mayors of Chicago, Memphis, and Jersey City were elected democratically, while

Oriental leaders were despots who clawed their way to the top."

"Just a slight change in wording and the whole picture takes on a different meaning," Hasi said, his face showing annoyance that politics couldn't be laid out like mathematics.

"Shall we go down below?"

"Hai," Sakamoto agreed standing up.

If I pay closer attention, perhaps I might be more eager for combat," I thought, following Hasi toward the fire room.

"We'll start with the year after you joined the navy, Debuchi. Those twelve months saw the continued process of a larger share of the world's market going to Asia. Manchukuo's per capita income increased dramatically with Japan's assistance."

"Make sure you show up for the evening meal," the Chief Cook recommended, slipping past us on his way up from dry stores inspection.

"I intend to, but what's so special about tonight?" I asked, ducking under the clipboard the Chief waved around in his exuberance.

"We're having rice and red beans, the omen of good luck," the thick-waisted cook allowed.

"He used to load lily bulbs for my father," Hasi said after the chief passed out of earshot. "My dad ran an export business."

The trip into the bowels of the ship provided a fascinating contrast to the rather sheltered life led by us university graduates.

"As I told you, Professor, engine room petty officers and firemen spend most of their waking hours in this artificial enviroment. They seldom have the chance for informal discussions on foreign affairs," the thirty year old Hasi repeated, waiting to assist Sakamoto up to one of the catwalks above the steam-producing machinery.

"Where are the engines?" Michi wanted to know, leaning on the catwalk rail overlooking boiler number 2.

The answer was not appealing.

"On the other side of that thick steel bulkhead with the double air-locked hatches," Engineering Officer Hasi replied, pointing to his right. "Don't worry. Should a catastrophic explosion occur here in the fire room, the engines won't be damaged."

I was more concerned with the possible harm to my body, rather than with any injury to the machinery after I saw at first-hand all the efforts going into developing pressures high enough to punch holes in steel.

The younger off-duty black gang sailors had poured into the boiler room to ask questions about international events during their high school years.

The first question came from a second class fireman, standing in front of the water tank for boiler number 2. His dark eyes were darting from unit to unit to make sure everything was under control. "Were the Chinese cities cleared of Western troops by 1936? That's the year I graduated from high school,"

The fireman's designation, equivalent to a seaman in rank, was an archaic holdover from the days when they shoveled coal into the firebox to heat the ship's boilers.

Sakamoto clutched the moisture-laded notebook to his chest. "No. But a good start had been made. Japan's industrial complexes and factories located in Hongkew were more secure."

"When I was in China during my second hitch in the navy," Chief Machinist Mate Inouye declared, never losing sight of the men checking on the evaporators and boilers. "Businesses run by the Japanese were replacing the Western establishments that had been created because of the unequal trade treaties."

"Hai," Michi Sakamoto agreed. "And Britain, the largest European investor, was stymied by a country made up of self-made provinces, and run by what the Western media referred to as Chinese warlords.

"I'm all for kicking the British army out of Malaya," Inouye shouted, his ever-busy eyes searching the fire room for machinery malfunctions.

Sakamoto seemed unsure of where to put his notebook. I climbed up on the catwalk and took it from him. Squatting down, I reached under the steel walkway and placed the journal on top of the boiler.

He went on to a different field of inquiry. "Did any of you hear Ruriko's radio program when she had a Tokyo bureaucrat on her show?"

"No," Inouye responded. The notebook was out of his line of vision. "It's too noisy in here, besides, we had a first-aid session on burns." The importance of the topic was underlined when the steam valve on boiler number I popped.

What's he doing here? I wondered, spotting Army Judge Advocate Geki Ibuse coming into the fire room.

Although both Sakamoto and Ibuse operated under the same time constraints, I had to admit that Inspector Ibuse had the bigger chore. The admiral wanted the murders solved before the new phase of the Pacific War began. He figured they'd never find the killer once hostilities started.

Chief Inoyue assigned a watertender to monitor the feedwater flow on boiler number 2.

"Let's break it off here, Professor," Hasi said. I felt the tension in the air as the crewman stepped up the number of checks on the machinery.

I grabbed the notebook and got down from the catwalk.

"Ibuse reminds me of *Oni*, the devil in Japanese legends," I remarked to the nearest fireman.

"Ibuse keeps a pet spider in a cricket cage," the fireman reported after making sure the Inspector couldn't hear his remark.

"I've got one more place to visit today," Michi informed me. "If you want to listen in, I'll meet you at the chart room in half and hour."

"I'll be there," I assured him.

I was standing in front of the navigator's domain when the duty quartermaster, who hated aviators, opened the door.

"What do you want?" the wide-bodied First Class Petty Officer Kato asked with a snarl reserved for enlisted flyers that weren't senior to him.

"I'm waiting for Professor Sakamoto."

"I'm not going to have an airman nosing around like some big shot in the spaces I'm responsible for," Kato said in keeping with his usual irritable mood.

Lt. Sakamoto showed up in an outfit I'd never seen before. "We're here to meet with the navigator," he said.

"Yes sir," Kato mumbled, unable to wipe the frown on his face.

"Commander," Kato said. "I've got Prof. Sakamoto and a non-commissioned aviator outside."

"Have them come in."

I lagged behind.

"And don't you look sharp!" the noble-browed navigation officer whose position intitled him to the rank of commander exclaimed, eyeballing the blue-gray uniform of the armored corps.

"This is our Naval Air Pilot, " Michi said. He preened, showing off his knee-high boots, and breeches, the suede gloves tucked decoratively under his wide leather belt.

"Aren't you going in with the infantry?" the navigator kidded, while Quartermaster First Class Kato bowed in Sakamoto's direction, then quickly turned his back on me.

I felt out of place in my regulation blue tennis shoes, but hoped to find a map containing information about the Malayan invasion.

"I appreciate your taking the time to brief us on the recent history of Manchukuo," Sakamoto said, oblivious to the scowl on Quartermaster Kato's face. "Start with a little background information, please."

Except for the coastline, Manchukuo is surrounded by communist forces. In fact, Russia had effective control of Northern Manchuria through its management of the railroad system.

"The usual accusations of duplicity came from the Western colonial powers. The move to independence effectively shut out all foreign countries from their local monopolies. The British-American Tobacco Company's Manchurian office put pressure on London and Washington to do something about it."

"No one has mentioned my great-looking green-gray landing assault team uniform with its color-blended shirt, anchors on the lapels, and epaulets," Kato murmured pulling out a pencil from one of the two big pockets on the jacket.

"What else happened, Commander?" I asked, my voice escalating when the hidden hand of Kato pulled the chair out from under me.

Fortunately, I thought from my seat on the floor, the navigation chart on the table above me had been placed upside down for security reasons--enabling me to read the part hanging over the edge while the two officers were engrossed in conversation.

"When Manchukuo increased its production of sheep, purchases of wool from Australia fell off in direct proportion," the Commander acknowledged, displeased with my falling off the chair.

Quartermaster Kato, in a fictional show of cooperation gave me a sickly smile, then stood back waiting for a reaction.

"We weren't able to get a vote for racial equality out of the Western nations and most of them refused to accept the new Asian country into their midst," the Navigation Officer said, his eyes on me as I reached up cautiously to get hold of the top chart.

"Have a rice cracker, Debuchi-san," the Quartermaster said pleasantly as I got to my feet. "It has *Ikeda's* special dip on it."

"Looks good," I said, enthusiastically, bolting it down in one gulp. "Urrgh! Water," I pleaded, tears coming to my eyes.

"What a baby," the shipboard sailor muttered. "All that racket over a mixture of toothpaste and hot pepper. It was guaranteed to add zest to that snack," Kato said with an evil smile, offering me a glass of liquid.

"Why wasn't the league more effective?" the Commander asked, glancing over to see what I was up to.

"Britain, with the urging of the United States, a non-member, did not want the league to have any real power," Sakamoto told him, noting his interest in my actions. "Instead, they wanted a few big countries with white majorities controlling the world.

"Thanks, I said in a strangled voice. Taking the glass in both hands, I drank the lemon-colored beverage as fast as I could."

"Any military clashes during your two-year tour in Manchukuo, Commander?" Lt. Sakamoto asked, ducking a spray of fluid, punctuated with a cry of anquish from me about carrying the rivalry between shipboard sailors and aviators too far.

"*Hai.* Manchukuo was so proud of its fledgling airforce that it became touchy on any unsanctioned flights across its border. Especially from Communist Mongolia--take your time drinking, Debuchi-san. There's plenty where that came from."

"How does that listerine taste?" Kato asked quietly. "I bought it on my last trip to Singapore."

"I'll kill you," I promised, struggling to keep my voice down, my face the color of the mouth wash.

"Didn't we have to provide the defensive forces for Manchukuo?"

"Most of it. At least until the country had time to complete its training cycle," the Commander said, pointing to the Nomonghan Incident campaign ribbon on his chest. "But the one memory of Manchukuo I'll always carry with me, was watching a Manchukuon Army Airforce pilot run his gloved-hand across his country's newly designed roundel insignia before climbing into the cockpit."

"What type of aircraft was he flying?"

"He was piloting a Ki-27 Fire Dragon built in Harbin, a Manchukuoan city with its own airfield situated near the Songhau River.

Within a short period of time, a quarter of a million Japanese resided in Manhuria. In less than a decade of its becoming independent, Manchukuo's per capita income was almost double that of China.

I scrambled to straighten out the pile of charts and take note of the information on the more important ones. Kato had me unnerved, his soft brown eyes in direct contrast to his contorted expression.

He crushed his foot against my hand as I reached for a fallen map. I never saw the landing team combat boot descending until it was too late.

Were there any special tricks the West used to gain an advantage in the Orient?" the navigator wondered.

"To move their goods tariff-free, the British and French had built railway lines in China," Sakamoto replied. This also allowed them to move their troops rapidly, as they continued to dismember the shattered nation."

"Did it give them the upper hand?" the chart room officer asked, using his arms to shield the maps for Southeast Asia from view.

"Not entirely," Lt. Michi Sakamoto replied. "At least thirty thousand

Chinese have been educated in Japan in spite of Western influence.

"The biggest problem for the West was the possibility of a trade deficit. Even after importing logs from the United States, Japanese plywood makers were able to deliver their products for $81.00 per thousand feet cheaper than America."

"Did America's election of a new president in 1932 increase our chances of better relations with America?" the commander asked.

"No." Roosevelt wanted to use sea power as a diplomatic weapon. And, because his mother's side of the family had made a great deal of money in the China trade, had a sentimental attachment to that country, he did not like the Japanese, and wrote racist articles defaming us."

"What were his appointments like?" Quartermaster Kato asked, trying to look innocent.

"Roosevelt, a Harvard lawyer and millionaire democrat, picked hawk Claude Swanson for his Secretary of the Navy. Then dipped heavily into the ranks of the prominent Republicans and staunch conservative Democrats for his administration."

I took note of the bayonet on the top shelf when Kato opened the map cabinet.

Taking a cue from America's 'Monroe Doctrine,' our country announced they had special rights in Eastern Asia," he ventured. "Because it was no radical departure from the stated reason for the 'Monroe Doctrine,' Japan did not expect any trouble from the United States. These special rights would be known as the 'Amau Doctrine.'"

"Seems fair to me," I said, wondering what that sharp pain was in my lower back area.

"That's because you haven't dealt with white supremacy," Sakamoto assured me. "President Roosevelt rejected Japan's 'Amau Doctrine,' but reserved the right for the United States to have the 'Monroe Doctrine.'"

"I hear we're going to use bicycles in Southeast Asia," the Quartermaster said, reaching up for a cabinet door.

"Which will bring back terrible memories to American businessmen. The first fears of Japanese competition in the United States were registered in 1896, when the reports of an imminent shipment of thousands of Japanese bicycles circulated.

"I hope they've kept them in good shape," I said, getting banged in the head with a cabinet door designed to stay closed in heavy seas.

"What other products bothered the West?"

"I don't know if it was a coincidence of not, but when Japan exported cotton, General Billy Mitchell asked for bombers and Secretary of State

244

Cordell Hull managed to remind us of the vulnerability of our cities."

"I heard you say that Japan shipped out of Usa, a coastal city, when American businessmen began putting USA on their merchandise."

Moving away from the plotting table, so Kato couldn't jab me again with the metal protractor, I decided the aviation element needed to go on the offensive.

The navigator asked. "What's the West's game plan?"

"They want Japan to accept a permanently inferior economic position or go to war, " Michi said, observing the pained expression on the Quartermaster's face. "If we decide on war, Great Britain and her Western Allies see no reason they can't squash us like a bug. They figure a Pacific War would be over inside of three months.

Having slammed into Kato's shoulder when I collided with him in an aborted attempt to get the navigator's log, I apologized and reached out to help him up. When I had a firm grip on both of his hands, I yanked as hard as I could on the one connected to the bruised shoulder.

"What's your biggest fear, Professor? the navigator asked, jarred by the yelp coming from his quartermaster.

"That America won't back off from using her fleet and airpower to protect the King-Emperor's Global Empire."

The navigator didn't bat an eyelash when Kato pulled me into a corner. "Looking at it from the Far East point of view," he said, "an economic and immigration arrangement between the Chinese and Japanese would be the start of a real Asian dynamo."

The commander's comment was inadvertantly timed to hide my grunt as I took an elbow in the stomach from the hostile Kato.

"Is it possible the West doesn't understand we're trying to free Asia, not make captives of them?" the navigator asked, his eyes missing some of the action.

When the Hell Springs Quartermaster was bent over, I raised my arms for a full-fledged polite bow, then closed my fist and brought it down on top of Kato's head with enough force to buckle his knees.

"A thousand apologies," I offered. "This unworthy aviator is too clumsy today to be in such honorable company."

"It's quite possible the West doesn't understand," Sakamoto said, drawing the discussion to a close when the commander turned to initial the navigator' log.

Feeling tired and bruised, I parted company outside the door after thanking Professor Sakamoto for taking me with him.

I heard the fugitive from a nightmare questioning Private Agi in the passageway as I started back to my bunk. I paused to listen in.

"What did you do for recreation last night?" Ibuse asked, trying to lull him into revealing something.

"Have you ever heard of the Japanese China Development Company?"

"What has that to do with my question?"

"It's a good place to invest your money."

"Perhaps you didn't hear me," Ibuse said, his voice taking on a more threatening manner. "I'm interested in your whereabouts last evening."

"I'll bet you haven't heard this piece of information," Agi said, determined not to let the Army Judge Advocate push him around. "Thirty years ago the Australians sent gunboats into China's interior. "Not only were they a long ways from home, but they stayed to collect Chinese railway fees at Tienstsin and   Peking."

"I'll ask you one more time," Ibuse glowered. "Where were you last night? And who were you with?"

"I was on the ship," the librarian-soldier said putting a piece of black licorice to his mouth.

"Okay wiseguy. I've heard that you've made friends with that street-tough back in Hell Springs. But you're talking to me now," Ibuse said ripping the licorice from his hand. "And I'd just as soon eat you for breakfast and throw your good-for-nothing bones over the side," Ibuse scowled, his reheated coffee-ground eyes coming to a boil.

"I wrote a letter and hit the sack early," Agi said, anxious to get away from the inquisition.

"That's not much of an alibi. I'll be talking to you again. Dismissed."

I took the opportunity to ask the Inspector a question. "Is it possible the killer got aboard the *Sky Dragon?*"

"I don't think so. Why do you ask?"

"I nearly got killed during a flight deck drill a couple of days ago. He may think I caught a glimpse of him back in Sasebo harbor."

"Did you?"

"Not enough to identify him."

"He's dangerous."

"I'm watching my step."

"Where are you bunking?"

"In the anchor chain compartment."

"Don't stay there alone."

"Thanks for the advice," I said slowly easing away.

I can't go whining to the master-at-arms that I'm afraid to stay in the anchor room by myself, I thought entering the compartment. I'd get laughed out of the service.

However, it did seem sensible to err on the side of caution, so I reached into the flight gear pile and got out my 9 mm pistol and placed it under the cot.

I was tired and overly anxious about the upcoming battle.

Chapter 31

Gun Platform

I had thrown myself on the anchor room cot without undressing. I fell asleep immediately, but the thought of Inspector Ibuse's eyes triggered off a weird dream.

I dreamt I was part of the Oriental Independent contingent going to a meeting in Honolulu--a glimpse out the aircraft window showed rows of battleships tied up to each other like school children holding hands, none seemed eager to fight for the King-Emperor.

Military aircraft were lined up side by side at their respective airfields--easy for the guards to patrol in case someone with darker skin dared touch their metallic surfaces.

"Sabotage!" screamed the guards, "Watch for sabotage! Only men with white coloring are capable of long distance seamanship or combat airmanship."

Someone shook my shoulder.

"What is it, " I groaned.

"Wake up."

I saw Kato through my bleary eyes. He was carrying a bayonet.

Sitting up in the dim light, I mumbled an incoherant question.

"I want to talk to you about your attitude," Kato said. "You're all alone here. It wouldn't be much trouble for the Trademark Killer to slip in during the night and cut your throat. See you later."

With that remark, he was gone and I hastily changed clothes.

It was now December 4, 1941 in the Western world, I realized. Three nights to go. I hurried into the passageway and found that Sakamoto had received a radiogram from Karatsu Hospital in Japan. The gist of Kimiko's message was: "The oil crisis has hit with devasting effect. Manufacturing plants are closing, classrooms are dangerously cold, hot water is unavailable, and finding an operating automobile or bus impossible. At this rate they'll have to use library books for fuel."

I followed a group up to the gun platform.

The Malay-bound convoy was still on submarine alert because of a

248

transmission from Black Magic 215.

"Professor, if we drive the British forces out of Malaya do you think they'll send their army back to reoccupy the country?" Kaine asked, standing on the forward gun platform gazing out to sea.

"You can bet on it," Sakamoto said, glancing away from a private who was using a piece of ivory-colored translucent paper and a wolf-hair tipped brush to paint the transport *Kuji Maru.* "We'll have to put up some sort of defense perimeter, and hope the Allies force the King-Emperor to keep his hands off other countries."

"But didn't you say that Great Britain's King-Emperor has a lot of influence with the United States?" Jun Kaine asked, thumbing through the paintings the soldier-artist had considered unworthy of his talents.

"Hai," the Professor answered, looking sad. "Unless America remembers the time when it wanted independence from England, and shows some concern for the Orientals, we're doomed in our efforts to free Asia within the next decade."

Only half-listening, the amateur artist dipped his brush into the black color to highlight the stark scene.

"Can't they see how much better off the Far East would be if it was economically successful and independent?" Jun asked, becoming interested in the calligraphy-like appearance of the painting.

"They don't care," Sakamoto advised him. "Control is all they're interested in."

I noted the dark squall line on the horizon and wondered if it was going to produce violent winds.

"Can't the East and West sit down at a table and come to some sort of agreement without resorting to war?" the artist asked irritably as I grabbed a section of the gun's canvas covering, intending to look at the twin 20 mm anti-aircraft weapon under it.

"Burma has been trying that route for years and has gotten nowhere," Sakamoto replied, stumbling over an ammo crate. "The white man's belief in racial superiority is emotional as well as economic."

Gunner's Mate Kikuchi, who was responsible for the 20 mm, limped forward, giving me a dirty look.

"How long have navy gunners been aboard merchant ships?" I asked.

"It's only been about eight months since the politicians in the Diet authorized naval protection for the merchant marines."

"There are still those in the political system that are trusting enough to believe that the Teutonics are going to stop invading now that they have most of Asia under military rule," Sakamoto allowed.

"I want to keep the salt spray off the gun's firing mechanism," Kikuchi complained, snatching the tarpaulin out of my hands.

"Where are you from, Gunner?" I said, not having asked him that question when he flew with me.

"Ikaruga," he replied proudly, his youthful face off-set by his steel-colored hair. "The home of the world's oldest wooden structure."

"Let's go get a cup of tea and talk about some of your interests," Sakamoto suggested to Kaine. "Tell me more about Miiko."

"Well, as you may have noticed at the navy store, she's about five feet tall, with shiny black hair and soft brown eyes."

"Does she have a job?"

"She works in the disbursing office at the Municipal Hospital in Nagaski. I just hope she can resist the advances of the doctors while I'm gone."

"Her parents?" Sakamoto asked, unable to observe the Gunner's Mate opening and closing his forefinger and thumb for the enjoyment of the seaman, indicating yak, yak, they're talking too much.

"Her father's a chemist and her mother used to work for the Toyota Motor Company. A year after they met, Miiko's father took part in the artificial fertilizer project which turned out to be such a huge success."

"How long have you and Miiko been going together?"

"Since high school."

"Was the meeting between you two arranged by the families?"

"No, we're too independent for that," Jun said, putting down the tiny bamboo brush when the talented private scowled.

"My mother knew Kimiko's family," Sakamoto said. "And I suspect she's doing a little match-making behind my back."

"You've never been married, have you, Professor?"

"No. I've been too career oriented. No woman has wanted to put up with my hectic schedule."

Gunner pulled the tarpaulin off the twin 20 mm gun and shook it just as the wind picked up, throwing the accumulated spray all over us.

Simulated air attack! Simulated air attack!" the executive officer shouted.

One of my buddies from Utility Squadron Five angled in from the northeast in the blue and yellow plane towing a banner behind him. It brought back memories of the time I looked over my shoulder to check the length of the tow line and saw empty space and tracers. They had shot the banner off. Any closer and it would have been my tail end.

"Stand back," Gunner hollered, kicking the tarpaulin out of the way. He slapped on the sound-powered battle phones and grabbed the 20 mm firing handles. "Feed those ammo cases into this slot," he ordered, shooting at the streamer.

The noise from the low-flying aircraft, cannon fire and empty brass casings bouncing off the deck mingled with the shouts from the gun crews deafened me.

I took my hands off my ears and looked down at the base of the uncovered gun as the utility plane sped off. "Who's been eating chocolate syrup?" I asked.

"What are you talking about?" the meticulous gunner grumbled, removing a mounting plate above the spreading liquid.

Feeling around for the source of the leak, he grabbed what felt to him like a human foot. "What the!" he yelled, quickly opening up the larger maintenance port.

As the sun entered the gun mount openings, my brain became forever imprinted with the visual image of a succession of shadows dancing to a silent song of death, across a face shorn of dignity and etched in pain. "There's a body in there!" I shrieked.

"Holy Torii! It's Corporal Mishima," Kaine cried, stooping over to take a closer look.

"I'll tell Captain Ohira and Inspector Ibuse," Sakamoto said, dashing from the gun station. Kaine headed in the opposite direction to tell the Sergeant.

"What an ugly way to go," the novice painter said in a panicky voice. "It looks like some obscene crucifix jutting out of a bloody stream."

Gunner agreed, trying not to stare at the body lying flat on its back with a bayonet protruding from its chest.

Ibuse is going to wonder why I'm at the scene of the crime again, I thought.

Chapter 32

British IX Regiment

The closer we got to Malaya, the more the situation took on the aspects of a losing game I once played against the Osaka Owls. Only this time, my fate was in the hands of the big league champions from Amsterdam and London. If I was chosen by destiny to be the first one in the batter's box, I had a hunch the Western team was prepared to counter with its latest multimillion dollar player. In the meantime, the other men in the 15 knot convoy had plenty of opportunity to dwell on the consequences of losing.

A petty officer pacing the deck told me he was worried about the possibilities of becoming a British prisoner. He was afraid of being branded, and sent to Christmas Island as a laborer in the phosphate mines, to work as many hours a day as the whites could force out of him, as they did his ancestors.

The small-boned, dusky-skinned, youthful-looking Coxswain's familiarity with rivers, creeks, and shorelines would be put to good use in Malaya. He had been born and raised in Tokushima, the water city, a place crisscrossed with canals and streams at the mouth of the Yoshino river. He had been chosen to drive an assault vehicle onto the beach.

Proud of his mother's Malayan heritage, he was anxious to free the country from Britain's armed forces.

"Did you join the anchor pool yet?" he asked.

"No. What's that?" I inquired.

"All you have to do is give your money to the barber and guess the correct time we'll drop anchor--the closest to the actual time wins the pool. The barber shop will be open in a couple of minutes."

"How much to get in the pool?"

"One yen."

"With the number of men on this ship, the winner's going to be a mighty happy man."

"I know it. Winning a fistful of yen for a Singapore blowout has the highest priority--after not getting shot," he said.

252

The facility no longer resembled the swank haircutting establishment it once did when the ship sailed as an ocean liner. The red and white striped pole had been removed, and the plush seats replaced.

Duty barbers, Nitta and Agi were behind their chairs and indicated a readiness to begin. Jofu Nitta was probably assigned at the request of Inspector Ibuse and Agi was designated to work there during the hours the library was closed.

The place was filling up, as a nervous Agi, sharpening up the straight razor, offered to take me next. "Would you like a shave, aviator?"

"No, just the standard trim," I said, noting the quiver in the amateur barber's out-sized fingers. "Didn't I hear you say you plucked chickens before you were drafted?"

"You only have a few facial hairs. I can flick them right off," he boasted, bringing the razor closer to my face. "I worked part time for the Kamakura Chicken Company before the army grabbed me."

"No shave," I insisted, quickly dropping my chin and moving my head further away from the sharp-edged cutting instrument. "I can get them with tweezers."

The ex-chicken plucker placed the razor back on the shelf, looking disappointed that he didn't get a chance to use it.

"What do you think about the murders?" Kaine inquired of Nitta, who jabbed at Sergeant Ogata's hair with dull scissors.

"We must have some sort of criminal element aboard," Agi said, his eyes darting like a trapped animal.

"I enjoyed that Peregrine Falcon airshow," Kaine remarked. "The Ki-43 gives us soldiers something to brag about, instead of worrying about the oil shortage back home."

"Too bad that Peregrine Falcon didn't take his arming switch out of safe and shoot up a couple of excess corporals," Agi kidded.

I noticed that Agi never looked over toward Yeoman Nitta when he talked.

"The West is expert at finding ways to worry Asia," Michi Sakamoto said, unsure of the amount of interest that topic generated. "They continually invent reasons for bringing about war in the Far East. Even though, under close examination, their reasons are self-serving and non-productive in the long run."

"Like what?" Private Agi asked, his question as unwelcome within the group as a case of flu.

"The masterful job America's newspaper magnate Hearst did in

253

educating the public into believing it was absolutely necessary to kill Filipinos and take over their land.

"That was more than forty years ago, wasn't it?" Nitta said, trying to short-circuit the Professor's narrative.

Navy Landing Trooper Banno, stood up. "How did Hearst get away with it?" he asked, knowing he wasn't going to be around to hear the answer. He'd already decided to come back when there were two navy barbers on duty instead of soldiers. The Chief Boatswain's Mate paused only long enough to give Agi his yen and anchor time.

He'd rather have a lady barber cut his hair, I thought, watching him start for the exit.

"Foul play," Nitta said, wanting to change the subject. "With all due respects to your former occupation, Agi-san."

"With all the higher education available in Japan and a ninety-five percent literacy rate," Chief Banno said, taking a seat again after deciding he had no better place to go. "You'd think that spooky Ibuse would have the murders solved."

"How come you want to be a landing trooper instead of staying aboard ship?" Lance Corporal Kaine asked Banno.

"Shiroko likes blue-green uniforms," the Chief Boatswain's Mate replied. "And that's not her only quirk!"

I listened closely.

"Like what?" Nitta asked, eager for a little juicy gossip.

"She makes me say 'tweet, tweet' before I kiss her."

"Holy Torii, why?" Three different voices asked.

"You've heard of those romantic European and American movies that were so popular with the girls?"

"Hai!" came from all sides of the barber shop.

"Since the Japanese film distributors always replace the act of kissing with twittering birds. Shiroko figured that's what gives the kiss its added zing.

"What does this Shiroko do?" Kaine asked.

"She works for the Navy's Judge Advocate General."

"You're a connoisseur when it comes to women, Chief. What does she look like?" Sakamoto asked.

"My mother, after seeing Shiroko's streamlined curves and gorgeous smile, immediately said, Yeh, but can she cook rice."

"You're exaggerating," Nitta claimed.

"Never!" he said with a hurt look on his face. "Not only is she good-looking, she also has a beautiful voice and is quite religious."

"How come I always get the women," Agi complained, "who wear clothes from the last century, baggy pants, straw hats, and work in the rice fields?"

"It might have something to do with the chicken feathers sticking out of your hair," Jofu Nitta suggested.

"There is a sad note to my story," Banno said. "Shiroko is the older sister of Corporal Hiko Daizen.

"My gosh!" they gasped. "That hits close to home."

"Who else aboard this ship is going in with one of the Navy Landing Teams?" Sakamoto asked.

"Too many for me to remember," Banno claimed. "In my rifle squad, I've got a quartermaster from Hell Springs and a yeoman who hunts bear in Siberia."

"I got two bears," Yeoman Nitta said, proud of his marksmanship.

"Where do you find time to read all your mail, Chief?" Agi asked the most senior navy man in the barber shop. "Scuttlebutt says you have a girl in every port."

"I can handle it," Banno said, his dark, half-closed eyes expressing confidence. "Are we going to be subjected to a morale-building speech by the Emperor every afternoon?" he wondered disrespectfully. "I thought he was powerless."

"Legally, yes," Sakamoto said, growing tense when the chicken-plucker reached for the razor again. "But similiar to Great Britain's King-Emperor, he has an enigmatic power that defies analysis. It's nice to have a unifying force to rally around in case of disaster. We could use more stability. The government in Tokyo has changed six times in the last three years."

"I blame that on the labor party," Nitta informed them.

"That's because you're a member of the downtown Rotary Club," Banno sniffed. "Who put camphor on the armrest?"

"Speaking of politics," Agi offered, his Osaka colloquial speech very noticeable. "Lots of oil tankers departed from what the Dutch refer to as the East Indies. The profits go to Amsterdam, not to the Indonesians."

"What part of the splendid and sophisticted area of Osaka are you from?" Ogata asked, one eyebrow up in the air, the other frozen.

"I lived in the northwest region near the Ina river, before I left for Sasebo," Agi answered, frowning. "What's the matter with your eyebrow Sergeant?"

Ogata arched his left eyebrow as far as it would go. "When I was in China, Macao to be exact, a Portuguese infantryman smashed me over the

255

right eyebrow with a rifle butt. The muscles in that area have shriveled up to a point where I can't move it."

"We had a baseball nut in here yesterday," Private Agi volunteered. "He said the stadiums drew upwards of seventy thousand people this year."

"Did he say anything about the Yomuri Giants?" I asked.

"No."

"When I was playing for a minor league team in 1937," I said. "An American ball player was seen taking pictures of the city from the rooftops. With all the talk of America planning to bomb our civilian population, it wouldn't surprise me to find out he was working for the United States Army Airforce."

"Does anyone ever talk about the future?" Sgt. Ogata asked.

"Television is the place to put your money," I said. "Tokyo baseball was the first sports event ever telecast."

"Any competition?" Sakamoto wanted to know.

"Television is still in its infancy," I said. "Besides ourselves, America, Britain, and especially Germany, are making progress in this field, but it'll take higher production figures before the price goes down far enough for the average man."

"Will we get oil in Malaya?" Kaine asked.

"Oil fuels the Global Empire ships that haul cheaply acquired rubber and tin out of Malaya for the benefit of British stockholders," Sakamoto replied warming up to the subject. "Ships are continuously departing Kota Bharu harbor. Malayans produce raw materials for the world markets, under the watchful eye of English overseers and the threat of physical harm."

"What's the name of that harbor?" Private Agi asked, placing the money wrapped in a piece of paper with the anchor time to one side.

"Kota Bharu, pronounced Ko-tah Bah-roo, a beautiful seacoast town in northeast Malaya," Michi informed them.

Kaine and myself gave our one yen and best guesstimate on arrival time to the former neck-wringing chicken-plucker before departing.

"I'll take all the money I can get from you suckers," Agi said, slamming it into the cricket box.

I watched him rub the insect's guts from his thumb and forefinger onto his working trousers. "Did you have to squash the cricket?" I asked, feeling revolted.

"Crickets don't necessarily represent good luck," Agi informed us. "Check the short life span on that one," he said, pointing to the tiny piece of fragile wing floating to the deck.

256

"How'd you like to go to the Captain's quarters with me?" Sakamoto suggested taking off for the weather deck.

"Very much," I said tagging along.

It was dark and drizzly, I noted, walking faster and tending to glance over my shoulder. I slowed down as we passed the anchor compartment and was startled when a black blotch moved out of the shadows.

"What's that?" I cried. But before I could make out its identity, it faded back into obscurity faster than a blotter soaks up ink.

"You're imagining things," the Professor rationalized.

Those sailors that were scheduled to take the army ashore were conducting their daily checks on the landing craft as we came abreast.

Water vehicles aren't my specialty," Sakamoto said. "Besides, I want and opportunity to use that classy uniform I wore in the navigator's office.

"Speaking of modern," I asked. "What was our education system like earlier in the century?"

"It continued to expand in an organized fashion," he assured me. "Your school, Rikkyo University had been founded in 1859. In the twentieth century, Japanese from all over the country were attending co-educational schools."

"How is..."

"Save that question until later," Michi interrupted. "Captain Ohira would like a more detailed rundown on the sessions we've been holding and has also invited our resident aviator along," he told Kaine.

"Maybe I'll get a chance to steer the ship," I said.

Stepping over a pile of coiled line, I moved up the walkway on past the pilot house to get a few minutes of unrestricted view from the bridge, it was the same scene the Captain and the Officer of the Deck had under observation.

As far as the eye could see, the lumbering transports rode gently over the swells, resembling unenthusiastic joggers more than track stars.

This contrasted sharply with the sleek destroyers, criss-crossing at high speed with almost animal-like exuberance, smashing head on into a wave, then turning to catch the wake left by one of its sister ships. To use an amusement park metaphor, the destroyers resembled a roller coaster ride and the transports a merry-go-round. Swinging the mounted binoculars towards the southern horizon, I caught a glimpse of the heavier and chunkier warship, *Painted Veil*, in the distance, presumably available to add its more deadly firepower to the upcoming battle for Asian freedom.

"I heard you ask Private Agi what the Emperor's name is again," Sakamoto said, talking to Kaine.

"Monarchies don't seem to be my strong point."

"What's the name of England's King-Emperor?" he quizzed.

"Louis the Fourteenth," Private Kaine promptly answered.

"Not Louis the Fourteenth. That was France. George the Sixth is the head of the British Empire."

"Is he the one who fiddled around with Marie Antoinette?" Jun asked attempting to show some interest.

"George the Sixth? No!" Sakamoto shouted, bewildered by Kaine's inability to keep the monarchies straight.

"I meant Hirohito," he said, exasperated.

"It was Lou. . . oh, nevermind, let's move on."

Pausing on the outside ladder leading to *Ikeda Maru's* superstructure, I scanned the horizon. Even though the ships in the fleet had their running lights on, I still couldn't see many of the N.Y.K. dethroned queen's floating subordinates.

The dim light produced one undesired effect. As *Kuji Maru's* searchlight swung in our direction it caught Inspector Ibuse head-high coming out of the shadows. The sardonic grin on his face etched by the artificial illumination turned Sakamoto's and my nerves to jello.

Ohira, an ex-merchant marine captain, looked right at home in the padded chair reserved for the ship's skipper. "How are your twin daughters and your lovely wife, Captain?" the Professor asked.

"Both girls want to be pearl divers. That's the hazard of living in the beautiful little town of Toba, home of the celebrated women pearl divers. How is Kimiko? And I assume this is our esteemed aviator."

"*Hai*, Captain, and Kimiko is fine, dozo," he said moving aside so I could utter my remarks.

"I am honored to be in you presence, Captain," I said, bowing respectfully towards the man with the dark, penetrating eyes, finely chiseled face, and faintly weathered skin that attested to his years at sea

After the conventional pleasantries were concluded, Ohira took a moment to instruct the officer of the deck, then asked Sakamoto to pretend that this was one of his standard sessions.

"Thank you, Captain," he said with the customary bow. "But would you mind answering a couple of questions concerning those who make their living on the ocean?"

"No, go ahead."

"Do you miss being on land?"

"During the last part of a long voyage, I miss the steep-roofed farmhouses, the log bridges, ferns, maple trees, trout fishermen, and the cherry blossoms," he said off the top of his head. "But most of all, my wife, Emiko and the twins.

"You can never tell when nostalgia will hit you. When I passed someone on the weatherdeck yesterday, I suddenly thought of a trip I took with my parents years ago through a camphor forest."

"But even though you miss your family, you stay in the navy."

"After I've been home for awhile the urge to go to sea becomes irresistible.

"Does the captain always go down with his ship?"

"Well, after undergoing an explosion a couple of years ago, the Japanese passenger liner, *Bokuyo Maru* sank. The captain of that ship was doing fine the last time I saw him, and figures to live to a ripe old age.

On the other side of the coin--rather than face a maritime board of inquiry, Capt. Edward J. Smith of the *Titanic* dove into the icy waters of the North Atlantic without a life preserver."

"Disasters at sea are very rare, I imagine," I said hopefully.

"Nature's whims aren't the only danger we face. Last year, even though we were neutral, one of Great Britain's warships stopped the passenger liner *Asama Maru* on the high seas and searched it."

"Go ahead with the question you were about to ask me down below, Kiyo," the Professor insisted, hoping to get to a new topic.

"Are you interested in ship disasters?" Ohira asked me.

"Not really."

"I just finished reading about the *Matsu Maru*. It sank in a collision at the turn of the century with three hundred lives lost."

"Too bad."

"And the *Kiche Maru* sank off the Japanese coast just before World War One with a thousand casualties."

"I'm more interested in economics," the Professor said trying to get him off the subject.

"Oh, in that case. You'd want to hear about the two Japanese cargo ships that sank in Tsushima straits with five million dollars worth of gold and silver bullion on board way back in the sixteenth century."

"Not really."

"I've heard that you deal in pocketbook issues. I imagine the colonies fit under that category," the skipper submitted, enjoying himself.

I excused myself and stepped outside for a second. An indistinct human shape stood at the bottom rung of the ladder. He probably wonders what an aviator's doing talking to the Captain, I thought. The ship had sailed into an area of heavier mist. The dampness and lower visibility were the first signs that mother nature faced a clinical depression.

Moving back inside, I heard Ohira ask, "Won't the additional competition when we set Asia free hurt our trade balance?"

I put my hand on the engine room telegraph out of curiosity.

"Don't move that!" Captain Ohira warned.

"I think we can hold our own in any trading," Sakamoto said in reply to the question. "It's certainly better than the present way of doing business. Colonies are profitable only if one has the ear of the political or royal authorities."

I stepped outside again. "Can I help you?" I asked when the shadowy figure placed his foot on the ladder leading to the ship's bridge.

"Can anybody go up this ladder?"

"I don't think so. I believe it's off limits unless you're invited up by the captain."

Although I couldn't see his face in the darkness, I had the feeling I had run into him before.

A housefly, known to Sakamoto as *Sea Bandit*, stopped rubbing his forelegs together, and left the handrail to follow a trail left by cracker crumbs and what I concluded to be the scent of mothballs. Its translucent wings were caught briefly in the beam of *Enchanted Shadow's* searchlight.

As I opened the door to the chart room, I wondered why someone would hang around the pathway to the bridge. Whew! I thought, I've got to check my sea bag for moth balls.

"Hai," I heard Sakamoto say, "To keep Asia from becoming a permanent toy for the West, someone has to stand up and take the heat-- and Japan's right-wing has decided to take on that task. What are your thoughts from a naval point of view, Captain?" he asked, curious.

"The navy was unable to stop a British squadron from threatening to bombard Japan some years ago, unless a certain city handed over $60,000 worth of yen. I understand Japan paid this protection insurance, much to the embarrassment of our fledgling sea service," the Captain admitted. "So you see, we have a score to settle."

"Please tell him about the destruction of your hometown, *Sensei*," I said, moved by the Captain's remarks.

"What I forgot to say previously, was that the British ships were equipped with the latest Armstrong cannon and their marines and bluejackets swarmed ashore and set the port on fire. We lost that mini

-war and British troops became the first occupation forces ever stationed in our country. They were headquartered on a bluff overlooking the harbor. Britain's battle-hardened IX regiment set up camp in hopes of staying permanently.

"The survivors, the port city kids, who remembered the reddish glow as the rockets maimed the population and destroyed their homes, became the grandparents of the soldiers and sailors you see on all sides of you," Michi declared with an uncharactoristic chill in his voice. "Chasing the British army out of Southeast Asia will give us the confidence we need to free the Orient from European rule."

"The West loves to burn down cities, and Kaine's scared to death of fire," I said.

"He had an Identical twin brother named Kikori," Michi said, turning to me for confirmation, his face taking on a melancholy look. He died in1923 as a result of a fire caused by the Kanto earthquake. He was only six months old at the time."

"That's a rough one. I'm sorry to hear that," the Captain said sympathetically, immediately thinking of his twin daughters. "But I understand his fear."

Captain Ohira used the voice tube to call for a pot of green tea and three cups.

I felt I had to contribute something. "Here we are on the high seas, taking a giant step to free Asia from Western control."

"Malaya, one of the great markets of the world," Sakamoto added, "will be held captive until some nation helps her engineer a prison break. What do you think our chances are, Captain?"

"Since the British army won't stay in their own backyard where they belong, the question is kind of academic," the Captain retorted, showing his fighting spirit. "Unless we knock out the American fleet it will be a nightmare. By the way, Professor, where are you in your sessions with the men?"

"I'm talking about the time when the U.S. was loaded with cheaply priced oil and was anxious to find a market for its surplus."

"Ah so!" the Captain said. "We helped build up their economy."

"In fact, when the big Texas oil fields went into production, there was so much crude oil available in the United States that a law was passed to keep the price per barrel from going lower.

"Where do you expect to go when your tour of duty on this ship is up, Captain? If you don't mind my asking."

"I hope to be assigned to the staff aboard the aircraft fleet carrier,

Dark Cloud.

"Three days from now and an hour after the bombardment of the Malayan beaches commences, we'll hit the American military forces to keep them from supporting the Global Empire's occupation troops."

"America doesn't understand how much Asia wants its freedom," Sakamoto said. "but won't hitting Malaya first give America a tremendous tactical advantage? Singapore will inform them whenever the battle starts."

"Can't be helped. The Pacific fleet, based in Pearl Harbor, will steam to the Far East in support of King-Emperor George VI," the Captain said grimly. "I'll have to ask you to leave now, Professor, I have to make plans for a fleet gunnery exercise."

Sakamoto got up immediately, gave a slight bow, and headed out the door, pausing only long enough to collect me and thank the Captain for the tea and talk.

I bowed in deference to the Captain's rank and thanked him for allowing my humble person to be part of the conversation.

This should be my last night in the anchor compartment.

Chapter 33

Fish Bowl

I followed Yeoman Nitta, who seemed to be shadowing Private Agi.

They went to the vicinity of deceased Corporal Kono's bunk, where Agi reached under and pulled out a tiny fish bowl. Its small opening was covered over with a piece of porous cloth.

"A nice, fancy goldfish," he muttered, looking at its orange coloring, bulging eyes, large fan-like tail and huge dorsal fin.

Turning to the adjacent bunk, he grabbed an expensive female Beta out of its container. After making a hasty and ineffectual check to see if there was anyone nearby, he threw it in the bowl along with the goldfish.

Where are they going now? I wondered, following the thief and his shadow.

Out on the weather deck, Private Kiroku Agi placed the little fish bowl down perilously close to the edge. "Fish," he said to the occupants. "You've been swimming in circles all your life. You must branch out and find out what the real world has to offer. Acting as your travel agent, I'm signing you up for a long cruise." With that, he kicked the fish bowl over the side.

"You'll have plenty of room for swimming in your new aquarium." I heard Agi shout down towards the waves, while Nitta made an unearthly cackle.

As the ship maintained a more southwesterly heading, I figured a dyed-in-the-wool aristocrat like Roosevelt would find it impossible not to put his rapidly expanding two-million-man armed forces and its four thousand M-4 tanks into battle on the side of European royalty.

"The only thing that could disrupt the American juggernaut spearheaded by its eight hundred Pacific based fighters and bombers when hostilities commenced in the far East," the Professor assured us, "would be some stupid mistake on their part."

Agi gave up any hope that the United States would agree to cut off armaments to a nation that controlled one-fourth of the world's population.

263

The convoy no longer needed fighter protection from *Sky Dragon*. The ships were now in comfortable range of army and navy aircraft based in Vietnam.

It was a busy day for the historians assigned to catalogue the fast moving events in the Pacific, and busier yet for Professor Sakamoto. He had less than seventy-two hours to turn the citizen soldiers into patriotic demons.

Agi burst out laughing when Kaine asked him if America might decide to fight for Asian independence instead of backing the King-Emperor.

"It's about as likely," Sukebator said, "as France giving Vietnam its freedom. Besides, Sakamoto believes the U.S. has already broken the Japanese navy's code."

"If we happen to be standing in this same spot a couple of days from now," Jun Kaine said, glancing out to sea." the Malayan mountains will dominate the horizon. Which reminds me, I better throw my knapsack in the assault boat," he announced nervously, after checking to make sure he had the netting and mittens that offered protection against mosquito-borne diseases.

When the *Ikeda Maru* came abreast of Cam Ranh Bay. I thought of catching a ride via a Vietnamese fishing boat. The French, and indirectly the British, were well aware that the fleet was passing by the big Vietnamese harbor heading south.

This Malayan-bound convoy must have the record for the worse kept secret in the annals of military history, I thought.

Captain Ohira sent word for me to relax. He said he was making arrangements for my trip via a seaplane tender.

Since I didn't know exactly when I'd leave the ship, I went to the anchor room to get my gear together.

Inspector Ibuse was there.

"Is that your wife?" he asked, looking at a picture I had placed on an anchor link.

"No. That's a nurse I'm going with at the present time."

"She's beautiful," the Inspector remarked, breaking out some pictures of his own.

"How old is your little girl?" I asked. "She looks like a charmer."

"Satsu's ten. Didn't I hear you say you had a brother?"

"Osamu, he lives in Sada, it's an eight hundred square mile island, twenty miles off the west coast of Honshu, opposite the city of Nilgata. It's the home of the crested Ibis, and is renown for its ballads."

"It seems like I've heard that name in reference to some governmental activity."

"That's where Japan banishes its gods. Emperor Juntoku was exiled there," I said with a sparkle in my eye. "I hope that doesn't disillusion you about their relationship to the Sun Goddess."

"No, I'm well acquainted with the West's interpretation of our legends. But it's going to be hard to convince America we aren't emperor worshippers now that they've seen the operetta *Mikado* by Gilbert and Sullivan.

"Something weird happened on my way here. I swear I smelled mothballs when I passed through a crowd of servicemen."

"Do you have any suspects?" I found his eyes devoid of any visible separation between eye color and pupil to be unnerving. It reminded me of uncomprehensible forces--something on the order of the pull of gravity. Falling into a bottomless pit was the first thought that came to mind.

"Is your brother old enough to be in the service?" Ibuse asked, in an effort to be friendly.

"Osamu's already in the navy. He's a rear-seat gunner in a torpedo plane squadron."

"I'd like to employ your help, Debuchi-san. Search your memory for any out-of-the-ordinary activities of Private Agi and Quartermaster Kato."

"Like what?"

"Any unusual phobias. Do either of them seem obsessed with rank, weapons, religion, or whatever. And does Kato profess a real hatred of soldiers?"

"You mean obsessions like Private Agi's, who's never without a paper umbrella?"

"A serial killer is usually a quiet upstanding member of the community. A loner," Ibuse assured me, quoting the party line without displaying any of his own feelings. "The type person you would never suspect. Just keep an open mind and let me know if anything occurs to you."

"I'll give it some thought," I promised, figuring it might be fun to play detective. "I can tell you this much. Talking to Quartermaster Kato is more dangerous than taking honey from a bear."

Finding myself with some time to kill after I'd finished packing my gear, I decided to listen to Sakamoto's latest motivation speech.

The Professor was in high gear.

"Admiral Halsey's task force is operating under wartime conditions, It has its torpedoes fitted with warheads, aircraft with live ammunition and dive bombers loaded with five hundred pound bombs. Any Japanese or unidentified aircraft aproaching the their fleet is sure to be fired on."

He had the men's attention.

A voice identifying himself as the ship's executive officer spoke out in an impatient torrent. "Did we do anything to cheat on our neutrality in the European War?"

"No!" Sakamoto snapped. "We're staying out of that squabble. We learned our lesson in World War One. But the Americans didn't. They stepped up their involvement. In October, American destroyers joined in combat alongside Royal Navy warships against a submarine wolf pack."

"Didn't Germany declare war over that incident?"

"No, but America kept up the pressure. The destroyer, U.S.S. Kearney was torpedoed with a loss of lives. Two weeks later, the United States armed merchant ship, Salinas, and her destroyer escorts, fought a battle with a German submarine. The Salinas was torpedoed and sunk."

"The Americans are at war," Sukebator declared.

"Not according to the White House. The American people haven't caught on yet to the way Washington operates. Saying one thing while doing the opposite is routine for them."

"Same thing with our House of Representatives," the legislator's son remarked.

Sakamoto continued. "The destroyer, U.S.S. Reuben James, was sunk convoying British Empire merchant ships that were carrying war supplies to the King-Emperor."

"Surely there must be some reason for America to risk her servicemen's lives to protect a European empire?" a man from the Taiwanese Mountain Artillery suggested.

"Sure! The pocketbook," Sakamoto declared. "Believing the British Empire will last many lifetimes, America hangs onto the Englishmen's coattails while listening to aristocrat Churchill call the people from China and Japan little yellow men."

I could almost feel the anger in the servicemen surrounding me.

"Suppose the countries occupied by the British army get their freedom?"

"Then America has bet on the wrong horse, and somewhere down the line will have a gigantic negative trade balance," he guessed.

Chapter 34

Castle Sinking

Later that morning, a float plane from one of the two seaplane tenders operating in the area picked me up.

Once ashore, I caught a ride in a Nissan half-ton truck. We headed south through Saigon on the way to Soc Trang airfield.

I reported to the squadron duty officer without delay.

"Happy to have you," the ensign said. "We need every pilot we can get our hands on. All hell's going to break loose within the next few days.

My heart beat faster, time was closing in on me. "Is it okay if I walk along the flight line?"

"Sure, get acquainted with our routine. Silent Storm fighters are the ones painted white with no trim. You've been assigned plane number 411.

I tossed him a thank you as I walked out the door.

My view of 411 was partially blocked by the back of a Caucasian male, who I assumed was a French civilian.

When he veered off in a direction away from the flight line, it enabled me to spot the large black lettering on the nose of the aircraft that spelled out *Mitsubishi Melody*.

I raced over, reached up and touched the words to make sure they were painted on, not just temporarily placed there with some sort of dark-colored chalk.

Life doesn't get any better than this, I thought. NAP Kiyo Debuchi had been stenciled in just below the canopy.

I made a quick circle of the aircraft and happily discovered that the squadron had placed the name on both sides.

Standing among the rows of naval fighter planes helped me shake off the apprehension I felt whenever I thought about tangling with the King-Emperor's subjects and their passion-driven opposition to Asian freedom and independence.

I put my hand on the cowling of the A6M2, Model 21, Zero. It was a beauty. Its white paint sparkled in the sun. Under that cowling was a Sakae 12 engine, capable of generating 1,000 hp. I ran my finger along the leading edge of the wing where the twin 20 mm cannons were located, then switched my attention to the two 7.7 mm machine guns jutting out of the upper section of the nose.

This plane was fast, maneuverable and sailor-friendly. Besides having long-range capabilities, it had numerous safety features to protect the naval airman in case he had to ditch at sea.

Having been given the opportunity to dilute the effect any previous blunders might have had on my record. I was determined to become a fighter pilot my shipmates could be proud of.

The pilot known as Ghost Leader, the squadron's commanding officer, confronted me. "I've got a job for you."

"Yes, sir."

"Did anyone mention seeing a yacht when the fleet passed by Cam Ranh Bay?"

"No, sir."

"That's funny. There's usually an American Admiral's yacht cruising outside the bay, spying on our ship movements. Take the Fire Dragon parked down at the extreme end of this flight line and conduct a fifty mile search pattern. See if you can locate that yacht."

"The Ki-27 is an army plane."

"I don't want to use a Zero right now, and we happen to have a Ki-27 that landed here when it ran low on fuel. The pilot is quarantined. He has measles."

"Yes, sir," I said, hurrying to change into my flight gear. When I got back to the flight line, I took a piece of masking tape out of my pocket and slapped a 411 on both sides of the nose of the Fire Dragon in place of the standard army number. Stepping back to admire my handiwork, something deep in my subconscious cautioned me not to advertise my presence on this mission. Ignoring the irritating warning, I jumped in the aircraft, started it, and headed for the runway.

An hour into my patrol and I still hadn't spotted the American yacht. Although the briefing officer had advised me that British and American planes were conducting a search in this area--he had also said with any luck at all, I probably wouldn't cross paths with them if I stayed on a southerly heading.

This seemed to be the best altitude for reconnaissance, I thought, tilting my head upward. The clouds above me resemble nothing more than shredded, dirty sheets and only partially covered the sky.

Aware that it was all clear below me, I trimmed the aircraft and let my mind drift back to thoughts of Vietnam. Although Professor Sakamoto mentioned Manchuria as a subject that turns the West blue in the face--I agreed with him that Vietnam sends their blood pressure even higher.

Farther on, I flew under a double dip ice-cream, cone-shaped, cumulous cloud formation and ran into light air turbulence. Easing back on the throttle, I readjusted the trim tabs, and let my mind drift again. The French had invaded Vietnam in the 1800s, and the Vietnamese, along with the Laotians and Cambodians, have been trying to get their freedom from Western occupation troops ever since.

Japan's move into Vietnam's airfields and naval bases which were established and controlled by the French military sent the West into orbit. Paranoid at the thought of having Vietnam obtain its freedom, America had imposed a trade embargo on Japan and seized its assets.

There must be a lot more to this Vietnam thing than meets the eye, I thought. Maybe it's the huge profits and tax from the opium and salt monopoly, or the promise of oil in the shallow waters off the coastline. Whatever it is, it sure makes the Westerners drool.

Glancing at the fuel gauge, I figured there was enough left for a little flat-hatting. While descending, I reflected on the hypocrisy of the West. They failed to freeze French assets or place a trade embargo on France during the last eighty years, but needed only forty-eight hours to take reprisal action against an Asian country.

Leveling off at one thousand feet to check out a momentary drop in manifold pressure, I wondered what the Western countries told their people about the permanent residence and dictorial powers of the French Foreign Legion in the Far East.

With the Nakajima engine running smoothly again, I put in some nose - high trim and and took the Fire Dragon down, down, down--down to where an engine misfire, a bird, or the slightest mistake handling the controls would make me a permanent deep-sea inhabitant assigned to a spot on the ocean floor set aside for aviators obsessed with low-level, high-speed flight.

A man-made object suddenly shattered the intense concentration so necessary for playing chicken with the wave tops. I yanked the plane around for a better look. A submarine broke the surface.

Climbing, I tuned in the convoy's frequency. "Riptide," I called. "Submarine sighted bearing 230 degrees, forty miles from you."

"Hai, hai! from Riptide. What nationality?"

"Dutch," I answered, getting a clear view as the sub surfaced. "It's pointed towards Indonesia."

"The odds are he knows the convoy's course. Riptide out."

I headed south along the Vietnamese coastline. Flying past the port of Haiphong, with Hanoi barely in sight further to the west, I got a quick glimpse of the fertile rice-growing valley, through which flowed the life-giving Red River.

Looking inland, I watched the contestants gather for the Miss Cloudburst contest. A dark, shapely whisp stepped boldly forward, followed by a billowing moisture-laden model, a curvaceous, loud-mouthed thunderhead, and an angry, gorgeous swirl, before being ovrshadowed by a chic, black drifter with flashing eyes--closer in--a soft, misty-eyed, cuddly creature beckoned me to step into her highly-charged bedchambers.

Swinging further south over the mouth of the Mekong River, I had a good view of the waterway whose journey began over two thousand miles away in China's northwest territory. From there, the gypsy-like stream swings down to provide a shadowy border between Thailand and Laos, then meanders through Cambodia and Vietnam. There its nine tribuaries form the Mekong Delta before it empties into the South China Sea.

On a sudden whim, I called for landing instructions and turned onto my final approach over the giant Michelin Tire Company's plantation outside of Saigon. I had decided to visit my old army buddy, Tomi.

I brought the plane in for a hot-landing on the extended runway, bounced, added enough throttle and height to roll the aircraft, then set it back down as gently as a mother with a new born baby.

I maneuvered between the long rows of Zeroes and Peregrine Falcons on the sagging taxiway and melted asphalt, wishing the plane had knee-action shock absorbers.

With aching muscles from holding onto the control stick so hard at low level, I followed the lineman to a parking spot near the tower. Two unenthusiastic Vietnamese labors dressed in black trousers and tightly buttoned white jackets swept the area in front of the aircraft.

After giving fueling instructions to the line mechanic, I got out of the plane and took off at a moderate clip for the command building. Conscious of the stiffness in my back and shoulders, I rotated my arms in a series of exercises to relieve the tension.

Brushing off a dark-green Peacock butterfly from my hand, I stepped into the entrance with a false show of energy, startling the secretary on duty. "Can I help you?" she asked, her eyes giving me the once-over for practice. Some interest showed in her face as she noted the petty officer first class emblem, but she didn't appear overly impressed until she spotted the pilot's wings on my lightweight summer flight suit. Her eyes lit up with the thought of steady flight pay.

"I'd like to get hold of the army first lieutenant who flies a plane called *Dolly,* please," I said taking an abbreviated look at the interior of the building constructed entirely from bamboo.

"Oh, you mean Tomi," the secretary said, her delightful Japanese speech lightily doused with Vietnamese words, the accent very noticeable. "You're in luck. He's scheduled for a flight and is almost always an hour early," she claimed, acutely aware of my soft, slow approach.

"Thank you," I said, pouring on the charm as she rose from behind the desk to show off her *ao dai,* a long, dark-green, embroidered, coat-like garment worn over tailored white trousers. "I assume he comes in early to see and talk to you. That's what I would do if I were based here. Tomi has all the luck."

"Why don't you ask the navy to station you here?" she countered timidly, her Paris earrings jiggling as she talked.

"I'm Kiyo Debuchi. May I have your name, please?" I asked, moving closer to the desk of this woman whose creamy skin was dusted with the light from the afternoon sun.

"Mieu," she said, moving her pencil aimlessly around the desk top.

"Isn't Mieu the Vietnamese word for salt? Your parents were wise to name you after such a precious substance."

Mieu nodded, keeping her mahogany-tinted eyes and long lashes lowered, too flustered to say more.

"Flying in here, I saw what looked like an elaborate road system," I remarked softly, giving her a chance to compose herself.

"The French rubber-plantation managers had the highway built," the secretary said, smiling now.

"That must have taken an awful lot of manpower and money."

"Forced labor, exorbitant taxation, and the French Foreign Legion as exterminators provide a powerful trio."

"How do the French get their money out of the country?" I asked cautiously.

"From the French-owned Bank of Indochina funneled through the Bank of Paris," Mieu answered bitterly. "It's easy to strip a country of its resources when you have the guns."

"I thought Paris was under occupation."

"British and American banks are still doing business there."

"You have to hand it to the Westerners. They know how to steal and act saintly at the same time."

"And they know how to shove you around," Mieu said, making pushing motions with her small, shapely hands. "Here comes your buddy Tomi. Early, just like I said."

"Greetings, future Ghost Leader," Tomi said cheerfully, walking behind a naval officer attaired in dress whites with a high collar trimmed in black lace.

Obviously happy to see my old pal, I executed an exaggerated bow.

"I see you've met the crown jewel of this old building," he kidded in a tone that resembled a cat's purr. "Watch him, Mieu; he's got several girl friends in the Far East."

"I'm sure he would have mentioned that before long," Mieu said coyly.

Embarrassed, I was steered by the army pilot towards the exit. I waved goodbye to the secretary who now looked pleased with herself.

We reluctantly left the cooler air provided by the revolving fan for the humid outdoors. "How've you been?" I asked.

"Pretty good. Lots of flying," he said, blowing a kiss Mieu's way as we walked through the doorway. "And you?"

I wished I'd had an excuse to talk longer to the attractive Vietnamese woman. "No personal problems," I replied, following him to the hanger area. "And like you, lots of flying."

"I see Zeroes parked everywhere I go in the southern part of this country," Tomi said, pausing to stare back at an inquisitive Sika deer looking over the shrubbery at us. "I thought you guys were supposed to operate off aircraft carriers?" he commented, combining a statement with a question.

"Obviously, Prime Minister Tojo doesn't believe the army's Ki-43 Peregrine Falcon is capable of handling the British aircraft."

"Hah!" Tomi said with joyful anticipation. "I'll give you a two thousand foot altitude advantage and still whip your butt.

"We're turning right at the parking lot. It's a short cut to the hanger area," he advised me, pointing out a large number of chequered swallowtail butterflies hovering over a patch of damp earth as he stepped around them.

"Have you been here long enough to form an opinion of the French Foreign Legion?" I asked, matching my stride to his five foot, six inch frame.

"They're ruthless fighters, backed by a tough regime in Paris. In 1930 they killed and deported over sixty thousand Vietnamese when a serious resistance movement started."

"How do the French keep such a rich country under control besides killing and deporting?"

"By destroying whole towns at the slightest sign of trouble," he told me, bending back a skinny branch hanging over the pathway. "What they don't demolish with firepower, they impoverish with mandatory wine quotas. Got to keep the wine-growers back home happy."

"What do you think of the upcoming Malayan campaign?"

"With the help of the Malayan people, the land battles ought to go as scheduled. And the Australians and British are due for a surprise in the air. But having to keep the Yankees from blindsiding us is bad news."

"I agree. It would be a fairer fight if the U.S. stayed neutral like we're doing in the European War. Do you think there's any hope of that?"

"No," he answered, speaking loudly enough to overcome the noise of the planes revving up for take off. "The gossip says that Roosevelt promised Churchill they will jump in immediately. You know he's not going to stand by and watch us throw the King-Emperor's armed forces out of one Asian country after another. And we will have lost the chance to cripple their initial striking power if we delude ourselves into thinking they will."

"We're caught in an ugly bind," I said. "Bankruptcy and possibly going communist if we don't fight, or facing a dozen or so white nations eager to get at our assets if we do fight."

"We could give in to all of Britain's demands," he declared. "We're going to pass behind the hanger on your left," he said, interrupting himself. "The flight line is on the other side."

"You mentioned something interesting, Britain's demands."

"The United States is doing the negotiating for the King-Emperor's claims," he noted before changing the subject. "You've been to Thailand, haven't you? What's the feeling there?"

"Thailand is boxed in. French troops on her eastern border, and British on the western side. She wants Asia freed from foreign control as much as we do. I'm sure she'll fight on the side of the Orientals."

"By the way. Do you still give your left glove a tug for luck?"

"I'm past that stage. I no longer need a crutch," I replied with pride.

"Oh, I almost forgot," Tomi said reaching into his pocket. "I've got a letter with 'Hisako' scribbled in the upper left hand corner of the envelope. It was hand delivered from Canton to the naval district in Japan. From there it went to Hainan where it was misrouted by N.A.S. Yulin to me. It's addressed to: *Mitsubishi Melody:* army business. Does the name Hisako ring any bells?"

"*Hai,* I'll read it later," I said, stuffing it inside my flight suit.

"There's your plane," the army aviator said, still doubtful about my ability to give up a superstitious habit so easily. "If you happen to take a detour to look over the landing sites in Northern Malaya, watch yourself; the British are trigger-happy."

"I will."

"I hope our paths cross often, Debuchi-san. Take care of yourself."

"Say goodbye to Mieu for me."

Out on the airstrip, I cracked open the canopy on the late model Ki-27 so I could hear the deep-throated roar of the Nakajima engine. It reminded me of a car with a blown muffler.

The bumps and ruts of the deteriorating tropical runway rushing at me seemed to flatten out as the plane approached take-off speed. A few more knots and she left the ground eager for new challenges.

I took the long way around to Phu Quoc, a sixty-mile-long amoeba-shaped island off the west coast of Vietnam that was to be my new base. According to the aeronautical chart, there was a group of small hills in the northeastern sector and a village called Duong Dong on the side facing Thailand.

Seventy-five miles southwest of Saigon, I passed within sighting distance of a Norwegian freighter.

I've got great news, Ghost Leader said, greeting me on my return. "You're on the list for promotion to chief petty officer. Congratulations!"

"We're having a saki party for you tonight," Nogi said.

By noontime, I was already into my second hop of the day in the Fire Dragon and I was worried. Had Jane and Hisako inadvertently placed me in this perilous position. Or was *Wen Kami* operating behind the scenes?

Unfortunately for my well-being. The most chilling of my fanciful daydreams now confronted me in real life. I refused to believe it was coincidental that a British PBY suddenly came into view just as the Malayan-bound convoy appeared over the horizon. Glass enclosed teardrop openings on each side of the plane made it easy to identify.

I'll bet those cricket-players feel superior to the Asians in that nifty, American-built, twin-engine aircraft of theirs, I thought, trying to make light of a dangerous situation. The plane can carry bomb racks and is equipped with plenty of gun stations.

In addition, the pilots believe they're playing a key role in the downfall of the last obstacle to the white man's conquest of the Far East.

I had a clue to their attitude from overhearing a conversation between two Royal Navy pilots in Shanghai: The big one, feeling jubilant after his victory in two games of squash that morning, said optimistically, "On the ground, the Japs are in trouble because they're myopic; they can't shoot straight like our chaps can. In the air, they're in worse shape, having to fly a bunch of fabric-covered aircraft with lousy engines."

"I hear the blighters will run at the sight of a white man," his pilot buddy suggested.

"You can say that again," the first one had claimed. "We'll cut those squinty-eyed creatures in half before they have a chance to get us in their sights, if they even use gunsights."

I had stalled around long enough. My last thought before returning to the task at hand was just plain absurd. I wondered if the British crew wouldn't rather be flying into the west coast of America. It's Saturday, the sixth of December in San Francisco. That town would be jumping tonight.

The PBY's radioman has undoubtedly sent out an urgent message to his home base pinpointing the covoy's location, I figured. And even more ominously, maybe the patrol bomber's going to drop a string of aerial mines set to detonate when the thin-skinned troop transports pass over them. Hesitation has always been my downfall, but for the sake of my comrade-in-arms, I had better take action promptly this time.

"I had never received the most valuable player award while playing with the Kabuti Kites," I muttered. "Nor did I ever win a batting title. I usually swung too late. But I do possess the opportunity now to have my name appear in someone's record book. Providing, I get up the nerve to act."

My reluctance to throw the first punch was weakened somewhat when I remembered the old literature term, *Castle Sinking.* It makes reference to an abandoned fortress.

By forcing us to give up any hope of freeing Asia, the West will make sure our future is as barren as that lonely, useless castle.

Rejecting all my built-in fear of starting an uncontrollable avalanche, I began closing the distance between us.

Halfway to the optimum firing position, I gave a tug to my left glove. A few more seconds and I had the bomber in my sights.

I was now out of excuses for not shooting. The target was in range.

My fingers trembled in their eagerness to have the struggle for Asian independence begin. Preferably by someone else.

My thumb hovered over the firing button, unsure.

I envisioned the multitude of guns on the bomber.

My thumb hardened and stood ready to begin its downward arc.

With the mental picture of an empty castle searing my mind. I took a deep breath and smashed down on the firing mechanism.

The seaplane shuttered as the 7.7 mm bullets tore into the compartment where the flight engineer sits--*I had fired the first shots of the Pacific War.*

My brain was immediately cluttered with second thoughts. What have I done! A radiotelephone call from Singapore to Washington will surely bring a batch of American home run hitters into the game.

"Too late now," I yelled. "Gunners, how do you like the flying ability of this poor, illiterate coolie?" I turned the Fire Dragon within the length of their aircraft and headed back for another try.

Looking through the flashes of light coming from my cowling-mounted machine guns, I saw the PBY's tracers from the tunnel gunner probing for my vitals. My cautious nature wasn't going to get in the way this time. I gritted my teeth and continued towards the enemy.

"I hit him again!" I hollered, as his windscreen was blown away.

Fighting the fierce air currents, the Catalina turned to give the gun in the starboard blister a chance to fire.

I shot the British gunner before he got me in his sights.

Not wishing to waste any more ammo on the fatally wounded plane, I watched the PBY finish up its final flight by plunging into the Gulf of Thailand, the first casualty of Operation Asian Independence.

Looking through the glazed canopy down at the blue water, I patted the telescopic gunsight, but felt no sense of elation, no adrenaline high. It was more like the feeling you get on Monday morning after a hectic weekend. The endless string of challenges that lie ahead of me somewhat dampened my enthusiasm. I was concerned whether the world would remember the new chief petty officer as a patriot or a war monger.

Following orders, I flew to Soc Trang and swapped the Ki-27 for the faster *Mitsubishi Melody* before returning to Phu Quoc.

I was sitting in the cockpit of my beloved Zero at midnight.

As briefed, one hour later I took off.

Thanks to my new attitude, I managed to be in the hottest spot just offshore of Kota Bharu when the convoy's warships opened fire.

The exploding shells hit the British gun emplacements as the bombardment escalated.

Minutes later, luck deserted the British Imperial forces when I detected a flash of moonlight off a Royal Australian Hudson bomber's wingtip. Another American-built aircraft.

Under a skyful of shapeless clouds, I steered the shiny white Zero alongside the aircraft built in Inglewood, California. Then getting the attention of the pilot, I pointed in the direction of Vietnam, intending to escort him safely down.

Instead of giving an affirmative signal, the Hudson's guns swung in my direction as we passed into an area of thunder and lightning. Not waiting until the weather deteriorated any further, or letting the thirty caliber machine guns locate me, I gave another tug to my left glove, rolled under the plane, pulled up, and fired at point blank range.

Dropping back in case the bomber blew, I watched it fight to maintain altitude before plummeting to the ocean. A lonely grave, far from home, for those foreigners who thought they had a God-given right to strip the Orient of its wealth and dignity.

I broke out in a big smile. The second victory against the Global Empire belonged to a navy plane.

My aircraft hadn't escaped unscathed. When I attempted to lean out the Sakae engine, it sputtered. Easing the mixture control forward, I noted the lever was almost to the full-rich position before the engine smoothed out. A bad sign with the air base an uncomfortable distance away.

Facing the possibility that some of the gunfire had found its way into the nine-cyclinder, air-cooled powerplant, I trimmed the aircraft for level flight, and doubled the scan of my instrument panel.

I'd gone only a short way toward Phu Doc when the oil pressure suddenly dropped. I quickly reversed course.

The safer course of action would be to make a water landing near the hospital ship and let them pick me up. But there was a big drawback to that choice. *Whispering Wind* happened to be at the rear of the amphibious fleet and I'd miss part of the opening day's action.

I chose to pancake the plane in next to the anchored *Ikeda Maru* instead.

Nonsensical thought: I wondered who had won the anchor pool.

I was still puttering with the mixture control when I passed over the first of the troop transports. At mast-high level and hoping my backfiring engine wouldn't get me shot down, I weaved my way through the maze.

Overjoyed at finding the wind in my favor and enough space on *Ikeda Maru's* starboard side, I gripped the control stick tightly, flew parallel to the ship's heading and maintained a fast-enough gliding speed to keep the plane from stalling. The ultimate outcome I left in the hands of my favorite shrine.

Approaching the stern of the ten-thousand-ton vessel, I had the flaps down, kept the landing gear in the retracted position, took a deep breath, and cut off the ignition, before dropping the plane into the sea about half-way up the length of the salt-stained ship.

The shoulder harness prevented me from being thrown forward during the initial contact with the water and was an absolute life-saver when it kept me tied into the seat throughout the secondary splash-down produced by the bounce.

I pulled the lever to blow up the flotation bags so the aircraft wouldn't sink. A cargo net was quickly lowered and a seaman assisted me onto the weatherdeck.

Temporarily confused by the continuous gunfire from the heavy caliber guns of the warships compounded by the wild water-landing, I was led to a bunk in sick bay.

Still somewhat disoriented, I fell into a disturbed sleep, highlighted ironically by a nightmare as the sky grew lighter.

In my dream, I found myself in a place called the Foldup Saloon on an unidentified beach lined with palm trees and a pink hotel in the distance.

Feeling lost, I found an empty spot at the bar and asked for a Nippon beer.

Before the Caucasian bartender wearing a flowery-patterned Hawaiian shirt had a chance to serve me, I was yanked off the stool by a man calling himself the Gold Dust Fireball.

A group of white men left their tables claiming I threw the first punch. They held up signs printed in longhand with catchy slogans like "Malaya is mine," "Britain defeated Burma three times," "Wake Island," and "India belongs to the strongest," They crowded in on me, I tried backing away. But non-Asians pushed in from all sides--slowly, surely, inching me into the nearest corner.

With a lifelong tendency towards claustrophobia, I panicked. I turn violent whenever a full-blown anxiety attack hits. Squashed against the wall with hostile Caucasian faces mocking me, the mental torture approached its crest. I held my breath to appease the internal demons, but the next spasm drove me mad. I started shaking--the first signs of a destructive convulsion. Another shudder and I threw all caution to the winds.

I quickly slammed my fist into the throat of an Englishman sporting a Malayan tattoo, then spun around, grabbed the nearest chair, tore off one of its legs--and took measured aim at the man the Britisher referred to as Yank. I smashed this opponent on the right fist with the broken piece of furniture and then savagely attacked the left one.

As a wild-eyed New Zealander yelling "God Save the King-Emperor" threw himself into the fight, I caught him alongside the head with the broken chair leg. I followed this up with with a judo chop to a Dutch attacker exploding in from the sidelines.

Scrambling over the fallen bodies, a pair of French Legionaires closed in. Spotting a window behind the juke box, I ducked away from a bottle-swinging Canadian dressed in a Hong Kong T-shirt, and tried to reach an open window.

A friendly face from Thailand blocked the Legionaires long enough for me to shove a chair next to the push-button music cabinet.

Screaming, "thanks!" to the Thai from the top of the juke box, I turned and executed a well-placed kick to the chin of an Australian getting ready to tear me from limb to limb in the name of His Royal Majesty.

When the British led, unenthusiastic Sikhs closed in. I dove through the open window into the shallow water behind the building. As the last cheer for Queen Wilhelmia died out, military police from two dozen non-Asian countries rushed forward to arrest me. Shaking my head to clear out the cobwebs, I wondered what the rest of Sunday, December 7, 1941, Hawaiian time, had in store for me and my brother Osamu.

Still in a partial daze when I went topside, I heard Sakamoto say that the United States industries had two hundred million dollars invested in Malaya.

On a happier note, I was glad my loved ones, with several exceptions, would be safe from the turmoil of battle, while I and men like me made our bid to free Asia from the white men who had conquered it.

The Professor's discussions had apparently been successful. The men around me were excited and motivated. Being part of an expedition to break those chains of bondage was exhilerating.

As anxious as I was to participate in this worthwhile endeavor, getting killed was not on my agenda. All the talk of dying for the Emperor was nothing but a distortion of the old proverb: "If you must die in battle, it is better to die for a cause."

Converted passenger liners filled with men, horses, and vehicles, are inviting targets for enemy bombers.

I finally remembered the letter Tomi gave me, and raced back to get it out of my jacket pocket.

I heard Inspector Ibuse's spooky voice as I strolled past the personnel office tearing open the envelope.

It was from Hisako: "I forgot to tell you about a Japanese sailor named Nitta," she wrote. "He was accused of stabbing a French gendarme with a bayonet last year while screaming obscenites against whites."

I stuck my head into the office.

Ibuse nodded in my direction.

"It looks like we can forget the hostility toward those who were promoted ahead of the killer as a reason for the murders," he claimed as I got near. "The corporal business was a red herring. A coincidence."

"Read this," I said, handing him the letter.

He grabbed the army files, after hurriedly scanning Hisako's correspondence.

"According to the family records, Hiko Daizen had some French blood, Gyo Mishima certainly had a Norwegian sailor in the family tree, and Corporal Kono was part Portuguese. And lastly, Atsu's Uncle Benjiro had Dutch relatives somewhere in the distant past.

"That does it," Geki Ibuse murmured, throwing the stack of army records on top of the cabinet. "I had better talk to Private Agi before he goes ashore. That bookworm would be the most likely person to have dug up this data.

"But first, let's check out the man who had direct access to this information," Inspector Ibuse said, heading for the landing team files on the opposite side of the administration compartment.

"We'd better hurry," I urged. "Some of the yeoman keep their helmets in the back of the filing cabinet and I noticed Nitta didn't have his on when we passed him in the companionway earlier."

"Look for his name under the N's," Ibuse ordered, glancing anxiously over his shoulder.

Staggered by the sight of so many filing cabinets, I quickly moved to the starboard side of the first row. Even though I was scanning rapidly, it was still taking a dangerous amount of time. And worse luck, although they were filed alphabetically, the navy's cabinets weren't labelled on the outside. I was at the third row before I even got to the C's. "How're you doing?" I asked, yanking open a drawer to check its contents.

"P's," he said, angrily, slamming a drawer in the next row closed.

When I thought I heard the door open at the other end of the compartment, I skipped over two aisles to where I judged would be the correct spot for the N's and found Ibuse already there.

He stooped over to open up the bottom drawer in the middle of the row. "Here it is!" he shouted. "And the helmet's still there."

A whiff of mothballs put my nerves on alert. I increased the number of times I turned my head to see if anything was behind me.

According to the family history section in his personal record," Ibuse said, "Jofu Nitta was born in Kuala Lumpur, Malaya on June I, 1920. His mother was Kesa Minowa. His father, Saji Nitta, was forced out of business by the British Secret Police and committed suicide in disgrace.

"After an incident in which little Jofu was bayoneted several times in the side and shoulder by a British soldier, Jofu's mother returned to Japan with her only child. She obtained employment within the Chinese community in Yokohama.

"By the time he was fifteen, Jofu had been picked up by the police for harassing a white tourist.

"At sixteen years of age he had been accused of beating up an elderly Dutch visitor. At seventeen, he was arrested for disturbing the peace when he screamed at Nami Tanaka for talking to an American businessman.

"I won't have to go ashore. I've got my man."

Nitta and I spotted each other at the same time. The moment he saw Inspector Ibuse standing by the navy filing cabinets, he realized he'd been uncovered.

I poked the inspector.

Even though the survivor of a dozen street brawls reacted quickly, the brawny sailor wasn't fast enough to go undetected by Ibuse.

Unless the ferocity of the expanding battle for Malaya made the JAG officer realize how minor Yeoman Nitta's crimes were in comparison to the destruction surrounding them, hiding was Nitta's only alternative.

He took off running with Geki right behind him. I followed at a more leisurely pace.

The Yeoman tore into the mailroom, shoving a heavy mail cart into Geki when the Inspector tried to enter.

From there we went to the linen storage room on "F" deck, then down a series of ladders to the fire room.

Entering the subterranean world, I paused and listened.

Giant boilers rumbled in their eagerness to supply power, and valves clattered like hail on a tin roof, interspersed with squeaks and puffs from safety devices releasing pressures high enough to blow out the side of the ship.

It was impossible to hear someone moving about. I shifted over to stand behind the noiseless salt-water evaporators.

Geki was up on the catwalk trying to locate the killer. He pointed in the direction of the entrance. I twisted around just in time to spot Nitta leaving the area.

He charged back up the ladder to the scullery on "D" deck with me right behind him. Unable to push the bolted-down tables into my path, he tore through the mess deck on "C", on his way to the hospital room on "B". He tossed an unused IV stand at Ibuse who had passed me by. The race continued on to "A" deck, where he tried to get lost among the hundreds of triple-tiered bunks in the crew quarters.

I arrived in time to see Nitta ease himself out of a bed on the far side of the compartment before Geki Ibuse, moving methodically from bunk to bunk, got to his hiding place. In his hurry to get out Nitta tripped on a hatch opening and fell with a loud crash.

"Here he is!" I hollered.

Picking himself off the deck quickly when he heard Geki grunt in satisfaction, he made haste for the weather deck with the pair of us not too far behind.

Geki and I checked behind the air ventilators. Ahead of us we heard an involuntary squeal as if somebody had stepped on something accidently. Looking towards the bow, I saw a coke bottle spinning aimlessly.

"Give yourself up," Ibuse shouted. "I'll have you zeroed in shortly."

Nitta stood on the roof of the captain's quarters, moaning over the fact that his hide-out alternatives had been drastically reduced. He was as high as he could go. "Unless," he wailed, looking straight up at the top of the foremast.

The inspector wasn't in sight. Nitta placed his palms on the fifty foot structure and leaned against it striving to get his breath back. There were no shells or aerial bombs from the British at the moment to distract his pursuers. He had hoped the landing phase would provide enough noise and destruction to make his escape nothing but a minor inconvenience. The voice of the master-at-arms joining in the search shocked him into action.

Jofu quickly but nervously climbed up the narrow ladder on the mast. Halfway up the vertical steps, he ripped off a piece of non-skid material on the rung ahead of him that had been loosened by the weather. Then being careful to avoid it, proceeded on.

I stayed on the sidelines. I was more than willing to be a bench-warmer until my turn at bat came up.

Inspector Ibuse, running frantically to cover every spot on the upper surfaces of the ship, plowed headfirst into the mast. Picking himself off the deck, he massaged his damaged nose. "Mothballs." he cried, with a strange expression on his face.

On a hunch he looked up at the towering structure above him and spotted the landing-team sailor.

Undoing the strap on his holster, he took a deep breath, and grabbed the first rung of the ladder, a handhold that looked about as wide as the hands on a grandfather's clock to me.

Yeoman Netta was crouched down in the crow's-nest with nothing above him but the radio antenna wire that stretched fore and aft like a clothes line.

Halfway to his destination, the Inspector's foot slipped off the bare rung, throwing him sideways. Grasping the side of the ladder with one hand while most of his body dangled in mid-air, he hung there for a moment--then holding tight with his right hand, he grabbed the next crosspiece with his left and proceeded upwards.

Nitta tried shaking the skinny ladder, but it was attached too solidly to the mast to provide any movement.

When Inspector Ibuse reached for the top rung, Nitta stomped on his hand, smiling when he heard the bones crunch.

Yelping, Geki threw his arm over the round crosspiece and heaved himself toward the murderous butcher. A viscous kick to the forehead bent Ibuse's upper body backwards.

Hanging by his legs, Geki twisted around enough to get his good hand on a lower rung. From this upside down position, he arced his feet up and over, letting them drop towards the deck.

Climbing back up, he managed to get his left hand on the lip of the crow's-nest where the Trademark Killer's boot couldn't reach it.

Street-wise Jofu Nitta took off his shirt and wrapped it around Geki's wrist like a rope, then jerked it downward, hoping to pull the Inspector off the rim. But Ibuse wriggled his hand free enough to get a grip on the cloth--forcing Netta to drop it before the tables were turned and he got yanked out of his sanctuary.

The yeoman intended to survive. "Get away from me," he yelled, taking out the sharpened bayonet from its holder.

His initial thrust impaled the Inspector's uninjured hand against the top edge of the crow's-nest.

Geki Ibuse jerked his hand away--deliberately letting the bayonet slice through the skin between his middle and ring fingers.

After a couple of tries with his bloody and shaking hand, the Inspector got his gun out.

The eyes from the Gates of Hell glared down at the man with the black holes. A temporary standoff.

I got plunked with a mothball that fell out of Nitta, pocket "It was a lousy good luck charm anyway," he said, frustrated by the turn of events.

Quickly adding a fudge factor to the distance he needed to clear the obstacles below, Trademark dove over the side.

Unfortunately for him. *Ikeda* took a near miss from a British artillery shell just as Petty Officer Nitta left the crow's-nest. The explosion rocked the ship sideways, straight into Trademark's path.

Jofu Nitta, flailing in mid-air as if this would slow down his inevitable descent, screamed in agony as he ricocheted off the cone-shaped foghorn on the ship's smokestack. The next thing I heard was a terrifying howl when he crashed onto the roof of the captain's quarters. I closed my ears to the shrieks undoubtedly caused by massive injuries sustained when he slammed into, and caterpaulted off of, the metal railing on the upper deck. The torturous fall ended with his impalement on a spike like stanchion whose rigging formed a grotesque resemblance to the Christian Cross.

Shaking off the remnants of the last several hours, I grabbed some landing team clothes and jumped into them. Doing my best to ignore the sound of fleet gunfire and angry aircraft passing overhead, I ran to landing craft number 4 to say goodbye to my cousin.

He'd just finished placing a curved-shaped side dish and a soup bowl inside a covered rice receptacle. "A pretty neat arrangement," he smiled.

"It's appropriate that your mess kit is made of tin, Jun," I said. "Since you're going to the tin capital of the world."

"Please forgive my lack of words," Michi said, coming up behind me while Jun Kaine was climbing into his water vehicle. "I have no way of explaining my feelings at this critical moment in our lives. Take care. I'll see you on the peninsula."

As the Lance Corporal took his seat in the assault craft, Private Agi reached around the Professor to place his paper hat over Kaine's steel helmet, whispering, "For good luck."

I watched the landing craft descend to the choppy sea, as Michi, using his knee as a table, penned a letter to Kimiko asking her to please wait for him.

Like any good infantryman, Jun had not forgotten to wrap his rifle in oilcloth.

"Keep your head down, Quartermaster Kato," the coxswain for boat 3 hollered from an adjacent landing craft.

Kaine was anxious to get to the beach, more worried about the venomous sea snakes that occurred in undulating patches ten feet wide and upwards of three miles long in these waters than the enemy's shore batteries.

Sergeant Ogata warned everyone to keep their hands out of the water.

"Fat chance," Jun Kaine hollered, his hands safely under his armpits. Heroics would have to wait until later.

As the defensive fire from land-based artillery grew more severe and more accurate, Kaine was hard put to think of anything to relieve the tension. "I wonder what Emperor what's-his-name is doing at this moment," he yelled, hoping for a smile when he couldn't come up with one of his famous joke poems. Quartermaster Kato looked grim.

"Now that he's headed for combat," I shuddered, "Kato doesn't appear nearly as aggressive as he did when I visited the captain's quarters."

Shellfire aimed at the assault boats churned up the water on both sides of Kaine's craft, tossing one of the vemonous creatures between Agi's feet. Jumping up, the terrified Agi used his bayonet like a stick. He jabbed frantically, in a desperate attempt to get the pointed part under its belly, hoping to toss it overboard.

.Hurriedly reversing the ends of the rifle, Kaine smashed at the snake's head. But the serpent slithered away each time the rifle butt crashed down. "Kill it!" Quartermaster Kato screamed as the viper wriggled in his direction.

Kato's shrieks grew louder as a near miss ripped a hole near the waterline, showering the attack boat with water and pieces of sea snakes

Aboard the *Ikeda Maru*, Gunner Kikuchi was firing as fast as he could. I ran over to give him a hand by feeding in the ammo. We downed one Hudson bomber, but a second one passing over the burning *Enchanted Shadow* bored in.

By the time the ship had pulled in its anchor and veered far enough north to get out of the conflagration, a Hudson had managed to hit the troop transport with a bomb that tossed me into the sea.

Banking away from its target left the attacking plane wide open for Gunner Kikuchi. He angrily poured 20 mm shells into the twin-engine bomber until it hit the water still going at top speed.

I turned green, then ashen, as my body bobbed up and down in sync with the waves. "My stomach doesn't want to go up and down," I protested, watching the detonations from shellfire just inland of the beaches.

As part of the mini-drama that demonstrated man's ability to affect the innocent, I saw Combat, the Calico cat, sitting atop of one of Sergeant Ogata's suitcases, floating toward shore like a first-class passenger on a Far East cruise.

My plan to take my mind off the mountains of seawater didn't work. I was terrified of the surroundings, and my perilous condition intensified when the frothy waves broke over my head. Jamming my elbows into the top of the life jacket, blubbering incoherently, I ducked my head, and tried using my hands for an umbrella, with the same measure of success one would have emptying out an overflowing reservoir with a teaspoon.

"Get in here," Kaine said, as assault boat 4 came within hailing distance.

"At least we got away from the snake breeding area," he yelped, involuntarily ducking as the shells passed overhead.

In an effort to blank out the horrifying scene taking place all around me, I tried thinking about the carrier force that would be striking the American fleet at Pearl Harbor in another hour or so.

Unable to join the one-sided air battle above me and feeling pretty patriotic, I asked for a rifle. Kaine ignored me and pointed to the words on a large sign fifty feet back from the water's edge. It said: "Beach of Passionate Love."

With ferocity a natural component of the air war, torn bodies lying crumpled on the sand, and men fighting for their lives in the treacherous water, it seemed like someone's idea of a sick joke.

"Apparently, one of the lesser gods had a distorted sense of humor," I said resentfully.

When it became shallow enough, we got out and staggered ashore. Jun Kaine found time to drag a limp and bloody body from the surf. The eyebrows without an arch, and the blank look in the once vibrant, gingerbread eyes only confirmed what he had suspected. With a sigh, he turned away from Mallory Agi, the reference librarian from Sasebo. The man's wonderful memory had been erased.

Concerned with the rattle of machine gun fire in the distance, Kaine suddenly became interested in finding the relative security of the shrubbery up ahead.

I picked up Agi's rifle lying in the shallows and tore off the oilskin.

Sea Bandit's wings fluttered and were almost torn off amidst the concussions from the heavy shell fire. After resting on my collar for a second, she lifted off and circled overhead before locating the target nature had in mind for her.

Spotting the open wounds on the soldier laying on the sand like a crumpled up paper cup solved her problem. Fluttering down, the housefly hovered over the body to make sure it was an appropriate birthing place. Landing softly, she felt her way to Private Second Class Agi's torn up flesh. There she deposited her eggs on a spot where the oozing blood would not flush them away. The cycle of life for a fly was to be kept intact. Housefly to eggs, to maggots, to housefly.

Under a hail of gunfire, infantrymen from boat 2, with me tagging along behind Sergeant Major Hozumi, headed for Machang airfield just inland of Kota Bharu, the initial landing spot. Convinced that Singapore's radio station had already sent word to the Western world that the Global Empire was at war with the Asians, we followed a Malayan freedom-fighter to the airport.

Kicking a discarded Exide battery out of my way, I commandeered one of the Zeros that had been quickly flown in from Vietnam. I chalked *Mitsubishi Melody* on it, and got ready for my first mission from Kota Bharu. Taxing out, I thought about my mother's frequent advice to find a girl and settle down. I knew it would be either Yukiko or Shiroko, and I leaned toward Yukiko. She was smart, beautiful and I missed her greatly.

Cockpit canopy open, engine at high power, helmet against the headrest, and with my neck muscles tensed in anticipation of a short-field take- off, I no longer felt as antsy as a hummingbird in an arbor full of honeysuckle.

I released the brakes and headed out at a fast clip for the runway. Straddling the centerline I got into the air in record time, calling out, "Silent Storm Four One One airborne."

Instead of an answer from the tower, I heard: "Tea Cup in trouble, I say again, Tea Cup in trouble."

Looking up the code names from a card on my kneeboard, I found out that Tea Cup was a fishing fleet off the southwest coast of Thailand.

The captain must have been trained in aircraft recognition because he was able to relay the following information: "Many Martin B-10 bombers, Curtis fighters, and Douglas A-24 dive bombers. All with Dutch insignia headed our way."

It'll only take me a couple of minutes to get there, I figured. This is an emergency. No need to call for permission to assist vessels under enemy fire.

I remembered Osamu saying there was a second cousin twice removed in the family that had once spoken to a samuri. That sparked my need for man-to-man combat.

"Tea Cup, this is Silent Storm Four One One," I radioed to establish contact.

I could hear the relief in the fishing captain's voice. "Your squadron has a reputation as a top-notch outfit. We need your immediate assistance. We've counted ninety aircraft on the horizon so far. How many planes in your party?"

"One."

"Say again."

"One Mitsubishi Zero."

Commenting to the fishing boats listening in on the radio transmission, the fishing fleet's captain burst into hysterical laughter. "We're expecting dive bombers, twin-engine bombers, and fighter planes any minute, and he says one Zero."

"Maybe it's Japan's leading ace," somebody said sarcastically.

"Silent Storm Four One One. We'll take care of it," a Japanese voice from Kota Bhara tower insisted. "We want you over the beach area."

Nine Brewster Buffalo fighters based fifty miles south of Kato Bharu roared over the landing site, eager for battle. The British airmen sounded short-tempered and in no mood to show mercy. Maybe their croquet game had been interrupted, I thought.

The Teutonics, confident of their natural God-given abilities and superior American-built aircraft, were poised to sweep the skies clear of all slant-eyed pilots before tea time.

A British pilot, and I swear he had on a pink fox hunter's coat over his flight suit, broke formation to bore in on his first objective, a Japanese dive bomber pulling off its target. Single-mindedly, the other eight Buffaloes went after a lone Zero calling itself *Mitsubishi Melody*.

I had pulled at my left glove too hard and managed to drop it. Like most of my fellow baseball players, I was fanatically superstitious. Without the missing glove, disaster would befall me.

Glancing up quickly from my cockpit search, I found myself as the preferred bullseye for a squadron of enemy fighters. This time I didn't give in to my fears. Without hesitation, I plunged into battle.

To prove to myself how cool I was. I started reciting John Masefield's epic poem, *Sea Fever*, as I angled in for a shot.

"I must go down to the seas again,
    to the lonely sea and the sky.
I must go down to the seas again."...
I was rudely interrupted by machine gun fire and a guttural voice.
"This is Major Dirk Van Mook headed for your tail, and you'll need more than that Zero to save your lousy Asian soul," he screamed savagely, in broken Japanese. Queen Wilhelmina had ordered her Royal Army Air Force into battle.
"Watch your rear view mirror," Van Mook roared. "I'm in the plane with bullwhip painted on its cowling."

As my guns grew hot and my aim steady, born-again-Christian Kenji Ito, hearing the exchange between me and Van Mook, tore into the enemy matching my poem with something that sounded like a sailor's hymn.

"Eternal father, strong to save,
whose arm hath bound the restless wave...
    Oh hear us when we call to Thee,
    For those in peril on the sea."

In the process of turning around after evading the initial onslaught of aircraft, I had a few seconds to think about my brother, Aviation Radioman Osamu Debuchi, before I picked out my next target. He'd be seated in the rear cockpit of a carrier plane enroute to colonial Hawaii's military bases about now and would be listening closely for the message that could send him and his companions back to the carrier with their bomb loads intact. The inbound aviators, cognizant of the fact that the war in the Far East had already begun, knew that there might be a skyful of fighters waiting for them.
According to Japan's well-rehearsed plan of action, the defending forces, unaware that the attacking planes had strict orders to hit only military targets, would be caught unprepared for a low-level torpedo run. A precision maneuver designed to leave the hospital ship, *Repose,* berthed at Pearl Harbor, untouched.
The battle to free Asia from the hated Western occupation armies was underway, and the probability of both my brother and I coming out of this war alive were slim. Many of us will die, Gegan Sukebator had predicted. But I knew other Asians will come forward to replace those losses. The West is kidding itself if it thinks the Far East can't win this

battle for independence in the long run.

I intend to hold Hisako Bayar to the promise she made me the last time I saw her. She said she'd recite one of Rudyard Kipling's most famous poems, outloud, in front of a crowd if I fired the opening shot. Even though I may not get the opportunity to see her regal figure, standing tall, mouthing the words: *"At the end of the fight is a tombstone white/ with the name of the late deceased/ And the epitaph drear: A fool lies here/ who tried to hustle the east,"* I'm sure her rendition of the final lines of the verse will enable my fellow countrymen to understand why I squeezed the trigger and plunged us into war.

A victory of sorts had already been achieved, I thought, closing in on a Brewster Buffalo. Yeoman First Class Jofu Nitta's broken body will slay no more. The serial killer whose shattered childhood taught him to detest the Westerners had taken his last breath.

Rather than be consumed by that kind of hatred, I let my professional side take over. Just because I had referred to the chattering of the machine guns as a militant *Mitsubishi Melody,* doesn't mean I'm not taking my occupation seriously. To prove my point, instead of patting myself on the back and chalking up one for the good guys each time I shot a European out of the sky, I found myself looking over the canopy sill to see if his chute blossomed and cheering when it did.